Books in This Series

By Death Series

Touched by Death

Haunted by Death

Chilled by Death

By Death Books 1–3

DALE MAYER

HAUNTED
BY
DEATH

BOOK TWO OF BY DEATH SERIES

HAUNTED BY DEATH
Beverly Dale Mayer
Valley Publishing Ltd.

Copyright © 2013
Second Edition © 2022

This is a work of fiction. Names, characters, places, brands, media, and incidents are either the product of the author's imagination or are used fictitiously. Any resemblance to actual events, locales, or persons, living or dead, is entirely coincidental.

ISBN-13: 978-1-988315-96-6
Print Edition

About This Book

Meg Pearce is haunted by a death that may never be explained, … and so she can never truly be healed. During the summer before she started college, she and her boyfriend went on a camping trip that ended with one of their friends disappearing. In one fell swoop of destruction, she lost not only a friend but her own innocence, her future, her best friend and lover, her everything.

Seventeen years later, Meg's career as an anthropologist drives her to seek understanding about why things happen and the answers for human behavior. Those questions that torment her have her returning to the same campsite of the tragedy that defined her life. A part of her hopes to solve the mystery that has plagued her for most of her adult years. Ultimately she longs to find a way to deal with the loss. Instead of gaining closure though, she stumbles onto a gruesome discovery that has her reeling back to the darkest time in her existence.

Detective Chad Ingram has spent the last seventeen years attempting to solve a stone-cold mystery—one that also stole his life and his true love.

Death seems supernaturally determined to shake up their lives for good or evil—only this time, Meg and Chad are both in the crossfire.

Sign up to be notified of all Dale's releases here!
https://geni.us/DaleNews

Chapter 1

THE CLOUDS SWEPT across the sky, whipped by a blustery northern wind. The sun was high, shining brightly over the lake and shore. It was a perfect summer's day at the lake. Not far from the water's edge, where multiple brightly colored tents sprawled, Chad Ingram followed his buddies up the beach for a short hike. Bruce and Josh, his best friends, were in charge of today's adventure. The girls had elected to stay behind.

This was their last camping trip of the summer, before college started next week. The long-standing group of three young males and their three girlfriends had made the most of the summer weather to get out and to enjoy their time together. This weekend, Tim and Bruce's cousins—Anto and Pero, who'd moved to the US a couple years ago—had joined them.

Chad liked them both, and Pero was easy to get along with. However, his broody brother, Anto, was, by contrast, hard work. But so long as he was on his best behavior, he fit into the group just fine. Some of the group had worked full-time for the summer, others only part-time, and one of their number was doing summer school. Making time together had been a challenge.

And they all knew it was the end of an era. And that making time for each other was important. Next week, each would start on the pathway of whatever future they'd chosen. This weekend was a last chance to let loose before life intruded. Good thing too. Futures were serious business.

Josh had organized this day hike, which was intended to be a fun couple of hours, exploring this side of the lake. With only T-shirts, shorts, and runners, they weren't equipped to do more. Chad liked to do at least one hiking trip a day when they were out. Not going too far and not putting out too much effort, just a break from the beach and swimming and beer drinking. Well, maybe not that last one, as several of them usually carried an open can of beer with them.

This was their second trip to the popular northern area of Washington State. They'd camped at the other side of this same lake earlier in the summer, close to where several members of Bruce's extended-family had cabins. That trip had been such a blast that they all wanted to come back and check out the opposite side of the lake, the less popular side. Where they'd first camped out were hundreds of cabins up and down the lakeshore. That area was open and sunny, with lovely sandy beaches. All of which made it a big attraction for kids and families.

This time the group wanted a different experience. They wanted seclusion, isolation, privacy, and a chance to enjoy their last bit of freedom, without having to follow curfews and noise restrictions.

And, from the looks of the tightly grown forest and steep incline on parts of the hill behind them, they had it.

The group took off up the hill in good spirits. Chad walked last in line, smiling at his friends' antics up ahead. Their laughter preceded them, filling the dense woods, even as the sun fought to reach into the old growth and the tightly grouped stick trees on the left. The air was filled with a heavy pine-scented atmosphere. Although the walk up the hill on the left side had started out easily, it hit the way-too-much-work-to-be-bothered-with category very quickly. Besides, they hadn't brought enough beer to fortify themselves for that much effort.

"Hey, Chadwickie, what's taking you so long?" Josh yelled back from up ahead. He'd been leading the group of males for the last ten minutes but had stopped to see what was holding up his friend.

"I gotta take a piss," Chad called out. "That beer is running right through me."

"Weakling! Jesus, you really can't hold your liquor, can you?" Raucous laughter filled the air.

"Ha, ha. I can hold it that way just fine. I wasn't the one slobbering all over the girls last night, like you and Bruce were."

Chad—or Chadwickie, as his buddies liked to call him to rile him—stepped farther into the dense woods and slightly off the path, then opened his fly. Immediately a bright stream hit the mossy ground and ferns in front of him. He tilted his head back and sighed with relief, enhanced by the mild buzz going on in his head. Life was good.

"Aren't you done already?" called back one of his friends, probably Bruce. "It's almost time to go back to the girls. You're taking so long."

"When you gotta go, you gotta go," Chad murmured quietly, with a contented sigh. He could hear his friends moving farther away, but they were still within hearing distance.

The stream went on and on. Finally he tucked himself back inside and zipped up his khaki shorts. He turned to look for his buddies. No one was in sight.

Shit.

"Hey, Josh? Bruce?" He spun around. "Where the hell are you guys? Anto? Tim?"

There was not a sound, not a whisper of laugher or a crackle of leaves. Nothing. Crap. Where were they?

"Pero?"

Just then, the sun went behind a cloud, and the air around him darkened, adding a sinister overtone to his growing fear. Crackling noises off to the left had him bolting to the right. "Hey, guys!"

Nothing.

Laughter from the way ahead wove through the air. He ran toward it. Tripping over roots and piling through bushes, Chad chased after his friends. They would hide from him for hours—or for as long as they were having fun—if he didn't find them first. They were all jokesters, him included.

But going for a two-hour hike as part of the group was one thing; getting left behind and lost was another thing altogether. *That* was not something Chad wanted. The group had been making hiking and camping trips for the last year. They had been a blast. But they'd all been on fields or beaches in open terrain, where it was easy to see the sur-rounding area, easy to pinpoint landmarks to avoid getting lost. Never had they been in woods like this, but, of course, that had been the attraction this time around.

Open spaces were fine; beaches were good—great even. This place was eerie in a good way. Kinda like ghost stories around a campfire, a creepy kind of good.

Besides, he knew his buddies, and he trusted them. This was all in fun. He'd take his hit now and dish out more to the others later.

Just to the guys though. The girls didn't prank like the guys did. And he should know. One was an ex-girlfriend and the other? She was the love of his life. There had been a little occasional camping with both his ex and his current girl-friend, but he hadn't gone out with Cia since last Halloween. He'd hooked up with Megan—or Megs as they often called her—in February. She was special. He'd had several girl-friends already, but she had been the first one to touch him inside and to make herself right at home with him. She belonged with him. He loved that connection, that special-ness of knowing he'd found the right partner.

His friends thought he was nuts and were always point-ing out other chicks and telling him to test drive a few more models before he made a decision. The thing was, he'd already done that. Cia had been one of the worst ones. And his friends just didn't get it about Megs. There was no decision to be made. It had been done for him. He couldn't explain this to someone who'd never experienced such a feeling, but Megs was his, and he was hers. End of discus-sion.

Chest heaving, he stopped his headlong rush and caught his breath, while he searched the hillside for his friends. Still no sign of the others. Shit. How far ahead could they be? The incline now looked to be a half-mile deep. He checked his watch. *Jesus.* They'd been gone forty-five minutes already. Given that they were close to the time of returning anyway, the others may have circled back toward the lake already.

And that was a damn good idea. They'd always said, if someone got separated from the rest, they were to return to base. Chad should have done that right off. They could be anywhere by now. He didn't want them to send out a search party looking for him. His friends would never let him live that one down. If it weren't for the steep incline, he'd be seriously worried, but the lake had to be down somewhere at the bottom, so how lost could he be?

Still, he'd go back to the girls, while he could still find his way and before he'd take the chance of getting really lost out here.

A flock of birds flew up in a cacophony of sound right behind him. He dashed around a huge tree trunk and slammed up against it, his heart racing in shock. Shit. Somehow a fun afternoon's exploration had stopped being fun. He took a deep breath, hating the nerve-induced adrenaline snaking through his system. A lot of country was out here.

And he was starting to freak himself out.

He'd never been lost or alone in the woods before. Didn't like it much either. Talk about feeling small and unimportant in the vast world of Mother Nature.

"Hey, Josh? Bruce? Very funny, guys. … *Where* are you? Pero? Anto?"

No answer from any of them. Shit.

He hated this. He couldn't see anything but more brown trees and moss and green bushes in every direction. That wasn't good. His friends were good people, but they were assholes when they pranked each other. Yet Chad had been as guilty as they were.

A branch cracked off to the left. His heart jumped, and he hid behind a tree. He held his breath. *What the hell was that?*

The undergrowth crunched as if someone— something—were walking heavily on it.

All other sounds had stopped.

He swallowed hard and slithered downward to the base

of the tree. After a long moment, he peered around the edge of the tree trunk. He couldn't see anyone. Yet he heard a stealthy noise—barely. Branches rustled; leaves slid against each other, and the birds had gone silent, as if they saw something which he couldn't. The noise could have been from an animal. A bear? But he wasn't so sure. It hadn't been his friends. He knew that. They didn't have the skill to move so quietly. They were all elephants.

But hundreds of cabins were here—and likely thousands of people, counting homes, campgrounds, and the park. He waited, still peering from his hiding spot, but he couldn't hear anything else.

Then it hit him. The noise had come from the direction of the lake. From where they'd left the three girls alone.

Alone. … Oh, Megs.

For the first time he realized how stupid they'd been. His heart went into overdrive, and he could barely breathe. Oh shit. Oh shit. *Oh shit!*

Taking a deep breath, he plowed through the brush the way he'd come, around trees, ducking under branches, jumping over fallen logs, and dodging the bushes that reached out to slow his progress. He had to get back. Something was wrong. He knew it. He just didn't know what.

He crossed what seemed like dozens of miles. He wished he knew where his buddies were right now, but it was the thought of the girls that scared him. They should never have been left alone, never.

He broke through the tree line, gasping in pain, his body trembling with panic, sweat coursing down his back and soaking his T-shirt. And, at last, he came to a dead stop.

Megs was there, with Stephanie. The two girls were in

the lake, floating on air mattresses about twenty feet from shore, talking and paying no attention to anything but their conversation. Relief washed through him at the sight of Megs's long, lean body stretched out under the sun. He bent over, struggling to breathe.

She was fine.

Even as he watched, she was pointing out something in the sky to Stephanie. He doubted they even knew he was here. Those two had been close friends for years and could talk about nothing for hours. Confused, he straightened slowly and looked around.

The area was peaceful. Normal. And this normality made him feel like an idiot for overreacting.

But where was Cia? She wasn't emotionally close to the other two females. And she wasn't the type to share confidences with other girls. She was all about the guys. And that had made it a little hard with all the relationship-switching that had happened within the group. Cia had been the one to break up with Chad, and a good thing it had been too. It had saved him the job. For all her good points, Cia came with a couple really negative characteristics.

Normally she could always be found sitting to one side, reading one of her never-ending books. He spun around, looking for her, but found no sign of her.

Maybe she was napping, as she'd been tired, complaining of the heat when they'd left.

"Megs," he called out, "where's Cia?"

Megs twisted around, saw him, and gave him a warm smile. "She went to lie down. She has another headache."

Right. Of course she had. Cia got major migraines. He'd never known anyone else to have them before. It had been quite an education, as they completely crippled her at times.

Feeling better, he walked to the water's edge and splashed cool water on his face. If anyone realized how completely he'd overreacted, they'd make fun of him for days.

As he straightened up, his face cooler and his heart no longer trying to escape his chest, he realized that the inner disquiet hadn't been fully calmed. Not able to let it go until he was sure, he walked over to Josh and Cia's tent. "Cia? Are you in here?"

He hated to wake her, but he had to know for sure.

The flap was down, so he lifted the corner and peered inside.

Empty.

He straightened up, cupped his hands around his mouth, and called across the water, "She's not here. The tent is empty."

Just then the rest of the guys thundered through the trees, half running, half crashing into each other, all laughing and joking. "There you are." Josh grinned at Chad, as he jogged over to him. "We got into a crazy game of hide-and-seek in the woods. We weren't sure if you were with us or not at that point."

Bruce and Tim approached, gasping for breath but still scrapping over who had arrived first and second.

"I wasn't," Chad snapped, hands on his hips, as he glared at his friends. "And no thanks to you guys. You could have waited for me."

The others grinned, totally digging him being pissed off. He couldn't blame them. If their positions had been reversed, he'd have done the same. No sign of the Novak brothers. Chad spun around to see them—Anto first, coming through the trees; then Pero, much farther down.

Damn. Chad faced the gathering crowd. "I can't find

Cia. The girls said she went to lie down and have a nap, but she's not here."

The responses came from all of them at once.

Bruce brushed off the news with a shake of his head. "Stop worrying. She won't be far away."

"Probably grabbed her book and found a shady spot to read."

"Anyone check the outhouse?"

Chad was having none of it. A horrible certainty had filled him. This was seriously bad.

At his insistence and, with the other two girls now back on shore, they spread out to search … everywhere. Grim-faced and sober, they finally regrouped an hour later.

There had been no sign of Cia.

She was gone.

Chapter 2

Seventeen Years Later

THE SUN SHONE through the windshield, warm and soothing after the tumultuous last few months. Meg Pearce stared at the wilderness through the passenger window, as Pete drove down the highway. She didn't remember any of this area. In fact, she'd been lost since leaving the highway. It had been a long time since her last trip here. That one had been so horrible that she'd managed to avoid coming back to the area so far. Only it was Pete's favorite spot …

And Pete had been insistent this time. As she hadn't told him the real reasons why she hated this area, and, as she'd run out of excuses, what choice was there now? She could explain, but she really didn't want to open up old wounds. She had enough relationship issues to deal with since her brother's death. So, if this helped, then she was all for it.

Where had the time gone?

Listless, she watched the miles speed by—just like the years had. These last months had been hell, months of emotional turmoil, handling of necessities and adjusting to the new status quo, which hadn't left much time for grieving. Worn out now, she was a mere fragment of her old self. She needed this rest and some time away—time to recoup her energy and her passion for living.

All that had disappeared with her brother's death and the changes and challenges that had come with it. Such as parenting his twelve-year-old daughter and dealing with Pete's unhappy reaction to the new situation. Not to mention Janelle's unhappy reaction to her new life. No wonder Meg's normal *oomph* had disappeared. But this was a vacation, and, as she knew already, if her mood sucked, so did Pete's and Janelle's. But if Meg could pull out of it and be cheerful, then she could usually get their moods turned around too.

"Hard to believe something like this exists, so close to civilization," she joked, partly because they were two hours out of Seattle and not that far from the Canadian border.

Janelle sniped, "Who said *this* was close to anything." She glared out the window from the seat behind Pete. "We're in the middle of nowhere," she wailed.

Meg smiled. It was a small thin one, but all she could manage on short notice. The last thing she needed was more of Janelle's histrionics, but, given that technology, which her niece appeared to depend on, worked only sporadically up here, Meg and Pete could be in for a lot more of the same. For herself, Meg was looking forward to being unplugged for a few days—or longer, if she needed to. Not that she'd left her cell phone behind. But that was only for business and safety issues. As for Janelle, one day of being unplugged was one day too long.

And, for Pete, he'd lightened up a lot, once he realized they were actually going on this trip. He'd been here many times over the years. He loved being in the bush, renovating this place, working with his hands. It's what made him so good at the construction work he did. Meg traveled for months as part of her work, making it hard to get time away with Pete. And, when she did, it was never here. *Never here.*

She wasn't looking forward to this trip but had to admit she could already feel some of the tension draining from her shoulders and spine. She took a deep breath of the woodsy air. It was so different from the smog of Seattle and from the wet coastal smell after a rain or the humidity of Haiti. That had been a tough job. It had ended on a good note, but the pain of what she and her team had gone through had been life changing.

Maybe that's why she had had this change of heart. With what she'd survived over in Haiti, followed by the events since her brother's death, surely Meg could deal with a seventeen-year-old ghost now.

She cast a quick glance to the back seat of the double-cab truck, where Janelle was pouting in the corner. These last few months had been hard on Meg, but they had been hell for her niece. Meg's brother's death in a car accident had been the latest of a long string of incidents that had torn Janelle's life apart. The first was her mother's death to disease, followed by relocation to Seattle to be closer to Meg and Janelle's grandparents. Her brother had always thought that Meg would be a good influence on his struggling daughter.

Being uprooted to Seattle—and unloved, as Janelle had put it—she'd been very unimpressed by the move away from her school and friends. She'd had a hard time adapting to her new social situation. And, at the same time, she had been still dealing with the loss of her mother.

Then months after slowly rebuilding a new life in Seattle, her father had been taken from her. Sometimes fate was a bitch.

Pete slowed the truck on the long stretch of empty road.

Meg leaned forward, wondering how he could find an overgrown turnoff in this mess of woods and brush. Even Janelle sat up and looked around.

"This is a back way to the cabin. It keeps the nosy neighbors from knowing when I'm here." Pete turned the truck onto a deeply rutted track, overgrown with waist-high grasses. Janelle groaned, as they drove onto yet another road, taking them deeper into the wooded area. It was darker and much cooler here, with tall spindly trees blocking the sun.

Meg knew it would open up soon. Good thing, as the darkness creeped her out.

Damn. Talk about old fears flaring up.

How many times had Pete vacationed here without her? Not that coming here alone had been his fault. She'd been the one gallivanting off with her job. She'd had a bad case of wanderlust all her life that had only been partially slaked after the Haiti trip. At least she hoped it had been. With Janelle now part of the family, Meg couldn't just get up and run off anymore.

Meg hit the button to open her window. Cool air spread through the warm cab. Having slowed down, there was a light breeze, but it was not enough. She wanted to gulp in freshness, innocence, and renewal. All things she so desperately needed to find again.

She leaned back and closed her eyes, willing her adrenals to hold on, hoping peace and quiet were on the way.

"You okay?" Pete asked, concern coloring his voice.

"Fine," she murmured, not opening her eyes. That was another thing on her list—to repair her relationship with Pete. This year it was as if they were brother and sister instead of lovers. Her job, a bone of contention a year ago, had taken second place to Janelle's sudden arrival into their world.

Since the two had bonded by the time her brother had died, keeping Janelle with her and Pete had been the natural option. Meg's only other sibling, Aaron, had moved across the country, while Meg had been in Haiti. That had been tough, as she'd been close to his teenage sons. She'd been happy to take in Janelle and, with the internet and cell phones, Meg had easily enough stayed in touch with Aaron and his sons.

Only Pete hadn't seen Janelle in quite that way. A temporary situation was fine. Long-term? Not so much.

Pete had wanted to start a family a few years back. He'd lost his own father in a car accident, while still a young man. It had been an accident he'd barely survived. Meg had seen the pain some of the injuries still caused him. He should have been able to relate to Janelle's loss, but instead it seemed to remind him of his own loss—and his inability to deal with it ever since.

Meg winced at the reality of the first mention of having a child being almost eight years ago. She'd been dragging her heels, knowing it would curb her trips around the world. Of course that had been part of Pete's *having kids of their own thing*—to keep her at home. Now, with Janelle, Meg had been home more. Only Pete wanted his *own* family. Not broken pieces of Meg's brother's family.

Letting her head roll to the side, Meg stared at the trees, as they slapped against the side of the truck. The ruts in the road were deep, and every bounce brought on a mother of a headache. The bright blue of the lake twinkled invitingly through the trees. It wouldn't warm up for another month, and, with the horrific storms in this area over the last few years, the lake would likely be frigid cold right now.

"We're almost there, aren't we?" Meg asked, hating the fatigue coloring her voice. She glanced over at Pete to find him staring at her with a raised eyebrow.

"Yes, just a few more corners."

A grin flashed as a lighthearted idea swept through her. "Stop the truck. Janelle and I'll walk ahead." A laugh escaped. "We'll probably beat you there."

She didn't give him a chance to argue. She pushed open her door and jumped out of the still-rolling vehicle. She motioned to her niece in the back seat. "Come on, Janelle. Let's take a shortcut. The cabin is up just a little way."

"No, wait," Pete said. "We're almost there." The powerful engine revved, as the front end of the truck dipped into a rut again, the large tires spinning in the air before catching the ground. "Meg, get back here," he shouted. "You don't know where you are going."

"You said it's at the end of the road." She laughed. "How hard could that be?"

Janelle giggled and jumped out, slamming the door shut behind her. She ran ahead, catching up to Meg quickly. Of course she didn't walk like an adult; she bounced, with her jet-black curls flouncing around her shoulders. Meg smiled down at her. She was a beautiful kid. Her mother's Spanish ancestry had given her beautiful creamy skin and midnight-black hair, so different from Meg's own pink skin and brown hair.

"Come on. The road curves up again. We'll cut through the trees and be drinking tea before he even gets there." The two waved at Pete and bolted through the trees on the right. With Pete hollering his protest into the wind, Meg laughed and laughed, chasing Janelle into the stick forest. It felt good to sprint, and the laughter sent delicious feel-good vibes down her spine.

Without much natural light and in crowded conditions, the pines had grown up tall and skinny, forming a tight wall. Meg frowned. She hadn't remembered this much overgrowth.

It had been years, but still …

She could see the road as it turned up ahead, so it wasn't as if they could get lost. The truck labored on behind them. Pete had stopped yelling, and, with the fresh air blowing across her face and rifling through her hair, Meg was already feeling better. And her headache had magically disappeared.

She and Janelle slowed to a stroll, just enjoying the moment together.

"How long are we staying here?" Janelle asked, walking at Meg's side. The running and dodging of trees had put a rosy flush on her young cheeks.

"Just for two nights. We'll head back on the afternoon after that." Meg smiled down at her. She held out her hand, her heart giving a slight bump when Janelle reached out to hold it. While her niece may look like her mother, she acted so much like her father as a kid that it brought both pain and joy to Meg's heart. "It's a chance to get away and a chance to relax."

"Like a spa?" Janelle asked hopefully, looking around uneasily. "Please say yes."

Meg laughed. "Not quite, but it will be fun."

Janelle looked at her doubtfully. "Promise?"

"I promise." She looked down at the trusting soul beside her, Janelle now pointing at something off to the side. A steep hill was up ahead, and, about one-third of the way down, a tree had fallen, now hung up on a ledge. Heavy storms and the spring thaw could do that. Mother Nature still liked to call the shots in her world.

"What's that?" Janelle asked, pointing again to the left.

"Nothing." Meg wrapped her arm around Janelle's shoulders. "Just some downed trees, or rocks—maybe from a small mudslide after a heavy storm."

"No, not that—I mean that shiny white thing over there."

Meg let her gaze travel in the direction Janelle had pointed at, skimming past, hesitated, and zinged back to rest on the round white ball. Her breath caught in her throat. Her mind screamed, *No!* Her muscles tensed, and her gaze hardened.

Then she relaxed. It couldn't be. Not out here. This was just the side effects of her job. She saw bodies everywhere. "It's just a rock," she said reassuringly.

It *had* to be.

No way a body would be out here. Of course her rational mind immediately kicked in and snorted at the thought. Hunters went missing in the woods all the time. A lake was close by, and all kinds of weekend warriors and partiers came up to get away from city life. A body could definitely be here.

One body in particular.

But she so didn't need to see one this weekend. A part of her wanted to tug Janelle away. Maybe come back in another day … or year, but … the rest of her knew she couldn't do that. She had to find out what they were looking at. Her conscience wouldn't let her do less. Not to mention she'd spent more than half her lifetime wondering when a particular set of remains would be discovered. That she was once again in the same general area where her friend had gone missing? … Her insides were shaking. It *couldn't* be.

She dropped Janelle's hand and told her, "Stay here. I'll take a quick look. Just stay here." She took a few steps in the direction of the white thing and glanced back to ensure Janelle remained in place. "I won't be but a second. Besides, if I'm any longer, Pete will win the race." With a big grin, she dashed across the short distance.

"No, don't." Janelle's panicked voice reached out to Meg.

Crap. Meg spun, her gaze darting back to see Janelle, frozen. Janelle, who had done nothing but deal with death for the last year. Janelle, who couldn't sleep and desperately needed this time away. Janelle, who didn't need the specter of death intruding here—because it had intruded enough already. And then she found her niece running toward her, fear clearly etched on her small face. Meg shouted, "Stop!"

Janelle came to a bumbling halt, her face scrunched up, tears forming in her eyes.

"Honey, don't come any closer. You might fall and hurt yourself. Plus this hillside could come down at any moment. I'm coming to you. Stay there."

Janelle sniffled, and Meg knew she had no choice. Since coming to live with Meg, Janelle was terrified of something happening to Meg and that Janelle would be left alone yet again. Taking out her cell phone, Meg quickly noted the GPS location of where she had stood.

"Auntie Meg?"

With one last glance at the rock, still too far away to be seen clearly, she started back to Janelle. "It's nothing."

With a big carefree smile, she grabbed Janelle's hand and ran up toward the road. The cabin had to be close. And she wanted it to be even closer by now. "Let's beat Pete!"

Laughing again and gasping for air, they crashed through

the tight brush onto the road just ahead of the truck.

Waving at Pete, they picked up their pace and raced to the cabin.

And beat him.

AN UNEASY TRUCE settled inside Meg—for the moment. She couldn't get that *rock* out of her mind. There'd been something about it. She'd been too close to it to ignore it and yet too far away to have recognized what it was. She was afraid it might be so much more than a rock.

She needed to return and find it to confirm. But how could she, without alerting Janelle? And she'd have to tell Pete, which could be a really bad scenario. She'd have to choose her words carefully and pick her timing even better.

Somehow.

Pete had a hell of a temper, and she didn't want to set it off. She didn't fear him, but Janelle had had enough distress in her young life. Even a healthy debate with Pete these days disturbed her. That girl needed to rest and to heal. That Pete and Meg were having more issues than usual just made it that much harder to keep the atmosphere friendly, open, and supportive.

If only she could take another look. And make sure. Her mind wanted that to be a rock. They didn't need death to intervene here. Not when this trip was all about finding joy in life again. But her heart? ... Well, her heart wanted to find her friend. She's been waiting for an answer for so long. What if she'd just found it?

"Earth to Auntie Meg?"

Meg started and then turned to smile at a frowning Janelle, peanut butter sandwich in one hand and an apple in the other. "How can you eat both of those together?"

Janelle grinned a big sticky peanut-buttery grin, then took a big bite out of the apple. Meg shuddered. She picked up an apple for herself and took a big bite.

"What were you thinking about?" Janelle asked, her mouth full.

Automatically Meg said, "Don't talk with food in your mouth." Then she winced, as she heard echoes of her mother's voice. "Sorry. That was instinct."

"Yeah, yeah." Deliberately it seemed, Janelle took an oversized bite and worked her jaws to munch it down to normal-size pieces, so she could swallow them.

Meg had to turn away. Before her brother's death, Janelle ate normal food normally. Now she seemed to delight in eating weird combinations in the most irritating ways. Was it to annoy Meg? Maybe. More likely it was for attention.

It had been a very tough year for them all.

Pete walked inside. "Did you leave anything for me?"

Meg pointed to the large sandwich sitting untouched on a plate. "That's yours."

She walked outside to sit on the top step. It was early in the afternoon, and they had two days ahead of them. Two days to rest. Two days to enjoy the great outdoors. Two days to not work.

Except … she *had* to go back to that spot.

"Who wants to go fishing this afternoon?" Pete sat down on the step beside her, half of the sandwich in his hand, the other half on a paper plate. The first disappeared in three bites, as Meg watched him. He'd always been a big eater, but being outdoors seemed to amplify this. He picked up the second half and demolished that in a couple bites as well.

"Not me. I'd be playing games on my cell phone, but, oh, you wouldn't let me bring it." Janelle pouted in the doorway behind them. "Of course you and Auntie Meg could go fishing, and I could stay here and play games on *her* cell phone."

"Not going to happen." Meg worked to keep her voice neutral. "We came to get away from all that. Remember?"

"I saw you use your cell phone when we were racing Pete," Janelle accused, her voice disgusted and pointed. "So how come you brought your phone?"

Pete slid a sideways glance at Meg.

Damn. She fumbled for inspiration. "I wanted to take pictures."

"Then how come I can't have my cell phone so I can take pictures?" Janelle jumped over the few steps and strode down the path, muttering, "Unfair."

For all her best intentions, Meg couldn't hold back a heavy sigh.

"Are you sure you want to raise her?" Pete asked, yet again.

"Yes," Meg said firmly. "Besides, no other family member can." And Meg loved her niece.

"She could go to your brother. Or even into foster care." Pete nodded down the pathway. "At the rate she's going, she'll want to go in the system."

"Only because she doesn't know how bad it can be." Meg stood, irritated at Pete's suggestion. She was unwilling to get into another argument on that same issue again. Janelle was her niece, and Meg was happy to have her live with them. In truth, she was delighted. She missed her brother. The grief was a deep ache that never seemed to go away.

And Janelle had already wormed her way into Meg's heart. The months of getting to know her before her brother's death had been a gift. It would have been so much harder to have her come to them as a stranger. This way, the bonds of love and friendship had already been established.

Even if Janelle were lashing out in anger and saying some of the most hurtful things Meg could have imagined a child saying, she knew that Janelle was reacting to the terrible situation and the major change in her life. She understood, even if Pete didn't.

Still, finding herself in the middle of the two of them and the constant warring, the constant role of peacemaker was wearing Meg down.

Not for the first time, she wondered what final toll her brother's death would really take on her own life. She'd thought she'd been through the worst.

Now she was beginning to realize that the turmoil had only just begun.

"WHAT IF I don't want to go fishing?" Janelle asked, her body rigid, glaring at the sun reflecting on the lake water. "I hate boats. I hate the woods. This trip is stupid."

"That's enough." Anger vibrated through Pete's voice, as he snapped at her. "We came here to enjoy ourselves, not put up with more whining from you."

Meg winced and stared up at the sky. She closed her eyes at the soft sniffles from her niece. Janelle went from anger and disgust to tears and heartbreak in a snap these days. Right now, Meg had to admit she'd like a good cry herself.

"Then go without me," cried out Janelle. "I'll stay here."

"No." Pete's voice brooked no argument. "Get in. We're

here. The least you can do is go out for an hour and give it a try." Disgust laced his voice, as he gazed down at Janelle. Pete had never been around kids much, and his first foray into them hadn't been easy. Meg was about ready to step in yet again, when Pete added, his voice softer, calmer, "You've never even been in a boat. How can you say you hate it? Come on. Just think of all the stories you can tell your friends when you get home."

Janelle perked up.

Meg closed her eyes on a whispered sigh of relief.

Another situation had been averted.

"Meg, you look tired. Why don't you have a nap, while we go out in the boat?"

Surprised, Meg stared up at Pete. Normally he would never voice such a suggestion. Inside, hope bloomed. An hour alone would be wonderful. She not only needed a break, she needed peace of mind. And that meant returning to the spot she'd marked with her GPS.

Pete stepped closer, whispering, "You know that she behaves differently when it's just her and me. Let me try this. Maybe we can get on a better footing. Just think. We might enjoy the weekend after all." He leaned over and kissed her gently.

Janelle, now with her life jacket on, climbed into the boat; then Pete pushed off. Janelle didn't look back at Meg.

Maybe that was a good thing. Meg was still dealing with Pete's first kiss in over a month.

In fact, it might have been much longer than that. Her heart was breaking, as she watched her partner and niece paddle out to the middle of the water. Just another sign of all that had gone wrong in her life. Maybe, just maybe, they'd hit a point where they could turn that around.

Feeling better than she had all day, she waved at Pete and strode back up the path to the cabin. She retrieved her cell phone and brought up the coordinates of the site she'd entered.

Knowing her time was short, she picked up a light jacket and a couple plastic food bags, wishing she had gloves with her. Hoping to avoid problems, she entered the coordinates of the cabin so she could find her way back. With a last look at the lake, where she could see Pete's and Janelle's heads close together, with rods in their hands, Meg took off into the woods.

The sun was bright and strong when she left the cabin, but, once into the deepest part of the treed area, the sun couldn't penetrate, and coldness ruled there. She closed her jacket and picked up the pace. If things blew up between Pete and Janelle, they could be back in half their allotted time. Meg had no excuse for not resting up. At least, not one she wanted to share with those two.

She checked her cell phone. She had to be damn close. Sure enough, the location should be just off to her left. She glanced around. The area did look familiar but not so familiar that she could have found this spot without having marked it first, as she approached it now from a different direction.

Please let this be a rock. She'd seen too many horrific things in her life to not check it out. Besides, death was her job. She dealt with it every day. But, as the last month had proven, dealing with dead bodies that you didn't know was a whole different process than dealing with the death of a family member. She'd never seen her brother in a morgue or dealt with the process of identifying his bones, like she'd done with bodies in Haiti and in so many other countries.

In those cases, the people had been dead a long time. The hole they'd left in the families was already closed and healed over. In many cases, the families themselves were deceased too.

Meg took several more steps to the left, shifted around a tree, and stopped. Yes. This was the right place. Taking her time to observe the area, she clambered over a fallen tree, feeling her fingers slipping deep into the moss growing over it. This was such a rich and different world from what she was used to.

Long green vegetation hung from branches high over-head. The leaves underneath her feet were spongy, decomposed. She knew the weather had changed over the last few years. What had once been dry and hazardous seventeen years ago had now become moist and musty. Heavy rainfalls and strong tree growth had blocked out the sun and had resulted in the ground becoming more boggy than dry in the lower-lying parts.

Looking up the steep incline behind the area, she could see an old mudslide had taken a corner of the cresting hillside above.

Carefully she worked her way closer to where she'd seen the odd bleached item. Her fingers clenched, making her realize how sweaty and nervous she'd become. *Please don't let this be human remains. Not this weekend.*

So much was at stake. And keeping death away from her personal life was hugely important right now.

She navigated under a low-hanging branch to a small hollow.

There.

She'd found it. Turning around, she checked to ensure she was still alone. She was, but what was it about being out in the middle of nowhere, in a dark and lonely place, to make someone worried that they were being followed? Her rational mind knew she was alone, but her emotions were all over the place.

Giving her head a shake, she surveyed the thick humus around her. Nothing looked askew from what she'd seen on her way over here. Now to double-check that all was good and to get back to the cabin, before the others noticed she'd left.

Still seeing nothing out of the ordinary, she closed the distance between her and the rock in two large steps and then bent down.

Shit.

Rocks didn't have structural sutures. Neither did they have occipital orbs on the front. This one did. It was definitely a skull.

Having almost convinced herself it would be nothing more than a weathered rock, she gulped for air, while her mind automatically cataloged the find.

Skull, small, a vertical forehead and rounded, so it was a female, likely Caucasian. The lower jawbone lay twisted slightly to the side. In spite of the moss and the humus, she noted the teeth were intact. They should get DNA and decent photographs to match dental records. And that's just what she saw on the surface. Tiny bits of material peeped through the dirt. There would be more, lots more.

She stared off into the horizon and swallowed several times. Her initial glimpse said a young adult female lay before her.

She closed her eyes and whispered, "Oh, dear God."

It couldn't be. And yet, … given the moss and the condition of the skull, these remains had been here a long time.

But seventeen years long? Possibly.

Surely not, but inside she hoped so. *Please, let this be Cia.*

She pulled out her cell phone to check for reception. She had less than one bar. Like that would do much. Still, she had to try. She quickly grabbed the GPS location from her cell phone and sent it to Chad Ingram at the Seattle police station. Knowing the chance of her message getting through wasn't good, she didn't waste any effort typing a lengthy message.

Her fingers fumbling, she finally managed to get down the words: **Body at location, please come.**

Chapter 3

MEG CAREFULLY MADE her way out of the immediate area, then, unable to help herself, picked up her feet and ran back the way she'd come. Inside, her heart pounded, while, outside, her skin chilled with the breeze, as she raced from the scene behind her.

Damn it.

Why here and why now?

Pete would be so pissed off when he found out. He'd blame her. Last year he wouldn't have. He would have laughed it off and said, *Trust you*. Not this year. He had so many good points, been so accepting for so long, but Janelle's arrival had changed so much.

Or was it Meg who had changed so much? She had to admit that was very possible. She was not the same person she'd been a year ago either. And maybe she wanted different things herself now.

How much difference a year could make …

She reached the cabin, hearing Janelle's excited voice in the distance. Thankfully it was coming from the lake. Meg rushed into the cabin, quickly washed her face, checked her appearance for twigs and moss, and then strolled down to the water's edge.

"Well, don't you look happy?" she said to Janelle, with a big smile. Janelle's face split into a wide happy grin that made Meg's heart squeeze. It had been a long time since she'd seen her so carefree. At least Janelle had had this moment. And maybe Meg could keep her out of the worst of what was to come.

She had to. Janelle had been through enough.

"Did you get a nap?" Pete asked, with a relaxed look on his face.

Obviously the fishing trip had been a resounding success. She shook her head and lied, just a little. "I tried but couldn't, so I went for a walk instead."

He nodded, reached into the boat, and pulled out two still-flapping fish. "And we caught dinner. That makes you the cook."

"Wow!" Meg laughed, enjoying the moment. "I can do that, but you are so cleaning those things, before I take over."

"*Eewww*, clean them? That's gross." Janelle backed up several steps, her face twisting in revulsion.

Laugher rolled across the lake. With Meg's help, Pete pulled the boat alongside the dock and tied up. He handed the tackle box to Janelle, the rods to Meg, and then pulled out his pocketknife. "I'll take care of these now down here. You two can go on up. A cup of coffee would go good right about now."

"Yes, boss." Meg smiled and followed Janelle up to the cabin. The sound of Janelle's excited laughter lifted Meg's sadness. For now, Meg would take what joy she could.

By the time Pete had arrived with the fish nicely cleaned, the coffee was percolating on the stove, and Meg had a salad washed and ready to go.

"Oh, lovely." She turned on the burner, got the pan hot, and added the fish. "Dinner will be soon, so let's set the table and get washed up."

Janelle made a moue, but Meg shook her head. "You smell like the fish you helped catch. So wash with warm water here or go back down to the lake for a dip."

Cringing at the second idea, Janelle came to the sink and scrubbed her hands. "I don't really smell like those fish, do I?" she whispered to Meg.

Holding down the laughter to a minimum, Meg whispered right back, "You smell much better now."

With a beautiful smile, Janelle turned to set the table. Meg stared out at the late afternoon sun, dappling through the trees. Damn it. Why couldn't this perfect family moment be extended for the weekend? Maybe Chad hadn't gotten her message. She brightened. That would be great. The bones had lain there a long time, from what she'd seen. They could remain there another day without harming anyone.

With that happy thought, Meg sat down to dinner.

An hour after dinner, her cell phone beeped. Oh no. She reached for it, wishing she'd put it on Mute.

Call me.

That was it. She glanced up, both Pete and Janelle staring at her disapprovingly.

She offered a small smile. "Sorry, I thought I had it turned off."

"So turn it off now." Janelle frowned, as Meg continued to stare at her. "It's not fair that you have your phone, and I can't have mine."

Meg couldn't resist a small eye roll as she murmured, "Slightly different scenario, kiddo. This is work, not games."

"I thought you told them that you were going away and not to call." Pete's voice was tight, cold.

She sighed. "I did."

"And?" How could his voice, already chilly, become like polar ice with that one word? So smooth and so silky, it sent chills down her back. She groaned lightly. "Please, can we talk about this outside?" She nodded at Janelle, who sat quietly, watching and taking it all in.

He frowned, then relented. "Fine. Janelle, clean off the table. We'll heat up some water to wash dishes when we come back in."

That invoked an immediate response. Meg went through the door before the last of the screeching could be heard. Janelle hadn't had a problem with helping out and doing chores until she'd lost her father. Now gaining any cooperation from her was a challenge.

"That girl needs a stronger hand," Pete said brusquely, as he followed Meg out. "You let her get away with too much."

"I know," Meg admitted, "but, right now, she's got a lot to deal with."

"And rules will help her deal with it effectively." He leaned over the railing at her side. "She'll appreciate you for it later."

"Maybe." Moodily Meg stared at the darkening sky. "For all the beauty here, there is a dark underside to this place." She felt more than saw his sideways look at her.

"That came out of the blue. I think it's time you changed your profession. You are always so depressed and negative these days."

"Well, this time, I have good reason." It was now or never. She wouldn't get a better time. Calmly she collected her thoughts and then explained what she'd seen and how she'd gone back to check and had confirmed what she'd originally suspected.

He just stared at her, the whites of his eyes bright in the

dim light. "You can't be serious?"

"Oh, very serious." She watched the emotions rush through his gaze. His features were always more closed than open, stern more than lighthearted. He'd been raised by a father who hadn't spared the punishment and had then died when he was seven. It had molded Pete into a strong but also hard man in his own right. Their decade together hadn't always been easy, but it had been rewarding.

"And what did you do about it?" he asked, his voice knowing and yet flat. As if realizing he'd have to make the best of it.

She winced. "I texted a cop in the Seattle department that I know."

"Texted?" He stared at her.

"Yeah." She held out her cell phone. "The reception is lousy. I was hoping the text would get through better than a call would."

"Was that the text you received over dinner?"

She nodded.

He sighed and looked up at the stars. "Was it really too much to hope you could leave work behind for a couple days?"

Now that wasn't fair. She hadn't planned on finding a skeleton. She hadn't gone looking for it; well, she had, but only to confirm what she'd seen the first time. She opened her mouth to protest, but then slowly closed it. It so wasn't worth it. She waited quietly.

"So is this person coming here? And, if so, when?"

"I don't know. He asked me to call, but there is no reception."

"Good. Then call when you get back home. Give us a chance to work on there still being an *us*."

With that, he turned and walked back inside, leaving her staring after him. Jesus. Were they that close to there not being an *us* anymore? Her throat seized up. She knew they were having major trouble; she just hadn't realized they were that close to the line.

And, if they were, how did she reconcile her own personal ethics with her personal life? And was her work, in this case, a deal breaker?

She should be calling Chad, and, if that didn't work, jumping in the truck and going back to town and raising the cavalry to come and help. But it was dark, and she didn't know the road. So it was foolish to leave at this time of night alone, and she didn't want to ruin her family's weekend. Considering that she had limited communication out here, would it matter if she waited overnight?

The remains had been there for years. Would another day or two make a difference?

"Auntie Meg? Are you coming inside?" Janelle's timid voice squeaked out into the darkness. Hell. Janelle, already dealing with enough right now, had been unsettled by Meg's exchange with Pete.

No. Given the circumstances, it wouldn't be wrong to wait until morning.

CHAD WAITED FOR a response at his desk, a desk he should have left hours ago, but it was hard when a haunting voice from the past contacted him about an event that had directed his path in life. And might solve the mystery he'd spent half his life trying to solve.

Had Meg even made the connection? She *must* have.

But then they'd all worked to forget that terrible night so

long ago. Maybe Meg had done a better job than Chad had.

She'd certainly forgotten about him, until now.

He'd tried to forget her but had failed. So he'd tried to honor their history instead. A history that included Cia, who'd disappeared without a trace that afternoon so long ago. A brash young group of kids, who'd gone for a fun weekend trip, had come home a group of ravaged adults, forever changed.

Being older, more responsible, and having had a prior relationship with Cia, Chad had felt connected in a bigger way. He also felt guilty. He should have tried to track whatever he'd heard in the woods that afternoon. That he hadn't had eaten away at him for years. In his nightmares, someone was always spiriting an unconscious Cia through the woods, while Chad had hidden away like a coward.

That guilt sat permanently on his shoulders, breathing with him, as he went about his days, waiting for something, *anything*, to blow the case open.

And now it had.

Going to see Cia's parents back then, and trying to explain, had been the hardest thing he'd ever done. Her parents couldn't handle the loss of their only child. The mother had died of an overdose of prescription drugs not long afterward. And the father? Well, he'd called Chad almost monthly, after finding out Chad had been accepted into the police force, asking if he'd found out anything new. Then he'd had a heart attack a few years back, still not knowing what had happened to his daughter.

Chad didn't want the same sad end for himself. Until now he'd been afraid that that was where he was headed.

How could Meg send him that little bit of information and leave him hanging?

He returned to his computer to dig for more information on the location, on any missing persons, and on Meg herself. He'd kept an eye on her progress over the years. As if unable not to, he'd watched her grow into a stunning woman and a highly respected anthropologist in her field. He'd taken a secret joy in finding out that she'd stayed single, but it wasn't something he wanted to examine closer. He also knew she had a long-term relationship.

What the hell had she been up to lately?

And who else had she told about her find?

MACK PICKED UP his cards and took a look, a pair of kings to start. Not bad, not great, but enough to put him in the game. As he tossed in his ante, his cell phone buzzed.

Damn thing.

"Hey, Mack, you gonna play or talk to the little wife all night?" Frank smirked.

Mack snorted. "Ain't her." No way would she interrupt his poker night, unless the house was burning down, and she'd called everyone else already. "It's probably work."

"You're not on call, are you?" Joe asked, tossing his cards on the table in disgust.

"I'm always on call," Mack growled. "I'm getting out next year."

"Ha, you say that every year," one of the guys said.

Mack was used to the ribbing. The group had been meeting for over a decade now. He knew them better than his own brother at this point. He pulled out his cell phone. His gaze locked on the text message. His mood dropped rapidly. Shit.

He'd known this day would come. He just didn't know

about the days after this one. In the beginning, he'd burrowed into this case like a bulldog, determined to prove one of the kids a killer and, therefore, to find the others innocent. But he hadn't been able to. He'd crossed a lot of lines back then and had been slapped back. He shouldn't have been on the case in the first place. He should have handed it off. Only he hadn't been able to. Not when his family had been involved.

But there'd been no answers. No closure—for anyone. For a long time, the worry and frustration had eaten at him. Then, with the passing of the years, it had slipped to the back of his mind. Until now …

"Is it really possible?" he murmured, shock rippling through his beer gut. A deep sense of inevitability gathered underneath. Could they finally have found her? Cia Barnes's disappearance was one of the most frustrating, perplexing cases of his career and the most personally unnerving.

Chad's message included the coordinates in a link. He clicked it, his lips twisting at the technology Chad had used. It was typical of the younger generation and always made Mack feel like a dinosaur.

His stomach rolled, as he recognized the area. Of course he did. He owned a cabin up there, like a lot of other people he knew.

And he'd spent weeks searching for the missing girl. His nephews, three of them, had been part of that group. Idiots. He stared off into space, doing the math. It had to be close to fifteen years now. Or maybe even more. And every time he'd seen his nephews, he'd been reminded of it. Bruce had been badly affected by Cia's disappearance. The other two had been less so but still disturbed enough. The youngest boy had died in a car accident five years later. He'd always wanted to clear his name. The older one, now mostly alone, had gone quiet, and he'd changed. He had nothing to do with Mack's family anymore.

They'd all been badly affected back then. Lives had changed and not necessarily for the better.

As Mack stared at the map, a sense of certainty, readiness, settled in his gut. Maybe now he could find out the truth and could close a chapter in his own life.

THE NEXT MORNING Meg woke, feeling unrested. An early morning chill had her pulling the covers up to her chin. The old blanket had seen better days, kind of like the cabin. She lay quiet, staring at the open timber frame ceiling over the bed, waiting for the unpleasant memories to slip back into place, hidden away with the pain and the sense of loss she'd experienced so long ago.

Maybe Cia had drowned, and her body had sunk to the bottom of the lake? That had certainly been a popular theory at the time. But the divers couldn't find any sign of her. Then it was a deep mountain lake, spring-fed, and apparently bodies often sank and stayed down. There were other possibilities but never any proof for them.

The guilt was bad, but not knowing was … the worst. Had Cia wandered off to join the hikers as a last-minute thought? And had she fallen and hurt herself so severely that she'd died? Or had someone forced her into the woods? Meg knew Chad blamed himself, but he hadn't been there at the time. He'd come back to find Cia gone, *but* she'd disappeared while Meg and Stephanie were swimming in the lake. Sure, they'd been deep in a discussion about their respective boyfriends at the time, but surely they would have heard a scream, a struggle, any outcry at all, if there had been one. They'd certainly heard Chad's shout.

But they'd heard nothing from Cia. *That* dark silence had persisted through Meg's nightmares. The boogeyman had nothing on Cia's attacker.

And that just led Meg back around to the situation again. They'd assumed that Cia had been kidnapped, stolen away in broad daylight. But they'd never had any proof. And just because Meg had found a set of remains close to where Cia had gone missing, it did not mean that these were Cia's. But Meg couldn't stop thinking they might be.

It would be a relief if they were. She needed closure on a most difficult time in her life. It was too late for Cia's parents, but others needed to know what had happened. Like the eight who'd survived the weekend. Not just Meg. She hoped that there would finally be answers and not more questions.

"Go back to sleep. Sleeping in late is one of the good things about a vacation." Pete's sleepy voice drifted up from under the covers, where he was buried. The country air held a chill that had her snuggling under and closer to him. Thankfully Janelle still slept.

Then she didn't have Meg's nightmares.

"You can't do anything about it right now, so sleep."

Meg rolled over and tried to do just that. And couldn't. She pretended to sleep. She did need rest, but inside, the tension coiled tighter and tighter.

A storm was breaking in her world. She knew it and couldn't prepare for it. But it was coming regardless.

Then she heard it.

A truck driving up the road toward the cabin. Would it turn in? The main road went on up and past the cabin turnoff.

Beside her, Pete stiffened, and the room chilled instantly. An eerie stillness took over. Her stomach knotted. Please, not yet. Please, not now.

She held her breath, listening, and, sure enough, the engine shifted, and the growl changed, as it slowed down. Even from inside the bedroom, she heard as the truck bounced over the ruts.

Her eyes closed. *Shit.*

Chapter 4

MEG SLIPPED OUT from under the covers, gave a slight shudder at the chill, and dressed quickly. It would take a few minutes for the truck to get to the GPS coordinates. She had no idea how long it would be before the driver would continue the drive to the cabin. If he even knew about this cabin …

She hadn't called Chad back last night. She'd tried but couldn't get any reception.

Maybe he'd come to check out the location alone.

What she knew for sure was that, if Chad had gotten the message, he'd come. No way he could ignore a body found in this area, any more than she could.

She hoped he didn't ask the one question she didn't have an answer for. *Where had she gotten his phone number?* In truth, she didn't remember the origin, but she'd kept it close for many years. As if waiting for this moment …

She should have told Pete about this part of her past a long time ago. It would be a little rough doing it now. Yet it was another thing she needed to do. Should have already done so, in fact. So why hadn't she? She mulled it over, as she made coffee. There'd been a lot she hadn't shared with Pete, too much really.

Had she just shoved it deep inside, never wanting to touch such a painful topic again? No one would blame her for that, except Pete. And he'd have a point. Partners shared their feelings, their fears, their lives. She'd traveled so much that, every time she'd returned home, there'd been almost a honeymoon air to their relationship. Then she would pick up and take off again. Why? And was she done with that aspect of her life now? She wanted it to be done with. She wanted that vagabond part of her to be settled enough to stay home and to raise Janelle. And to be happy with that life.

It needed to be, or Janelle would suffer. Meg winced, as another truth hit home. Janelle would suffer—like Pete had suffered.

Moodily she stared out the window. Life had been good to her, but had she been good to life? She hadn't been all that concerned with Pete's feelings every time she packed up and took off. She'd been a willing participant in a job that took her anywhere and everywhere.

Her last job in Haiti was a prime example. She'd gone over to retrieve a man's family, who had been killed in the massive earthquake over a year ago and buried in a mass grave. That job started out simple but said nothing about the horrifying twists that she and her team had experienced in the meantime. Poor Jade and Dane, the two of them had gone through hell, but, like the phoenix, they'd risen stronger and happier than ever.

Meg was jealous. And that was just stupid. She had Pete. They'd been together for years and years. They knew each other inside and out. And that's where she stalled. Because the truth was, she hadn't shared with him that defining moment that had sent her on her path around the world and away from him. So just how honest had she really been? How well did he know her? And if *she* hadn't shared—had he?

So how well did she really know him?

Her interior foundation, that of knowing she had been on the right path with the right person, cracked a little more. She bowed her head, struggling to breathe. Dear God, this hurt.

And it was far from over. This crack was just the top opening up, leading to the crevasse below.

Her life was splitting apart. … All she could do was grab on to it and try her best to survive. It was now. It was here. It was time.

"Is the coffee ready?" Pete's heavy voice growled from the bedroom. "Sounds like that's the end of the sleep we'll get tonight."

She caught back a sob, rubbed her cheeks, and answered in a somewhat casual voice, "Yes, it's almost done." Walking back to the coffeepot, she heard the bubbles furiously working away inside. She turned off the burner, threw a cup of cold water inside to calm the grounds, waited a moment, and then poured two cups.

Picking hers up, she walked outside to the low-hanging veranda. The cool air bit her cheeks. It was the dead of summer, but, up here—with so many trees blocking the sunlight, adding in the winds, before the heat of the sun hit—it might as well be autumn.

Across the water, the sun had already crested the hills on the other side, but the long, warming fingers hadn't reached her yet. Too bad, she was cold inside and out. A buzz in her pocket had her reaching for her cell phone to read the incoming text.

Where are you?

She stared down at her phone, then out in the direction of the trees where she'd sent him. There really was no option. She quickly answered. **Coming.**

"Are you going to meet them?" Pete's voice spoke from the other side of the screen door. A barrier she couldn't miss.

With a quick nod, she said, "It will be easiest this way and the fastest."

"I'll stay with Janelle."

She turned to give him a thankful smile, didn't detect a response, sighed again, put down her empty cup on the railing, and walked away.

It took ten minutes for Chad's truck to come into view. At least she hoped it was his truck. She'd only caught sight of him a handful of times in the intervening years. They had a lot of history, and it didn't help that she'd loved him for a long time. She'd gone camping that fateful weekend, knowing he was the man for her and knowing that their relationship was strong enough to survive the upcoming college year apart. Knowing, no matter what, they could make it through the worst life could throw at them.

And, as if challenged, Cia had then disappeared, and that disastrous weekend had split them apart almost instantly. And it had kept them apart for years. So much for *forever.* … So much for *knowing* anything …

She had to admit to being excited about seeing who he was now. He'd been tall and rangy as a young adult, not yet fully grown into his height. He'd had promise though, and she hadn't been alone in seeing it. Chad had always been popular with the girls. Dark hair, dark eyes, with that whole bad-boy thing going on, he'd been the love of her life—until her life as she had known it had come to an end. They'd never officially broken up, but everything had come to a paralyzing halt.

She'd gone on to college alone. There'd been the odd

phone call, the odd unexpected awkward meeting, and the reviews of the case for a few months, then less and less as time had marched on.

Until now.

Her footsteps slowed, as she approached the single vehicle. Was it him?

She took a deep breath, wiped her hands on her jeans, and stepped around the truck.

Only she couldn't see anyone.

She checked the coordinates on her cell phone and realized he'd likely parked and walked from here to the site. She followed.

"Megs?"

It was Chad. That same deep voice she remembered so well, that same old nickname. A surprising warmth washed through her, filling her heart. He'd been such a special friend. She turned slowly and saw him.

"Chad." Her smile was tremulous but real. "And it's Meg now."

He was older now, and more filled out, but still with that same charming grin splitting his face, giving her a glimpse of the young man she'd once known and loved.

In two strides he was at her side. His arms opened. She stepped inside, instinctively loving the way his arms closed tightly around her. For just a moment, she relaxed into his comforting embrace. For just a moment, she let herself slide back in time—and enjoyed the closeness. He squeezed her gently before stepping back, his hands on her upper arms, holding her still, so he could look at her. His gaze warmed, as he stared down at her. "Damn, you look good."

So did he. She couldn't believe the heat churning up her insides. She hadn't had anything to do with him in so long, and yet it was as if they were back at the beginning of that fateful summer, when they'd been so in love.

She opened her mouth to speak, but he snatched her up again and squeezed her tight. When she was freed this time, the words exploded from his mouth. "I couldn't believe it when I saw your text. Nothing like spiking my attention with the one hope I'd lived with all my life." He stopped, then corrected himself, quietly added, "We've *all* lived with."

Tears came unbidden to her eyes. She sniffled slightly. "So true, that nightmare has haunted my days and nights and colored my actions, even when I wasn't aware of it."

He shoved his fists into his jeans pockets. "I hear you." He stared off into the trees, his Adam's apple bobbing up and down several times. "When I think back to all the times, when I wondered, worried, and felt that I could have, should have, done more …" He ran a hand through his hair. "I just hope this is her."

"No way to tell yet." Meg walked closer to the site. "Did you see it?"

"No. I was just searching the area, taking pictures before entering the scene." He glanced at her. "You're the expert in this field."

Her smile slipped. "I had to do something." She glanced at him. "Like you."

Their gazes met in understanding, and, on that note, they approached the area cautiously.

Standing on the one side of the moss-covered tree lying in front of them, she pointed out the gleaming white item in the half light. "That's the skull showing."

"And you've checked it?" he called back, as he took several large strides forward and then squatted. "Sorry. Of course you have."

She approached but stayed off to one side. She allowed her gaze to roam the area slowly, as she searched for more bones, clothing, items, … anything to identify the body and to understand what had happened. The ground was a muted display of greens and browns, and, in the dim light, they blended together, making everything harder to see.

"What can you tell me from the little bit you've seen?"

Taking a deep breath, she verbalized her instant cataloging of the scene. She waited a beat. "You know this is likely to be a crime scene." He shot her a direct look. She nodded. "We're all expecting that Cia died by someone else's hand."

"And yet we don't know for sure that this is her." He studied the ground around the skull, as Meg watched.

What appeared to be years' worth of organic matter decomposing to rich humus hid most of the evidence.

"And it could be a dumping ground or even an accidental death." He straightened. "I've already called help in. A team is on the way."

"Of course you have." She laughed, even while shaking her head. Chad had always been extremely proactive. "Even without seeing the body."

"I didn't need to, as I did my research on you instead."

Her eyebrows shot up. "Really?"

"If you say a body's here, then I'm sure there is." He straightened. "Now tell me that it's Cia, and I'll do everything I can to find the bastard who did this and to hang him from the nearest tree."

Except that he wouldn't. He wanted to. She wanted to. But they were both professionals, and, unfortunately, taking the law into their own hands couldn't happen.

"So tell me. Is it her?" He stood and stared into her eyes, as if willing her to give him the answer he wanted to hear.

"Not so fast," she said in a gentle voice. "I can't identify her just like that." She shrugged. "I can tell you this female is Caucasian and is of the approximate age as Cia was when she vanished, but beyond that ..."

"That's a good start. And it says that it *could* be Cia." He glanced down at the gleaming skull. "Are you sure there's nothing else you can tell me?"

"Well, this girl didn't die from a bullet to her forehead," Meg quipped, recognizing her need to ease a difficult situation with humor. In the distance, she heard the sound of approaching vehicles.

"There is that." He pinned her with a direct look. "Damn, Meg. After all these years, what are the chances?"

"My vote?" Meg thought about location, the length of time the skull had likely laid here, the thickness of the humus. While she knew it was just guesswork at this point in time, there were her instincts, her gut feeling. Abruptly she said, "I think it's her.

His breath whooshed out. In a low voice, he added, "So do I."

CHAD WATCHED MEG leave. He understood she was here with her family. And that felt wrong to him. The last time she'd been here, she'd been with him. But that wasn't the only thing different. Still tall and slim, Meg had revealed a calm maturity now, a sense of going through hell and coming out stronger for it. He'd seen her name mentioned in several articles and always heard her spoken of with respect.

He was proud of her. She'd become a hell of a woman. Then he always knew that she would turn out to be someone special, that she would mature into the promise he'd always seen in her. Cia's disappearance had been difficult, but Meg had gone on to do well regardless.

Chad's life, meanwhile, had been waiting for this moment. And everything else had been put on hold. He'd never married, never had a family. Hadn't done the traveling he'd wanted to or built that log house he'd always planned to build. Everything had been consigned to the category called *later*.

A life interrupted. He sighed and ran a weary hand down his face. Maybe now he could pick up the threads and carry on.

Still staring in the direction where Meg had disappeared, he wondered how she'd been able to pick up her life and to carry on. Instead of it being something he should be happy about, it made him edgy. As if she had no right. And that was just stupid.

Being female, she hadn't come under the same cloud of suspicion as he had. Although being *the replacement girlfriend*, as one cop had called Meg back then, she'd certainly been heavily questioned.

Their relationship hadn't survived Cia's disappearance. None of their relationships had. Six guys and three girls had been in that original group. Three pairs and three spares, and they'd all known each other. All had spent a lot of time together. He'd trusted them. Now he could barely remember the details of their lives.

Yet it felt right having Meg here at this time. Her finding the body had to do with that whole life-interrupted thing.

He heard the sound of a truck in the distance. Good. That should be his team. He wanted to get moving on this scene and to find the answers and, once and for all, put Cia's case to rest. So he could finally get on with the rest of his life.

MEG HATED TO leave Chad and the site, but she wanted to check up on Janelle. Make sure that Pete hadn't gone fishing and left her to wake up on her own.

Besides, Meg couldn't do more at the site now that the team had arrived. Chad had been fully engrossed with taking care of business. She wanted to be a part of that team but hadn't been asked. Better she took care of things here first.

Her empty coffee cup still sat on the railing, where she'd left it. Almost a message. As if it waited for her, just as Pete had done all those years.

Another heavy sigh slipped out. Seemed to be all she did these days. There was so much trauma and so many adjustments. But such was her life right now.

Pete had put up with a lot from her. She could only hope he'd put up with a little more.

She walked inside the cabin and thankfully found both Pete and Janelle sound asleep. She couldn't deny the sense of relief at not being questioned about being gone so long or about bringing her work once again into their home. And there was coffee. Feeling that she'd been given a reprieve, she filled her cup and snuck back outside to enjoy it.

Once settled on the veranda, Chad filled her mind. He looked the same. Older, more mature, harder even, as if he'd seen a lot more of the darker side of life than most people had. Then so had she. They were so much alike; even the paths they'd taken had been along the same lines. What they'd had back then had been so special and so short-lived that she felt like she'd been looking to repeat it ever since— but hadn't found a way of doing it.

She frowned and stared down at her swirling coffee. Life with Pete had been good. It was just different. It didn't matter if it hadn't been the same. Pete was here and now.

Chad and she had gone their own ways a long time ago. It was not as if they had a relationship to go back to, not anymore.

Melancholic and borderline depressed, she couldn't fathom a way forward.

Then she heard the sound of more vehicles. She wondered which anthropological specialist they'd brought in and realized yet another truth. She wanted—no, needed—to be part of that team. She *had* to be involved, to know for sure that no mistakes were being made and that no shortcut had been taken that would stop them from getting to the truth.

And yet she had no right to be involved. She shuddered.

Her cell phone rang. "Hello."

"Are you busy?" Chad's strong voice came through, loud and clear, as if he were standing beside her.

She almost looked to see if he was. "Not more than I was a few moments ago when I left you. Why?"

"I need an anthropologist. The team came without an archaeologist or an anthropologist. They've been trying to find one who is available but aren't having much luck."

"I want to," she answered slowly, knowing he needed a specialist to collect the remains and to work on their identification, "but that might not be a good idea, given our potential connection with the victim."

"But we don't know who the victim is at this point. There are many missing women cases. And your name on this list of consulting experts came up, *and* you're here on the spot. And there is the weather factor, with a storm possibly tonight. We have limited options. If you can give us a hand collecting the remains and the evidence, it would be a great time saver. The longer the remains stay here, the less chance we have of collecting all the evidence. And, once the media find out, more people will be here, digging around …" He left the rest hanging.

She understood. The media would latch on to the discovery within hours, if not sooner, and then there'd be the curiosity seekers. The team must collect everything before then.

It's what she'd hoped for. The opportunity she hadn't expected to be offered.

"I'm on my way." She disconnected and stood.

"Where are you going?" Janelle's soft voice crept through the screen door. Meg instinctively hunched her shoulders. With yet another sigh, she opened the door, placed her mug on the counter, then hugged her niece. "Some men need my help for a couple hours. It's just down the road. I won't even need to take the truck."

She peered into Janelle's eyes, hoping she understood and was okay with it. But a maturity well beyond her twelve years stared back at her. "You found a body down there, didn't you?"

Meg wanted to lie, wanted to keep death out of the cabin, only it had already crept in. She whispered ever-so-softly, "Yes. I did."

There was no change in Janelle's gaze, but she hung on Meg's every word.

"I will be back as soon as I can. I promise."

"Take me with you."

The plea was so soft and hesitant, it almost broke Meg's heart. She gathered Janelle into her arms. "I can't, honey. That's no place for a child."

Or for a niece who had too much death in her life already.

Janelle pulled back, her body vibrating in outrage. "I'm not a child anymore, Auntie Meg."

"I know." And Janelle had been through so much that she'd grown up more than most other kids her age. "But in the eyes of the law you are." She smiled down, tugging a stray strand of hair off Janelle's face. "I'll be as fast as I can."

Janelle's gaze bored into Meg's, as if by will alone, she could force Meg to return faster. "Promise?"

With a lopsided smile, Meg promised.

"And, if she isn't, we'll go down there and drag her back up here." Pete's smooth voice spoke from the living room behind them. Still tucking his shirt into his jeans, he nodded at Meg, adding in a slightly colder voice, "So be quick, or we'll be the first two of your curious public."

She winced. It was so not the role she wanted Janelle to be in. And she understood Pete's warning. Not liking it, but knowing it was the best she'd get under the circumstances, she dropped a kiss on Janelle's cheeks and headed for the door.

Only as the screen slammed behind her did she note that she hadn't kissed Pete goodbye. Again.

Outside in the fresh air, racing down the path to the work she loved, she could leave behind the anger, the sense of oppression, the uncomfortable changes that life had forced upon her. She loved both Pete and Janelle more than life itself, but that life had become incredibly wearying lately.

She could only hope better times were coming.

And maybe this was just what she needed. Inside, a building excitement took over. What if they'd finally found Cia? Meg could leave that part of her life behind.

And finally get on with her future.

Chapter 5

CHAD AND HIS team were waiting for her.

She nodded to the others, listened to his brief introductions, then went to the truck. They'd brought suits and supplies. She geared up, grabbed her gloves and several tools, and moved carefully to the remains. On the way, she murmured to Chad in passing, "Thanks."

"You're welcome. Figured you would like to be in on this one," he said, with a knowing look in his gaze.

She paused, gave him a quick glance. "In all ways," she said, then bent down and got to work.

The work over the next few hours was painstaking. As she concentrated on the remains, Chad stayed close by but out of her way, while the rest of the team went about mapping the scene, photographing, and marking finds. The bones were scattered and, once located, were marked. Trees had fallen over time in a crisscross pattern, keeping the bones relatively contained.

Meg worked on the torso. Under and surrounding the rib cage, tiny rotten pieces of material poked through the surface debris. As Cia might have been only in a bathing suit at the time of her disappearance, that would also fit. Some materials had decomposed entirely, others only partially. Some had never deteriorated. The lab would determine more. The original color of the material was no longer identifiable, having been stained some kind of deep woodsy color.

All the moss that grew on and around the bones had to be collected and returned to the lab to confirm no evidence was in the foliage. The team had set up commercial lights to assist in the collection process, giving a weird sci-fi glow to the area.

In spite of her best efforts to remain neutral, her heart pounded as she lifted each piece of bone and examined it, looking for answers. The bones had been cleaned by Mother Nature, giving further proof of the length of time the body had been exposed to the elements.

"The remains are scattered. We'll need to search for all the pieces." She glanced around, looking for other markers. Considering the location and the fallen trees, that made sense. There were signs of animal activity, and that was to be expected too. "Both femurs are missing."

"We have a femur over here," called out one of the other techs from beside her. Straightening, Meg winced as she realized how long she'd been bent over in that position. She stretched slightly, gave a slight moan, and then stepped back to hand over the last of the bones she'd tagged to be moved to the truck. There was more to do, but the work was moving quickly. She glanced at her cell phone. Not bad timing; even Pete shouldn't be too upset at her for this.

She made her way over to where the femur lay. Picking it up carefully, she noted the head appeared to have fused. That placed the victim between the ages of eighteen and twenty-four. Cia had been eighteen at the time of her disappearance. Given the length of time, which she could only estimate ...

Chad held up a tape measure—their gazes meeting. He

quickly measured the length of the femur, while she did the mental calculations. "The victim was right around five feet tall."

A long hard breath shuddered free from Chad. "And Cia was five feet tall—*a hair over*, as she liked to say."

Meg nodded. She closed her eyes. Then straightening her spine, she said, "Let's finish this."

The excavation was time-consuming to do properly. With the evidence of animal activity around the remains, Meg wanted to ensure she had every bone possible. Two more of the ribs lay at her feet off to the right, and a couple pieces of the spine were on top of each other to the left.

The skull was next. She moved it onto a large sheet and examined it carefully. She kept her feet firmly in place to avoid shifting anything, just in case she lost something important. She found no head wounds, no indication of a blow to the head as the cause of her death. There were small animal marks, but the top of the skull was amazingly undamaged. The lower jaw bone, in similar shape, was placed next to the skull. She was happy to see large healthy teeth and even happier to see the molars. Not only could they pull DNA from them for identification but they certainly put the age of the victim within the seventeen to twenty-two range, which was another point in favor of these bones being Cia's remains.

As Meg scooped up the debris from around the head, a smaller white bone caught her eye. She lifted it carefully and held it up, her professional eye immediately understanding that she was holding the hyoid bone.

The breath gushed out of her chest, and, for a moment, she couldn't breathe. It was too early to make a formal cause of death, and she, for all she wanted to be in on the examination of these remains, might not be the one to find the official cause of death. Yet this bone gave her a lead in that direction. It had been fractured.

And it answered one question—in her mind, at least.

Chad leaned closer. "What did you find?"

She looked over at him, her eyes wide, knowing the sheen of tears in them was unmistakable. An eerie silence filled the air. Several of the team walked closer, as if understanding something important was about to happen.

"This victim"—she swallowed back Cia's name—"was strangled." Then she couldn't help herself from whispering, "Cia was murdered."

CHAD STARED AT the small bone in Meg's hands. He swallowed hard. They'd known it. There'd really been no other answer.

But knowing it wasn't the same as proving it. And he knew it was too early for conclusive identification, but, given everything they knew so far, he was sure they'd finally found Cia. And that made his spine freeze. At this moment in time, everything locked down, as he realized what had happened here seventeen years ago.

His gaze fastened on Meg's, knowing that she was thinking the same thing. The sadness in her eyes, the inside knowledge of what Cia had gone through—that same knowledge was streaming through his mind. Strangulation wasn't easy to do effectively. Cia, so tiny and petite, would have fought like a tiger, claws and teeth if she had had to. But, given her size, there wasn't much hope of her throwing off an adult male attacker.

Chad nodded, breaking their locked gazes. "Okay. Let's

finish this. Let's take Cia home."

WITH CHAD'S WORDS echoing in her mind, Meg returned to the job at hand, focused and determined to do her part in solving this mystery. Her heart hurt from Cia's pain and the sense of fear that Meg could swear still lingered over the area, so strong and thick, as if she could reach out and touch it. Meg knew it was the memories, the inside knowledge that made this job so much more difficult for her.

But the same inside knowledge also made her the right person to be here—helping to take their friend back home.

The hours went by, as Meg worked on with incredible thoroughness—to the point of overkill. But she refused to let up. She didn't dare miss anything.

As the last of the bones were collected and packed for transporting, she walked back to where she'd found the skull and bent down for one last look. Something glinting below the skeleton suddenly caught her eye.

She crouched lower and carefully scooped up the next layer, including what had caught her eye. It was a necklace. Using her fingers, she gently tried to clean it, but it was as organic looking as the debris around it. It was a small simple heart-shaped pendant. She remembered all the girls wearing them back then. Turning it over, she found something inscribed on the back of the heart.

"What did you find?" Chad dropped down beside her. His breath caught, as he saw what she held in her hand. His voice hoarse, urgent, asked, "Can you read it?"

Using a flashlight, she tried to read the inscription. She could barely make out the words. *Oh God.* Her heart squeezed, and her breath locked deep inside.

Wordlessly she held it up into the light, so he could read it for himself. He whispered reverently, "*For Megs. Love you always.*"

They stared at each other. Pain, fear, and understanding filtered into his gaze.

"Meg, is that yours?"

She swallowed hard, closed her eyes, then opened them to look directly into his worried dark eyes. Then she nodded and whispered, "I think so."

CHAD LET HIS gaze wander over Meg's devastated face. Tears were in her eyes. He hadn't thought about the cost to her personally of taking on this job. He'd been thinking of the cost to her *not* being involved. From what he knew about her, from his research and the articles written on her, she was very exacting in her work. She was a perfectionist that coaxed the most from the evidence. He needed that, both professionally and personally.

And now he'd hit a snag he could never have foreseen.

But first things first; he motioned at Larry to take over the chain of evidence and to document everything that had just happened. With one last glance at the necklace, he nudged Meg into putting it carefully in the bag, where it was sealed and written on for the evidence tracking.

He tugged her to her feet and walked her back out of the circle. "You did your job. Let them finish this up."

"You know my being here is a problem now, don't you?" She stared at him, dazed and unfocused.

Shit.

Who could have prepared for this? The best thing was to follow procedure and to carry on. It's what they all did best.

Process the evidence and see where it led them.

And if it led them to the woman standing corpse-like in front of him, then he'd follow it there—and find a way to clear her name. The prosecutor would say Meg had been wearing this necklace when she'd fought with Cia, as she had killed her. The necklace had fallen off during the struggle, unnoticed by Meg at the time.

Chad had no doubt she'd had nothing to do with Cia's disappearance. Stephanie had also backed up Meg's statement that she had never left her sight. In other words, they'd provided each other with alibis. And that could be another problem.

He watched in silence, as the techs continued working the crime scene.

Why would that necklace have been here? After all these years …

"When did you notice it was missing?"

Meg glanced at him, her gaze unfocused, as if churning back through the memories. "I don't know. I don't remember a time that sticks out." She shrugged helplessly. "Who can remember that long ago? I missed a lot of stuff back then. We packed in a hurry, left in chaos."

How true. Back then Chad had been taken to the police station. He didn't even know who'd packed up his stuff. Just that he'd gotten it back at some point in time. It had been hell. She was right. Who could remember?

And it was a small, relatively insignificant item that could have been removed at any time. Before Cia had gone missing or afterward. Cia could even have taken the necklace to wear herself. Either borrowed it, as the girls had often done before, or stolen it from Meg herself. In fact, if Meg had it there at the camping trip, everyone had access to it.

But why bother?

Unless Cia had taken it herself … or someone had wanted to implicate Meg.

And that meant one of their camping group—who else would have known about it? And that was just wrong. He'd sworn that his friends were innocent at the time.

But he was older now and, hopefully, wiser.

He would swear Meg had nothing to do with Cia's disappearance, and Chad knew he hadn't. That left six others. Could he, in good conscience, *still* say they were all innocent?

It had been so much easier back then to band together and to choose to believe in a stranger abduction. Chad knew now that those were the hardest kinds of abductions to deal with. Strangers who picked random victims for weird reasons that lurked in their minds. This made it hard to track them and even harder to find a pattern in their behavior, making them almost impossible to catch.

With nothing surfacing in the case over the years, the stranger abduction theory had seemed more and more likely. But was it?

Did the necklace even change anything? Or just confirm that someone had it in their possession. Hell, for that matter, Meg could have lost it while they were all out searching for Cia. "Could she have borrowed the necklace from you?"

Meg frowned, her head tilting to the side, as she considered the concept. "It's possible. We shared clothes and jewelry and make-up all the time. I'm not even sure why I would have had it with me that weekend. Josh gave it to me."

"Josh? Then Cia wouldn't wear it, would she? She was going out with Josh at that point."

"I know. But she'd been bugging him for jewelry, so maybe wearing it was to put pressure on him. As if saying, *See? I know you bought this for Meg. Prove you love me more by buying me something better.*"

"And of course the last line, with the overtones of *See? I know you loved her more than me. This just proves it. You didn't give me a necklace.*" He couldn't quite keep the bitterness out of his voice. Cia had been a lot of things—fun, pretty, smart—but she'd been conniving to boot. She wanted things, expensive things, all the time.

"It's not an expensive piece, just a trinket really. I kept it because Josh gave it to me." She kicked the dirt at her feet.

Chad felt his heart start. "You weren't upset when you broke up with Josh, were you?"

She gazed at him, blinked, then finally understood. "Oh no, I wasn't. It was not good for either of us. Yet he was my first serious boyfriend. I wanted to honor that time in my life, and so I kept it. And obviously I didn't care that much because I can't remember losing it or even being aware of losing it."

That sounded like the Megs he knew. And his mind immediately wondered if she'd done anything to honor their relationship?

And, once that thought entered his mind, he couldn't let it go. They'd been more-than-good together. It had been the best relationship he'd ever had. He'd had several since then, but they hadn't been the same. They hadn't been Meg. How sad was that?

And why was that?

He hated that instinctive answer in his head, in his heart. Because his was a life interrupted, to be continued, so to speak. It was way down the road, waiting for when Cia came home.

As he stared around at the organized chaos working to claim Cia, he wondered what that meant for him, … for Meg, … for them … now.

MEG RETRACED HER steps to the cabin, walking slowly, carefully, afraid a misstep would send her world listing again. It felt as if it mattered where she placed her feet. Somewhere along the line she'd gone off the track of the life pathway she'd expected to be on. It had taken a hard right, and she'd forgotten to stay on course.

Now she felt suspended, weak, hurt, and injured in ways she couldn't understand. Her thoughts and emotions were left hanging.

Chad had to follow the evidence, and he would. She knew that. It was also the right thing to do.

The necklace had been a shock. It *was* hers. At least she thought it was. The inscription stated her name. And she had no reason to believe another Megs was in the vicinity. Or another Megan, for that matter. She'd been Megan all through school, but her friends had called her Megs. A nickname her mother had abhorred. So, of course, Meg had encouraged its use.

After Cia's disappearance, Meg knew there was no going back to Megan or Megs. That was a time of schoolgirls and innocence.

She'd lost that.

Then there was the whole guilt thing. Her adult mind knew she hadn't done anything wrong, but a part of her was stuck in teenage mode from that time and couldn't shake off the guilt. She'd been there. On the spot. At the time, she and

Stephanie had been deep in gossip. So involved that Meg hadn't seen Cia go to her tent or even leave for a walk. Meg certainly hadn't noticed Cia being carried away.

That was the worst thing. How could someone disappear right from under their noses without anyone noticing?

She approached the cabin silently, wishing her heart wasn't so empty and her head wasn't so full.

No sounds came from the cabin. It would be good if Pete had taken Janelle fishing to get her mind off what Meg was doing. Maybe she should have lied to Janelle, but the child was old enough to understand what Meg did for a career.

She opened the cabin door and entered. The place was empty. Sighing, she snagged an apple from the cooler and returned to the veranda and followed it around to the other side of the house. She could see out onto the lake, but the boat was nowhere in sight. She walked to the lakeshore and still saw no sign of the boat. Good. Maybe they'd enjoy their trip and come back happy.

Happy was something *she* hadn't felt in a long time.

She strolled down to the end of the dock, enjoying the way the water lapped at the edge of the wood. Once at the end, she surveyed the lake, looking to see her family.

Only there was no sign of them.

Unable to stop the jittery feeling inside, she walked farther along the beach, climbing over rocks and ducking under low-lying branches. She could try texting Pete, but he'd been the first to suggest they leave all electronics behind this weekend. So chances were good he'd been the first to ditch his. He hated the damn thing anyway. Not much of a sacrifice for him.

For her on the other hand, … yeah, she loved all electronics and made no excuses. She used as much up-to-date technology for her work as she could, used cloud-based storage for everything all the time and always stayed connected, both professionally and personally.

She was a creature of today's world. Pete was a bit out of the loop in today's technological world. Janelle had been born in this era and didn't understand that the tech hadn't always been here. In fact, she complained when the internet was slow, when her songs wouldn't download fast, when her pages wouldn't load immediately.

Meg chuckled. Janelle was a child of the instant-gratification generation. Meg could only wonder what the next few generations would be like.

With perfect timing, her cell phone rang. Glancing around guiltily, Meg answered it. "Hello, Chad."

"Are you okay?"

She had to stop and think before answering slowly. "I can't say that I am fine, but I am holding."

"Good." The obvious relief in his voice warmed her. "I was worried about you. Finding that necklace really threw you."

"Didn't it throw you?" she asked quietly, only a tiny bit of bitterness leaking through. "Didn't you, for one moment, wonder if it had come off in a struggle that ended Cia's life and that I hadn't known about the loss at the time?" Even as the words burst loose from her, something inside her recognized the hard ball of fear that she'd never quite managed to let go of. Instead she'd kept it stuffed down deep inside. And now there was no holding it back. Torrential waves of emotions rolled over her, making her bend over, gasping for breath, trying hard to hold back the contents of her stomach.

It was the fear that she would be found guilty of some-thing she *hadn't* done. She'd been so afraid that somehow someone would find her guilty.

"No." The response blasted through the phone, instinctive, reactive, righteous. "I definitely did not think that. You, more than anyone else, should know what I went through that weekend. I *know* you had nothing to do with it."

She had gone through so much hell back then that she thought she would never sleep again. She knew she hadn't done this horrible thing. She also knew Chad hadn't. But they'd always worried they'd go to jail for a crime they hadn't committed, as so many other people had.

Still, his natural response, the absolute belief in his voice, was a soothing balm to her raw emotions. A slight bitterness continued to leach through her soul nevertheless—albeit now at a slower rate. "But your knowing won't stop the cops from looking at me sideways and from digging deep into my life to see if they can find a way to pin this on me."

"I'm a cop. Remember?" Chad took a deep breath. "I know this is tough. It's tough for all of us. And ... I will admit that it'll get worse, before we can solve the case and put it away forever."

Meg added, "You shouldn't even be working this case. Your bosses won't let you. You know that, right?" Meg wiped her dry eyes. There should be tears; they were inside her soul, just not ready to fall yet. "It's stupid. I have wanted to find her for so long. I have needed closure on that part of my life, ... and, now that it's here, now that we might have found some answers, ... I don't want to go there. I'm afraid this is a Pandora's box, and I'll regret ever having opened it."

"Don't say that. We didn't do anything to her, but we've been punished, and have been punishing ourselves, as if we had. This is our chance to get at the truth. We owe it to ourselves. And we owe it to Cia. She didn't deserve whatever happened to her." The force and conviction in his voice had Meg straightening her body and running her hands through her hair.

"I know. I have to believe this is for the best, but it's hard." She sighed and admitted, "I've felt so alone all these years. Finding her brought everything slamming back."

"You are not alone. You have your family. Don't isolate yourself. Share this with them."

She stared out over the lake and wondered about that. In fairness to Pete, he hadn't been given entrance to that part of her life. She'd shoved her history into the same damn hole as the rest of the mess. "Pete doesn't know."

Silence.

She winced, understanding the myriad questions her statement must bring up. She was being forced to examine a few of them herself. Why hadn't she shared? And, if she couldn't share before, why, after ten years, couldn't she share now? And was it Pete? Or was it her? And the big question— what would she do about it going forward?

"I'm sorry."

That surprised her. She frowned. "Why?"

"Because this is too big for you to hold inside. You need someone to hold you, even just for a moment. Troubles shared are easier troubles to bear."

"And do *you* have someone to share this with and to hold you at night?" This time the silence was awkward, uncomfortable. She bowed her head and pinched the bridge of her nose. "I'm sorry," she said softly. "I had no right to ask that."

"It's fine." But, when he spoke again, it obviously wasn't

fine. "I have had several relationships since you, but none of them strong enough to last. And, like you, none of them were close enough to share this with."

"We've always been alone, haven't we? Always waiting, always isolated." Now there was no holding back the tears in her eyes. Tears for the lives impacted on and destroyed by Cia's disappearance. When he didn't answer, her anger flared at him, at herself, and at the situation. She snapped, "Haven't we?"

The slow, deep exhale whispered through the phone, mingled with and supported his soft answer. "Yes."

Chapter 6

MEG DIDN'T KNOW how long she been sitting on the end of the dock. She should have been making something to eat. Or, if she was lucky, Pete would have caught more fish for her to cook. Truly she didn't care either way.

Her mind was fixated on the necklace. What she had deliberately withheld from Chad was now a nasty, festering suspicion inside her. For all Cia's good qualities, the fact remained that she had some not-so-nice qualities as well. For Meg, it was wrong to say bad things about dead people, but there it was. And Cia had always been jealous of Meg and of what Meg had had.

It wouldn't be the first time Cia had *borrowed* something of Meg's. Also it would have twisted the knife into Josh, something else Cia had liked to do.

Not for the first time, Meg realized that, had Cia lived, Meg would not have stayed friends with her. They hadn't been good friends even then. They'd been part of the same group. And that was different. There'd been an air of finality to that last summer. Meg had known that they were going their separate ways, once college had started. She couldn't even remember each person's plans. Theirs had probably changed too. Meg had planned on becoming a dentist. She laughed at that now.

Chad had planned on becoming an engineer, along with one of his best friends, Josh. So much had changed …

The soothing sound of splashing water brought her attention back to the lake. Pete and Janelle. At last. … As she glanced at her cell phone to check the time, she realized she'd only been waiting a half hour. Not bad at all. As she watched them come closer, she realized Janelle appeared to be dozing, her head resting on her arm, the other trailing in the water. Pete, in front, was rowing smoothly and steadily. This was his favorite type of relaxation.

He was lucky to indulge as often as he could. The cabin had been his uncle's, and he'd left it to Pete in his will. There'd been such a wealth of satisfaction on his face, when the property had been signed over to him. The timing had been such that Meg had been on the verge of leaving on yet another job. Then Pete had left too, his truck loaded with tools and supplies, to make the modifications to the place he'd always wanted to be done.

She waved at him as they came closer. He nodded but was silent. The soft dip and pull of the oar in the water continued at a steady pace for a few moments, until he brought the boat alongside the dock. Meg grabbed the bow and held it steady, while Pete turned around and noticed Janelle. "Hard to believe she's still asleep. She's been out for a good hour."

"She must have had a bad night," Meg said quietly, reaching for the rope and tying up the boat. Pete worked his way to where Janelle lay and gently picked her up. The boat rocked, but Pete held steady until it stabilized. In four strides, he was up on the dock. Grabbing the tackle box, Meg then followed the pair up to the cabin.

Her phone rang before she'd taken a dozen steps. It was

Chad yet again. With a cautious glance at Pete's back, she answered softly, "Hello."

"I'm heading back into town. I'll call you when I get the paperwork sorted out."

She knew what he meant. His choice of anthropologist hadn't turned out to be the best one, now that her necklace had been found with the remains. "Fine, we'll be here for another night. Then we'll head home tomorrow afternoon."

The door slammed closed in front of her. Damn. "Or maybe we won't. I don't know yet. I haven't had a chance to talk to Pete."

"I wouldn't leave it too long," Chad warned.

"I know."

"Anyway, I'll speak to my boss, but, considering you did the excavation, it should be you doing the examination. I know there are some issues, but are you willing to follow through, if I can make it happen?"

"Yes." And that's what she had wanted. What the protocol was for this sort of situation in Seattle, she didn't know. A case-by-case basis, she would assume. "You didn't have to ask."

"You're not heading off for distant parts right way, are you?"

Not anymore. But he didn't know about her brother's death and the other changes in her life. "No. I will be home. I'm trying to figure out my own career at the moment."

"Good. I'll get back to you."

A warm smile bloomed inside her at his reassurance. "Thank you."

"Don't thank me. Help me to catch this asshole. He's ruined everyone's lives for long enough. It's time we ruined his."

CHAD HOPPED INTO his truck and prepped for the long trip back. He was hungry and tired, yet excitement, … eagerness, had lit a fire in his achy muscles and had kept his brain moving. The techs weren't done yet and probably wouldn't be for another few hours. Before heading back to town, he wanted to drive around and take pictures, catch the lay of the land. He'd already downloaded maps of the region on his GPS but wanted to see for himself what cabins were here and how far away they were from each other.

He'd come here time and time again, looking for Cia, searching for any evidence that could shed light on her disappearance. It was an obsession at first, then a hobby. Over the years, the trips had gotten farther apart. He hadn't been here for five years. But that didn't stop him from downloading the latest images of the area every time Google Earth updated them. He had topographical maps, aerial maps, and satellite photos. His original folder had become a zippered briefcase heavy with data.

He'd done some research on the owners of the cabins seventeen years ago, and then, when he'd been able to access the databases once he was in law enforcement, he'd gone deeper.

But he had found nothing useful.

He knew it was too early to confirm the remains as Cia's, but there were good grounds for assuming they were. He'd spent an hour taking pictures and then marking off a grid, noting where the three pairs and three spares had their tents set up all those years ago. Definitely they were within walking distance, but not the *carrying a person* walking distance. Not unless that person was in awesome shape and bloody strong. That was another reason to let Meg off the hook. Back then, she'd been called gangly. She'd grown into her height and had filled out some. She could probably have lifted Cia—tiny doll-like Cia. But Chad doubted that Meg could have carried Cia that far.

No, this had all the markings of a male aggressor. He winced. He knew all too well what often happened to women in those situations. He could only hope that Cia's end had been mercifully swift.

He'd noticed Meg's enforced calm, as she'd gone through the process of collecting the remains. It had been that strong silence that had him watching her carefully. This was difficult for her. For him too. But she'd maintained a professional demeanor the whole time. Until she'd found the hyoid bone—and then her necklace.

Chances were good that Cia had been strangled to death, given the current evidence. And that was a downright personal way to kill someone. Was it someone who'd known her? It was that question that kept bringing him back to the group of friends who'd gone camping so long ago.

Sure, she could have wandered off on her own.

But she hadn't strangled herself.

THE CABIN WAS largely silent as Meg entered. Waves of disapproval emanated from Pete. *Geesh*, what a surprise. *Not.* Janelle sat up on the old couch, yawning. "Auntie Meg?"

"Yes, honey, I'm here."

Janelle gave her a tired smile. "Good. I wondered how much longer you would be."

Meg laughed lightly. "And imagine my surprise when I came back to find you both out enjoying the sun, fishing on the lake."

Janelle brightened. "You were home before us then? I wanted to wait for you, but Pete said no, that we couldn't spend our whole lives waiting on you to walk away from work."

Her childlike delivery did nothing to impact the overtone in Pete's words. The message was so typical of Pete. She refused to glance at him. She dropped a kiss on the top of Janelle's head. "I'm glad you went fishing. Was it fun?"

Janelle shook her head. "There were no fish," she complained. "And it was hot. I got really tired."

"And you had a nap, all of which is good." Meg straightened up. "I guess that means I need to find something for dinner, seeing as how you guys didn't catch anything, *huh*?"

Janelle grinned. "I want grilled cheese."

"Really? We're out here camping, and you want a grilled cheese?" It had to be Janelle's favorite meal. And it was so not high on the healthy food list. Then sometimes one needed to toss the list in the garbage. And this weekend, the list probably should be burned.

"Pete, what about you?"

"We brought hamburgers. We can't keep raw meat past today, so it's hamburgers, regardless of what anyone wants." On that categorical note, he walked over to the cooler and pulled out the sealed and dripping bag from the ice. He slapped it on the counter and proceeded to make patties.

An awkward silence followed. Meg glanced over at Janelle, who was biting her lip nervously. Meg wanted to run away and hide. When did a person hit overload, and when did it all become too much?

She didn't dare hit that point. Janelle needed her. And Meg didn't think she'd ever been needed before. Her parents were almost past child-rearing age when she'd been born, and, while they had done their duty by her, their relationship had been an independent one. It still was. Meg called them on special occasions, but they'd moved to a warmer, drier climate a long time ago. And now their cool relationship had chilled even further. She'd just always assumed it would improve, but it hadn't.

With a reassuring smile, she turned to help Pete get out the rest of the fixings for the burgers. Pete walked outside to light the barbecue. She watched him with sadness in her heart.

"Auntie Meg?" Janelle came up beside her to stare out the window at Pete. "Why do you stay with him?"

Her breath caught in her throat. She tried to smile but failed. Still to her, honesty *was* the best policy, so she answered Janelle's question, "We're just going through a bad patch right now."

"Really?" Janelle picked at a piece of lettuce. "I don't remember ever seeing a 'good' patch."

Meg looked at her sideways. "This last month has been tough for all of us."

"You weren't happy before Dad died either. He always wondered why you felt you had to settle for this, when you could have found someone to love instead."

"He didn't say that to you, did he?"

"Not to me, but to Grandma on the phone. I overheard him."

That hurt. It was also all too possible. Darren had been closer to her parents. Then he'd been a lot older. Did they really believe she didn't love Pete? Surely not. Pete and she had been together a long time. They had gone through a lot to get here. He loved her, even if he didn't show it. And she loved him. But lots of relationships went through a cooling-off period.

She didn't want to think it was any more than that, but Janelle wasn't ready to let it go.

"You guys don't hug. He never kisses you. You don't hold hands. I thought people in love did all that."

People in love? Were they that different from people who loved each other? Meg was stumped for an answer. She tried a different tactic. "Some people are more demonstrative. Other couples are happy to touch less." She shrugged. "I guess Pete and I are in second group." There was a long silence. Meg looked up from the tomato she was cutting. "What?"

"You always hug and kiss me," Janelle noted.

So true, but Meg didn't want to make the obvious connection. She knew there were problems with her relationship with Pete, but she didn't want them pointed out by anyone, much less by her too-observant niece.

Thankfully Pete came in then to say the burgers were ready.

Dinner was a quiet affair. Janelle could barely eat; her eyes drooped with fatigue. Meg eyed her carefully. The fresh air would have made her tired, but it should also have made her hungry. She didn't eat enough as it was now.

But then Meg was having trouble getting down her own burger. Finally she managed to finish it. She cleaned up the dishes quickly and suggested a walk, but the others declined. Janelle grabbed a book and went to her bed. Meg suspected few pages would get turned before Janelle crashed for the night. Maybe sleeping the weekend away was a good thing to do at this time. Then again, it was hard to know what was best.

Pete headed back outside to clean up and to pack up the

barbecue. Meg took a seat on the veranda, as she waited for the kettle to boil for some tea.

"So are we leaving in the morning?" He stood, hands on his hips, glaring at her.

She glanced over at him in surprise. "Why? I thought the plan was to leave in the afternoon."

"We were, until you found another excuse to work. Don't you have to go deal with the remains?" The cool tone of his voice spoke of suppressed curiosity.

"Not necessarily." She relaxed back into her chair. "There are other qualified people back in Seattle. They just couldn't get someone to come out here today."

"And why did it have to be today? Surely tomorrow would have been soon enough. You found the body yesterday."

She sighed. "True. Having reported it, the media would likely hear, and then any number of strangers could come traipsing through the area. That's the worst thing to have at a crime scene." She pointed at the cloudy sky. "Also, the weather is set to change. No one wants to lose the evidence."

"Crime scene? Evidence?" His voice rose sharply. "How do you know a crime has been committed?"

"We don't." She tried to reassure him. "It's just that we treat each scene as if it were and hope the evidence proves it wasn't. This person could have died a natural death." She didn't of course, but it wasn't Meg's place to say so.

"Could you tell the sex?"

"Of course. The remains are those of a young woman."

The silence was oppressive. He gave a harsh bark. "She hardly died of natural causes then, did she?" He got up and walked to the far end of the veranda. "Odds are she was murdered. Then you already knew that, didn't you?"

She closed her eyes. Her professional and personal lives were once again butting up against each other. Since when had it started doing this? It never used to be an issue. And since Janelle's arrival in their home, Pete knew Meg wouldn't ever be leaving again. So why was there this continual discord?

"What, no answer? You, whom the experts call on for answers, have nothing to say now?"

Inside, her stomach sank. He was in a rare mood. And she didn't need any more emotional storms right now. But almost as if he realized he could push even harder and take a bigger cut out of her heart, he pushed deeper. "Oh, right. It's confidential. You can't tell me."

"Yes," she murmured quietly. "It's a police matter now, but that's not the point. I only collected the remains. Tests have to be done in order to determine the cause of death."

"Bullshit," he roared. "You'd know. Within minutes of seeing her body, you'd have known if Mother Nature had taken her or if she'd died by her own hand or someone else's hands."

"Lots of times, yes, I know, but sometimes I truly do not know. There are no one-answer-fits-all-scenarios here."

He snorted, disgust and old anger filling his dark features.

Meg watched him warily. She wasn't comfortable with this man she lived with anymore. Where was the man she fell in love with? Or even a year ago? That man was calm, funny, accepting. This one seemed to do nothing but pick away at small things in bitterness and anger.

Without warning, his fist lashed out and slammed into the railing post. She winced as blood flew from his ripped knuckles. She jumped to her feet and started toward him, but he turned and held out his other hand. "Don't come any closer. This is your fault."

She gasped. "My fault? That you were an idiot and punched the wood?"

Oh shit. At the word *idiot*, he locked down and became shadowed, as if icing up. His gaze turned almost black. "I. Am. Not. An. Idiot."

"I didn't mean it that way," she said, hastily backing down. She took a deep breath. "I'm sorry. I guess we're all touchy right now."

He stared at her, with no give in his expression.

She didn't know how to cross the impasse dividing them. He was so on edge right now, anything could set him off.

And that she didn't need. She'd seen more than her share of what happened to women when they came too close to a man's wrath.

She turned and quietly walked back inside. Closing the screen door softly behind her, she left him alone to his righteous anger. She paused at the doorway and looked back at him, searching the growing darkness, hoping to see some softening. When there was none, she realized they'd crossed yet another invisible line.

One she wasn't sure could ever be crossed back over again.

HE STARED DOWN at his cell phone. Jacob, the owner of the café, had called. Said there were a mess of cops at the lake. And an old set of remains had been found.

Interesting …

He smiled, a cold smile of anticipation.

Wait until Stephanie heard. She might have tried to change herself, but some characteristics were too ingrained for that.

Not that the location was a guarantee of finding what they were all hoping for. It might reveal Cia's remains. Then it might not.

Now that everyone, most likely everyone anyway, knew, what would they do next?

Chad and Megs would race around and try and solve the case. Of course. They were two do-gooders with brains and vengeance on their minds.

Stephanie would huddle and quake and shake and hope that Cia had died of natural causes. But she knew inside that this wouldn't be the case. Had she ever voiced the reason for her own breakdown? Did she even know it? Or was that inner fear, that inner knowing, that had destroyed her all these years?

She was so weak. She loved all the excesses, and they loved her. Her emotional state had been evidenced years ago. Unlike him, for he'd planned that weekend. Not that events had turned out the way he'd intended.

So many people in this world let life just happen. Randomly. These people were the victims of circumstances, the pawns of the world. Others, those like him, were the chess players, moving things around cunningly to suit their own needs. They planned ahead and took care of what needed to happen, in order to achieve their own ends.

They were the rulers of this stupid world of peons.

People like Megs and Chad were the enforcers of this said world. And that was such a joke. They might have turned into enforcers. Back then though, they were just victims, other victims of his actions.

People like Stephanie were the garbage in the street. He could have taken care of her a long time ago. But enforcers needed someone to enforce. The Stephanies of the world were perfect. They needed people. And people need to be needed.

Just think of Stephanie's life and how many people had been needed over the years to keep her alive and functioning. There were all the cops who had arrested her for drugs, prostitution, and petty theft, if that's what shoplifting *was called in the mug books. Then there were the counselors, the ministers—how many different religions had she joined, trying to save herself? And the doctors, nurses, and emergency workers helping to save her life after overdosing or taking a bad hit of drugs.*

And that was only in the first few years …

He shook his head. These people needed Stephanie. People like her gave them all a sense of purpose. Stephanie, in fact, gave them a reason to go to work each day and to earn a paycheck.

As for Stephanie herself, she should feel good about herself. Look at all the busyness she was creating. Instead of being depressed, she should be cheering. Of course, being depressed was good for business too. It meant more rounds of doctors, therapists, and drugs, prescription ones this time. So easy to get hooked on those, wasn't it?

Now, with a new set of remains to fuss over, he'd bet she was a real basket case.

He smirked.

He hoped they all were.

Chapter 7

MEG WALKED INSIDE. It was still early, but the sun had gone down, adding to the darkness caused by the overgrowth of trees. She was tired from her restless night and emotional day, but she knew sleep couldn't be further away. She curled up in the one single chair in the living room and stared out over the water. She couldn't stop thinking about the necklace and that last day so long ago. And the conversation that went on over and over again in her head.

"Did Cia tell you?" Stephanie asked. "She's slept with four of the guys here, and she is planning on doing the next one this weekend. The last one of the group she turned down. You know how she likes to do the chasing."

"No way." Meg listened to Stephanie's litany of complaints against Cia. Meg's mind was buzzing, as she tried to figure out who Cia had slept with. Chad, for sure. After all, they'd gone out for months, although that had been a while ago, so … "Who else has she slept with?" Meg asked.

"Ha, you don't know, do you?" Stephanie laughed and laughed. "What is Chad like in bed? I've often thought about it. He's really cute."

Meg grinned. "Chad and sex are like chocolate and peanut butter—they naturally go great together."

"That's what I figured." Stephanie giggled. "And Cia said something similar."

"She did?" Meg turned to her friend, outraged. She looked back to the shore, where Cia sat on the beach, looking like the perfect model that she was. All that perfect creamy skin was getting sun-kissed. She wouldn't burn. Instead lucky Cia would end with a lovely golden glow. Everything she touched was perfect.

Megs—tall, with long wavy brown hair—would never look perfect. "So who is she planning to seduce this weekend? And does Josh know?"

"Oh, I doubt it." Stephanie giggled. "He'd kill her if he did."

Such prophetic words.

Even after seventeen years, Meg had remembered them. She'd known Josh well back then. She'd gone out with him for a couple months herself, but she hadn't gone to bed with him.

It hadn't felt right. She hadn't had the same instant need she had had with Chad.

Had Josh known about Cia's plans? Had the man she'd selected known what she was up to? Maybe she was testing the waters.

Meg couldn't even think of who it could be. There was Chad, Josh, and Stephanie's boyfriend, Bruce, who was also one of Chad's best friends. Those two had been together for years. And Bruce's cousins, Anto and Pero Novak. It was the first time they'd come camping with them. Both were dark and intense looking. All the girls had giggled over their good looks.

But not Megs, she'd barely noticed them. She'd only had eyes for Chad. Other than these people, the only other person there that weekend had been Tim. She'd thought he might be gay, but he'd never mentioned it. She'd wondered about him, as he'd studied the brothers as much as the girls had.

She hadn't spoken to or seen Tim since that weekend. She thought she'd heard something about him living overseas for many years.

Meg rubbed her eyes, wishing the memories would leave her alone.

But she couldn't stop thinking about Cia's conquest … and the one guy she'd turned down.

In the background, she heard Pete come in and go to the bedroom, probably for the night. For herself, she didn't even want to join him. However, if she didn't, there'd be a bigger fight tomorrow. She could sleep out here, but …

The door slammed behind her. She turned around in surprise. Then she heard the truck start up.

Shit.

Where was Pete going?

And more important—was he coming back?

CHAD WELCOMED THE city lights. He was hungry and tired and pissed. He'd gotten nowhere with his phone calls to locate another anthropologist. Seemed as if everyone was out of town or didn't want to make a decision. And a decision needed to be made.

He'd driven for hours around the area where they'd found Cia, renewing his memory of the layout, noting the cabins, old and new. The popular lake had developed into quite a summer destination. And he had learned nothing new. Of course he hadn't. But they had the remains. With any luck, they'd find evidence that would point to her killer. And he had no doubt Meg's findings would prove out. She was highly respected in her field, and, on this case, more likely than on any other in her career, she would want to find the truth.

And so did he.

His phone rang. A favorite restaurant was just around the corner. He pulled into the parking lot and checked the number. It was Stephanie's.

Needing food before tackling that phone call, he entered the restaurant and ordered himself a big steak and baked potato. Alone, tired, and caught between edgy excitement and energy-sucking frustration, he stared moodily at his cell phone. The GPS coordinates Meg had sent showed clearly on his phone. This was it. He knew it. But he couldn't *know* it for sure, not until the lab went over everything and found something he could work with. Then again, he knew about the necklace. Could it be Meg's own necklace? Was there any chance that Cia would have made another one just like it to piss off Josh? She hadn't been the nicest of females, and, when she wanted something, she went after it like a cobra.

Josh would have been helpless against her wiles. He'd been lovestruck from the beginning and could barely do anything but stare at her all the time. It had been a big joke back then. But everyone knew he would cheerfully give Cia anything she had wanted. But that honeymoon phase hadn't lasted. Toward the end of their summer, Josh had asked for advice about how to break up with Cia. He wanted to start college as a free man. He was also afraid that Cia had been cheating on him.

Breaking up was easy. No reason to kill her to end the relationship.

Another call came in. "Is it her?" Stephanie's harsh voice cut through the phone, reminding Chad that more than just his life had been affected by Cia's disappearance. Other people needed closure too.

"I can't confirm it until the tests come back, but, given the age of the victim, the proximity to the location, and a few other determining factors," he paused, then finally said it, "I think so."

"Holy Christ." Stephanie cleared her voice. "After all this time."

"Yes. Finally."

After a solemn pause, she asked almost diffidently, "Could you tell how she died?"

"Not officially." He knew that wouldn't go over well. Stephanie's life had spiraled out of control after that fateful weekend. She never did go to college, and a cycle of booze and deadbeat relationships had followed. Somewhere in the last few years, she'd straightened out. She now worked at a grocery store and had been in a relationship for longer than a year, although that had recently broken up.

"And unofficially?"

"Unofficially she didn't likely die by natural causes. However," he stressed, "we don't know much yet."

She took a deep breath. "We knew it had to be, but I'd hoped, so hoped, that she'd just gone for a walk and had gotten lost."

"And yet we had how many people out there looking for her?"

"But we never found her back then, and now her re-mains are found in relatively the same location?" Stephanie asked, "So how come we didn't find her back then?"

"That's just one of the burning questions we need to answer."

"Someone really killed her?" Stephanie's voice thickened,

and she swallowed hard. "Was … was it one of us?"

Just then his waitress arrived, bearing his plate of food. What had seemed like a great idea when he'd pulled into the parking lot, now looked like sawdust before him. He closed his eyes and sagged against the back of his seat. "I hope not."

"We'll have to go over it all again, won't we?"

Her voice was so plaintive, so despondent, it made him ache inside. That was one question he could give a definitive answer to. Only she wouldn't like the answer. "Yes, we are."

"AUNTIE MEG?" JANELLE'S voice called through the darkness. Meg startled. She'd been sitting in the same chair for hours, waiting for Pete to come back. And he hadn't. And he might not.

That would be fun.

She reached Janelle's side and sat down on the edge of her bed. "What's the matter, sweetheart?"

Janelle's tears flowed. "I miss Daddy."

Oh Lord. Meg's heart hurt. She laid down beside her niece and gathered her into her arms. "I'm so sorry. I miss him too."

And the floodgates burst. Janelle burrowed deep into Meg's arms, and all she could do was to hold on tight—a pillar in a storm of emotions that asked questions and raged at the unfairness of life, yet offered no answers. The storm seemed to last for hours, and, for the first time that evening, Meg was grateful that Pete wasn't here.

He didn't have much patience with Janelle's emotional bouts. Meg locked down inside and rarely indulged in tears.

Janelle was a whole different case. Meg dropped several kisses on the girl's temple and held her close. Her own tears weren't far off. He'd been her brother, and she missed him too. They hadn't been super close, and she was sorry for that. He'd been a stalwart supporter. He'd been there for her all those years ago, and she needed to be there for his daughter now.

Poor Janelle, she'd lost so much. And there was no guarantee that life hadn't finished ruining things for her yet either.

As Meg knew only too well, fate had the power to piss their lives right down the drain, again and again.

Finally Janelle sobbed her grief and misery out, with only the occasional hiccough coming through. After another long few moments, Meg pulled back slightly to look down on Janelle's tear-stained face.

Janelle had fallen asleep.

Meg hated to disturb her. In fact, she hated to move, period. A night sharing the bed would be a good answer. She wouldn't have to face Pete when he returned, and Janelle wouldn't have to be alone tonight.

She moved to reach for a folded quilt at the end of bed.

Janelle cried out, her arms instinctively tightening. Her actions squeezed Meg's heart even further.

"It's all right, honey. I'm here."

"Don't go," Janelle whispered, her eyes closed, sleep just a breath away.

Meg managed to tug the quilt over her shoulders. She settled down deeper into the bed, nudging Janelle back slightly so there was room for the both of them. "I won't. I'll stay here all night."

"Promise?" The little voice was muffled further by the quilt pulled so high, but Meg heard it, and the pressure on her heart squeezed even tighter. Janelle was precious, scared, and she needed her.

Meg could do no less than be there for her. In a soft voice, hugging the little girl close, her own heart over-whelmed with love, she whispered in Janelle's ear, "I promise."

INTERESTING. ... SO they did find Cia's body. That gave him pause. Had he left anything behind? He'd racked his brain over it for a full hour but couldn't think of anything that he hadn't thought of before. There could be a hair or two, but they'd camped together over the weekend, so a hair wouldn't be definitive evidence in this cold case. Besides, there would likely be the girls' hair there as well. Those girls shared clothes, hairbrushes, and jewelry.

So why not men?

He smiled. The police had taken long enough. And, if Cia's remains hadn't been found accidentally, she could have lain there for another twenty years.

Still, this way was more fun.

So long as the cops didn't figure this out too soon. ... And, speaking of cops, it was interesting that Chad had given up engineering to go into law enforcement. What a waste. Chad had some serious brainpower. He'd have made a fine engineer.

Megs had become an anthropologist. Who'd have thought she was smart enough for that? And then Stephanie, ... that she'd turned out to be a drugged-up whore was no surprise. She'd been man-hungry since way back when.

The other guys had changed their plans for their futures too.

It made him feel good. Powerful even.

He'd done something that had made everyone reevaluate their lives.

That was good—great, in fact.

Without Cia's disappearance, they'd have continued on in their meaningless ways. He'd made them stop and think and do something better with their lives.

His actions had given them purpose.

Really they should be thanking him.

Chapter 8

M EG WOKE WITH a start. She lay still, almost frozen in place. Her mind raced to orient herself; after years of traveling, it was instinctive. She was in the cabin but not in her bed. Then she heard a sound, a snuffle.

Janelle.

The stiffness slid from her shoulders and spine, and she relaxed into the mattress and groaned. Her body ached everywhere. Janelle's body had sprawled from top to bottom and from one side to the other during the night, with Meg trying to take up the least amount of space on the edge. No wonder she hurt.

A noise outside had her looking toward the window. Trees swayed on the other side of the glass, a long branch stroking the pane with each brush. The clouds looked gray and crowded.

Still, it was light out. And that meant morning. Considering her evening and night, she'd take that as a good sign. And then she remembered.

Had Pete returned? Or had he left them stranded in his cabin?

She hoped not. But it wasn't the end of the world if he had. She could hitch a ride, if any of the techs were still working, and, if not, well, she'd call someone for a ride. Unbidden, Chad instantly came to mind. He would never leave two females stranded.

Ever.

She snuck out of bed, careful to keep the covers over Janelle. For all that it was technically summer, a chill filled the air and a bite of ice hit the floor. She hadn't planned on sleeping fully dressed, but there were definite advantages to it now.

Walking quietly out to the kitchen, she put on coffee, her answer to the world's ills. Then she walked out to the veranda and saw the truck.

Relief washed through her. He'd come back for them. Thank God for that.

Using her cell phone, she checked the time. It was only 6:30 a.m., her normal waking time and hours ahead of Janelle's. She smiled at the reminder of Janelle's horrified protests at being woken before ten. Noon was more her style.

She checked on Pete and found his bed empty. Her breath sucked in hard. He was an early riser, but she hadn't heard him or was that what had woken her this morning?

She stepped out onto the veranda and gasped at the cool air. There was no sign of him. Maybe he'd gone fishing. She strolled down to the water's edge.

The boat was there, but Pete wasn't.

Slightly disconcerted, she walked back to the cabin, not wanting Janelle to wake up alone.

The inside of the cabin was quiet and calm. She poured herself a coffee and checked her cell phone. She had a little bit of reception but not much. It was too early to call Chad, and she hadn't kept in touch with the others from that long-ago weekend. In fact, she'd gone out of her way to distance herself from them.

Now she felt the pull to reconnect. They would understand and would be going through the same emotions and issues she was. And they'd also be looking for answers.

She looked at her contact list. She had only Chad's number. As she stared at the small unit, a text came in. Talk about synchronicity. It was Stephanie. How the hell had she found Meg?

Did you hear? They may have found Cia.

That was all, but it was enough. Knowing the news would get out soon enough, Meg responded. **Yes. I found her.**

Oh God. Are you okay?

And, just like that, the years dropped away, and Meg reconnected with her old friend. The texts came back and forth, hard and fast, as they caught up. Meg hated learning about the bald truth of Stephanie's life, as she offered it up in pieces, but Meg so understood. She had buried herself in work and had tried to focus forward, whereas Stephanie had buried herself in illegal stuff and had wallowed in her past.

They'd both been haunted by that one weekend. Anger rose, sharp and cutting. Anger at the person who'd so carelessly tossed away beautiful Cia. Anger at the same person who'd destroyed so many lives and so many hopes and dreams.

They'd been forced to live with something no one should have to.

The relatively unknown group of survivors who felt guilty for *not* being the victim of violence was phenomenally large. Many clung to a support group because those were the people who understood. So many more avoided the support groups because they couldn't talk about their own experiences and didn't want to remember and rehash the same events over and over.

Meg had avoided the groups. Stephanie had just recently joined a group.

It was a case of each to their own.

"Auntie Meg?" Janelle stood sleepily in the open doorway, rubbing her eyes. "What time is it?"

"Wow. It's almost eight o'clock." Being up this early was unusual for Janelle, but she'd slept in the boat yesterday and had gone to bed early last night. "Aren't you up early?"

"When are we leaving?"

"Good question," Meg said lightly. "Pete has gone for a walk. We can ask him when he returns."

With that, Janelle turned around and went back to bed.

If only Meg's life were so easy.

Pete walked through the front door a few moments later, a lighter, calmer Peter. Meg smiled brightly at him, so happy to see the return of the old Pete she knew and loved. "Hi. Did you have a good walk?"

He nodded. "I thought, given the circumstances, we should probably head back early. I went to the roadhouse in Wistery last night. Apparently the locals have already heard, and they've been talking to the media."

"Shit." And yet life went on. People would always talk, and the media would always listen. "Well, let's hope the techs are done with the crime scene."

"I just walked the area, and it seems like they are, at least initially."

"Ah. Yeah, I wanted one last look, before I leave too."

"Go now," he urged. "I'll grab a coffee and start packing up."

Feeling much better, Meg tossed him a grateful smile and ran.

CHAD LOGGED ON to his computer at work. He'd already called the lab and had his ass reamed out for pushing. He could wait like every other detective was doing.

He understood, but he didn't like it. Still, he had lots he could do. This wasn't technically a cold case. It was Daniel's case, but Chad had always thought of it as Mack's case. Then it had almost finished Mack's career. He'd caught it when it was fresh but hadn't disclosed that three of the suspects were close relatives. Daniel had taken it over, and Mack had been disciplined and almost kicked off the force. Seventeen years had dimmed the events for everyone, but those involved. Mack had kept on Daniel about the case over the years. And so had Chad.

Good thing the three of them had come to terms with this years ago—uneasy terms, but cordial, at least in public. Mack's heavy hand had made the young Chad into a man, but he'd become a detective on his own. Badge in hand, he'd stopped by Mack's desk and showed it to him. Mack had smiled and slapped him on the shoulder. "I knew you'd make it."

Those words had helped bury some of the animosity between them. Chad had felt like a loser for a long time. Hell, the same damn feelings of insecurity had even threatened to overwhelm him at times. He should have gone after that person in the woods. That he hadn't had haunted him every day. And now, maybe he could do something about it.

Finding Cia's remains would break the case wide open.

He'd asked Stephanie to keep quiet for the moment but realized he'd asked a lot of her. He'd given her Meg's phone number, suggesting she call her. The two had been close once.

He'd already contacted Josh and Bruce. He'd stayed in

touch with both of them since that fateful trip. Hadn't seen much of either of them in over a decade, but, with phones and texts now, staying in touch was easy.

Now he thought about contacting all the others from that weekend, only this time it would be in an official capacity. He wanted to go over their old statements first. And then see if they would change them this time. The years could do funny things to the mind. Forgetting was normal, but sometimes the stuff that popped out of people's mouths was the truth that they hadn't wanted to express before, out of concern for both the dead and the living.

MEG WALKED SWIFTLY through the trees. She couldn't believe the change in Pete's mood, but she was grateful for it but also surprised. A little sprinkling rain had started.

The rain made walking under the tree canopy a wet experience, as the rain slid off the trees and soaked her. She didn't need her GPS to find the right location. The pathway was imprinted on her brain. And the yellow tape let her know when she'd hit the right area and also made her steps falter.

The surge of mixed emotions made it difficult to continue. She stared at the stark reality, with a deep, dark stillness inside. Yet also an overwhelming sense of relief. They'd found her finally. They could now bring Cia home.

Meg had almost given up hope.

And to think she'd been the one to find her. So close to their camping spot, and yet just far enough, deep enough in the woods that Cia had been missed all these years.

Rain dripped on Meg's cheeks. She swiped the moisture away and realized it wasn't rain at all. Tears had formed in the corner of her eyes and had poured down her face. Oh, dear God, poor Cia. What had happened to her friend? And had it happened right away or had the poor girl been held captive for a while? Please not that. Much better to think she'd gotten into a fight that had gone bad.

But to think that, after all this time, her friend had lain here all alone, waiting to be found.

Meg's shoulders shook, and she started to sob. For years she'd kept that pain stuffed down deep inside. Now, alone, she could let it all out.

She collapsed onto a log outside of the taped area and let her emotions pour out. This wasn't why she'd come here one last time, but, now here, it seemed like the only thing she could do.

She needed to honor her friend. And she needed to say hello after all this time. And most of all, she needed to say goodbye.

Now Cia could go to her family and be buried with them. And, although this final send-off could happen now, closing the door forever would have to wait until they'd caught the bastard who'd done this to her.

It was time.

THE DRIVE HOME was slow, the rain pounding harder with every mile. Just driving through the slick ruts had Meg clenching her teeth and wondering if they should have stayed until the weather had changed again and the roads had dried up. She couldn't imagine being stuck in the cabin with a weeklong bout of this weather. Yet it could be days before it cleared. Besides, she needed to be back in Seattle.

As for Cia's remains, she hoped that Chad had worked

some magic, but, either way, she'd follow the progress of the case through him. She could get on with other aspects of her life. After her emotional outpouring at the site, the walk home had left her feeling cleaner and more renewed than she'd felt in a long time.

And that allowed her to see the next step in her life. She had to get Janelle back on track, but more than that, Meg needed to get her relationship with Pete back on track again too. Or, and she winced at the thought, she needed to change the track. As much as it might hurt to contemplate this, Janelle was now part of her life, and the two of them were a package deal. If Pete, who had said for years that he had wanted a family, couldn't deal with it, then so be it.

Having been away from home so much, she'd always considered the condo as being primarily his, although they had both picked out where they would live together years ago. He'd chosen the furniture, while she'd been gone one time; he'd painted the walls another time.

And, if they were splitting—again came that pang to her heart—then where would she go? What options did she have? Her brother had left her some money, and there was his house. She'd put it on the market recently, not knowing what else to do with it. The small brownstone was not someplace Pete would live.

But what if Pete were no longer part of the equation?

All this hinged on whether Pete was prepared to take on Janelle. If he were, then maybe they should look at moving to a new location anyway.

The more she thought about it, the better she liked the idea.

She turned to mention the idea to Pete and realized how tired he looked. She said, "I'm looking forward to going home."

He swiveled his head to look at her. "You mean, to get back to work, don't you?"

"I don't have a job right now, remember?"

"Aren't you going to be handling the remains that you found?" he scoffed. "Of course you are!"

Damn. He was pissed again.

She stayed quiet. With any luck he would calm down before too long and could be back to normal by the time they were home. Thank God Janelle was asleep. It seemed like it was all she'd done this weekend.

Maybe it had been a good thing, given Pete's disposition. The hot and cold reactions were wearying.

They were heading for a major storm, and she wasn't looking forward to it. In all her years with him, he'd been reasonable and easy to talk to. Now he was cold and distant, alternating between angry and angrier.

Not quite true, he had had moments like the one this morning when he had reminded her of the man he used to be. It was Janelle's permanent presence that seemed to have finished him off.

Or maybe Meg had been the one to hit the wall. Certainly this weekend she had. Her emotions were all over the place, and anger simmered just below the surface. She realized how much she hated these confrontations, and the more regular they were, the more she hated them.

Change had to happen, and it was looking more and more like today might be the day it would.

HE WANTED ANSWERS. Answers about what they had found and what test results they were getting done and how would he

get those.

He could ask Stephanie, but would she know anything? Not likely. And Megs? Well, she wouldn't likely give him the time of day.

So Chad was the best option, unless old Mack was still alive and kicking. He'd always been good for a beer and some chatter. Not that he'd give anything away, but he'd be a place to start.

Not his choice of victims and such a pain to dispose of afterward.

But he needed to stay on top of the news somehow. With Cia's remains now come to light, what were the chances that a few of those loose ends that he'd discounted as not mattering all those years ago might just matter now?

After all these years?

Surely not.

Something needed to happen, and finding Cia's remains definitely counted as something happening.

He gazed down at the long history of his life and wondered at the juncture in that history and the direction it had led him in ever after. Did he regret the impact of his decision so long ago? No, not really. Sure, his life had turned out differently than he'd planned.

But planning as a teen was like throwing popcorn in the wind and seeing where the pieces would land. He'd done something similar, then chosen from among the pieces he'd liked.

Now, some of those pieces had hooks and might be coming back to snag him.

Or maybe not …

He'd gotten very adept at being the predator and not the prey.

Chapter 9

MEG FELT THE thunderclouds building within minutes of being home. She needed Pete to hold off, until she could find something or somewhere for Janelle to hang out, so she didn't witness the explosion. Hell, Meg didn't want to witness it either. Yet she knew it was the only way to clear the air—one way or the other. At the moment, the *other* was starting to sound damn good.

Luckily Janelle came running to the kitchen, while Meg was wiping out the cooler. "Can I go to Linette's place, please?"

Janelle was almost dancing in place. Meg already knew the homework had been done, and it was perfect timing, as far as she was concerned. "Absolutely but home at five o'clock, please. And make sure you have your cell phone turned on and no leaving Linette's place."

With a big grin, Janelle took off. Linette lived in the same condo complex, making for easy access between the girls. Linette was a regular visitor and a nice girl. Also, she was a good student in school, which, if Meg were lucky, might rub off on Janelle.

Meg heard Pete yell, "Don't sl—"

Slam.

Meg let out her pent-up breath slowly. Not a good start.

"Damn that kid," Pete snarled. "She has to stop slamming the door." He walked in with his arms full from unloading the truck. "And she has to start cleaning up her own mess."

"She'll learn." Meg busied herself with drying the cooler. She didn't know how to open up the subject.

"Will she? When?" He snorted. "I could be dead first."

Meg winced. "She's not that bad."

"Says you. She's nothing but work."

Now that wasn't fair. "Not true. We're just not used to having kids around. We have to learn to get along too."

"No, I fucking don't." He slammed his load of cups and jackets, and a half-eaten apple, onto the table. "I didn't sign up for this."

Here it was, ready or not. She took a deep breath, grabbed the edges of her frayed control and said, "Then maybe we need to talk about that."

"Talk about what? That it's her or me?" He pointed a finger at the closed front door, through which Janelle had just disappeared. "Oh, I get the message all right. It's her all the way apparently." His voice clipped through the message with military precision and left her gasping from the cutting words. "We were fine until she arrived in our home."

She couldn't hold back. "So let's talk about whether you still want me if she comes as part of the package."

Now it was out in the open.

He stopped, stared at her, the muscle in his jaw pulsing. Fire burned in his gaze, but not a fire that warmed her or made her feel welcome. There was something cold, empty, and final in his eyes.

Forever final.

She hated that this was it. He hadn't said it, but she knew.

His mouth opened, and she caught her breath, waiting, half hoping for a rescue and a change in direction, but knowing it wasn't to be. And she wasn't sure she wanted one. Not at this point.

Then his jaw snapped closed, and he turned around very carefully and stalked into the master bedroom. She heard him opening closets and drawers. She swallowed and closed her eyes. Dare she follow him and push the issue? With her rock-solid foundation having turned to quicksand, she didn't know where she stood. And she needed to.

Instinct told her to leave him alone. Her gut said run. Her heart was beyond speech; it had swelled to the point of bursting from the sense of this achy loss inside.

Closing the cooler lid carefully, she placed it on the table and stared at the items Pete had dumped in a pile. Some of it hers, some of it Janelle's, and none of it mattered. Still, everything needed to be cleaned up. He'd always hated a mess.

She should leave. Go and pack an overnight bag for her and Janelle. Pick Janelle up at her friend's and go to a hotel for the night—or for the week. A half sob escaped. She didn't know what to do.

With a heavy sigh, she rubbed her face with both hands, hating the pressure in her chest and the indecision of what to do, yet knowing she had to do something.

And then he did it instead.

"I'm going away for a day or two." He stood cold and implacable in front of her, with an old scuffed hockey bag in his hand. Fully packed, he didn't look like he'd be home anytime soon. And from the edge to his voice, and the jut of his jaw, it was clear he didn't plan on explaining himself either.

She nodded slowly, holding back the tears that wanted to pour out but instead standing dry-eyed in front of him, as relief warred with the pain of his leaving. "That might be a good idea." She wanted to say more. She needed to say more. They both did.

Yet neither spoke.

He nodded and walked out, without a backward glance. He closed the door so very quietly and the very gentleness of this gesture added to the finality of his actions.

At least this time she was no longer at the cabin without transportation. She could thank him for that much. She had a roof over her head, a bed for the night, and a place to keep Janelle that wasn't a cold impersonal hotel. And her car was outside—her brother's car. She hadn't bothered buying one, as she'd been traveling for so much of the time.

Then none of it mattered now. Her life was splintering around her, and the relief at finding Cia's remains had been replaced with a feeling of regret. And inevitability.

She put her head down on her arms and burst into tears again.

CHAD'S PHONE RANG. He glanced at the time; it was four p.m. He picked it up off his office desk and answered.

"Detective Mack Monroe here. I hear you've found a breakthrough in our old case."

With a smile, Chad leaned back in his chair. "Hey, Mack, how are you doing? Did you get my text?"

"I did. And I'll be doing much better when you tell me what I want to know." Gruff, brusque, and a loner, Mack was a bulldog, following a lead until he found the answers he needed. Then he stood by the case, until he had caught the asshole who had got on the wrong side of his file. He just didn't care about those who got in his way or those he might damage through this process.

"We might have found the remains of Cia Barnes."

"About damn time." Mack coughed several times. "Give. I want the details. All of them."

With a short eye roll, Chad told him what he knew. What he'd already told Daniel.

Silence fell when he was done. Chad could almost see Mack thinking things over. "Who'd have thought it would take that long for her to be found?"

"I know. It's been a long time. I'm just hoping that we can close this one now."

"I bet you are. You didn't like being on the opposite side of my interviewing skills, did you?"

"No," Chad answered emphatically, hating the reminder of how Mack had taken the guilt-ridden young Chad and pounded him into the ground, looking for a confession. He'd felt like a lowlife, and Mack's constant hounding had been brutal. It had changed Chad forever. Even now he had a hard time forgiving Mack for that. And Mack didn't give a damn. The real problem was that Chad had felt Mack's suspicious gaze turned his way more than once in the ensuing years, as the case hung between them. Even though Mack had almost gotten kicked off the force himself in the process, he'd never let Chad forget.

Still, Chad was a man now and a damn good detective. He understood the lengths they were forced to go through sometimes in pursuit of a resolution to a case. But he'd never been the bastard Mack had been. He'd also come to understand it was Mack's fear for his nephews that had driven his behavior. Fear was a powerful motivator.

For that reason alone, Chad had to admit to being suspicious of Mack. He'd been at his cabin that weekend and close enough to have killed Cia himself. Only Chad hadn't found that out until after Mack had pushed the innocence out of him forever—good thing too, or Chad might have pushed back …

"I'm still having trouble processing that Megan Pearce found the body. She just 'happened' to trip over it, *huh*?"

"Yes." Chad hated to see the suspicion rest on Meg's shoulders, but he knew that it was normal at this stage. Everyone and everything would be reexamined. Like it or not, their lives would be put under a microscope again, and that included his own life.

"So where do we start?" Chad would have deferred to Mack even if he hadn't been the original detective on the case back then. Some men just commanded that type of response.

"It's time to bring everything back up and take a fresh look. I'll talk to Daniel. Plus, I want to talk to the labs. Wish I'd seen the site myself."

"I did contact you, but you never answered," Chad reminded him.

"Yeah, I know. It was my poker night." He coughed a harsh, raspy sound that made Chad wince.

"You still haven't quite given up on smoking yet, have you?"

"Hell no." Mack coughed again. "And you still haven't stopped nagging. Just like my wife."

"Yeah, I can't imagine why she hasn't stopped," Chad joked. "Maybe it's because she doesn't want to be alone in her old age."

"Sure she does. She'll hate having me underfoot all the

time." He paused. "So what aren't you telling me?"

Chad sighed. "I was waiting for you to stop choking. Under the body we found a necklace. It's hard to make out the inscription after all this time, but it appears to say, *To Megs, with love.*

"Megs?"

"Yes. Megan—Megs. It was Meg Pearce's nickname." Chad stared across his desk at the far wall. "Obviously Meg couldn't have strangled someone and wouldn't then have left her own necklace behind."

"Unless she didn't know it had gone missing. It could have come off without her noticing in a girl fight." His voice hardened. "Strangled?"

"That's what Meg's preliminary observation says."

"What a big coincidence for Megan. Not only does she find the body but she was one of the suspects at the time of Cia's disappearance. And, the icing on the cake, she finds her own necklace with the remains."

"I know. Strange, isn't it?"

"Yeah, I think so." That same laconic voice that had caused Chad so many nightmares when he'd been interviewed rang through the phone. Chad let out his breath slowly, as he formulated his thoughts. It wasn't just Meg that Mack was asking about. It was also about whether Chad believed in Meg and, if so, why. "I was there when she found the necklace. She was surprised and horrified."

"She could be playing to both scenarios," Mack said in a noncommittal voice.

"True enough, but she was also completely distraught over finding the bones."

"Again, she could be playing to both scenarios."

"Maybe, but she didn't do it," Chad said, tired of this. "I

know that for sure."

"Right. So, now here's the next question." Mack paused, and Chad braced himself. Mack was always good for shock value. "Are you still in love with her?"

Ah, there it was. The one question he'd avoided since receiving that text message. How did he feel about her now? She'd been the love of his life, until their lives had blown up. Lack of trust, horror at the unimaginable, not knowing how to cope, all of those factors and more had played a part in her breaking up with him. If they'd had more time together, or a stronger, longer-lasting foundation before life had blown up, they might have made it.

However, at the time, everyone had scattered. Chad had gone morose and angry, until he'd finally turned it around. He had realized that Mack and the rest of the cops didn't have any answers for him, and Chad would have to find them for himself. He just hadn't expected it to take seventeen years.

He'd always figured when they found out the truth, he could go to her and tell her that she was free, he was free, and that it was time to move on—together. Only the years had gone by, and he hadn't found any answers either.

"And the telltale silence." Mack laughed so hard that he started coughing. "You still care."

"I don't know what I feel," he admitted quietly. "I've barely seen her since that weekend."

"And that means nothing, as you well know. Your life together stopped—waiting for you to solve the crime."

"Only she went on with her life." And he knew it wasn't fair, but there was a smidgeon of jealousy, almost anger, underneath his acceptance. Of course he wouldn't have wanted her to be alone for all these years. She was a beautiful person. She deserved to be happy. No, he wouldn't wish that on anyone.

"And so did you."

Chad startled at Mack's dry comment. "Yes, but not quite the way she did."

"What? So you're mad she made a better go of doing without you than you did doing without her?"

That sounded so wrong when put like that. Juvenile. "Stupid, *huh*?"

"Ya think? Sounds like perfect timing now. Don't waste this opportunity."

"I thought you said she might be our perp?" Chad hated that about Mack. He always twisted things around and forced Chad to look at life in a different way.

"I said she might be. You're the one who is so gung ho that she's innocent." Mack's derisive tone sent Chad's back up.

"She *is* innocent."

"Good. I'm still trying to figure out why the hell you aren't at my desk, so we can haul all the evidence back out and take another look." And he rang off.

Chad shook his head and stared at his dead phone. Typical Mack. And yet different. There was a hint of excitement in Mack's voice. And that was good.

Maybe this time they could find the answers they both needed.

WOW. AND DOUBLE wow. Megs and Chad back together again. Well, not together-together, but still close together. Who would have thought this could happen? Then he hadn't foreseen this happening at all. Life was like that for him. He looked

forward but only a day or two at a time. Certainly not seventeen years down the road. What a waste. Life was for living, not worrying about what might happen too far down the road to see.

He shook his head. What a joke.

Still, this was an interesting turn of events. Not one that required action on his part. He was happy to observe and to see where it led. To see what Chad did and to see what Megs did.

She was the center to all this anyway. At the time, he'd been dumbfounded, waiting for the fumbling idiot police to lock in to the truth—and lock him up for the rest of his life. Then, after realizing they'd missed it altogether, he'd found it as funny as hell.

Everyone had focused on Cia, as if to say that this whole mess revolved around her. She would have liked that. They'd missed the salient points and, therefore, had missed the center of the whole issue. From a point way off to the left, the authorities had fumbled around blindly. Of course they had never found anything. What was there to find? Well, Cia of course, but she was nothing but a whiney whore anyway.

No. No one had thought to look closer at Meg back then.

He smiled. Well, they would now, wouldn't they?

Chapter 10

JANELLE BARRELED INTO the kitchen and skidded to a stop. "Auntie Meg? What's wrong?"

Meg frowned, trying to pull her thoughts back to the moment. "Why do you think something is wrong?"

Walking toward her slowly, Janelle appeared to search Meg's face. "You're baking. Mom only baked when she was upset."

And what did one say to that? When would Meg stop feeling like she was stepping on ghosts? Meg stared down at the batch of brownies, ready to pour into the pan. She instinctively headed to chocolate when she was upset, and baking brownies had seemed like a good answer.

Now ... not so much.

"I'm sorry, honey. I was craving chocolate."

She watched as Janelle took several slow steps forward, her face a mixture of confusion and hope. "So, you are okay?"

She had to laugh. "I'm much better now. Just seeing you puts a smile on my face."

A beautiful smile lit up Janelle's face. And Meg realized how little time she'd taken to say something nice. God, she sucked as a mother. Her brother should've chosen better.

"Auntie Meg?" Uncertainty threaded through Janelle's voice. "Now something else is wrong."

Meg schooled her features, hating that Janelle was so sensitive. "No. Honey, I was just realizing how poor a job I've been doing, looking after you." Meg walked closer and enfolded her in a gentle hug. "This is such a learning curve for me. I'm sorry, but you need to have patience with me."

Janelle's arms crept around Meg's back, and then she hung on tight. Tears came to Meg's eyes, and she cuddled her. Such love was here. And Pete wanted nothing to do with it.

How sad.

"Where is Pete?" Janelle pulled back slightly to look up at Meg. "Is he here?"

"No." Meg gave her a bright but shaky smile. "He's gone for a day or two."

It took a moment, then Janelle's face brightened. "Really?" She stepped away. "That is great."

"It is?" Meg asked curiously. "Don't you like Pete?"

A shadow whispered across Janelle's face, as she danced away from Meg. "He's okay."

"But only okay?" Meg pressed gently. Did Janelle really not like Pete? And if not, why not? Maybe separating would be a good idea, if only for Janelle's sake.

Janelle's dancing slowed, and she stared down at the floor.

Meg caught her breath. "Janelle, can you tell me what you don't like?"

She caught a glimpse of Janelle's uncertain look, before she hid her face behind her hair. Meg took a step closer. "Janelle, please tell me. It's important."

Her niece stilled, her shoulders hunched. Inside, Meg's stomach clenched. "Honey?"

So soft and gently, Meg had to lean closer to hear Janelle

say, "He scares me."

"When he's angry?" Meg asked gently.

Janelle nodded and then added, "And he's always angry."

Meg wrapped an arm around the girl's shoulders. How could you explain that the anger was because he didn't want her? She couldn't say that. It would devastate her. "He's going through a lot right now. That's why he's left. To rest and relax and to sort some stuff out."

There was silence, and then Janelle whispered, "Is it wrong to hope he doesn't come back?"

The breath gusted out of Meg's chest. Here was another difficult question. "No. It's not wrong. Let's just hope that, if he does come back, he comes back happy and wanting to be here." She wasn't ready to share her own plans, not until she had arrangements in place. Too many questions and no answers would only increase Janelle's insecurities. Better to wait until tomorrow. "In the meantime, I have some decisions to make. Just know that you will be with me no matter what. Okay?"

Janelle smiled. "Okay."

"Now, how about I get these brownies in the oven, so we can have one after dinner?"

And now Janelle beamed.

For the first time in months, Meg enjoyed the evening with Janelle. There were no tantrums, no whining, and no sign of tears. All because Pete had left.

Later that evening, after Janelle had gone to bed, Meg knew a corner had been turned.

Pete may have chosen a few days away, but that time and distance had also given Meg the clarity to see what she needed to do.

She wanted to move out—before Pete came back. Even

if it was only a temporary move, she could see tonight just how much improved Janelle was, without being in that constant negative atmosphere.

But moving out wasn't so simple. She had a house to go to, so that was a gift. But she'd have to contact the real estate agent and pull it off the market, at least for the moment. It was only a few miles away, so Janelle could at least stay at the same school.

Only Meg would have to deal with Janelle's emotional state, if she moved her back into her old home, the home where she'd lived with her father. Meg probably should never have removed her in the first place. At the time, it seemed that staying with all those memories wouldn't be a good idea.

She set about making plans.

The more those plans formulated in her mind, the clearer her understanding became. The emotions settled inside.

This was the right thing to do.

With a notepad, she started on a list: pack up, contact the Realtor, grocery shop for the house.

The house would be clean in the sense that it was good enough for house buyers to come by and look, but she'd have to change out the bedding. Janelle hadn't brought much with her to the condo, just a couple suitcases. The rest was in the fully furnished house that Meg had pushed off as a problem to solve into some distant future, like when the house was sold. Instead this was looking like a godsend.

She studied her bedroom. She'd never been a clothes horse and being ready to travel at the drop of a phone call hadn't given her much time to accrue much. What she did have was boxes of treasures she'd brought home from her travels. They were in storage until she and Pete could buy a bigger house. They were well past that point now. Meg had a healthy bank account, and, although she needed to sort out her professional future in town, she had the qualifications, experience, and the references to find something, somewhere, to make her happy.

After Janelle's school year finished, they could talk about changing locations. Maybe by then, Janelle would have settled in.

Either way, they would start a new life together.

LATE THAT NIGHT, Chad walked into his bedroom, turning on the television, as he headed toward the shower. He stripped down, dumping his clothes in the hamper, before stepping under the hot water. The water sluiced down his back, easing the tension that he'd been unable to get rid of all day. He needed answers.

Hell, he'd needed answers for a long time …

He stayed under the water for a few minutes longer and then shut off the soothing heat. Drying quickly, he wrapped the towel around his hips and headed back to his bedroom.

He made it to the doorway of his bedroom and stopped short.

"Breaking news tonight. There may finally be a break in the Cia Barnes case. A set of female remains has been found in the area where she disappeared seventeen years ago—"

"Shit."

"We'll have more of this latest news in a few minutes from our own Mike Clifford, who is outside the apartment of Stephanie Thornton. She was one of the girls who was camping with Cia on that fateful weekend when Cia went missing."

"God damn it. Not Stephanie. She can't handle this."

He reached for his phone and called her. Stephanie had been through so much. She didn't handle stress well.

Or anything else, for that matter.

He texted her immediately. **Don't go outside. Don't answer the door. Media. The news is out.**

After sending the message, he tried to call her again.

Still no answer. He tried several more times, as he stood in front of the television and half watched the news coverage. The reporter was going on about the mess that had happened, but so far there was no sign of Stephanie showing up. They didn't appear to be saying anything they hadn't said dozens of times already over the years.

Thank God.

If they found out about that damn necklace, that would be seriously bad for the case, bad for everyone, and really bad for Meg.

The public would convict her in a heartbeat.

STEPHANIE WHIMPERED. SHE tucked deeper into her closet, hating the lights from outside that flashed into her ground-floor bedroom, with the headlights and camera crews outside.

Damn it. Bruce should be here with her and protecting her from them.

She wanted to go back to the way things had been before, when Bruce had still been her best friend and lover. She'd tried to resume a normal life after Cia, but their relationship hadn't been strong enough to handle her slide into alcohol. When she'd added the drugs, Bruce had walked.

She'd gone on an all-out bender then. She'd woken up

years later, hating who she was and what she'd become. She'd hated Bruce for giving up on her.

She couldn't do this again, not alone anyway.

It had damn-near killed her last time, and at least then she'd had Bruce. She should have been the one to die, not Cia. It would have been so much easier than this long, slow torture. Tears burned in the back of her eyes. She'd shed so many over the years that they never fell anymore.

She'd used drugs, alcohol, and men to dull the pain, to hide the fear, hoping that one of them would finish her off. Instead she'd survived. It had been two years since she'd made the decision to live, to forget, to move on, and to acknowledge that she'd suffered enough. Two years of feeling like maybe life was worth living. Two years of thinking she could do this. Two years since dumping the bad habits—*all* of them.

And she had finally started talking to Bruce again. It was only texting so far, but that door had been opened. For that she was grateful.

And then they had found Cia, and everything had come rushing back: the pain, the terror, the endless nightmares, the *what ifs*, the constant looking over her shoulder. She didn't even know what she was looking for. She just had that incessant sense of being watched.

A cry escaped before she could suppress it by shoving the bottom of her shirt into her mouth. Shudders racked her body. She tightened her grip on her knees and rocked back and forth.

Now—as if those years recovering from the trauma had never happened—she couldn't stop looking over her shoulder again. She remembered the sly looks, accusing stares, uncomfortable silences. The cops had been bad, and the whispering from friends and family had been even worse. But the media? … They had been horrible.

And now the media had found out about Cia's remains.

And worse—the media had found *her*.

MEG COLLAPSED ON the bed, exhausted from too much thinking. She was exhausted too from the turmoil in her head. This was way too much stress. She pulled a blanket over her legs. Sleep couldn't be further away.

Just then her cell phone rang.

Chad said, "Cia's case was on the eleven o'clock news."

"So it's started." She took a deep breath. "They haven't found me yet."

"They found Stephanie." Chad's voice lit up the room. "She thinks she's being watched, and she's getting hang-up phone calls." He took a deep breath, exhaling noisily. "Lots of them."

Meg winced at that last bit. She asked cautiously, "Watched? Like stalker type watching?"

"Yes, to the first question." He sounded distracted. "And although it could be nothing, she's pretty scared right now."

"Has she seen anyone following her?" Meg sat up, brushing her hair back over her head, hating the thought.

"No." He cleared his throat. "That's part of the problem. Since Cia's remains have been found, Stephanie's become very emotional. She went off the rails when Cia first disappeared. You may not have seen it, as you left for college as soon as you could. I don't know what you know about her history through the years, but she lived pretty rough for a while."

Meg had been under such emotional stress for so long

that she had no trouble relating to Stephanie's problems—or her method of handling them. She murmured, "I'd heard."

"Yeah, well, it's hard to tell at this point if this is something serious or not. I figured I'd better check and see if you'd had any similar problems."

"No." Thank God, but then she had to wonder if she would have even noticed with everything else going on in her life.

"I'm not trying to panic you." Chad's voice soothed her nerves. "Obviously you both need to take extra precautions right now."

She pulled her knees up to her chest and tightened the blanket. "Great, just what I don't need right now."

"Why?" He backed up. "What's wrong?"

"Pete's not here right now." She waited a moment and then said quietly, "He's moved out temporarily."

He sighed. "I'm sorry."

Inexplicably her eyes burned, as she fought back the tears. She mumbled, "Thanks."

"Does that mean you're alone?"

"I have my twelve-year-old niece here."

"And you have a safe, secure place, right? Locks, alarms, and a security system?"

"Yes. At least, I think it's decent." She thought about it. "However, as we know, there's always a way to get in." Moodily she played with the fringe on the blanket, hating the thought, the necessity of having to reexamine the issue. "Are you expecting trouble?"

"No, but we have to consider that finding Cia may have blown something wide open." His voice sharpened. "And this may have alerted her killer."

Meg caught her breath. "Are you thinking Steph's hang-up caller was Cia's killer?" She shook her head. "That doesn't make any sense. This guy kills a girl, and then, seventeen years later, he's stalking another one? It's more likely the media checking to see if she's at home."

"How do we know that Cia wasn't stalked in the first place? There were other campers at the lake and another campground on the other side." He added thoughtfully, "Not to mention the dozens of cabin owners there over that weekend."

"It's possible, I suppose." Thoughts twisted in Meg's head. "Is there any reason for Stephanie to be nervous now?"

"What do you mean?" Chad asked curiously. "You mean, nervous about Cia's death? That would only be if she had something to do with it. And we ruled her out a long time ago."

"Maybe she knows something? Or is protecting someone?" Meg sighed. "Sorry, I'm grasping at straws, trying to reach for an explanation, the same as I have done for the last seventeen years." She stared across her bedroom, wishing Pete was there. At least she wouldn't have to worry so much about an intruder. "I know Stephanie didn't have anything to do with Cia's death. I was there with her the whole time."

"The *whole* time?"

"Yes, except for my trip to the outhouse. Yet Stephanie was in the same place where I'd left her. She wouldn't have had time to kill Cia and to move her."

Silence.

Meg chewed on her bottom lip. "Chad? What are you thinking?"

"I'm just wondering at the concept of more than one killer. It's not something we'd—I'd—given much thought to before."

"Two people working together killed her?" Meg fell silent as she thought about it. "That's pretty awful to contemplate. I kept myself sane all these years by convincing myself that it *had* to be someone I didn't know who killed her."

"If that's the case, why did you walk—no, run—away from all of us?" he asked, a hint of accusation in his voice.

She let her breath out slowly, carefully. "Because I couldn't be sure of anyone anymore." And that hurt her to admit—even to herself.

"Even me?" The tone of voice was right, but the barest hesitation, that diffident note made her realize what her absence had done to him. She'd hurt him badly. In the process, she'd hurt herself. Her fear had torn them apart and had destroyed the special relationship they'd had together. And she'd never meant to do that.

"No," she whispered, the tears that were never far from the surface now rolled down her cheeks. "Not you. Not then and not now." She sniffled.

"Then why?" he cried out, his voice cracking from emotion. "I tried to call, but you were never home, and you never called me back. I stopped by, and either your dad or your brother wouldn't let me in." He swallowed hard, the sound clear through the phone lines. "Finally your dad told me to let it alone and that you were trying to rebuild your life and that I should do the same." He cleared his throat. "I wanted to hate you. I tried to, … but I couldn't."

She hadn't known about the visits. However, the calls were on her. She'd run from the devastation of that weekend, from the horror of the investigation, from the reality that life was no longer nice. Or fun. Most of all, she'd run from the realization that bad things did happen to good people, and sometimes there was no escape.

"I'm so sorry. I just couldn't handle anything more." And she was sorry. For so much. She didn't even know how to explain it, but she tried. "The police were looking at me because Cia was your ex. They were looking at you and suggesting to me that you'd killed her and how well did I know you? I just didn't know what to think. They made me so confused. I had no idea what was going on, and I just ran and went to college and never looked back."

"Never?"

She winced. "I tried not to. I thought that if I could just keep moving forward, then I wouldn't have to face that time in my life again."

"And you are okay with that?"

There was disbelief, curiosity, and a hint of derision in his voice. She deserved it but didn't like it. However, he deserved an answer. "I tried to be. But it always felt …"

"Unfinished?"

"Yes." She gave a wry laugh. "To be expected, I suppose. Maybe now that will go away too."

"I'm not sure I want it to go away."

His voice was so faint that she wasn't sure she had heard him correctly. Her breath caught in her throat. "Pardon?"

"I said, I'm not sure I want it all to go away." And this time there was no doubting the strength of his voice.

Only she wasn't sure exactly what he meant. Stumped, she said nothing.

"No response?" he asked wryly.

"I'm not sure what you are saying." She tried to keep her voice light. "Care to clarify?"

"I'm saying I don't want to be relegated to your history. I don't want to be part of your life that goes away." He paused, sucked in his breath, and then let the rest of his words pour out. "I know this isn't the best time. I know you're dealing with a potential breakup. I guess I just want you to know that I'm here." He paused for a long moment, then added thoughtfully, "In fact, … I always have been."

And he hung up.

"WAY TO GO, Chad." He stared down at his cell phone and groaned. "Smooth, really smooth."

He hadn't meant to say that. Any of it, but the words had slipped out before he could call them back.

And now he didn't know what to do.

Hanging up like that was also stupid. Teenage stuff. And, in a small way, he almost felt that way. As if finding Cia's remains had sent them all tumbling back in time to that frozen part of their lives and to the emotions from back then. Insecurity, betrayal, horror, and … anger.

Meg was the one part of his history that he was hoping to reconnect with. In his head, they hadn't broken up—they were on hold, until Cia's disappearance had been resolved. And how arrogant was that?

Very. And he didn't care. He had to put it out there.

But his timing sucked.

Meg was dealing with a difficult breakup of her own. Good timing for him, in that she was breaking up, but really bad timing in that she needed … time. And although her relationship was on the rocks, that didn't mean it was over, though he could hope.

A text came in. Stephanie. He read the single-word message.

Help.

Shit.

MEG WALKED TO the window again and stared out into the black of night.

Emotions rolled through her. Could Chad have really been holding a torch for her after all these years? What had he said? Something about not wanting to be kept in the past? She pondered the years gone by. Would she ever contemplate returning to her childhood sweetheart? And so fast? Surely that wasn't smart.

She groaned and stretched out on the bed.

Why had he said that *now*?

Talk about bad timing. But her traitorous heart said, *Think of it as a second chance. A chance to correct your course— to get back onto the path you had planned on taking with him.*

But she knew there was no going back. Not to a time of innocence.

But he's not asking you to go back. He's asking you to meet up with him again. The diverged roads were curving back to each other and, once again, becoming as one.

God, how appealing was that?

Visions flashed across her mind of Chad's smiling face, as he had held her tenderly in his arms, the gentle look in his gaze, when she had woken to find him staring down at her, as if she were the most precious gift. The joy of holding hands and being together, fitting together like they were meant to be. And they *were* meant to be. They had spent hours making plans and sharing hopes and dreams. They were going to be together forever.

Forever had lasted one summer.

Then she'd left and had never even said goodbye.

Sitting here in the lonely darkness, Meg realized that *she'd* avoided meeting him, seeing him, because then she could avoid having to do just that—saying goodbye. That way, the door stayed open … just in case.

Now that future was here. And one door in her world was closing. Was she ready to walk through the other? So soon?

Yeah, talk about shitty timing.

TIMING WAS EVERYTHING.

And before the cops learned anything new, he had to find out what they knew now. Just in case he needed to take care of loose ends.

Stephanie was the weakest and easiest link. He would have thought that the years of substance abuse would have taken care of her eons ago but apparently not. How could her body have survived all these years?

It had been interesting, watching her suffer, but even that joy had waned. And now it was too dangerous. He'd loved the grateful sound in her voice when he'd called her to talk. To invite her for coffee.

She'd been so happy to connect again. She was so pathetic.

God, he loved it.

He waited outside the coffee shop, nursing his drink. He'd chosen a remote spot with very little traffic. He had gone in as part of a crowd and had walked straight out with his cup. Just in case there were cameras, he'd kept his face down and his hat on. He didn't want to avoid anything. But neither did he want to be memorable. Not that anyone was looking for him … yet.

Stephanie was driving. He'd chosen a place just too far away for her to walk and not convenient for her to take a bus.

He wanted her vehicle. It was much easier to travel that way. He had a pair of stolen plates in his bag. It would be easy to switch them around, and no one would be looking at the car-plate combination.

Only she was late.

Typical female—wants to meet but can't be bothered to show up on time. It was bullshit. He allowed a little of his loathing to leach through. Females were bitches. In heat when they thought it would get them something and conniving mouthpieces when they didn't get it.

A small dark blue compact drove into the parking lot.

About time.

He put a big smile on his face and waved.

Chapter 11

CHAD RACED TO Stephanie's apartment. She hadn't answered her phone since he'd received her last text for help. The older cement building had been around longer than she had, but no graffiti was on the walls, and the hallway was clean. Not that Chad spent any time checking.

She had a ground-floor apartment, and the glass doors to her small patio were closed. Inside, he knocked on her door.

No answer.

He pounded again. "Stephanie. It's Chad. Open up." He put his head against the door and listened. No sound came from inside. "Stephanie!"

The door on the left opened. A tiny head appeared. Bright eyes under an almost pink scalp, with a ghost of white hair, peered out. "Are you looking for Stephanie? There's nothing wrong, is there?"

Chad walked over to the frail but hopefully nosy neighbor. He pulled out his badge. Her eyes lit up at the sight of it. "I'm looking for her. Have you seen her tonight?"

The head bobbed. "Oh yes, she went out with a friend."

Finally a break. "Did you get a good look at him?"

This time the woman shook her head. "No, I didn't. She told me about him, as she was leaving to meet him." The birdlike woman frowned. "I can't remember exactly what she said." She pointed to her watch. "I remember the time though, because I was waiting to watch my show." She beamed up at him. "It was just before eight o'clock."

"And she didn't say anything about where they were going or what they were doing?"

The wispy cloud of white hair about her head bounced. "Oh no, but she was so excited. She was real bubbly, like a young girl again."

Chad nodded. He glanced back at Stephanie's apartment. "I'm afraid she might be in trouble."

"Oh dear, I haven't seen her come home yet, but sometimes she doesn't, you know," she said almost apologetically. Chad could see the woman being accepting of Stephanie's old lifestyle. As Chad studied the paper-thin skin, he couldn't help but see the decades of rough living she herself had experienced.

"Damn." He glanced back at Stephanie's closed door. What to do now?

"I can see if she's home. Just in case I missed her." The woman pulled her keys from the pocket of her oversized sweater. Then locking her door, she walked across to Stephanie's. "I come over all the time to spend time with Chester."

"Chester?"

"Yes, her big tomcat. He's a baby, gets really cranky after too long alone."

Didn't they all? Chad quickly checked his phone. No more texts. *Damn, Stephanie, where are you?* The little old lady already had the door open and had gone in before he could stop her.

"Wait." He was too late. He raced behind her. He stopped in the open living area and gave the place the once-over. Not much had changed since his last visit. The place held few furnishings, and what was there were old and faded. Still, the place was spotless and showed no sign of a disturbance. He smiled to see it so clean. It matched the new Stephanie. She'd cleaned up her act both inside and out. Now, if only he could find her alive and well.

Walking through the one-bedroom apartment, he found Stephanie's neighbor sitting on the double bed, stroking a very large gray cat. The cat appeared undisturbed at Chad's presence.

"What are you looking for?" the neighbor asked curiously, her gaze following his every move.

"Anything that might tell me who she went out with and where they might have gone."

"Oh, I don't think you'll find anything," the woman replied in that chirpy little bird voice.

He spun around. "And why is that?"

She beamed. "Stephanie said it was a secret."

MEG COULDN'T SLEEP. She wandered around the apartment, a cup of herb tea in her hand. Their bags were half packed and possessions half sorted. She couldn't focus. Her mind spun endlessly from Cia to Pete to the media to the mess of her life.

It was too early to call in a few favors to find out what evidence had been pulled from all the material she'd sent back. She should be the anthropologist who examined the remains. She'd collected them. She wanted to be the one to examine them. She'd been in at the beginning; she needed to be there at the end. And yet she could understand the naysayers. Authority thrived on red tape, rules, and creating hell for people. She knew that. Still …

Chad would share what he could, if only to get her professional opinion on the case. That might have to be enough.

It was also too early to contact the people she needed to in regard to the move to the house. And too early to call her friends and talk it over with them. Then who would she call? She'd deliberately kept people at a distance over the years. They couldn't hurt you that way.

She was tempted to call Jade. Of anyone, she'd understand. And she'd offer constructive suggestions. Jade was nothing if not practical. That she had Dane at her side just rounded out Jade's world perfectly.

Once again, Meg walked to the stack of bags on the floor. She couldn't stop feeling that Pete could be back soon. He'd said days, but … it could be just overnight. Or he could be back within a few hours even. Confrontations were not her thing. Look at her history—she always ran when things got tough, except with Pete. Then she might have hung on too long.

And why did she think that might have had something to do with cutting out too quickly on Chad?

She collapsed on the living room couch, not liking the look she'd taken into her character. She hadn't meant to run all those years ago, but it didn't change the fact that that was exactly what she'd done.

Maybe Chad wouldn't want anything to do with her when he got to know the new Meg. She wasn't Megan or Megs anymore.

All those years when Pete had been okay with her absences, she'd been overjoyed that he had been so accepting. But why had he been so accepting? Surely that wasn't normal. Shouldn't he have wanted to spend more time with her?

Jade could be away from Dane the odd time, but she would never choose to be separated. Meg had damn near run at every chance she'd been offered.

And here she was—running away again.

She stared at the bedroom door, then at the heaped bed that she had no hope of getting into tonight. And she needed to finish packing, so she could get them moved, while Janelle was at school.

What she didn't take, she had to be prepared to leave behind. So she'd been tossing stuff out as she sorted. And that had created another problem, as memories overwhelmed her. They also highlighted that Pete was not the same person she'd originally fallen in love with, and she didn't like the new person in the way she'd loved the old one.

Then her mind swung to consider the old Chad and the new version.

That she didn't know who Chad had become was another disturbing thought. That she was even considering Chad in that light again bothered her. She'd never been unfaithful. She'd never even been tempted. And while thinking of him in that light wasn't crossing the line, there was a sense of having done *Chad* wrong by having a relationship with Pete.

And how did that work?

It didn't. It was stupid.

But it's how she was beginning to feel. And to right that wrong from so long time ago, she had to level the field again. Good thing she'd already decided to move out and to leave Pete.

Her inner voice piped up. *Except you haven't yet made the final decision that your relationship with Pete is over. You have come to that point but have shied away from making that final decision.*

But inside you have.

And you have to go with your gut.

"Auntie Meg? What's the matter?"

She spun around to find Janelle rubbing her eyes and looking ready to cry.

"I'm sorry. Did I wake you?" She walked over, glancing at the clock in the living room at the same time. It was past two in the morning. "Let's get you back to bed. It's a school night, and you need sleep."

"I *was* asleep, but something woke me up." Her voice wavered.

Meg tried not to wince. Janelle had had such horrible nightmares when she'd first arrived. "More nightmares?"

She nodded.

Meg needed to keep Janelle from seeing her overly-heaped bed, as this so wasn't the right time for explanations. Meg wrapped an arm around her niece's shoulders and gently tugged her back toward her room.

"Come on. Let's get you back to bed. I'll stay with you, until you fall asleep again."

Besides, Meg knew sleep was beyond her tonight. She cuddled up to Janelle, waiting until she fell back asleep.

CHAD STOOD ONCE again in Stephanie's apartment. He had posted a bulletin on her vehicle and plates, and her description had been sent out to all divisions. He ran a hand through his hair. His stomach was knotted, and his nerves churned.

He'd done what he could do—and, as was so often the case, it wasn't enough.

Three hours had passed since he'd received her text—three hours of frantically searching her old haunts, knocking on doors, and sending out alerts.

So far, nothing. No sign of Stephanie or her vehicle.

Gloves on, he started going through her apartment. Closets, drawers, and all surfaces were checked for notes, address books, diaries, something to show who she'd gone out with. And it had come up empty. He walked into her bedroom again and started dissecting her bed. He found a notebook under her bed. He picked it up and flipped through it.

It appeared to be meandering thoughts, disjointed in time, with no dates or names. He tried to make sense of it all and skimmed over several pages of writing but found the rest of the book empty. As the book was covered with a thick layer of dust, none of it appeared to be recent. He dropped it on the bed and went to the night table. The drawer was stuffed with books—romance novels, if the covers were anything to go by. At the bottom at the back was a small jeweler's box. He tugged it out and studied it. The velvet box was old, burgundy in color, some spots worn right through the nap. He opened it up to find two small necklaces, with a single silver heart pendant.

He lifted one and turned on the lamp to see it better. The silver heart looked familiar, so he turned it over to see a simple inscription. *To Stephanie, with love.*

The words alone made him sit up and take notice. That had been the same wording on the necklace they'd found with Cia's remains. Only in that case, the necklace had had Meg's name on it. Same style, same look. It would take the techs to match it any closer than that.

But it somehow followed … that the same boyfriend

gave the girls this gift?

And that might mean Josh. Again. Stephanie had gone out with him before hooking up with Bruce.

He closed his eyes. His best friend back then had been everyone's friend. And the girls had loved him, *all* the girls. All the time there'd been a lot of envious looks directed his way as he switched his partners on a regular basis back in school, but, at the same time, he was solid. And even though he had had a lot of girls, he was with only one at a time. He never cheated. And he didn't need to—they all just lined up for their turn.

That also meant he had no reason to kill any of them.

He'd been smitten with Cia in the beginning, but that had worn off quickly. He'd known they were done, and Cia was eyeing her next boyfriend. Josh hadn't cared. He'd also had other interests and had planned to break up her with after the camping weekend and before starting college.

Did Josh have it in him to kill? Accidentally maybe. Premeditatedly? No. Chad would bet his life on it.

Instinctively he wanted to say Josh had had nothing to do with Cia's disappearance. But was that fair? He needed to take a new look at everyone. That's what Mack had said too.

They would start fresh. Go over everything with a magnifying glass and tweezers, if necessary.

This time they would find the truth. And, if Josh had killed Cia, then Josh's ass would get nailed.

Chad closed his eyes.

He hoped it wasn't his best friend.

MEG WORKED THROUGH the night. She collapsed at two a.m. and woke up at five a.m., and then she carried on. She had the bulk of her belongings sorted and bagged—a stack she was taking and a stack that she wasn't. Then finally, just before time to wake up Janelle for school, Meg remade the bed, took one last slow look at the bedroom that held so many loving memories. They'd warmed her for so many long cold nights. And now there was nothing but icy sadness.

Fatigue had taken over. She swayed, overcome with pain and grief.

Then she heard Janelle get up and go to the bathroom.

Meg poured steel into her back and pushed back the hot ball in her throat to be dealt with at another time, yet again.

One of these days that space inside would explode from the pressure—but not today.

Today was big. And the knot in her stomach was a fear that ate away at her insides. She was afraid, now that she'd started, that she wouldn't get out in time, before Pete came back.

With one last glance around, she closed the door on her past and turned to face a sleepy Janelle—her future. And, for the next hour, Meg could do what needed to be done.

She could get through this.

"Good morning, sleepyhead. How are you feeling?"

With Janelle promising to get dressed quickly, Meg headed to the kitchen to make breakfast.

Janelle left on time, and the moment the door closed behind her, Meg kicked into high gear. She lugged her bags to her car and stowed them in the trunk. When that couldn't hold any more, she filled the back seat. It took several trips to get these loaded. In the front passenger seat, she loaded the bags she was giving away to charity.

Puffing with exertion, she raced back upstairs, feeling as if she were running out of time, her nerves jangling every time she heard a truck or saw a tall man. In Janelle's room she stopped to take stock. The place was relatively neat, but Janelle still had dirty laundry, school stuff, and some other items that she'd chosen to take to Meg's. And they all needed to be packed up and returned to her old house.

For just a moment, Meg wondered if she was doing the right thing. Maybe they should move to a neutral setting.

But, no, she didn't have time. If Janelle didn't like being back at her old home, then it would only be temporary. But she had to go now.

It took another hour and six more trips before Meg took a final look at Janelle's room, then at the rest of the apartment.

She took the stairs on the last trip and walked to her stuffed car. She'd go to the closest Goodwill store and get rid of those items first.

Unlocking her car, she opened the door. A voice called out from behind her.

"There she is. Megan Pearce."

She spun around only to see a TV crew, racing toward her. The cameras were a dead giveaway. "Shit."

She hopped in, locked the door, and turned on her engine.

"Wait! We just want to talk to you."

Just as the reporter reached her car, Meg peeled out of the lot. So much for privacy. Damn good thing she was moving out. In her rearview mirror, she watched the crew climb into their van in an attempt to follow her, which was so not going to happen.

She took several corners in an effort to lose them and took the long way to run her errands.

The last thing she needed was to talk to the media.

They'd made her life hell once. She wasn't signing up for a second round, if she could help it.

But how long would it be before they tracked her down at her new location?

STEPHANIE TREMBLED. SHE lifted a hand and watched as her whole arm shook. Her chest rose and fell in short gasps. It felt as if she'd been running for hours. She'd been on the run before, but she'd forgotten the adrenaline rush or the pain as the shock wore off.

If it wore off …

Damn, she was scared. She kept her eyes closed, knowing that the whites of her eyes would shine in the dark of the night.

The problem was that she didn't know what she was running from. She should have met Bruce for coffee. Now she figured she'd taken a wrong turn in life again. And that she was being followed.

But by whom?

She slipped around the dingy corner into a back alley she knew all too well. No one could find her here. She was in the world that she'd struggled so hard to get out of again.

But right now it was a perfect place to blend in and to hide away.

She had to stay safe. She didn't know who had killed Cia, but she knew it had to be one of those guys she'd camped with. She couldn't trust any of them.

Not now.

And she wanted to live. For the first time in a long time, she *wanted* to live.

Chapter 12

M EG SCRUBBED HER face, then put on heavier makeup than normal—but she was deluding herself that she'd camouflaged her exhaustion—then walked out of her brother's house. Her muscles ached and her back was telling her that she'd done too much. Yet what were the options? The bags had to be unloaded and unpacked and the cleaning had to be done. The house had been empty for months. And there wasn't any coffee. She needed to shop for food and a few basics.

The lab came first.

She drove her brother's car to the Forensic Support Services lab and parked in the staff parking lot. She'd been a consultant out of this office off and on for many years. She could only hope her earlier phone call had brought the results she'd hoped for.

Inside, she identified herself and strode down to Stacy Carter's office, a forensic pathologist. Of the same age, the two had been friends for years. Professional colleagues at first but that had quickly morphed to mutual respect and a developing friendship. A friendship she'd called on this morning.

Stacy looked up, a warm smile breaking across her face. "There she is. Meg, who can't take a weekend away without tripping over a body."

Meg smiled wanly. "Too true and you're not the first to bring up that point."

"Pete, *huh*?"

Meg winced. "Yeah, it was the last straw for him."

Stacy's chocolate-brown eyes widened in shock, and the smile fell away. "Oh, no, I am so sorry." She stood and walked around her desk to look Meg in the eye. "You two have been together a long time. Maybe you can work this out."

"Maybe." Meg shrugged. "Yet I may not want to anymore." She stared around the office, not certain she was ready to talk about it, but she didn't have too many people she could share this with. Stacy was one of them, so she took a deep breath and explained about everything that had happened since Darren's death and Janelle's arrival in her world.

When she was done, Stacy reached out and gave her a hug. "I'm so sorry. You've had a rough couple months. But you are doing the right thing. Janelle needs you. Obviously Pete doesn't."

Meg gave a half laugh. "That's one way of putting it. Thanks."

"And these remains you found, you believe them to be of your old friend?"

Meg, relieved to be onto other issues, nodded. "All of the evidence points in that direction. Obviously DNA tests will need to be done to confirm it, but the victim is the right age, height, and in the right location."

"And the necklace?" Stacy was always a direct person. Meg appreciated it. It was so much easier to deal with.

"I think it's mine."

"Hence my role?" At Meg's nod, Stacy added, "Okay. I'll

do the examination. You'll observe. The process will be videotaped, with audio to ensure you aren't touching the bones or compromising the evidence. Yes, that's overkill."

Meg laughed. "In our business, nothing is overkill."

Stacy smiled. "How true. But, if this goes to court, we both have to testify."

It was such a pleasure to work with a professional. "Exactly."

Stacy led the way to the lab. "Now, let's go see if we can help your friend."

CHAD WALKED INTO one of the many empty rooms at the station. He felt like shit. There'd been no sign of Stephanie. He didn't even know which places she haunted, and neither did her neighbor. Stephanie hadn't contacted Chad and hadn't shown up for work.

He'd called her friends, but no one had heard from her. On the off chance, he'd texted Bruce but hadn't heard back from him. For all intents and purposes, she'd disappeared.

If it hadn't been for her last cry for help, he hated to say, he would likely be considering she'd disappeared with her druggie friends for a few days.

But maybe that *was* her cry for help. Maybe she'd been hoping that he'd stop her before she spiraled out of control again and went back to her old ways.

But what if this disappearance wasn't her return to bad habits? What if it was connected to Cia's disappearance? The timing was suspicious, coincidental, and convenient.

With that thought uppermost in his mind, he headed for the room Daniel had booked for this process. He stood in the doorway. Daniel should be here already but apparently wasn't yet. The room wasn't empty though. Boxes had been stacked two high at the one end of the table.

He couldn't contain his excitement as he strode closer. It had been hard moving from being a suspect in a disappearance to a cop and now a detective in his own right. Especially with Cia's disappearance always hanging over his head. From Chad's point of view, this find had been a long time coming.

Finally they could catch the asshole who had killed Cia.

"Figured you would show up early." Mack walked in, hitching up his pants. He carried a chipped coffee mug filled with coffee in one hand and a stack of files in the other. "Just not this early. Daniel isn't even here yet."

"I'm not that early," Chad protested, then grinned sheepishly. "And so what if I am?" He shoved a hand through his hair. "Any news on Stephanie?"

Mack shook his head and dumped his files on the table at the opposite end of the table to the boxes. "No, but her disappearance might have nothing to do with Cia's case. Stephanie's disappeared into the streets many times before. If she's relapsed, then that's on her, not on you." He looked up and studied Chad. "Are you sure you're ready for this?"

"Are you? I've been ready for seventeen years, and there's no way to know about Stephanie," Chad snapped, then reined back his impatience. "But, if her disappearance is related, … I want to find the bastard and her, … fast."

"Yep, me too. But, for me, this is just one of many cases I'd like answers to."

"Yeah, but it's the only one that happened in your backyard."

Silence.

Chad looked up, caught Mack's narrowed-eyed gaze, and grinned. "Do you really think I don't know who owns each and every one of those cabins?" He added smoothly, "Besides, you're Bruce's uncle, not to mention Anto's and Pero's uncle as well."

Mack dropped his gaze to his folders, a thick frown forming on his pug face.

Chad studied him. "I know that you shouldn't have been on the case back then. I know about you almost getting kicked off the force over it all. Does that bug you?"

"No. You just surprised me, that's all." He shuffled through the folders. "Now, if you're done, maybe we can get to work. Daniel should be here any minute."

Chad filed that reaction in the back of his mind and turned to the top box. He moved it down beside the first and opened the lid. Instantly all thoughts of Mack's cabin flew out of his head. This was the gold mine of evidence laid out before him.

Finally. Now he could get the answers he'd always been looking for.

Maybe he'd be in time to save Stephanie. Inside, he doubted it. He hated to think of it, but he was afraid it was already too late.

MACK WATCHED CHAD burrow into boxes, like a child who'd found lost treasure. Chad had lost a lot back then, his innocence being at the top of that long list.

Mack had been so sure that Chad had killed Cia Barnes. And Mack had had no doubt that Cia was dead. Years of experience said the odds were not in that young girl's favor. Those same odds also said it was one of those six young men from the camping trip who'd killed her.

And three of them were from his own damn family.

That had been tough. His other family members called him, day in and day out, crying and screaming for him to do something. And he had a big family. They'd nagged him endlessly. Over the years, the case had ended up being the one taboo subject at any family gatherings. It was as if, by ignoring it, the three men would be innocent.

Sure, Mack had seventeen fewer years on the force back then, but he'd been sharp, and he'd understood the vagaries of human nature even then. Chad had headed the suspect list. Mack admitted to having leaned on him pretty hard, hoping for a confession in order to clear his nephews. Instead Chad had held up, and Cia's case had remained unsolved—and a permanent worry to eat away at Mack.

But Chad had gone from a shocked, scared innocent to a bitter realist and an even more scared man.

Mack had seen the change before his eyes. The memory saddened him. At the time, he'd been glad of it. He'd wanted the smart ass to grow up and to see the pain he'd caused Cia's family and friends and to feel the full force of the law and to be scared and to need to feel the heavy hand of punishment. Mack had done a lot wrong back then. Almost ruined his career over the choices he'd made. However, he'd done it to try to prove his nephews innocent.

Then one day, Chad had walked into the station with his own badge.

Now Mack grudgingly admitted he *might* have misjudged the guy. The young kid had grown into a solid young man. But … leopards didn't change their spots, and killers never forgot what they had done, no matter how long it was between kills. That meant this kid was *not* off the hook.

And this was very suspicious timing for Stephanie to go missing. If she had panicked about the remains that had been found, she had had an interesting way of reacting. Stephanie was a drug addict, who, if she'd ever known anything incriminating, had either forgotten about it or had lost the credibility to prove it a long time ago.

Also interesting was that the only person who thought she was missing was Chad, and Mack only had his word on her disappearance. Something he would have to point out to Daniel.

But Mack had seen people act in a lot of ways. So far as he was concerned, while Chad was looking through the evidence for suspects, Mack would take another look at *him*.

MEG WAITED OUTSIDE the school grounds for Janelle to walk out. She'd texted her already, saying that she'd pick her up.

Now, seated in the car, with the heat pounding down on her and after the fullness of her day, Meg just wanted to close her eyes. Exhaustion had nothing on her. She wanted nothing more than to go home and sleep.

And that so wasn't an option.

She had to face Janelle first.

"Auntie Meg? Are you sleeping?"

She laughed at Janelle. "Get in the car, silly. I admit I'm tired, but I'm not sleeping."

"Sure looks like it to me," Janelle muttered. "Can we go home, please?"

Uh-oh. Meg cast her niece a quick look, then turned on the engine. She drove to the house, wondering how long it would take.

Two blocks apparently.

"Auntie Meg? I thought we were going home."

Meg changed lanes and took the next left. A couple moments later, she pulled into her brother's driveway and drove into the garage. She turned off the engine, twisted in her seat, and turned to look at Janelle.

In a calm, quiet voice, she said, "We are home."

Janelle's eyes widened uncomprehendingly. She frowned. "What do you mean?"

With a buoyant smile, Meg unlocked the door and got out. She waited for Janelle to grab her backpack and join her. She closed the garage door with the button at the side of the interior door. Then she unlocked the door to the house. She returned to the car and opened the trunk, and started unloading the grocery bags she'd stashed in the back. When she walked into the kitchen, Janelle stood in the center of the kitchen, staring at her.

"A little help, please." Meg gasped as one of the bags started to slip. Janelle jumped forward and grabbed it before it fell. "Start putting away stuff, and I'll go get the rest."

It took ten minutes before the groceries were unloaded and put away. Janelle grabbed an apple and a spoonful of peanut butter—and again stood in the middle of the room, right in front of Meg. "Now what's going on?"

Blowing a strand of hair off her face, Meg smiled. "I would have thought that was obvious by now. We'll live here from now on." She studied Janelle's face, looking for some inkling of a reaction. "If that's okay with you?"

Janelle was quiet, as she munched on her snack. "It's fine by me. Why?"

Meg wanted to prevaricate, but that wasn't the best way to move forward. "I have thought a lot about my relationship with Pete and decided that the best thing would be some time apart."

Instead of the happy reaction she'd expected, Janelle frowned. "Have you broken up with him?"

"Not yet. He went away for a few days to consider our relationship, and I decided that I wanted to be gone before he came back."

"And will he be mad at us?" Janelle asked, her eyes narrowed, her voice cautious.

"I'm not sure." Meg smiled. "Maybe he'll be relieved."

"Did you leave him a note or something, so he knows where we are?" Janelle's voice rose in fear.

Meg tilted her head. "You are concerned about him?"

At that, Janelle dropped her gaze to her apple.

Meg caught her breath. "No. You're worried about him being angry?"

Janelle lifted her face slowly, uncertainty shining in her beautiful eyes. Then she gave a faint nod.

Right. That fear factor again. "Ah, honey, Pete might get angry sometimes, but he's not dangerous." She hoped. Meg walked over and wrapped her arms around her niece in a comforting hug. "Not to worry. I'll speak with him about our future soon. But, as the condo is Pete's, I felt this was the best interim home we could have, as long as it doesn't bother you."

Janelle glanced around. "No. It won't. Dad and I didn't live here very long anyway." She spun around. "It's bigger than the condo, and I can have my old room back. It still has some of my stuff in it."

"Right. I've brought everything—at least, I hope I have everything—from the condo. Go on up and take a look. Set about organizing your stuff, and I'll start dinner."

At that, Janelle took off.

Meg sagged against the kitchen counter and dropped her

head backward, before slowly rotating it to ease the knots building up all day. Why had she thought this step would be a hugely difficult deal? It had been easy.

She'd expected endless questions, and instead there'd been essentially nothing. That didn't mean the questions weren't still coming, but, for now, conflict had been averted.

She still had a few more loose ends to tie up, like the security system needed a second look, but that could be tomorrow's job.

Tonight they'd be fine. Besides, no one knew where they were anyway.

STEPHANIE WOKE UP alone, cold, and scared. The sun was up, reaching into the back alley. God, she was still alive.

She wasn't sure she deserved to be. And she wasn't sure she wanted to be. The place reeked with vomit and urine … and something else she didn't want to think about. But this is what she had to deal with. She straightened, hating the pain in her back, the agony of an empty belly yet again. She didn't dare go home, but that's where she wanted to be.

And damn her for being such a fool as to lose her cell phone. She couldn't even remember where her car was at this point or even where she was in relation to it, for that matter.

God, Stephanie, you're such a loser.

Then she remembered being followed. And ducking out of sight and then running for her life. Had she shaken him off?

Or was he on the street waiting for her. *Shit!*

Chapter 13

C HAD LEFT THE office late, frustrated and depressed.

With Daniel, they'd opened the boxes, gone through all the evidence and every statement, and then set up a new board with position locators, indicating where everyone had been at the time of Cia's disappearance. Then they set up a timeline of events.

It had been a futile exercise. He'd bet the new material they'd worked up would be exactly the same as what he had at home. He was counting on it. Yet he would spend the evening checking it out. He'd taken copies of what he could photocopy and had taken pictures of the rest.

The answers had to be here.

Somewhere.

Once at his apartment, he cleared off his dining room table and unloaded the work he'd brought home. Then, with the same precision he'd used at the office, he reopened and set up the case files he'd kept at home.

He had just sat down to work when his phone rang. *Josh*.

"Who killed her?" Josh began without preamble, a hard edge to his voice. When Chad didn't answer fast enough, Josh's voice rose. "Damn it, Chad, who fucking killed her?"

"Easy, Josh. I don't know who killed her." He cleared his throat, knowing Josh needed answers as badly as he did. "It's too early to say yet. We don't know anything at this stage."

"Damn it."

There was a dark silence, then Josh growled. "Is it her? At least tell me that."

That much Chad could give him. "We think so. Right height, age, location. However, DNA will be weeks before confirming. They are looking for dental records to compare." He waited.

"How could we *not* have found her?" The pain in Josh's voice made Chad wince. "We searched for days."

"I don't know about you, but I went back several weekends, hoping to find her—or something that would explain what had happened to her."

"So did I, over several weekends as well. I couldn't forget about her. Who could? Damn it. When I heard the news, I knew it had to be her."

"Me too. Meg found her, you know."

"Meg who?"

"Megan. Megs. She goes by Meg now. She's an anthropologist. Has a mess of degrees. Like a lot of us, she switched her name to one the media didn't know so well. She went on with her life and became someone."

Josh gave a harsh laugh. "Glad someone did. I sure as hell didn't."

"That's not true, Josh. You might not be an engineer, but you're doing something you love."

"Surveying for a company that is given contracts *by* engineers is not the future I had envisioned for myself. We were both planning on engineering, but ..."

Chad didn't want to get into that discussion. Too many years had passed to worry about a change in career paths now. "It's also not doing drugs and curled up in a back alley somewhere."

"Stephanie is a great way to put my life in perspective." Josh sighed. "I wished I'd done things differently though."

"Don't we all?"

"Do you? Do you wish you hadn't gone into law enforcement? You've spent every day trying to hunt down the killer."

"I know, and, since we found Cia's remains, I'd like to think we have a chance now to find out what happened. So that—"

"So that we can get on with the rest of our lives? Oh, don't worry. I've thought the same thing. But what future? We've lived with this hanging over our heads for so long. I didn't do it. You didn't do it—but we might as well have because of how we've let it affect our lives. It's been criminal, that's what it is. Yet we aren't criminals."

"No, we aren't." Chad tried to ease the conversation down a notch, but Josh was just gearing up.

"But that's how we've been treated. Since then, I feel like I'm always being watched. That, if I don't pay a parking ticket as soon as I get it, I'll go to jail for life. It's as if I slipped through on that one transgression, and now the law is looking for another way to nail my hide and to throw me in jail, as if that's where I should have been all this time."

"He—"

"Do you realize that if we'd been convicted of accidentally killing Cia, we'd be out by now?" He snorted. "Instead we did nothing, but got a life sentence anyway."

"Stephanie is missing," Chad finally managed to say. There was no easy way to say it.

Silence.

"Missing—how?"

"That's just it. I don't know. She sent me a text asking

for help. Just the one word. *Help.* Nothing else and nothing since. She's not at home and hasn't been home since then. No one has seen her since she left in secret to meet a 'friend.'"

"Shit. You think something has happened to her?"

"I don't know." Chad stared out the window. "Yet I'm afraid something might have."

"She could just be meeting her dealer. After quitting her drug-taking, any meeting with him makes him a 'secret' now. Had you found out, you'd be pissed at her, same for anyone else in her circle. She always was a drama queen."

"And a nervy one. I know. However, I can't get the timing out of my head."

"That Cia's remains have been found and that Stephanie has gone missing? You don't think she had anything to do with Cia's death, do you?"

"No, I don't—or Meg, for that matter. But what if Stephanie didn't tell all the truth back then? What if she knows something, or what if the killer thinks she knows something?"

Josh laughed. "That's your cop's instincts getting to you. Chances are, she's shacked up with someone, and her cell phone battery has died. How many times over the years has she called you to get her a place to sleep at night? Help with getting her out of jail? Help with finding her rehab assistance? She has even called you to help her rent an apartment because she had no references. She'd only rented the flop-by-the-hour ones before then."

"I remember." Talk about memories that Chad would not like to resurrect. "She had no one else."

"Hell, of course she didn't. Even Bruce finally had enough, and she had him on speed dial for years. He's still sweet on her, but he still walked away. Hell, we all walked away, once we realized she was on a downward slide and looking to take everyone down with her."

"And I walked away too." Chad groaned softly, hating the rush of painful memories.

"Hey, man, don't hold yourself to blame for that. At some point there is no helping those who won't help themselves, at least not if they aren't interested."

"I know." Chad stared at the wall, with all the case information. "She's been doing so much better these last few years. I'd like to think she's turned a corner. She's called several times since the word got out."

"She'll have it rough if the media finds her." Josh sighed. "That would send her into hiding."

There was silence. Chad had nothing to add. Josh was right.

"Funny about Megs, though."

"Meg," Chad corrected automatically. "What's funny?"

"Look at what she does for a living, and then she's the one who finds the remains." He snorted. "Almost like it was meant to be."

"Merely a coincidence."

"I thought you didn't believe in those."

"It was Meg's first time back in the area since that weekend. She was staying at one of the cabins down a way. It was a fluke she even found the remains. While she'd be better prepared than most people at finding them, it still hit her hard, when she put the facts together."

"Yeah, I imagine. How is she doing?" Josh's voice changed, deepened, making Chad wonder if he still carried any lingering emotions for Meg. "I presume you've talked to her since?"

"Yes, I have, and she's holding. She's good people."

"I know. She always was."

There was that odd twinge in his friend's voice. "You aren't still hung up on her, are you? I thought you got over her a long time ago." *Like before she started going out with me,* but Chad didn't say that last bit. There was no point.

"I did get over her. I was just wondering what she's like now. Look at how Stephanie turned out. It seems like Meg went in the opposite direction. She chose something so focused and so demanding that it's like she has to be in control, ready in case of a repeat event."

"That's because she blames herself. If she'd only kept a closer eye on Cia, she would have known what had happened to her, that kind of stuff."

"No one could keep an eye on that girl. I always wondered if she'd crept off on her own to meet someone. She was my girl, but I knew it was over. She was already looking for her next mark. In a way, I was too. It was more so for my ego than anything else." He gave a self-deprecating laugh. "Now I'm used to getting dumped."

Chad sighed. "Oh no, did Kim leave?"

"Sure did. The minute the news hit the wire and the phone calls started, she bailed, saying she hadn't signed up to live with a murder suspect."

Shit. "I'm sorry, man." If anyone had been dogged by the bad press, it had been Josh. Another prime suspect from that weekend because, when things got rough with his relationships, the cops always brought up the fact that a prior girlfriend had disappeared. And then the women usually left after that.

"Anto was the lucky one, dying like that. A head-on collision and, *boom,* no more suspicion, no more threats or lingering doubts from supposed family and friends."

"Yeah, except that he's dead."

"And safely out of everyone's suspicious eyes. I don't know about you, but dying was the easy way out. Staying alive and dealing with this shit has not been fun."

Depression had always been an issue for Josh, ever since that weekend. Now every time he came up against another hurdle, he seemed to drop down further and further. So far, he'd always managed to pull up again, and, maybe this time, they could solve Cia's case, and that would stop the vicious cycle. They all needed a break from their pasts, Josh more than most.

Then there was Stephanie.

Chad was afraid it was all too much for Stephanie. She might never survive this—regardless of her reason for disappearing. He wasn't sure he could help her anymore, not if she'd gone off the deep end yet again.

MEG WAITED UNTIL Janelle went to sleep, a chatterbox right up to the end, before slowly walking back to her new bedroom. She sat on the bed and stared around. She'd put away her clothes and had stored as much of the other stuff as she could in the bottom of the closet. She kinda felt like she had deserted Pete.

And that felt wrong, but she was too tired to change it now; maybe on the weekend.

She collapsed on the bed with her arms above her head and tried to relax. Today could have been so much worse. Thankfully it had gone relatively smoothly. At the lab, she'd observed so intently that Stacy had laughed at her a couple times, saying it felt like she was back under examination by her toughest profs.

Meg hadn't meant to be that intense, but sometimes she didn't dare have anything go wrong—or have anything important get missed.

And nothing had been. Sadly not much to see. Meg was convinced they'd found Cia, but outside of cause of death being confirmed, Stacy had found nothing new. She'd pulled DNA that would be tested against that of Cia's father, but, after having gone through the bones and having the rest of the soil sifted and looked at for evidence, they hadn't found anything new. That hadn't made Meg happy, but it was what she'd expected.

She wanted to tell Chad. However, for many reasons, she shouldn't call. She groaned and reached for her phone. She had just as many reasons *to* call. Besides, it would be nice to connect. She had been feeling a little disconnected all day, and she'd expected to hear from Pete by now. That meant he was staying away longer than planned or had come home and had found her gone and hadn't come after her.

He would likely know where she'd gone. It's not as if she had any number of places to go to. This choice made sense, but he might not see it that way. And did she care if he hadn't come after her? No. She would be relieved when that final conversation was over. Until then, she was waiting. And that was uncomfortable.

First things first; she dialed Chad's number, trying to ignore the fact that she'd called Chad instead of Pete.

"Meg, I heard you were busy today?"

That surprised her. "Did Stacy call you?"

"No, Daniel and Mack spoke with her."

"Oh, *Mack.*" Damn, just hearing that man's name was enough to send the willies down her spine. "I thought he got kicked off the case."

"Yeah, it's technically Daniel's case, but you know that Mack won't ever stay out of it."

"Oh, yeah, I remember him—built like a crushed cement truck and with an attitude to match."

He started laughing. "That sounds like him, but I've come to respect the work he does."

"Bet that wasn't easy." She thought it might have been damn difficult. "He was an asshole to us."

"Yeah, but then he figured one of us had killed Cia."

"I suppose. Still doesn't make him a nice guy." She remembered how terrified she'd been of the detective. The hard look in his eyes had given her nightmares for months.

"Well, not sure he is now either, but he's good at what he does."

"Except that he couldn't find Cia's killer either."

"True. First, did you find anything on the bones? I tried calling several times today, but your phone went to voice mail." He gave a short laugh. "And I drove past your place today. The media were all over there."

"Yes, I barely avoided them this morning. I haven't been back there since." She groaned. "I should have mentioned it before, as the damn media could make it look like I skipped town." Quickly she filled him in on her night and day. Toward the end, she yawned, then yawned again. "Sorry. I'm exhausted."

"With good reason. Sounds like you need a good night's sleep."

"Or two or three. I just wanted to see if you had anything new." She hated the hopeful note in her voice, but, damn it, one of them should have found something.

"Nothing. We're going back to the beginning and taking

a fresh look at everything. We will have to come around and speak with everyone again."

"Oh, *fun.*"

"I know. It's not what we want either. I have other cases to work on too, and this is Daniel's case, not mine. So expect a call from him soon."

"Thanks for that positive note." She didn't want to speak to anyone again. "I so don't want to remember the details from back then."

"We have your statement but expect to be questioned to see if you want to change or add anything."

"There isn't anything," she said tiredly. "I gave as clear an accounting as I could back then. Nothing has changed in my head, just that I am seventeen years older, wiser, and more cynical."

"Aren't we all?" He paused. "Have you eaten?"

She smiled and ran a hand through her hair. "Yes, I have Janelle to maintain some semblance of normality for. I really don't want her affected by this."

"You know she will be. As much as we'd like to avoid it, the families are always affected."

"I know. Doesn't mean I like it. She knows I found a set of remains, but she doesn't know anything about whose remains they may be or how they are connected to me."

"You might want to tell her. It's not a good thing for her to find out from someone else."

"I know." She considered the issue but didn't like any of the options. "Damn."

"Sorry. I'm going to contact the others."

"*Ugh.* That's a tough job. How is Pero doing? Last I heard, he was recovering from a car accident that killed his brother, Anto. But that was like eleven, twelve years ago.

Pero was okay but … his brother? … Yuck.”

"He was a good friend. I didn't realize you didn't like him."

"I liked Pero. None of us girls liked Anto. And I never told you because he *was* your friend." She smiled at the memories. "He was important to you, and you were important to me. So I put up with him."

"I never knew."

"No," she reminisced. "Lots of things you didn't know."

He laughed. "No way," he scoffed. Then he paused for a long moment, before asking curiously, "Like what?"

She laughed. "Oh, I don't know. Lots of things. We were so young and intense. I was scared to screw it all up, but I did anyway."

Damn. Meg closed her eyes. She shouldn't have said that. Waves of emotional exhaustion hit her in never-ending painful ebbs and flows. It was the only reason she'd said that. It wouldn't have slipped out otherwise. But it had, and now she had to deal with it.

"What? No. That's not true. You were perfect, always."

"So not true," she whispered. "I was horrible, just horrible, back then."

"What are you talking about?" His voice deepened. "You were never horrible. It's not in you."

She stifled back the tears, hating the weakness threatening to overtake her. She should never have called him. Her throat was clogged, and she couldn't get the words out. She swallowed several times, but that hot ball in her throat refused to budge.

"Is this to do with Cia?" His voice broke through her pain.

"Yes," she replied. "You know that, when she disappeared, we were gossiping about her? *About* her. That's like how horrible we were. … She was dying, and we, … well, we were sniggering about her."

Just the memory burned hot and hateful in her head. God, she hated how she had acted back then.

"Christ, Meg, you were barely eighteen. Everyone gossiped. And everyone gossiped about Cia. Jesus, she got around." He sighed. "If nothing had happened to her, that would never have been an issue, but, because something did, it put a spotlight on each of our behaviors at the time." He groaned. "Remember what I did? I almost went out of my mind, knowing she'd died because I'd been a coward, too chicken shit to find out what that noise was."

"No, that's not true," Meg cried out, shocked out of her self-pity. "You could have been killed yourself."

"And maybe I could have stopped it before anyone got hurt." He gave a harsh, short laugh. "Instead I've spent every day wondering *what if …*"

"Like the rest of us. We all wondered if our actions could have changed the outcome, and, of course, there is no way to know."

"Exactly. … This has ruined all our lives, but we can't let it control us forever."

"Like Stephanie." Meg sighed. "I feel so sorry for her. I should have stayed in touch, but I just couldn't handle it."

"Yeah, we got that. I stayed in touch early on, but I was struggling too. Then, by the time she hit the streets, even though I tried for years, I couldn't help her anymore. She contacted me a few years ago, saying she'd cleaned up her act, asking for help."

"What kind of help?"

"To get some counseling, help her find a place to live,

that kind of thing."

"You've been a good friend to her." The sound that came through Chad's end of the phone made her wince.

"Not good enough. She's missing right now, and I've done all I can do, but there's still no sign of her."

"Shit." Her reaction was as much for the worry and frustration in his voice as for the fact that Stephanie was missing.

"Exactly." He sighed. "Everyone is assuming she's taken another dive into the drug scene to forget."

Meg sat up and crossed her legs. She ran a hand through her hair. "Has she done this since cleaning up?"

"Unfortunately, yes." He added, "Once after losing a job. It was a slip-up but not a bad one."

She winced. "Some events are enough to shake even the most stable of us."

He gave a short laugh. "And no one would consider her stable."

"No." So true but they'd been good friends at one time, and Meg wished Stephanie had had an easier time of it. "Well, I hope she shows up soon. Otherwise …"

"Yeah, I know." He cleared his throat. "Enough of Stephanie for now. With the media out hunting up anyone connected to Cia's disappearance, I suggest you keep a low profile for the next week, while we work on the case."

"Will do." She stood and walked to her window, where she peeked out from the side. "The street looks clear. They haven't found me yet."

"Good. Let's keep it that way." His voice deepened. "I wouldn't want anything to happen to you."

She sighed. "You know the timing really sucks, don't you?"

"I know." His voice lightened so much she could almost

see his smile in her mind, "I'm just letting you know your options."

"Really?" She laughed. "Is that what you call it?"

"No pressure," he stated firmly. "I'm here if you need me or if and when you are ready to see if we have anything worth rekindling."

She both loved and hated the shiver of delight slipping down her spine at his words. He'd always had that effect on her.

After saying good night, she murmured a few moments later, "What a concept." Maybe that's why she'd gone for Pete. Stable, solid, and comfortable Pete. He'd never take her camping and have someone get murdered. No, but he had taken her to his cabin, where she'd found a body.

Maybe she was destined to live a life that always touched on crime. Certainly she could have focused on that with her work, but she'd chosen a more humanitarian way to use her education and skills. Yes, crime was often involved, but she'd spent so much time working on old, oftentimes large cases that the crimes, for all their horror, were distant and, therefore, easier to deal with.

Opening a mass grave to identify bodies from an earthquake was much less personal than identifying Cia's body found in a lonely faraway place in the woods. The mass grave in Haiti had had an additional creepy criminal aspect to it, but that had been a one-in-a-million-lifetimes' chance of occurrence.

She'd gone through enough horror back then. And she'd never told anyone at the time about her own history with Cia. It wasn't something she wanted to share. It was something she *couldn't* share.

Tuesday Morning

CHAD WAS STILL trying to gulp coffee before shooting out the door on the way to work, when Daniel called. "I'm calling them all in, including you."

"Shit. A little warning and a little time for them to arrange their lives would have been nice." He threw back the rest of his coffee, then called Meg.

"Good morning."

Her voice, warm and welcoming, brought a smile instantly to his face. Then he realized she'd lose both when she realized what he needed.

"What's up?" Her voice had cooled. "Chad?"

"Sorry, just giving you a heads-up. Daniel called. He wants everyone in the office today for questioning."

"Really?" She gave a choked laugh. "Well, I can make it, but I wouldn't be so sure about the others. Let's see. Anto and Cia are dead, and Stephanie is missing. Besides you and me, that doesn't leave many. Josh, Pero, Tim, and who? Bruce, right?"

"Right, only Josh, Bruce, and you live in town. Tim is in Europe, and I have no idea about Pero. I haven't heard from him or about him for over a decade."

"I'll go straight there. Let's get this over with." And she hung up.

Damn. Chad knew it was asking a bit much without warning, but he'd hoped for a better reaction than that.

He grabbed his keys and drove to work. At the station, he was surprised to find Mack waiting with Daniel. Chad asked, "Did you reach everyone?"

"I will," Daniel said. "No worries there."

At his tone of voice, Chad spun and looked at him. "What's going on? What have you found out?"

"Stephanie is now officially a missing person. I went to her place. Found this." Mack tossed a small evidence bag on the table.

Chad walked over and checked it out. "Right, it's similar to the one found with Cia's remains."

"Right. And according to Stephanie's statement, she was Bruce's girlfriend at the time. But she has the same type of necklace as the one we found with Cia's remains."

"True enough. But she also went out with Josh earlier. In fact, the guys all bought them, as they were all the rage. What one girl had, the next one must have or something better. As they were all friends, it was easier to just buy the same. So either Bruce or Josh could have bought it for her."

Daniel, shoving his long sleeves up his arms, asked, "Are you sure?"

"Look. A lot of friends were in our group. Some came on one weekend but couldn't go on the next. But, within that group, a lot of the couples changed and paired up with others. In fact, the more I've thought about it, it was only a couple hours' drive away, so anyone could have known of our camping plans and taken advantage of Cia being alone."

Mack just stared at him. Derision was clear in his gaze. "You got to take off those rose-colored glasses, boyo. One of you six males killed Cia, mark my words. There wasn't another friend making the drive out there just to pick her off. Neither was it a stranger or a random killing. No." He stabbed a finger at the files in front of him. "It was someone in your group."

Chad glared at the files under Mack's thumb. "I damn well hope not."

"Both of you calm down," Daniel snapped. "And if you can't be impartial about this, then I don't want you anywhere near me or the case, until I find the bastard."

"I *am* impartial." Chad wanted to note that Mack was not being impartial, but that wouldn't help his case. In fact, Daniel could shut out Chad. But that wouldn't help anyone. Mack only wanted to clear his nephews. Chad wanted to clear *all* of them …

"Just because I don't want it to be a friend doesn't mean I'm not going to follow the evidence." He picked up the bag with Stephanie's necklace in it. "This is hardly evidence. It just proves that Cia and Stephanie may have had the same boyfriend."

"Not Cia. Meg. That necklace had her name on it."

"And that could mean nothing." Chad explained, "Cia wasn't the nicest or easiest girl to be friends with. She might have borrowed the damn thing, or she might have stolen it. I can almost guarantee that she wore it to bug Josh. He'd bought it for Meg but hadn't bought Cia one. She'd wear it just to push him into buying her one."

"And then he killed her in a fit of temper?"

"Josh? Hell, no. He didn't, doesn't, have much of a temper. Although, given the years this mess has put us through, I'd have to say he's likely to have developed one. I called him this morning, and he was already trying to dodge the media."

"Good. Let's hope he's pissed enough to say something incriminating."

"Whatever."

"I don't want you in on the interviews."

Chad knew that was coming. "Fine, but I'd like to listen in."

Daniel stood and towered over the portly Mack. He seemed to consider that and then nodded. "Fine. Just let me know if you catch anything. Megan is waiting, so Mack will start. Maybe seeing him again after all this time will jog something loose."

Oh, shit. That was so not likely.

Chad followed Daniel and Mack out the door. It would be a hell of a day. And it had only just begun.

STEPHANIE STARTLED AT the noise.

"There you are, Stephanie. What's the matter?" The man laughed, his voice coldly amused. "Remember me?"

Christ. Stephanie bolted for the far end of the street, dashed into another alleyway and came up against a blocked exit. Her heart pounded, as her instincts screamed at her to run.

She didn't recognize the man or his voice. But, God, she knew the fear.

"There's nowhere to run." The man came closer.

She spun around, searching for a way out, when she felt something prick her arm.

How had he gotten so close, so fast?

"That wasn't so bad, was it?" His voice stretched and receded, as the walls in front of Stephanie twisted and warped into a weird shape. She fell against one wall, her body sliding to the ground.

"Have a nice trip. And this time, please die."

Chapter 14

MEG SAT IN the small room and waited. She didn't flinch or fidget. She'd been here before. She wasn't a scared young girl anymore, and she hadn't done anything wrong. She worked on the side of the law now herself. Mack might try his scare tactics, but Meg was no fool. She'd already contacted her lawyer and had a brief conversation with him.

He'd offered to come in, but Meg didn't want to take that step yet.

She wanted to help the police. She wanted Cia's killer to be caught, and Meg damn-well wanted her life back.

She checked her cell phone for what had to be the tenth time in the last half hour. Still no contact from Pete. As much as she wanted a peaceful end to their relationship, she couldn't help but worry. She hoped he was all right.

The door opened to let Mack in. "Are you late for something, Miss Pearce?"

Meg looked up. "No, I'm not."

His gaze drilled into hers. She stared back, quietly, calmly.

"Good. I'd like to have you tell me again what happened on that day Cia went missing."

"And correlate it to my old statement?" At Mack's nod, Meg said, "I can't add anything. However, to the best of memory, this is what I remember." And she launched into her story. Thank heavens she'd clarified that point with her lawyer. How accountable could one be for discrepancies between two statements on the same event taken seventeen years apart? Not much apparently. Given gaps in memories and time passing, she could remember only so much. When she was done, Mack handed her a copy of her old statement. She read it with interest. And found it to be the same. "Well, nice to know age hasn't affected my memory that badly. Yet," she added, with a small smile.

"And now we come to this necklace." Mack tossed a small bag at her.

She picked it up, expecting to see the same necklace she'd excavated at the site. Instead inside was a shiny newish-looking one in the same style. She turned it over and read the inscription and laughed. "Typical of Josh. He never could figure out what to get people for presents."

"Josh?"

"Stephanie's old boyfriend, I think after me and before Cia, yet before Stephanie hooked up with Bruce." She gave him a crooked smile. "But who could remember? Back then, it was musical boyfriends."

"For you?" Mack's gaze, dark and intent, studied her carefully.

"Not really. I went out with Josh for a couple months. Then about six to eight months later, I started going out with Chad." She shrugged. "That was it for me."

"And what about Cia?"

Meg tilted her head. "Again, it's hard to remember. She'd gone out with Chad before me, but months earlier. Then she went out with Josh at the same time I was going out with Chad. I think she'd been out with Bruce a few times as well. As for the others Cia may have dated, I don't know."

"And Stephanie?"

Meg winced. "That I am not sure of. She was going out with Bruce and had gone out with Josh for a short while. Who else? Honestly, I don't know."

"Did she ever talk about her boyfriends?"

Meg thought it was an odd question to ask now, but given that Stephanie wasn't here to answer questions herself, maybe not. "All the time. It was typical girl talk."

"Did she mention anyone else?"

"What do you mean, anyone else? Any other boyfriends? Wannabe boyfriends? I don't understand."

"Cia's remains were found, and, right away, Stephanie goes missing. Is it too far a stretch to believe that maybe the same male did something to both of them?"

"I wouldn't like to think so." Meg felt her heart sink. "That would be horrible."

"But you are not a fool. So who else did Stephanie mention?"

With a sigh, Meg slouched back into her chair and cast her mind backward. "Stephanie loved keeping track of other people's relationships."

"But you didn't?"

"No." She smiled lightly. "I had my own, and I was really happy with it."

"If you were so happy, why did you break up with him?"

There was no mockery in his voice, but his tone was too even. Too … something. … She couldn't figure out what it was. "I guess you had to be there to understand."

His gaze narrowed, darkened. "Try me."

She stared back calmly. "No."

His eyebrows shot up. "Really?"

"It has nothing to do with the case." She added carefully, her tone even and controlled, "Our break-up happened after the crime and in no way impacted what happened beforehand."

"For all I know, you two were in on Cia's murder together. After your unholy pact, you couldn't love each other, knowing what you'd done together and split. You've hardly spoken since." He smiled. "Have you?"

"No, we haven't." She'd be damned if she'd give him more than was required.

Just then the door opened, and Chad walked in. Meg stared at him. She didn't smile. This scenario was awkward enough without any sign of friendship—or the signs of anything more—showing through.

With a hard look, Mack nodded to him. "Did you have something to add?"

"Meg, you said that Stephanie and you had been gossiping while out in the water. Was anything in that conversation indicative of who Cia might have moved on to next? Or who she *wouldn't* move on to?"

Meg frowned, trying to remember. "I remember some of it. Although I'm sure I brought this up back then. Stephanie had been talking about who Cia had slept with and who she hadn't. Stephanie never did tell me the names though. She did say Cia had slept with four of the guys who were on the camping trip and was planning on sleeping with a fifth that weekend."

Mack leaned forward. "That weekend?"

Chad shook his head. "Couldn't be, she was sleeping with Josh on that trip. She was sleeping in his tent."

"I know. That's what I'd been trying to figure out when

you called out to us." She shrugged. "I never did get the name from Stephanie. I also don't know if Stephanie was telling the truth. She loved to stretch the truth and loved to gossip." She stopped and forced herself to correct her words. "We all did, but Stephanie thrived on it."

Mack stepped in. "You're sure you have no idea who Cia had planned to sleep with?"

Meg shook her head. "No, none at all." She shrugged. "Considering who was there, there weren't that many choices."

"Already sleeping with Josh, had been sleeping with Chad here …" Shuffling papers, Mack asked, "Don't know about Bruce, so that leaves Pero, Anto, and Tim. Was there time for Cia to disappear to meet up with this mystery date?"

Chad stared at Meg. She stared back. Chad shook his head, saying, "I don't know. I wouldn't have thought so."

"I don't know for sure." Meg lifted her shoulders. "And we never saw Cia after she went into the tent."

"*If* she went to the tent …"

"Right." She switched her gaze back from Mack to Chad. "And if she didn't, she could have walked off. We'd always considered that she might have run after you guys to join the hike. I hadn't considered she might have been having a tryst." Even that old-fashioned word seemed wrong. She tried to look at it from a different perspective and then shook her head. "No, I can't see it happening."

"And of course she didn't," Mack said, "because someone killed her. Most likely, she was meeting a man or someone pissed at her, who'd found out about the meeting."

"Josh?" Chad snorted. "It wouldn't have been him. He didn't care. He was breaking up with her anyway. Even Stephanie and I knew that. You could see it was over."

"*Over* is one thing." Mack tossed down his pencil and sprawled back, stretching his legs out in front of him. "Having someone stepping out behind your back with a buddy is another thing."

"True, but it does happen. I can't see Josh being so angry that he'd kill her over it. And if he had, where is the other male in the picture? Had he come upon them afterward? And then killed her? Because, if he'd come up on them earlier, he would have seen them and said something."

"Not if both were involved."

Both Chad and Meg frowned at Mack.

"What?" Meg asked cautiously.

"What if Josh came upon the two of them, got angry, and Cia was killed in the fight."

"And then both of the men made a pact of silence?" Chad asked, studying Mack. "It could shake out that way. We've certainly seen similar cases, but not with Josh."

Mack turned on him. "Oh, and why not? Because he's a good guy? Because he's your friend? Because of what?"

"Because he's too honest." Meg couldn't stay quiet. She knew how awkward this was for Chad, as well as for her. Yet she doubted that Josh was guilty. "Besides, the second man is hardly going to cover for the murderer, certainly not in the long-term. He'd done nothing wrong, so why should he?"

"Bullshit. Cia's death might have been accidental, a crime of passion so to speak, happening while hot tempers raged. But what about afterward? Panic would have ensued. Then cold reason would have taken over. If Cia's current boyfriend and her new love interest were both there, they would have both assumed they'd be held responsible. Or one could convince the other they wouldn't go down for this alone."

Chad frowned, and Meg could almost see him considering the issue. "We wondered if there were two of them," Chad admitted, "but I hadn't considered Stephanie and someone else."

"Stephanie? Why her? How? I don't understand." And Meg didn't. How had they gone from Josh to Stephanie? Nothing made sense. She hadn't once seriously considered that Cia had gone to meet someone. It had been one of the many suggestions tossed around at the time, but it had so lacked in reasoning that it had been dropped.

Over the years, the idea had popped up from time to time but was then dropped again. Watching the men pull out the idea and turn it over and over yet again made her nervous. It was one thing to consider one of her friends as a murderer but *two* of them? ... *That* was hard to believe.

"On the other hand," Mack suggested, "Stephanie might have known something or might have been helping someone. She was easily manipulated and easily coerced. And, if she had known something, she would have been too scared to tell."

"Or too scared of getting someone else into trouble," Meg noted, easily seeing that aspect. "I suppose that would also help explain her decline into drugs and all."

"How is that?" Mack stared at her.

"It's just that, if she were hiding something, she'd feel guilty and would need to handle that guilt somehow. The easiest way would be to try to forget, and how does one do that? Substance abuse is the most common way."

"By the same token, I'd expect some long-term reaction from Josh, if he'd been involved." Chad explained further, "Definitely anger is there, but moreover the damage to his life because of this event. There's no guilt. No sadness.

Nothing to indicate he's hiding anything."

"This, after seventeen years, is to be expected." Meg sighed. "Think about it. After all these years of keeping this information hidden, it would feel normal. It would feel natural. There might be an underlying tension that permeates everything, and that tension may snap at some point, but not unless something jars it."

"But having found Cia's remains—that is a pretty big jarring." Mack added, "Our killer has to be worried."

"Josh isn't showing any sign of that."

Mack snorted. "Why would he? He doesn't know we are close."

"Are you close? Do you have anything to pin this on Josh?" Meg shook her head. "If you couldn't pin it on him seventeen years ago, nothing was on the body that could do that now either."

"Not true. Now we know the cause of death and the location of the body in relation to the rest of you at the time."

"And what about the necklace?"

"A necklace I suspect Cia *borrowed*," Meg said, "but who could say after all this time."

"When did you notice it missing?" Mack asked.

"I *never* noticed. At least I don't remember ever noticing it had gone missing. It wasn't an important piece for me. And, after that weekend, we all packed in a rush, and our emotions were everywhere. If I'd noticed it missing then, I would have just assumed it had been lost in the chaos of the investigation."

"That's no help."

She stood. "No. I wasn't much help then, and I can't add anything now."

"Except for the gossip on Cia's lovers."

"True, if the gossip was the truth." Meg nodded. "Now, if we could find Stephanie, maybe we could ask her."

"What about the other males? Do you know much about them?"

"I was less with them than anyone else. Chad"—she looked over at him—"you would know more about the guys than I would." She walked to the door. "I knew Bruce and Josh, but I had only met Pero and Anto a couple times before that weekend, outside of passing them in the school hallways. As for Tim, I can't even remember his face." She shrugged. "I know some were related, but I can't remember now who was related to whom."

"Bruce was a cousin to the brothers. Their family had come over from Croatia, when they were little. I think Bruce's mother was their aunt," Chad said and nodded sideways to Mack.

"And Bruce's family had a cabin on the other side of the lake, right?" Meg asked, not quite understanding Chad's head motion. "Where we camped that first time?"

Chad nodded.

"I want to go back." The words ripped out of her throat so fast that she didn't realize what she had said.

Chad snapped, "No."

"I need to." She stared at him calmly. As she thought about it, she realized she *really* did want to go back. She wanted a chance to explore and to look for anything that might give them some answers. She knew it was too late, but she couldn't get it out of her mind that maybe, ... just maybe, she'd find something else. "If we now know where she was found, and I know where I was and where Stephanie was, we can walk the route and time the distance from one spot to the next. It will help sort out who could have been where. And maybe catch someone in a lie."

"No. We were all in the woods together—and lost most of the time. We can't pinpoint their location like that."

Mack looked over at him. "Except you gave us a pretty clear map of where you heard the other person. If we take your statement as fact, that rules the three of you out, therefore we need to plot out where everyone else was at the time."

"And we could do it on a map, but it would be easier if we went there and measured it out," Meg repeated.

"We did that last time, and it didn't help," Chad added slowly, as if thinking this through, "but there are better tools available to us now."

Meg checked her cell phone. "I've got to go. If you drive out there, let me know. I want to come. I can help." She nodded to Mack and Chad. "The sooner we figure this out, the sooner we can find out who did this. At the moment, I'm seriously thinking it must have been Anto."

"Why?"

She groaned. "Because he gave me the creeps back then." She stared at Chad. "And I'm going back up there."

"You're not going alone." Chad's voice brooked no argument.

She smiled gently. "Good. I don't really want to go alone. Janelle has a sleepover at her friend's house tonight. So my window to travel is now." And she walked out. She had almost made it to the front door, when Chad came running up behind her.

"Wait up."

She stepped through the door to the top step, before turning. "What's up?"

"I'll go home to grab some equipment, copies of everyone's statements, and a map. Then I'll swing by and pick you up." He headed back inside, without giving her a chance to respond.

Meg made it home in record time. She packed a light bag, made a quick call to Deirdre, Linette's mother, and explained that Meg wouldn't be at home but available by cell phone. "We'll try to get back tonight, but just in case …"

Making sure she had everything she thought she would need, she packed extra gloves and a large flashlight. She wanted to hike to the top of the mudslide, as she had been able to last time. Remembering the heavy rain, she grabbed a warm jacket and put on hiking boots. She realized Pete might have gone to his cabin. It was his place to hole up. She didn't want to intrude or to get involved in an argument. It was bad timing, or, as the old saying went, worse timing.

A sound outside had her grabbing her keys and cell phone, lifting her bag and letting herself out of the house.

Chad waited for her in the same truck she'd seen at the excavation site. Good. At least it would make the trip. He hadn't mentioned staying anywhere overnight. Hopefully it wouldn't be required, but she'd packed just in case.

And didn't that thought make her heart race. Knowing how Chad felt about her made her both uneasy and, yeah, … excited about the coming night. She'd spent a lot of nights with him, but sleep was the one thing they'd never managed to do. But then young love and the heated nights had been all about exploring their passion and expressing their love. It was something she'd never experienced since.

"Ready?" he asked.

She looked at him, wondering if a hidden meaning was in that question, then realized it didn't matter, even if there was. The answer would still be the same.

Clipping the seat belt firmly in place, she settled back and said, with a smile, "Yes, I'm ready."

CHAD TOOK THE highway on-ramp and pulled smoothly into traffic. They had a long drive ahead of them, but he enjoyed driving. He hadn't mentioned staying overnight anywhere because Meg had enough to deal with.

"I've been thinking about Stephanie," she said.

"What about her?" He took his eyes off the road long enough to search her features. There'd been a note of … he didn't know what, something hesitant, maybe even fearful. "Are you worried about her?"

"Of course. Even if she's gone back to her old ways, it would still be bad news. Anyone who makes it out of that dark hole has made a huge change in their lives. Sliding back into it again, though …"

"It's hard to know in her case. It isn't the first time, but she's been clean and sober for a long time now."

"She sounded so normal when I last spoke to her. That conversation made me more aware of who she is today and how disappearing doesn't seem normal for her."

"Oh, it's normal. It's just that you didn't see much of Stephanie before reconnecting. So your view is slightly twisted."

"Meaning, if I'd known her these past years, I wouldn't be surprised by her actions?" She settled back into her seat. "I wonder if that's true."

She went as if to speak once more. He waited. When she remained silent, he asked, "What?"

"I guess I just wondered if you were still looking for

her?"

He frowned. "Constantly—I was out last night, driving around her favorite haunts. I've been asking her old employers and friends, but there's no sign of her."

"But that just reinforces what I mean. If she'd gone back to the bottle or drugs, she'd be visible. She might have gone away inside, but physically she'd be somewhere. Right now, it's as if she's just disappeared from the face of the earth. That takes more skill than she has."

"Skill?" he asked. "Are you suggesting someone might have helped her to disappear?" It did fit that she might have wanted to run away. "Honestly I hadn't considered that."

"Either willingly or unwillingly, I just don't think she knows how to drop so completely off the grid on her own. And whoever is helping her could be friend or foe. No way to know yet."

"It won't likely be family. She cut ties with them years ago, and then they reciprocated when she ended up on the streets."

"But that could have changed in the years after she cleaned up her act."

"True." He pondered the issue. "She has no credit cards and hated bank cards because she used to steal them from other people. She used cash only."

"But did she have money to plan ahead? I understood she was pretty much living from paycheck to paycheck. One paycheck alone won't get her too far."

"And she got paid every Friday. Five days at minimum wage buys a bus ticket across the country and not much more."

"Exactly."

He glanced at her again. "Who would help her?"

Meg shrugged. "I have no idea. I don't know who her friends are."

"She was supposed to be meeting a friend in secret, according to her neighbor."

"And did she have a bag of belongings with her?"

"No." And that's why he hadn't considered that she may have left for a few days. But then, why tell the neighbor about the secret meeting? Was it to throw someone off the scent, and, if that were the case, why the cry for help? Maybe it was because she'd changed her mind about it.

"Then ..." Meg dropped her head on the back of the seat. "Hell, I don't know. Unless this guy, not that we know it's a guy, but this person, whoever, would be the last person to have seen her."

"Precisely."

"Damn. That could be anyone who doesn't want the police to call on them. It doesn't mean they were looking to hurt her. They could be helping or they could be—"

"Her drug dealer." He sighed. "Sorry. I didn't mean that to come out as harsh as it did." He opened the window slightly to bring in fresh air. "I'm just frustrated. I've done as much as I can, and still it's not enough."

Her tone weary, Meg said, "Is it ever?"

"Sometimes."

Silence filled the cab of the truck. Chad knew the odds of finding Stephanie were good. Given her history, she just might not be in decent shape when they found her. Finally he said, "I have to believe this time it will be enough."

He glanced over to see her reaction and realized her head had fallen against the passenger door. He glanced at the road, then back over at Meg, but her chest rose and fell in a steady, relaxed manner. She'd fallen asleep.

MEG CAME AWAKE slowly. The steady movement of the truck rolling down the highway had lulled her into a comfortable, relaxed state. The truck engine soothed her soul. She'd needed her nap. It seemed like her nerves were just waiting for the rest of her body to follow through.

She yawned and rolled her head toward Chad.

"How are you feeling now?"

She smiled. "Better. I've been running on empty for a long time."

"Not healthy." He smiled to cut the criticism in his words.

"I know, but sometimes it's unavoidable." She straightened to look around. "Where are we?"

"We're coming into Wistery. I thought we could stop for a break and pick up some coffee and maybe a bite to eat."

"Food sounds good. Coffee sounds even better." The long stretch of countryside had gradually morphed to the odd house here and there. She saw the sign for Wistery next. "Good. It's just a few minutes down the road."

"The roadhouse is right here." Chad slowed the truck and went around a series of hairpin turns and, as he pulled out on the other side, she saw the sign.

"Stan's Roadhouse?"

"We stopped here that camping weekend and picked up treats."

"Really?" She glanced at him in amazement. "Are you sure? I don't remember that at all."

"Not much I don't remember from back then." He pulled the truck to a stop in front of the café and turned off the engine. "Ready?"

Still stunned at what he had remembered over what

she'd forgotten, she nodded. "Let's go."

Inside, the air was cool, and the restaurant empty. "I guess they don't get much business."

"It's early yet. The lunch crowd won't be here for a bit."

She glanced at the clock on the wall. It was just after eleven a.m. "We made good time."

"Good. We have lots of work to do. We probably should have held off and left early tomorrow."

"Too late now." She smiled and walked up to the front counter.

"I'll grab this." Chad stepped up beside her. "My treat." He studied the menu for a moment, then ordered a couple large sandwiches to-go and an extra large coffee. Then he turned to her. "What do you want?"

"Not that much," she murmured. "I eat like a normal person, but the sandwiches sound good."

With a smirk, Chad doubled his order and then snagged a couple wrapped muffins and coffee cake slices at the counter. He walked over to the cooler and pulled out four bottles of water to add to the order.

"We didn't come well prepared, did we?" She eyed the stack at the counter. "Then I wouldn't have packed for four days anyway."

"This is just for today. We will be working. That means keeping up our strength." With a big grin, he unpacked a muffin and took a large bite. "I missed breakfast."

She shook her head and made a trip to the ladies' room. On her way back, she noticed a couple people walking inside. She didn't know them but knew the town enjoyed both the benefits and the detriments of summer residences. She wondered if the business struggled to stay afloat in the winter. Summer would be fine, but as for the rest of the year?

She wasn't so sure.

Glancing around, she saw Chad paying for the lunch. She watched while he finished, picked up their bags, and joined her at the door. "Ready?"

She laughed as she pushed the door open to step outside. "Seems like you've been asking me that a lot lately."

He grinned. "And I'll continue to ask."

At the truck, she took the bags from him and waited while he unlocked the doors. Hearing something, she turned around, gave the parking lot a wide sweeping glance. The place appeared empty. Shrugging, she placed the bags on the seat and went to climb in, when she saw something out of the corner of her eye. She turned and looked at the big window in the front.

Someone stood there, watching her.

Shit.

Pete.

"MEG? IS THERE a problem?"

Meg, startled, turned back to Chad. "No. No, there isn't."

He studied her. She made no move to get into the truck. In fact, she turned to stare back at the restaurant. Chad leaned over, so he could see what she was looking at. A few people were seated at the front tables, but they appeared to be in conversation among themselves and not concerned with Meg.

"Meg?"

"Oh, sorry." She gave a sheepish smile and clambered in. Slamming the door closed, she took one last look at the window and sighed.

"Did you see someone?"

"I thought so," she admitted, "but he wasn't there when I looked the second time."

"He?"

Her breath gusted free in a heavy *whoosh*. "I thought I saw Pete."

"Your boyfriend?"

"Ex-boyfriend," she corrected. "I have moved out."

"Does he know that?"

"I don't know," she admitted. "He hadn't returned home by the time I left, and I have yet to hear from him."

"Would he have come out here?"

"Definitely. He loves his cabin, comes every opportunity he can."

"Then it could be him." Chad thought about that, as he drove the truck back onto the highway. "Will that be a problem?"

She glanced his way, her face troubled. "I hope not."

He raised his eyebrows at that. "Good thing you didn't come alone then."

"I don't think he'd be a problem. Pete has never been violent."

"Good." Chad picked up speed, so they were going at just over the limit and thought about what she'd said.

And what she hadn't said.

WITH ANY LUCK, Stephanie would take a bad trip into hell and stay there. It might take a while. He should have stayed and finished the job.

But, this way, it was all on Stephanie's head. She'd be yet another overdose and yet another dead junkie—no big deal.

Stephanie's friends would sigh and would whisper about how hard it had been to kick the habit, and, after a respectful few moments, they'd take a trip themselves.

After all, it was hard to go straight in life.

And he needed to move on. Get more loose threads tied up.

Getting caught after all these years was so not on the agenda.

Chapter 15

MEG TOOK A large bite of the half sandwich in her hand. She'd avoided talking about Pete, but that didn't in any way stop her mind from twisting about him. Would he understand she'd come here for work? Even if she wasn't getting paid, she was helping to solve Cia's case. But then he didn't know about Cia because she hadn't told him about her.

He did know about the grave though.

She stared down at the sandwich. Ham and cheese heaped with vegetables. And it tasted like cardboard. She dropped her hands and leaned her head back, wishing she hadn't seen him. Now she couldn't stop thinking about him and what had been and all that it could have been.

The warmth oozing from Chad made her feel bad, yet good. In fact, right now her emotions were all over the place.

"How's the sandwich?"

"It's good. I'm just tired."

"Eat up. It will ease back the fatigue." Chad drove with one hand. The other held the sandwich he had partly scarfed in a few bites. He'd already eaten a full sandwich. Meg looked down at her uneaten half of one and realized he was right.

She took another bite and chewed slowly.

"Are you scared of him?"

She shook her head, swallowed, and answered, "No. I just haven't cleared things up with him. It feels awkward. We're not together, and we're not apart. It's over, but I haven't told him."

"You haven't spoken to him at all?"

The disapproval in Chad's voice made her realize the situation from a man's perspective. "No. I left before he returned. I really felt it was over when he walked out, that he knew it and that I knew it and that he was giving me time to get out."

"But?"

"But, because we haven't had that final conversation, it feels incomplete."

"Do you know when he's due home?"

"No. Normally he'd text me, call me, … something, but this time there's been nothing. Which I guess is reasonable if we have just broken up." She stared moodily out the window, as she finished her sandwich. "Then I never contacted him either."

"Maybe you should."

"I was just thinking that, but I doubt he'll answer." She brushed her hands off, scrunched up the sandwich wrapper, and stuffed it back into the to-go bag. She grabbed her phone and texted Pete. **Where are you?**

She waited. Nothing.

"No answer. He comes out here to get away. Hates his cell phone at the best of times." She couldn't believe the relief she felt. It had been a shock to think she'd spied Pete at the restaurant. And the fear of a confrontation had kept her on edge, worrying.

She was back at Pete's favorite place with Chad but without Pete. How would he react? It was not as if she'd planned this, but Pete wouldn't know that. She didn't want him thinking she'd broken off with him to start up with a new guy—or worse, having been engaged in an affair while still with him.

She was still mulling things over, when Chad slowed the truck. She sat up and surveyed her surroundings. "This isn't the same place."

"No. I wanted to go into the park from the side of the lake and take a look around first."

She barely remembered where they'd first camped, except it had been pretty. Another ten minutes of driving through the trees, then the tree line opened up to show the lake sparkling in front of them. In spite of her worries, a happy sigh escaped. "Regardless of the circumstances, it's a pretty spot for Cia to have lain all these many years."

He glanced over at her in surprise. "That's a nice way to look at it."

Chad parked the truck, and they both hopped out. The campground road went farther around the lake. From where she stood, Meg could see dozens of camping spots had already been taken. A large grassy area was up ahead with picnic tables and the occasional barbecue stand.

She shook her head and laughed. "I barely recognize the campground. It looks so different."

"They've done a lot of work over the years. The trees have grown. Another dozen or two cabins have been built over there." He pointed to the left. "Most of those cabins weren't there back then." He turned around and nudged her to pivot too. "Most of the ones behind us are new too."

"Wow. This place sure is popular. I was afraid the roadhouse couldn't make a living all the way out here, but loads of people are here." Rows upon rows of summer homes and houses stood tall in front of her.

"Let's go to the water's edge." He took her arm. "I want to show you something."

They walked down the path side by side; Meg couldn't believe how developed the area had become on this side. She would never have recognized it. And, from Pete's side of the lake, this couldn't be seen from either the deck or the cabin. She had no idea any of this existed. Janelle would love it here.

"I also brought maps of the area—from seventeen years ago and now."

"That's smart." She walked to where the water lapped the rocks. "What did you want to show me?"

He pointed to the left. "The road continues on around that end of the lake and goes up the hill on the far side. If you follow the line all the way over there …" He moved his arm in the direction they were talking about. Now she was looking straight across the lake.

"There's the campsite we stayed at last time. And you found the remains over to the right, … by that darker clump of trees."

She shook her head at the short distance. "It was so close to the camping spot?" It had seemed much farther at the crime scene.

"Close enough for it to have been one of us, but, if you see the cabins along the road there"—he pointed—"it's also well within the distance of anyone who'd been at the cabins at the time."

"But how many of those cabins were there back then?"

"About three-quarters of them, and the ones that were there were empty that weekend … supposedly." He stared at her. "As far as we could tell at the time, we were alone over there."

"But that spot is within easy reach by anyone on this side too. In fact, we were clearly visible to anyone on this side of the lake."

"Correct."

"It's not even, what? … One-quarter mile across? A good swimmer could swim it, but a power boat could cross in no time at all."

"We would have heard power boats. And we did. We heard several of them. Remember, some people were out waterskiing that day? Besides, anyone could have driven around the lake, parked, and traveled the last bit on foot."

"True. And … we saw canoes and kayaks, as well. There were a lot of people at the lake then. It was the end of summer."

"Exactly, so what are the chances that all those cabins on the far side and at the end were not occupied?"

"If many on this side were, then odds are that many over there should have been too."

"Well, at least some of them. Instead, according to the police report, *all* the cabins were unoccupied."

She stared at him, back at the long stretch of cabins, and then said slowly, "That doesn't seem right."

"It doesn't, does it? Only I haven't found anyone who'd seen residents at the cabins."

She tried to think back. "I can't remember myself. Were there lights on?"

"I have pictures from back then. I should dig them back out and see what shots we took at the time. Maybe there were night shots."

"There were!" She turned to him. "Remember? We were taking pictures of the campfire and our tents?"

He nodded. "I'll have a look when I get home." He glanced sideways at her. "What about you? Do you have pictures?"

"Maybe—I gave the film to the detectives at the time." She stared at him. "I have no idea what happened to it."

He narrowed his eyes. "They developed mine to get a look at the pictures."

"And did you get all the pictures back?" She studied the cabins, now brimming with life on the left. "Too bad it was before the digital age. We'd have so much more information available to us today."

Hearing the sounds of trucks pulling into the lot, she glanced back and asked, "What now?"

"I have some help. We'll measure everything we can and time it. Then map things and compare them to the statements we have from everyone who was there, as well as from those at the cabins."

"That's what we came for, but I'm grateful to see a crew to help."

"No way we'd get it all done in time." He started back up the path. "Let's get started."

With one last glance toward the cheerful, sunny shores, she followed behind him to find the crew unloading the equipment. Some people she recognized, and some she didn't.

As the teams were setting up, she stared out across the water, wondering how Cia's remains could have stayed undetected for so long. The site was steep and rough, dark and thickly populated with trees. The cabins weren't close, but they were accessible.

Just not *easily* accessible, but *someone* had known about the remains. And she was determined to find out who it had been.

CHAD SPLIT THE techs into teams. He left one group at the campsite to start surveying and took the other over toward the old campsite with Meg.

He parked roughly in the same spot as he had years ago. Then he explained the plan to the team.

He handed the maps and pins over to Meg. He followed behind her—with the laptop and the rest of the supplies—to the nearest picnic table. Meg already had the map spread out and pinned in place and was leaning over it, studying it carefully.

He gingerly unloaded his armful and leaned over beside her. "Find anything interesting?"

She murmured, without raising her head, "The whole thing is interesting, considering we have inside knowledge. How long does it take the killer to meet Cia, kill her, and stash her so she'd never be found?"

"Or perhaps stash her temporarily, then come back and move her."

She screwed up her face at the thought. "Kill her, hide her body, then come back later and move it? That wouldn't be fun."

She stabbed a finger on the map at the point where the closest cabins were located. "Unless, desperate to hide the body, he may have taken a chance on an empty cabin."

Chad took a deep breath. "That's all too possible."

MEG STUDIED THE closest cabins. "Weren't they all checked out thoroughly back then?"

"They checked out what they could. According to the records, a thorough search of all the premises was made."

"And they didn't find her. Either because she wasn't there, or she was so well hidden, or someone was protecting our killer, or the cabin owner was the killer." She straightened up to walk around the picnic table. "So we have to go back to the owners."

Chad murmured, "I wasn't sure whether you remembered or not."

"Remembered what?" She continued to study the map.

"That Mack is Bruce's, Pero's, and Anto's uncle. And he owns a cabin here."

Shock hit her first, then disbelief, then a slow burning anger. She raised her head slowly to study Chad's closed face. "Really? Now I know why he was such a hard-ass to us back then. He was trying to prove his family innocent by making us guilty." She stared out at the water, hating the bitter memories and the fear that his name could still bring up in her. "That bastard."

She shook her head. "And although he seemed nicer this time, I can't say I trust him." She frowned. "I don't know that I trust many people anymore."

"Except for me, you mean." He grinned, as she gave him her narrow-eyed look. "Just keeping it out there …"

"Are you ready to go back to the site?" Needing to get away from the subject of Mack, she raised her eyebrows, looked at her boots, and added, "If so, let's go."

With that, he left one of the crew at the campground and led the way to the crime scene. It took them a good twenty minutes to reach it. Meg noticed Chad seemed to be timing their walk and making notes as they went along. It made sense.

She just couldn't imagine any of the kids they'd camped with having the brains to make and carry out an elaborate murder scheme. More likely Cia's death had been an accident. And it was just dumb luck that her body had stayed hidden for so long.

They continued to walk on in silence. Then Chad stopped abruptly. She stepped up beside him. "What do you see?"

"Nothing. No signs are left that we were here at all."

She studied the layout and frowned. "Any of the locals could have ripped down the tape, and tourists could have taken it as a souvenir. You know it happens all the time."

"*Hmm.*"

She approached the area surrounded by fallen trees and stopped to take a closer look. She knew the techs had searched for hours, and she trusted that they'd done their jobs, but that didn't make it easier to believe nothing more was to be found. They needed evidence that would point them in the right direction.

"Are you okay?"

"Yeah, I just wished we had found more."

"Always. But we could tear up this whole side of the lake and still find nothing." With a grim look he pointed. "I want to go up there. I want to see for myself."

CHAD STUDIED THE hillside, as he climbed up the steep bank. A huge fallen tree hung on a small ledge, almost at the top of the precipitous hill. It would have been a challenge to have carried a body up here. Chad didn't remember the ridge from before. But, if Cia had planned to meet her killer here, that would have made it easier. However, it would have been difficult to imagine anyone carrying her up here. And Cia hated hiking. So she must have had a hell of a reason to make this trek. With a final scramble, he reached the crest and climbed to the solid top. He offered a hand to help Meg up the last bit. She'd barely broken a sweat. He loved that she had stayed fit all these years. "There's the campsite." Chad pointed it out for her.

She crouched to peer through the branches of the surrounding trees. "Years ago it would have been much easier to see."

"Yet we wouldn't have seen anyone up here from down there." He pulled out his phone and texted John, the tech who was working the campsite. From where they stood, he saw John read the text, then study the hillside, where they stood. His phone buzzed. "John wants us to move around to confirm if he can see us."

They shifted around and watched. John's features weren't clear, but they could identify him. Yet he couldn't see them.

"That answers that question. We're completely hidden."

"And we would likely have been hidden on this hilltop back then as well." Meg stepped to the other side and pointed to the cabins below and to something else as well. "Look. Is that a pathway?"

"Shit." He moved behind her and searched for where it started. "It also connects to a well-worn path down below. Come on." He led the way to where two paths joined up.

"How come we didn't see it before?" she asked, behind him.

"It's the angle. It's completely covered with leaves and branches. If you didn't know it was here, no way you'd accidentally stumble across it. Plus we were looking up. It's hard to see, unless someone is walking on it."

They slid down the last bit and landed on the path they'd seen. They stopped to look back the way they'd come. Scrambling down the hillside left a dark gouge in the earth, but leaves were already drifting down to hide their tracks.

"Let's go." Chad led the way up the new path that veered uphill to the right of where they were.

"This place is full of trails."

"I suppose that's no surprise, given the years, the population, and the summer influx of tourists."

"But this isn't the most hospitable location for hiking." She caught her breath, as she crested the rise to stand beside him. "Or maybe it is. This is gorgeous."

The whole lake had opened up in front of them. Between the trees, the blue water twinkled and shone happily. They could see clear across it.

"Obviously more than a few local people would know about this spot," Meg said.

He smiled at her grimly. "It's time to canvass the locals again."

"Go for it. I'm staying here for a bit," she retorted, staring at the beautiful vista. With the sun barely reaching through the trees, the air was heavily scented with pine. A gust of wind blew toward them, lifting the leaves and dropping even more.

"I'm not leaving you alone up here."

MEG TURNED TO look at him in surprise. "Why?"

"For several reasons, but the one I'll go with is that a murderer is still walking around free, who is probably aware of what we are doing here right now."

She wrinkled up her face. "Nice thought. *Not.*"

He smiled. "Is there anything else you want to look at while we're up here?"

"Lots." And there was. "I think this whole place needs to be explored. A dozen bodies could be here. How do we know Cia was the only victim?" She turned to look at him and raised an eyebrow. "Or had you already considered that?"

"Considered and dismissed." He shrugged. "At least until any evidence comes up that points us in that direction."

"Including Cia—until now." She studied his face. "They had some bad storms a while back, didn't they?"

He snorted. "Are you kidding? The weather patterns today versus the weather patterns of seventeen years ago? No comparison. I don't know whether it's because of global warming or what, but this area has been hit with a lot of storms. As you said, a few bad ones came through a couple months ago."

Meg now ignored him. Cia's remains must have slid down from where they'd first climbed. That small ledge up ahead wasn't a large space, but it was big enough. And that fallen tree could hide many things. She pointed to the one area in question. "I want to go back over there."

He never questioned her reasoning, just returned where they had started. It was a rougher climb getting back up. For every step she took, she slid back, as her feet tried to dig into the hillside to grab hold. The slippery leaves made her boots slide more than climb. Finally they made it the top, and, with her chest heaving, Meg gasped for air. "That wasn't much fun."

"No. The ground is still wet from the rain."

She walked a few steps back from the edge, afraid it might all go. "It would take someone in good shape to climb up here."

"Maybe and maybe not." Chad pulled a folded map from his pocket. He studied it for a moment, then pointed to a spot. "Look. This road goes farther up. It should pass somewhere nearby." He turned to look up the slope, then pointed. "Somewhere up there. And it's much easier to come down a slope like this, than go up one."

Why hadn't she considered that? It was much easier to see their position on a map than from within the heavy tree growth. "So they could dump the body easily enough." She kicked the heavy leaves at her feet. "And, in this ground, it would be easy to bury the body."

"If they cared to …"

"True enough." Some killers never buried their victims, either wanting nothing to do with them once dumped or enjoying the sight of their handiwork again and again. Turning a professional eye on the scene, she studied the ledge and the hill above it. "You can see where some of the dirt and soil have eroded. That tree falling would have caused a mess of damage too."

"This area was searched when we found Cia's remains. No one found anything."

The ledge was close to fifteen feet across and almost completely buried under this massive tree that must have come down in a storm. The tree had fallen with the trunk downhill, hanging off the ledge. Large roots had dug into the soft dirt, keeping the tree in a weird hanging balance. The heavy branches lay uphill and across this ridge, but, in the process, they appeared to have knocked away a large portion of the original ledge. Hence, the mudslide that sent Cia's remains down the hill.

Meg looked at the tree, seeing more dirt and leaves already layered on top of it. "Look." She pointed down to where one of Chad's team stood at the site of Cia's remains. The tech was planting a large pole in the ground to use for measuring distances. "After a couple years in that lower position, this mudslide has become almost natural looking. It's completely covered in leaves and deadfall now. That tree didn't come down this year. It must have been down for at least a year—if not two to three years ago. I'm sure an expert can confirm."

"And the locals might add something."

She walked to the far side and looked over the edge.

Chad grabbed her arm. "Careful."

Standing beside her, he pointed to John, now walking around the campground, cell phone in his hand, talking into it. "The campsite is still easy to pinpoint."

Meg turned her back and tried to peer on the other side of the tree. It was huge. With a backward glance at Chad— still facing the lake and talking to his team—she slowly climbed on top of the tree trunk. Once up, she balanced and walked several steps forward to where the branches were thickest at the top of the downed tree. She crouched down and peered between the bark and tree limbs crisscrossing everywhere. She couldn't tell for the darkness and the dirt if anything valuable were in there to find or not.

"See something?"

"Can't tell. It's hard to see," she called back.

"Here's a flashlight if that helps." He hopped up onto the log behind her.

And Meg felt it move. "Shit."

"Whoa. I'm off." He jumped down. "Careful, that's not very stable." He moved around slightly to come up on the side. "See if you can reach it." He held out the flashlight for her. She shook her head. "Just toss it."

He gently lofted it into the air, and she snatched it safely. "Got it."

"Good, take a quick look, then get off in a hurry. We don't want the whole thing going down."

She turned on the flashlight and faced it into the shadows. Had the techs searched this closely? There—more sticks, more leaves, more dirt. She cast the long halo of light over and around the space, making sure she got a good look.

Then she stopped. Her heart raced. She could just make out something jammed under the branches. She caught her breath. Something white. Something round. Something dead.

Shit.

Another skull.

Chapter 16

MEG LISTENED TO the discussion with half an ear. She knew what she'd found; she just couldn't reconcile it with being related to Cia's murder. Had she been killed by a stranger after all? And by a serial killer, no less? Had he been here, dumping a previous victim, seen Cia on the beach, and snatched her?

Meg's mind spun, even as plans were being put into motion around her. It had been hours since they'd first discovered the second body. Hours of phone calls and plans being made, maps pulled out and looked at, and people talking. And yet more talking.

She knew the next steps were incredibly important. They needed to excavate that entire ledge, down to where she'd found Cia's remains. No way to know what else might have gone down in the mudslide. She'd only seen the one skull up there, so exactly how many would they find? The ledge was big enough for dozens.

What she did know was that this was a whole different issue now. More than one set of remains changed the nature of the killer. And the profiles of the victims all came into question. And who had had access to this location?

So often, bodies were dumped where no one ever found them. Hence, killers made deals with the police to give up their victims' locations.

She sighed heavily, hating the ache in her heart that seemed to permeate her whole body. She'd be sore tomorrow. And that sandwich she hadn't cared about eating on the drive in was long gone. She would need to find more food soon and some coffee too.

They were waiting for chainsaws and the men to operate them. The tree needed to be removed carefully, so as not to disturb the remains caught in its branches. The tree was big and old and would be taken out section by section.

A cup of hot liquid was shoved into her hands. She stared at it in surprise, then with dawning delight. Coffee! "Thank you," she murmured, blowing steam upward to bathe her tired eyes.

"Are you cold?" Chad asked, sitting down at the picnic table beside her.

"No, I'm fine." She smiled reassuringly at him. "Just a little overwhelmed."

"With good reason."

"It changes everything and nothing. I can't help but wonder if that weekend created a serial killer out of one of our friends or if a serial killer found a conveniently close victim."

"Too early to tell. You'll make yourself crazy thinking about it right now." He took a sip from the hot cup in his hand. "The men should be here soon. I'll take them up to the scene and have them start sectioning off the tree from the bottom."

"I'm coming." She stood.

"Why not stay here and rest?"

She shook her head. "No, I need to be there. It'll take hours, so let's get started." Determined to do her part, she walked in line behind the techs leading the three men with three saws. "Or maybe it won't take that long."

BUT IT DID.

Not only was there little room for anyone to stand on that ledge, but no one could work at the area Meg had marked off to search for bone remnants and other evidence, not until the tree was dismantled and carried out of the way.

She and Chad stood at the second ledge and watched the work in progress. Chad had already photographed the area several times and appeared to be intent on cataloging every step of the process.

She couldn't blame him. These pictures would be valuable.

"Could this place be visible from the aerial photographs?"

"No, I've gone over the old aerial photographs many times. Once Google Earth is updated, I will get those updates and compare them to the older versions. The tree growth is just too thick in here for the satellite to be of much help."

One of the men had finished cutting the lower half of the tree into long slices, and the other two men were cutting each into removable pieces. Then the other guy moved higher up and cut off another segment.

"Once he has that piece out of the way, we'd be better off removing branches or parts of branches." She motioned to where the larger branches on the ledge dominated. "He'll be an hour doing that easily."

"I doubt it." Chad smiled. "Maybe twenty minutes, tops."

And Chad was right.

Impatiently Meg waited until the last section had been cleared enough for her to stand in, then led the way back to the remains. She studied the branch pattern, looking to open up the space, while not disturbing anything below. The man operating the chainsaw had had the same idea. He started removing the branches on top first, and, with Chad's help, lifted them clear, and laid them to one side.

They did that for the next four big branches, then the chainsaw guy separated branches from the trunk and began chewing into the wood, until all that was left was the top ten to fifteen feet of the tree and its branches propping up the main trunk. Systematically, with both Meg and Chad helping, they removed the last of the branches from the ledge.

When the final smaller branches were removed, Meg pulled out her camera and took some pictures. Not a lot to see at this point, just the leaves from the fallen tree and the dirt the branches had snagged to pull down on top of them. She stepped back and studied the area.

"Are you good to go?" Chad asked.

"I need my tools and gloves." And so much more, she thought, but didn't say it. He knew what she needed. They'd been here before. She turned to smile at him, but he'd taken off down the hill. She watched until he made it to the truck and grabbed her bag. He started back up.

Hearing a sound, she turned around with a smile. Her gaze landed on the main man who'd operated the chainsaw. She nodded to him. "Thanks for the help and for being so careful …"

He wore a hard hat and earmuffs, with a full shield protecting his face. Even so, she recognized something about him.

He grimaced, pulled off his hard hat and nodded to her. "You're welcome, Meg."

She gasped in astonishment.

"Pete!"

CHAD WAS ALMOST to the path where he'd stood with Meg earlier when he heard her cry out. He searched the cliff edge in panic, but she still stood where he'd left her. And she appeared fine—but maybe not so fine after all. She was stiff, and, although she was talking to the man in front of her, she wasn't smiling. Chad couldn't hear the conversation, but just something about her demeanor worried him.

And had she said *Pete*? Was he her boyfriend? That wouldn't be good. But his appearance wasn't totally unexpected. Chad wished he'd been there to see Pete's reaction. And to meet him. Who was this man who had held Meg's love for over a decade? It would be interesting to know him.

With his arms full, Chad hoofed his way back up the hill on the path. At the path junction, he scrambled up to the ledge and almost lost his load.

"Easy. Let me help." Meg reached out and half unloaded her gear. "I should have come and helped you."

"Not needed. I managed just fine." He straightened and caught his breath. Pete wasn't here. "Where did our chain-saw operator go?"

Meg winced. "Home. It was Pete. He got a call asking him to come and lend a hand here."

"Pete?" He studied her face. It was normal. Not stressed, upset or angry. "Are you two okay?"

She shrugged. "He didn't have much to say, just a hel-lo."

"And that's it?" He didn't know what to say. "Isn't that a little odd, considering you've moved out?"

"Yeah, well, I told him that I'd moved out for a few days to think too." She smiled grimly. "Maybe I should have said more, but it was really not the place."

"How did he respond?"

She smiled. "He nodded and said he understood. He also said that he was sorry about the mess I found here and that it was a sad business."

"Yeah, isn't that the truth."

He watched as Meg turned her attention to the scene in front of them, effectively killing off the conversation.

MEG DIDN'T WANT to discuss the totally awkward meeting with Pete. He looked good. Happy and at peace.

She couldn't ask for more. The one thing seeing him again had done for her was that it had helped her realize the truth—that it was over. She had had a few pangs of sadness, a twinge of grief, regrets for what had been, but, at the same time, she no longer felt that pull. What they'd had before had died a slow death this last year. Although they were both to blame, her maybe more than him, there was no sense of guilt.

An era had passed. As for her, she was just grateful this meeting had been in private. He'd seemed to understand. He'd been friendly, and she couldn't ask for more at this point.

Now she had something else to focus on, and she could park Pete where he belonged—in her past. She walked carefully to the area which had been marked off. She stood and studied the ground, looking for a place to start. Then she got down to work, clearing away the bits of branches and searching the layers underneath. A skull was up on the left, against the hillside, and a femur tip sat on the right. It had yet to be determined if they were from the same body. She suspected that, as she dug into this mess, likely to be more than one body here. A tap on her shoulder had her turning to face Chad. "What?"

He pointed to the left, several feet in front of the skull. Covered by leaves and small sticks, easy to miss because of the full eye sockets, was yet another skull.

Sadness crept through her tired frame. "Damn."

"It's what you expected though, isn't it?"

She nodded, her gaze moving slowly across the surface and back to the hillside. Her gaze zipped past and then back again. There was a jaw bone, still partially attached to another skull. "There's number three."

"I wonder how many we'll find before we're done."

"Too many. Let's get at it."

STEPHANIE SMILED AT the gruesome clown face in front of her. Weird. ... Then a lot of things in her life were weird. Tonight was the most bizarre. One minute she'd been rushing into a coffee shop, and the next thing her head hurt, and she was here. In Clownsville ...

She peered through the darkness, trying to sort out the strange images from the truth. If she hadn't known better, she might have thought she'd taken a bad acid trip. Unfortunately she'd experienced more of those than she cared to remember. Was this another one? It had to be; nothing else made sense.

Her head lolled to one side. She tried to straighten it.

Only she had no strength to keep it up. Breathing was about all she could do. And sleep. She was good at that part.

And forgetting.

She'd spent a lifetime trying to forget her life. For the most part, she'd done well, … maybe too well.

Her eyes fell shut. She tried to open them again but couldn't.

Her stomach heaved, and wild crazy colors zinged through her mind. Her surroundings spun and twisted. As for her stomach? God, her stomach …

She curled into a tight ball and buried her face in her hands.

Please, let this be over *soon.*

Chapter 17

MEG STRAIGHTENED SLOWLY, almost crying out as the twinge in her back struck again. Damn, it had been a long night. And it was still ongoing. She stopped to look around. Eerie shadows from the big lights filled the small space, as teams in white worked quietly away in the darkness.

It was a scene out of a horror movie—or her life. How many times had she been in a similar scenario before? There'd been almost too many times to count them.

This excavation had been going on for hours. So far, five skulls and multiple sets of bones had been collected. What bothered her was that these bones, all skeletonized, were old. As in no fresh body had been placed here for at least ten years. Had the space filled up, and the killer moved on? But, if so, where to?

Or had he stopped killing? If so, why? Anto came to mind. Death was a hell of an excuse.

So far, she'd found only young female skeletons. That didn't mean there weren't children or males in here though. Putting the bones together would be a fun puzzle. And that also meant that the jumble of bones that they had assembled earlier—from what they had thought of as Cia's remains— could, in fact, be from some of these skeletons. That might explain the missing bones. Of course animal activity would too.

"How are you holding up?" Chad joined her, a thermos in his hand.

"Is that coffee? And, if it is, how come you have some, and I don't?"

"I'm sharing it with you." He smiled at her, but his gaze was searching, as he studied her face.

"I'm fine," she said brusquely. "Or I will be when you catch this bastard."

He poured coffee into the thermos cup and held it out for her. "Working on it. Can you tell whether these victims died before or after Cia?"

She shook her head. "Given the level of decomposition, I can't tell here. I may never tell you what you want to know with any level of accuracy. Within a couple years, it is difficult. If we can ID some of the women, find out when they went missing, we'll get some time frame to work with. I doubt any of them have been here much longer than fifteen years, but I can't say for sure."

"Do you want to take a break and sit in the truck and warm up?"

Holding the thermos cup to her lips, she tried a sip of the hot brew. It slipped down her throat, easing some of the dryness that had set in the last few hours. "Thank you," she whispered, before taking another sip.

"You're welcome. Are you sure you don't need a break? Food and drink are coming for everyone. Should be here in minutes."

She brightened at the idea of food. "That would be good."

A shout beside her had her spinning around in time to watch yet another corner of the ledge collapse and slide down the slope. The team working below easily moved out in time, but the layer filled in the space, forcing them to clear it away to get below it. A light rain had started meanwhile; *so not* what they needed right now.

"We need to hurry. It's degrading fast."

"I know." He nudged her toward the path. "A truck has just come in. That will have the food. Let's catch a few minutes. We're two too many up here as it is right now."

In that, he was correct. With a wary eye on the unstable edge, she handed him the empty thermos cup before carefully making her way down to the ever-widening path below. A light flashed on in front of her. "Thanks."

"Hey, it's late, and we're tired. Let's not have anything else happen."

She passed several other team members going up. One held a huge cookie in his hand. She eyed it hungrily. "Hope you left me some of those."

The tech laughed. "Only if you get there fast."

At the truck, a circle of people stood, eating. Meg walked closer, when a large hand landed on her shoulder and directed her to the picnic table that held a couple open spots. "Sit. I'll grab food."

Too tired to argue, she sat down and gently massaged her neck. She stared out at the lake. The moonlight was playing tag with the gently rolling waves. It would have been beautiful, except for the surreal look to the campsite, full of vehicles and white-suited personnel.

They'd found a dump site. As depressing as that reality was, it was also hugely positive. Hopefully they could identify these victims and bring them home to their families. That would make it all worthwhile. Then hopefully they would find the killer through what he'd left behind. ... That thought made her want to rush back to the scene. They would have yards of dirt and humus to sift through, looking for small bones and evidence. Some they would never recover. It just wasn't possible. However, some of the evidence that they would find should surprise even the killer.

And that was the good part.

She already knew a lot about him. He despised women, tossed them away like garbage, after using them as he wanted to. He picked young Caucasian women, between the ages of sixteen and twenty-six, and she might even narrow that down in the lab. He was physically fit and likely middle-aged at this point, but she wouldn't count on it. It seemed that the killers were getting younger and younger, and this one had been killing for fifteen years already. It wasn't out of the range of possibility for their killer to be her age, give or take a few years.

Most likely he was too smart, and, for him, people as a whole were a big joke. Yet he was stupid. Look where and how he'd left the bodies. Right above a popular camping spot. He hadn't even bothered doing a decent job of burying them. So far, they'd found blankets and plastic at the site. From the dirt on top, he might even have collapsed part of the hill above on top of the bodies. He must have figured the bodies would never be found, or, if they were, who cared? It's not as if the cops would ever find *him*.

Well, she sent a silent message out to the killer. *You're wrong there. We will get you. And it'll be soon.*

CHAD, AFTER MAKING sure Meg was safely ensconced with food and drink, headed back to his truck. Mack hadn't shown up, and Chad was pretty damn sure this wasn't his poker night. That he wasn't here said a lot. And Chad didn't like it at all. Daniel was on his way though.

Chad dialed Mack again. The phone went straight to voice mail. "Mack, where are you?" And he hung up the phone. Sure, Mack could be anywhere, but anything to do with this case and missing people sent up alarms. No one was likely to suspect a cop, but that didn't mean a cop wasn't part of the bad team. Chad paused. Was he thinking Mack had had something to do with this, either personally or by association? No, surely not? But then what would exclude him? He had a cabin on the lake. He had access to the files and could have doctored anything he wanted to at any time.

What about motivation? There was none. That was the problem. Many males were the right age group, healthy enough or strong enough to commit this type of crime, but they must have a reason to do what they did.

Mack had no reason to be involved, unless he was protecting someone—like his nephews.

Shit.

That wasn't enough to look at him as the killer. Yet it was enough to wonder if there wasn't a connection that needed to be looked at closer.

A call from the campsite caught his attention.

It was Meg.

MEG WATCHED, AS Chad loped over. He raised a brow at her. "What's up?"

"They found something." She frowned up at him. "They want both of us up there."

"Let's go," he said immediately. "Let me grab a bottle of water to take with me."

She nodded, polishing off the last of her apple. She

picked up her garbage and tossed it into the can and turned to climb back up the hill. At the base, she stopped and looked up. She glanced off to the hillside, thrown in darkness in comparison to the lit-up area. She swore the trees were closer together, as if protectively watching over those they'd hidden for so long.

Stupid. But it made her feel better to think Mother Nature had been an active caretaker all these years. This was no longer just about Cia. It had become so much more.

As she stood waiting for Chad to join her, she realized that she was waiting partly because going up that hill one more time looked like too much effort. She dropped her head forward and massaged the back of her neck.

"Tired?"

"Of course." She smiled a little grimly at him. "Then we all are. Let's get this done."

Once again at the path to the ledge, one of the techs called Chad over. "We've found another skull and a necklace."

"Shit. That makes six women."

"Seven," Meg corrected. "Cia."

He stopped and looked at her. "Do you still think it's her, when we now have six more young women? We made the preliminary identification based on location, age at death, her approximate height, age …"

"And the necklace," added Meg. "Let's not forget that."

"That's the other reason why we called you up." Another tech, a woman this time, walked over and held up a bag. "This last victim had this on her."

The bag held a small silver necklace.

Meg gasped. "It's almost the same."

Chad took the bag and held it up to the light. He shifted

it so he could see the small heart-shaped pendant on the necklace. "It is the same. The question is …"

The tech spoke up, "It's got an inscription on it."

"Oh no," Meg whispered. "Please not."

Chad handed her the bag. "Hold it." He pulled on a pair of gloves, then opened the bag. He poured the contents into his palm and held up the small heart-shaped piece.

His voice soft and deadly, he read, "To Megs, with love."

Meg cried out softly.

ANGER LIKE CHAD hadn't felt in years flashed into existence at the pain he saw in Meg's eyes. There was no longer any doubt this nightmare had gotten so much bigger. But the impact on her? … That too had grown proportionally larger and much more damaging. "It's not your fault," he said more harshly than he had intended, but, even as he watched, her eyes in the early morning light appeared to be great big orbs of pain. Haunted by memories. Haunted by unanswered questions. *Haunted by Death.*

Chad carefully poured the chain and its devastating message back into the evidence bag and handed it over to the tech. "Take good care of this."

"Not to worry," she said. "I'll put it with the others."

Meg, still at his side, froze, her gasp hard and terrified. "Others?"

Chad put an arm around Meg's stiff shoulders, willing her to keep it together. He understood what she was going through. "Yes, we've found four already."

"Exactly the same?"

"Yeah, they all appear to be."

Meg started shaking. The techs had returned to the section where she'd been working.

With no one watching, Chad tugged Meg into his arms and hugged her, tight and hard. "Hold it together. If you want to be in on this, I need to know you can handle it—whatever 'it' may be."

She stiffened and stepped back. She nodded, her eyes still dark and haunted, but she took several deep breaths. "I'll be fine. Thanks for the reminder."

"I know more than anyone what this means. We need to understand everything, so we can nail the bastard."

Grim-faced, she nodded. "I'm with you there. Let's fry his ass."

INTERESTING STUFF. … They'd found the dump site.

He pondered what difference that would make. Not even two hours' drive from Seattle meant millions of people were close enough to be considered suspects. None of the locals would be stupid enough to have a dump site in their backyard, so to speak.

He checked his cell phone yet again. Still no official news.

That was good. The longer they took, the better for him. Besides, they wouldn't find everything. He sat back in his truck and smiled at the thought of all those busy bees at work, cleaning up his mess, trying to analyze his motives and to sort out his victims.

Again, all these people should be happy. He had given them jobs and had kept them employed. Kept their paychecks rolling in, so they could get drunk on the weekends. He turned his attention to other factors. Stephanie. What should he do about her—if anything? Cia had told him that Stephanie knew. But, if she did, why hadn't she said something years ago? Or had Cia lied to him all these years?

And he hadn't stayed free all these years by being stupid. No, Stephanie would have to go but not in the same way as his girls. He laughed, the sound reverberating inside the truck. She just needed to die—the same way as she'd lived.

Pathetically.

Chapter 18

FINISHING HER PART of the job wasn't fast or easy, but, by the time the early morning sun's rays came through the trees, Meg knew it was time to go home. She didn't need to stay as long as she had, but knowing that more victims could be here had kept her searching—just in case.

They'd found six new female victims—six women to bring home, potentially giving six families some closure. And Cia—if it was Cia. In her heart, Meg still believed it, but here were other victims to consider now.

The one thing she hadn't mentioned was, in contrast to Cia's petite stature, two of the other victims were tall, easily over five foot eight, and two others were close. That was directly opposite to Cia. Had that been on purpose? Or was it because there had been a lack of choice in victims, or was it not a factor at all?

Seven victims, so far. How many more would they find before this was done? She stood at the edge of the ledge and stared toward where the highway curved above them through the trees. Techs and cops had been working, searching the highway area since the light had first broken through; so far, little else had been found. A woman's shoe, or what was left of it, and an old rotten blanket. Both had been bagged and tagged.

They might belong to the victims or the killer. Or to no

one related to these deaths.

They really were in a guessing game.

Chad stepped up beside her again. He'd been the Saint Bernard of watchdogs tonight, always seeming to be there, just in case he was needed. She didn't remember him being so solicitous but, then again, look at the situation.

The sense of being looked after was new and different. She'd been with Pete for years, but she couldn't remember such concern. Maybe it was because she'd always been so independent before, boldly tearing around corners of the world that most people wouldn't dare tread and doing a job most people wouldn't want anything to do with. She'd come and gone and had known Pete would be there when she got back. He was always happy to see her on her return, but she never saw that same concern that Chad had shown her these last few days.

Then she'd been knocked off her emotional feet a while ago. Maybe she looked like she needed looking after now.

Also … she kind of liked it.

"Home time," he said, a weary smile on his face. "We'll get you back, so you can sleep. The remains will be waiting for you in the morning." He gave a short laugh. "Make that tomorrow morning."

Good. She nodded and, too tired to speak, helped collect the gear she'd used, now to take down the hill for the last time. Still, she didn't want Chad leaving if it was just to take her home. She could grab a nap in the truck, if that were the case. Better they do what needed to be done than leave. "Are you done here?" she asked. "Because, if not, I can grab a couple hours in the truck and save you the long drive back again."

"Not happening. I'll be back tomorrow and likely the

next day. We have doors to knock on for starters." He motioned around her. "However, we have men on it."

"Right. Surely the neighbors must have seen or heard something." She stumbled over a tree root and would have sprawled face-first but for Chad's restraining arm. "Thanks."

"Easy on this next bit." He explained, "We've done so much climbing, we've packed the area down, but that's brought the roots up."

"I'd like to do a trip through here later, when I can see better." She gave him a wan smile. "And when I'm not so tired."

"That's possible. First, some rest."

"Amen to that." With him supporting her, he led her to the truck, then unloaded her armful into the back. "I have to go speak with the others. Get in. I'll be just a minute."

She nodded and struggled into the cab. It was just as cold inside, but being even this much closer to going home helped.

Leaning her head back, she closed her eyes and let some of the stress roll off her shoulders. Even though she'd seen similar scenes before, they never failed to hit her hard.

Those poor women and poor Cia. She'd never had a chance.

At the same time, the likelihood of the killer being one of her old friends was minimal—until you factored in the necklaces. Necklaces she'd been trying hard to forget. The implications were too horrific, too nasty to let sit quietly in her psyche. She'd been involved in lots of serial killings and knew that most of the killers had personal issues with one of the victims, usually the first one. Whether the victim was a stand-in for someone they couldn't kill or was the real target of the killer's rage, it was personal and usually about an emotionally charged relationship.

Her eyes drifted closed. Maybe after a nap, she could convince Chad to take her right to the labs. By the time they reached Seattle, Stacy was likely to be starting her day. Meg would help. This was no longer a simple job.

She sighed heavily and let the drowsiness take her deeper.

Her last thought as she went under was that not many people had used her nickname, *Megs*. She'd been Megan in school and only Megs to her close friends back then. Only a few came in that category. It was someone from way back then.

Someone who had hated her.

Someone who had killed her by proxy, … over and over again.

Seven times over.

CHAD WALKED BACK to the truck with John, one of the other team members, at his side talking. "We need to take another load back. Maybe you should drive one of the vans and let the doc drive the truck."

"I'll ask. I know she's pretty tired though."

"Yeah, it's been a long night for all of us."

"And we're not done."

John snorted. "We could be at this for days." He spun around to look back at the site. "Just look at that place."

Chad pivoted to stare at the stripped hillside, crawling with workers. "I know, depressing."

"And in a way, smart."

"Why's that?"

"It's dangerous enough to keep people away. Animals

have been at the bones but not in a big way. He's used something to cover up the smell somewhat, but nothing hides the smell of decomposing bodies. It's high up, so the smell didn't stay down low. Up there, the breeze is more likely to take the odors upwind. Accessible from the highway above and yet still walkable from below, if he wanted access."

John's tone was normal, but the admiration made Chad's stomach heave. He searched John's face carefully. In this game, the killer could be anyone. And given that killers often returned to the scene of the crime and could be found in all sectors of life, law enforcement had had their share of bad eggs too.

John turned, caught Chad's gaze, and laughed. "Hey, it's okay. I'm doing a research paper on serial killers. That's why there's the interest."

Chad chuckled. "Good thing. I was about to check your history."

"I'm not old enough for these killings. Not unless I started in elementary school." John grinned. "Yet this guy has stayed hidden for a long time, so he's got some balls."

"And that's an assumption you can't make ever." Mack, grizzled and growling, walked toward the two of them. "This guy could be behind bars right now for another dump site of bones we've already found and prosecuted him for."

Chad stared at the rumpled detective. When the hell had he shown up? And where'd he come from? "About time you showed up. What's the matter? Holiday hours for you or something?"

"I'm here. Damn middle of the night, you know?"

"Yep. Been here all the night myself." Chad nodded toward the hillside behind Mack. "Found six sets of remains."

"All killed a long time ago." Mack snorted in disgust.

"The killer could be married and have kids by now."

"And this could be one of twenty dump sites for his victims," John said enthusiastically. "Who knows how many he's killed."

Both Mack and Chad stared at the tech. He grinned and shrugged. "Hey, this is a great case."

Mack turned his back on John. "And you're taking off already?" he asked Chad.

"Been here a long time. Meg's finished, so I'm taking her back. I'll grab a couple hours, then return."

Mack spat on the ground and nodded. "Sounds good. I'll head over and get up-to-date on the case." He turned and walked away.

Chad murmured, "I bet you will."

"You two got a problem with this case? A little territorial dispute, by any chance?" John asked.

Hating that he'd let anything show, particularly with someone who had so much interest in the case, Chad shook his head. "Nope. This is Daniel's case. The original missing person's case was Mack's from a long time ago."

"And now?"

Chad walked over to his truck. "Now it's bigger."

MEG WOKE UP, as the truck door opened. She straightened up, her brain—slow to realize she'd been asleep—was slow to click into their location. She didn't recognize where they were.

"I'm going in to get some coffee. Do you want one?"

She blinked at Chad a couple times, trying to shake the sleep from her eyes. "Yes, please."

He smiled and shut the door, walking toward the café at

the truck stop. She pulled out her cell phone and checked the time. It was almost seven in the morning. Wow. If they were lucky, she could go straight to the labs. Not that she'd had anywhere near-enough sleep to function at an optimum level. Still, she didn't want to miss anything.

She hopped out of the truck and went into the shop to use the washroom. Giving her face a quick scrub, she returned to the restaurant, feeling better. Chad was in the process of paying for the drinks. She walked over, realized she was hungry again. Stepping up behind Chad, she ordered half-a-dozen muffins to take with them.

"Good idea. Hope several of those are for me."

Tossing him a cheeky look, she shook her head. "Maybe, after I'm done."

He scoffed. "You won't even eat one."

She chuckled. "We'll see."

Back in the truck, he drove back onto the highway. She opened the bag and handed him a muffin. She took a bite of hers. "*Hmm*. It's still warm."

"Good. Nights like this, we'll take our comforts where we can."

"And the sustenance as well. The nap helped a lot. I was thinking you could drop me off at the lab. I could get started with Stacy."

"Nope. You are going home. Maybe after a few hours of sleep and a hot shower, you can reevaluate where your energy level is at. Then decide. Not what's in your best interests but what's in the best interests of the case."

"Damn." He was right. She polished off her muffin, took a sip of her hot coffee, and said, "I'll text Stacy. Update her on what's happening." She brought out her cell phone. **Stacy, need help and need to help. We found six more**

victims and four more necklaces. Same inscription.

She waited a long minute and then sent a second text. **Please help me.**

CHAD WATCHED HER in concern. He took a sip of his coffee and glanced her way. She was starting to show the wear and tear around the edges. He felt like a damn mother hen.

The necklaces had changed everything.

Finding the old dump site had opened up the field again to other serial killers, including those already incarcerated. It was one thing to consider a friend who had killed by accident or in a passionate rage. It was quite another to consider that he'd carried on killing. And, if he had, why had he stopped?

"Anto again," he whispered, under his breath. Could it be? He'd been a great guy most of the time. Moody but solid. Chad groaned. Or not. The killer could have just changed his dump site. And considering Canada was so close, he could have just crossed the border to a new life.

"I was thinking about Anto too." She sighed and stared out the window. "Nice to have spent half my life wondering if my friends are killers. *Not.*"

"I hear you. Anto could have been the killer, and that would explain the victims in relatively the same time period. And why the killing stopped. If we can ID the bodies, all female, and find one who went missing after Anto's deadly accident, then it would rule him out."

"Yeah, none of us girls liked Anto."

"And here I thought all of you were swooning over the brothers' accents."

Meg smiled at the silly memories his words brought to mind. "There were some. But, of the two, Anto was the scary one. Something was just off about him. Even Cia didn't like him." Meg shrugged. "Not that we ever knew much about either of them."

"I had several classes with Anto. He was not quite two years older than his brother but behind a year. So he played catch-up, taking some extra courses in my year, even though he had enough credits to graduate."

She frowned. "I wonder if that's the one guy Cia turned down."

Chad took his gaze off the road briefly. "How would that play out with the necklaces?"

Meg stared at him, seeing through the tunnel of time so long ago. Answering slowly, she said, "I never really knew him. I only met him through the group, and I was always with you." What she didn't add was that she'd had eyes for no one but Chad. She'd been so lost in love that she'd not even noticed other men. "When did he die?"

"Five years roughly after Cia went missing, I believe. I'll have to check my notes."

"Five years and seven victims in that time? That's possible," Meg said.

Chad nodded. "But remember. The killer might not have stopped killing. He could have just moved."

"True enough. We should check the surrounding areas," Meg added thoughtfully. "Who knows what we might find."

"A couple cadaver dog teams are coming out. They'll do a sweep of the area. The next dump site could be a state over."

"And then there could be no more."

"Let's hope so." He glanced over at her. Her head was back, her eyes closed. Reaching to his dashboard, he put on the country radio station and kept the volume low. With any luck, she'd sleep the rest of the way home.

"It has to be one of us." She turned her head toward him, her eyes bare slits. "You know that. And he hates me."

Not much Chad could do but acknowledge the truth. "I know. Every time he killed one of the girls, he was killing you."

"So …"

"It'll most likely be one of our friends." He pounded the steering wheel in frustration. "But those girls didn't die *because* of you."

"Really?" She narrowed her gaze at him. "It's me who this asshole is killing in his head. It's not just Cia on my shoulders now. All seven young women have lost their lives because of me."

"No," he snapped. "This is on him, not on you. You are not responsible for the horrible things people do because of their emotional issues. Maybe Cia's death could have been a crime of passion—the one that started all this—but the others? No way."

He gently clasped her fingers and gave them a squeeze. "You have to keep this in perspective. Otherwise this, more than anything you've gone through so far, will destroy you." He took his eyes off the road for a long moment. "And that we can't have. There are people who need you. Janelle needs you. I need you."

Her fingers tightened on his, making him smile.

There, he'd said it again. Just in case she hadn't gotten the message so far. That she hadn't responded didn't matter. She had to be mixed up and confused. It could be a long time before she was ready to try another relationship. Chad had to be patient. After all, he'd already waited seventeen years. What were a few more months?

"Thank you," she whispered, the utter weariness in her voice making him wince. At his questioning look, she added, as her eyes drifted closed, "For being there."

JUST LIKE OLD times. Chad and Megs are together. That pissed him right off. Then everything pissed him off these days.

That dump site, for one. Who'd have thought that spot would get found?

On the one hand, he was ready for those remains to be found and dealt with. As long as they were dealing with the part that didn't involve him.

On the other hand, he wanted to keep his secret. And maybe go back to his little hobby. With a difference. He'd spent a lot of time building his little hideaway. Just in case.

He'd be really pissed if they found that.

Chapter 19

MEG DRAGGED HER sore, aching body into her house, as Chad unloaded her bags.

"Shower, then to bed. A couple hours' sleep, and you'll be as good as new." Chad took the bags to the bottom of the stairs and looked around the kitchen. "This is nice."

"It was my brother's house. It seemed like a good idea, when I needed a place to move in to."

He nodded. "Sorry about your brother. I don't remember him well, but I recall that he was always a happy guy."

That made her smile. "So true. Darren always saw the sunshine in life."

"You have a lot of that too."

She shook her head vehemently and then put a hand to her temple at the pounding from the movement. "No. I might have when I was younger, but it's been a long time. I would have said I was *balanced* now, but I realize a lot of that is a front. I was waiting for closure to move on with my life."

"It's happening." He turned to leave. "I'm heading out."

She trailed behind him, all too aware that he had to be as tired as she was, if not more so. She'd managed to sleep on the way home. "You're not going back to the site right away, are you?"

"I'll go home and sleep for a couple hours, then drive back." He stepped out onto the front porch. "Will you be okay?"

She smiled. "I'll be fine. I admit I want to rush to the lab, and I'm jealous you are going back out there. I need to take another look around, but I'm also needed in the lab." She glanced at her watch. "Janelle will be home this afternoon too. So shower, sleep, then lab and family."

"Good. I'll check in on you in a few hours." With a final wave, he walked out the front door. She watched until his truck drove down the block and turned the corner. Then, with a wide yawn, she headed upstairs for a hot shower, wanting nothing more than to collapse in bed.

HOURS LATER CHAD stopped by his office to check his email and phone messages. There was a message from Josh.

He dialed the number on his office's landline and waited for Josh to answer. While waiting, he checked his cell. Unfortunately nothing new on Stephanie.

And neither was Josh answering.

Then he tried Bruce. He might or might not be in town, but Chad wanted to connect in some way. They usually talked every couple weeks.

When he'd left the office yesterday, Daniel was supposed to contact the remaining four males from the original camping trip. Had he? And, if he had, did he learn anything new?

Josh should have come in for the interview yesterday. And that was probably what the calls were about. Chad called Stacy, but she wasn't answering her phone. Then why would she? She'd be in the lab, working on the evidence that had been shipped in.

His phone rang. Mack.

"Are you coming back?"

"Yes, just catching up with things at the office. What's going on there?"

"Lots of legwork still to be done. The techs have finished and are packing up. The weather is getting ready to start pissing down again."

"Not good. We've been hampered by bad weather since we found the first set of remains."

"True enough."

"Did you talk to Josh yesterday?" Chad asked abruptly.

"Yep, I did."

He volunteered nothing further. "And the other three?"

"Couldn't get a hold of Bruce, and Tim is in Switzerland. He'll call me tomorrow."

"Okay."

Mack said abruptly, "You know that it's one of you."

There was the dig Chad had been half expecting. "It's not me and not Meg, nor Stephanie. Anto is dead, so that leaves four males."

"*I* can count." Mack's voice was cool, hard. "And there are still five males."

Shit. "Are you back on that track again?" Chad snapped, his anger flaring to life. "I've spent my life trying to solve this case. For the last time, *I did not kill Cia.*"

"Silence came first. "Yeah, I hear you." This time Mack's tone had lightened.

Chad closed his eyes and tried to pull back the hot rage. It was an old accusation that, no matter what, he couldn't escape from the suspicion of being involved. Wrong place at the wrong time—it had just ruined his life. "So, what about Pero?" He kept his tone neutral.

"I'm still trying to track him down. No one has heard

from him in years."

The disgust in Mack's voice made Chad smile. Being family, Mack had a better chance of getting in touch with Pero. From what Chad understood, the Novak brothers hadn't been all that friendly with Bruce's extended family, as it were.

"I've left a message with family members."

"Right." As if that would work. As the less well-known of the group, he and his brother had come under suspicion as much as the others. Then the car accident that had taken his brother and father had sent Pero to hell and back physically. The last thing he would want would be to go back to that painful time in his life and talk with the cops again.

Hell, anyone could understand that.

"I'll call him," Chad offered.

"You do that, but I want to be there when you talk to him. Bring him in and let me know when." His voice hardened, as he added, "Got it?"

"Got it." Chad ended the call, getting some small satisfaction from the childish move. He walked to his board and checked his notes on Pero's contact information. He dialed and waited. Nothing.

No one had heard from Pero in years. Not since the accident. Several had gone to see him at the hospital, but he'd been in bad shape. His recovery had apparently taken years.

Chad had visited him around the same time, but Pero didn't want company. He'd been angry and grieving and hurting in a big way. Broken pelvis, shattered face from going through the windshield, and that had been just for a start. Pero had also lost the rest of his immediate family in that accident. His mother had died years earlier.

After that, they'd lost track of each other. Like the rest of the group, no one wanted to stay in contact. It was uncomfortable yet addictive at the same time. No one else knew what they'd been through. No one else understood. The connection was something they wanted, yet, at the same time, they didn't want, as it was a reminder of a horrible time in their lives.

So some, like Meg, ran as far away as they could get; and others, like Stephanie, couldn't get away. No matter how far or how much they struggled, the same issue always kept bringing them back—to this.

MEG WOKE UP achy and tired. She'd slept for hours—hours when dead bodies and dead friends ran screaming through her mind. Waking up to a film of sweat on her skin and a pounding heart hadn't been nice.

She sat up slowly, hating the bone-deep weariness. Just that little movement brought tears to her eyes. She couldn't imagine how she'd feel by bedtime tonight. Moving carefully, she stepped into a hot shower and let the water run over her sore muscles. She only had three hours until Janelle was out of school. She'd hoped for more, but she'd slept the time away.

Feeling more refreshed, she dressed quickly and decided to forgo coffee. She'd pick one up on the way to the lab. However, she needed food. The last of the muffins had been left in Chad's truck. She hoped he was enjoying them. Her stomach growled. She opened the fridge, removed the cheese. She cut herself a decent slice and then chose an apple to go with it.

Within minutes, she was driving to the lab to meet Stacy. Her visitor's pass got her through to Stacy's office, which, of course, was empty. Under the same circumstances, Meg would be in the lab too. And Stacy was just like her. A spare lab coat hung on the back door of the lab. She put it on and stepped into Stacy's domain.

"About time you showed up." Stacy's cheerful voice called out from the far side of the room. "What is this, summer holiday hours?"

Meg laughed. "I could use a holiday, so if you're offering …"

"Ha, I'm planning a trip to Belize in the fall, if you want to come along." Stacy was involved in a six-way puzzle of bones, as she laid out the skeletons. "Come. Give me a hand. I'll be all day putting these pieces together."

"It's quite a mess, isn't it?"

"Yeah, to say the least. It's so much easier if you find one skeleton at a time." Stacy walked over to the fourth table in the row of six and laid down a femur, below a broken pelvis.

"You've done well so far." Meg joined Stacy to study the various partial sets of skeletons laid out on the tables and felt overwhelmed with sadness. "This is really terrible."

"They always are. Don't just stand there." Stacy nodded toward the bags and boxes on the table. "Get busy."

MACK STUDIED THE map that Chad had left behind at the site. It was an aerial shot, showing the lots of each place on the lake. Chad had marked out the exact location of both evidence sites in relation to the highway and the lake. Then, with careful penmanship, he had drawn in the name of each owner with the letters T or O beside them. He frowned.

What kind of code was that?

The techs were busy packing up. Men were out, going

from door to door, knocking on all the cabins. Finding out what anyone had heard or seen, if anything.

He doubted anyone had. It was a long time ago.

Glancing around, he noted a line of cabins on the right that he wanted to check out himself. Walking around the chaos, he headed in the direction of the first cabin. He remembered that sucker going up years ago. He'd been young, just in grade school. But his grandpappy and his pappy knew the family doing the building. Back then, everyone knew each other. Everyone helped each other.

This cabin had been built by a lot of hands, and it was one of the earlier ones, before the place became fashionable.

Mack walked up the long pathway to the first cabin and knocked on the old wooden door.

As he looked back at the long line of years behind him, he realized that last thing still hadn't changed.

Everyone still helped each other out.

Sometimes they had to.

Chapter 20

CHAD ARRIVED AT the campsite to find it virtually empty. The techs had gone, and, although he could see Mack's truck, he saw no sign of the man. He opened his phone and called him. And heard a phone go off a few feet away.

"I'm right behind you," Mack growled. "You should try looking first."

Chad rolled his eyes and, disconnecting his phone, turned to face the grizzled detective a couple feet behind him. Mack appeared to be in a royal mood. "Where are we at?"

"Nowhere, as usual. No one saw anything. No one heard anything. No one knows anything."

Chad shook his head. Why wasn't he surprised? It was so typical of people. Everyone kept to themselves. "Have you contacted everyone?"

"Everyone who's here. At least a good couple dozen cabins are empty."

"Give me the address of those not here, and I'll track down the owners and call them."

"*Nah*, I'll do it. I know most of them anyway."

"Maybe it's better that I do it. More official."

"They aren't murderers here," he snarled. "It's the dumb kids who like to visit that raise hell around here."

Chad glared at him. "We didn't raise any hell. We were quiet. Just out to have a nice weekend trip before the end of summer."

Mack didn't say anything, but his lip curled down.

Chad tried to be reasonable. "Look. I know you consider this your backyard and blame us for bringing this mess to your doorstep, but we came here because of Bruce. Remember? Your nephew?"

"I know who Bruce is. And that was the first trip you guys made here. But the curfew was too early for you, the place too crowded, so you headed to the far side of the lake next time, where you could cause some trouble."

"For the last time, we didn't cause any trouble."

"There was booze, and you were all underage, a girl went missing, now turns up murdered. What do you call that?"

Chad had heard it over and over again from so many people, and it always pissed him off. There was no presumption of innocence for those living under the shadow of having gotten away with murder. That was a joke. He'd lived with that shadow for seventeen years.

He wanted out from under it. And he wanted Mack to get the hell off his back.

"And let's not forget that you were at your cabin that weekend, and, for all I know, you decided to walk on over and take out a young girl for yourself," he snapped, his voice harsh, cold. "Pretty easy to make the evidence disappear when it's your case, isn't it?" As Mack's face darkened, Chad added, "How did it become your case anyway?"

"Because I was here, when you idiots lost her." He scowled. "Someone had to take control after you punk-ass kids trampled the place."

Chad snorted. "Right. And how come your search parties never found her body when it was here the whole time?"

"And can you confirm that? For all you know, she was held captive somewhere for a week or two, then killed. Unless your 'professional' can prove otherwise, and I wouldn't trust her word anyway."

"Hey, knock it off." Daniel joined them. "They can probably hear you two fighting on the other side of the lake, for Christ's sake."

Chad glared at the two of them. Daniel was Mack's age and had been around just as long—if not longer. Daniel was good people, but the older set tended to stick together.

"Whatever. Just make sure that those addresses of the ones you checked go down in the file, or you can bet your ass I'll be walking around and disturbing each and every one here to find out who you missed and why." Chad strode past them, his irritation and anger vibrating through him. Christ, would this never end?

"Hey, wait up." Daniel ran behind him. "Take it easy, will you?"

"Why, so you can rag on me too?" Chad unlocked his truck door and opened it. The frame was jerked out of his hand.

"Calm the fuck down. You are not driving in a temper, and, although Mack usually has that effect on people he works with, you should be used to it."

Chad glared at him, hating to hear the sense in the words. He struggled for control, when he just wanted to drive away and to tear up the pavement. But that was suicide.

"Fine, I'll calm down. But Mack is done accusing me with his sly digs. If he's got proof of my involvement, then he better pony up, or I'll be heading to the captain myself.

Mack couldn't nail this on me seventeen years ago when I was a scared kid, and he can't now. I'm not a kid anymore, and I'll be God dammed before he ruins my life any more than he already has. He's a fucking asshole, and the evidence points to him just as much as it does to anyone else. And you can bet I'll be taking that to the captain too."

Out of nowhere, Mack appeared, fury flashing on his bulldog of a face.

And he charged.

MEG CHECKED HER cell phone. "I have to run. Janelle is out of school now."

"And you're back at her old house?" Stacy made a shooing motion with her hands. "Go. Just come back tomorrow." She smiled and returned to the work in progress.

Meg said, "Thanks. I'll be here bright and early."

She was already texting Janelle, as she took off her lab coat and grabbed her purse from the locker, where she'd placed it earlier. She could have stayed longer. Janelle wouldn't want to be coddled, but the fact remained they were still uneasy with their new living arrangements. She would just as soon help make the adjustment easier. Janelle would also be happy to hear that Meg had spoken to Pete—at least, a little.

Janelle hadn't responded by the time Meg made her way to her car. The traffic was surprisingly light. Still tired, she drove home carefully, grateful when she pulled into the garage and shut off the engine. She grabbed her purse and cell phone and unlocked her door. Inside she checked her phone again. Still no message from her niece. Glancing at the clock, she realized it was still a few minutes early. Meg could have driven to the school and picked her up.

A big yawn escaped her. She needed more sleep, but it would ruin the night ahead if she tried to nap now. She'd go to bed at the same time as Janelle.

First, some food. She rummaged in the fridge and pulled out the fixings for a sandwich. She didn't know what Janelle had had for lunch, but chances were, she'd be hungry when she got in.

By the time she had two sandwiches, sitting and waiting, Janelle still hadn't texted. Meg picked up her phone and called. Her niece would either be staying late because of homework or was walking home. Hopefully she could improve her marks now. Teachers hated it when the kids' cell phones went off, but it was after school now, so Janelle shouldn't get into trouble.

The phone rang and rang. Irritated, Meg canceled the call. Had Janelle left her phone at school, or was she in detention?

Her stomach growled. Meg put on the teakettle and sat down to eat her sandwich, with her eye on the clock. Every ten minutes, she called but still got no answer. By the time she'd finished eating, she was dialing the school and had managed to catch the principal, before he left for the day. "Hi, Meg, glad to hear from you. Janelle is doing much better these last few months." Meg winced. Janelle might have been doing better a few months ago—but this last month with Pete? So not. "Good, I'm glad to hear that."

"Yes, I'm really happy for her," he said in a chatty voice. "She's had a tough year, but she's handling it well."

"I've been waiting for her to come home this afternoon. She's not answering her phone. Have you seen her?"

"No. Not this afternoon." His voice deepened. "I'm in

the main office. Let me check the book." There were sounds of papers being turned. "Oh, here she is. It says she signed out twenty minutes early."

"She signed out?" Meg's throat closed. With great difficulty she swallowed and asked, "Are you saying that she left with someone?"

"Yes," he hastened to assure her. "I can't read the signature though."

"Oh God."

"You didn't know?" His voice sharpened. "Who could she have left with?"

"I don't know." Think, damn it, *think*. "She had a sleepover yesterday. Did Linette sign out as well? Maybe they were under the impression that it was to be for two days."

"It must be something like that." His voice lightened. "I'm looking through the names, but it doesn't look like it. No sign of Linette having signed out."

Meg turned all business. "I need to see that signature. Stay there. I'm five minutes away."

"But—"

She hung up, lunged for her purse and keys, and ran. She was close to twice her stated time, but he stood in the office, waiting for her.

"Here it is." He pulled a book toward her, open with a page of signatures. He stabbed at one signature.

She studied it. And realized it wasn't legible or familiar.

"Have you contacted her friends? That would be my first thought."

Meg held up her cell phone. "I'm dialing as we speak."

"Linette, hi, it's Meg, Janelle's aunt. Is she there with you?"

"No, she said you were picking her up early."

Meg's heart sank. She raised a trembling hand to her forehead. Working to keep her voice calm, she asked, "How did she know that?"

Silence. Then Linette said in a timid voice, "I don't know. I thought she got a text, but I don't know for sure."

There was a fumbling sound, and then she heard Linette call out, "Mom, can you talk to Janelle's mom?"

Then an adult voice came on the phone. Deirdre said, "Meg, what's the matter?"

"Janelle didn't come home. There's an unreadable signature signing her out early from school."

"Unreadable?" Deidre asked cautiously. "You don't recognize it?"

Meg choked back a sob. "No. I don't."

"Can you think of anyone who might have taken her from school? An uncle? A grandparent? And there's no reason to think it has to be a male. Is there an aunt or a best friend who could have planned a surprise?"

Meg's mind raced, as she tried to come up with a logical reason for someone, anyone, to have gone anywhere with Janelle.

Deidre asked tentatively, "Meg, what about Pete?"

"I thought of that," Meg said steadily, and she had. "It's not his signature."

Another silence.

"Is there any reason why he'd try to hide his signature?"

"No, there'd be no need to. He's been in her life for a long time. There'd be no reason to try and hide it." Meg thought for a long moment, then blurted out, "She isn't answering her cell phone."

"That's okay. The girls were playing games on their cell phones all last evening, and they almost ran down their phone batteries. Janelle forgot to bring her charger last night."

"Damn." Meg cast a worried look at the principal, who stood nearby, waiting to help. "Okay, if she calls, let me know."

"I will. And let us know when you find her."

"You bet." Meg hung up the phone and studied the signature again. There was no hesitation in the penmanship. Whoever had been using that signature had been doing it that way for a long time.

She lifted the book and handed it to the principal. "May I get a photocopy of this page? Of the signature? Please."

"Sure. That, I can do." Happy to have a constructive way to help, he warmed up the machine and quickly printed off a copy for her. "Let me know what else I can do."

She nodded. "I will."

"What will you do?"

"Call the police."

And she dialed Chad's number.

CHAD TOSSED MACK back several feet and surged forward to lift him off the ground and throw him back farther. His phone rang in his pocket. He ignored it, fury still riding him hard, as he glared at Mack scrambling to his feet. Daniel stepped between them. "God damn it, Mack. What the hell are you doing?"

Mack lowered his head, as if to plow forward again, bloodlust in his eyes. Daniel stepped toward him. "Back off. You're both on duty. So knock it off."

Keeping a wary eye on Mack, Chad stepped back a little and rolled his shoulders to ease the tension. As much as he'd like to pound Mack to the ground himself, it wouldn't help. And one of them needed to keep their cool.

He'd had enough of Mack's goading.

Mack glared at his old friend, and then his gaze settled on Chad. His face turned fierce, and, for a moment, it was as if time stood still, as they waited for Mack to choose his next move.

Chad watched his muscles tense.

Then Mack eased back slightly, and the dangerous moment passed.

As Chad watched, Mack turned and walked away.

Daniel took a deep breath, then muttered, "Stubborn bastard."

He spun all the way around to face Chad. "Why did you goad him?"

"Because I've had enough. For seventeen long years, I've listened to his accusations. I've had a gutful."

Daniel studied him for a long moment, then grimaced. "And maybe you should have done this a long time ago. But stay away from him now, until he cools off."

Chad said, "I'm going back to town. Better we work on different angles of this case."

Daniel nodded and walked away.

Chad hopped into his truck and headed back the way he'd come. He never should have left the damn city. Better he work the computer side of this investigation. Mack was okay on a computer, but he wasn't the best. Chad, on the other hand, knew he was good.

With any luck he'd be home in just over an hour, and the need to get back pulled on him. He slammed his foot on the gas. It wasn't until he hit the city limits and was only a few minutes from the office that he remembered the phone call. He blamed the confrontation with Mack for that.

He pulled out his phone and checked his message.

"Shit."

MEG DROVE HOME slowly, following the path Janelle would most likely have taken, if she were going home. Meg searched every block, every crosswalk, and even waited outside a small corner store, until she was sure there was no sign of her niece. All the while, she waited for Chad to get back to her.

Inside, her stomach acid churned her guts to sewage. Everything had knotted in fear.

Where was she?

Meg couldn't handle it if something had happened to Janelle.

Meg had lost so much already. Immediately she was assailed by guilt. She should be thinking of poor Janelle. She had to be scared, terrified.

"Please. Whoever you are, please look after my niece. Please don't hurt her," she whispered, and her whispers became prayers that she barely recognized.

She pulled into the garage, her hands shaking so much she could hardly put the car in Park. As she exited the car, she realized Janelle might have come home in the meantime or left a message on the home phone. She ran inside. "Janelle, are you here?"

The kitchen was empty. Meg ran through the main floor, then upstairs. "Janelle? Janelle!"

No answer. The house was empty.

She ran down the stairs to the landline and hit the button. There were no messages. Not one.

"Damn it, Janelle, where are you?" she wailed. Back in the kitchen she stared down at the sandwich she'd made earlier for Janelle. Meg's phone rang, and she snatched it from her pocket, hoping for a call from Janelle.

"Oh thank God. Chad, Janelle's not here. She was signed out from school twenty minutes early. She got a text, at least according to one of her friends, who said I was picking her up early." She gasped out the words so fast, she couldn't catch her breath. Finally she took several deep breaths to calm down.

"Take it easy. We'll find her. I'm sorry I didn't get this earlier. I'm almost back in the office now and just walking down the hallway. Did anyone see her leave the building?"

"I don't believe so, without canvassing a school full of kids to find out. The school secretary had to leave early, so the principal was doing double duty and wouldn't have been watching. He said he hadn't seen her this afternoon."

"Have you tried her phone?"

"Yes, but she's not answering it. More than that, she was at her friend's house for a sleepover, and she forgot her charger."

"So she can't call. Her phone is likely dead now or will be soon."

"Yes. I spoke to her friend's mother, and both girls ran their phones down last night."

"Okay, so I know you've been thinking about this, but who would know she's there? And who would be comfortable enough with a school setting to understand that they'd have to sign the child out?"

"I don't know, but anyone familiar with the school or any school. It's pretty standard procedure in this day and age, I imagine."

"*Hmm.* I need a recent picture and some basic description. I'll get an Amber Alert out immediately."

"Right." She hated this, but it was a necessity. She quickly gave him a physical description as her laptop turned on. "I'm powering up the laptop to find a digital photo to email to you."

"Good. And, when you've done that, sit down and make a list of all the adults you know in town who know about Janelle and where she goes to school."

"Right. That might take a while."

"Not really. You've been pretty focused on rebuilding a life with Janelle. So the list can't be all that long."

"Am I including even the real estate agent?" Meg had a document up on her laptop and was trying to add in the people whom she knew. And who knew about Janelle. She put down Pete and Deidre, Linette's mother. And Sam, Linette's father. Who else?

"Did the Realtor know about Janelle?"

"Sure, I contacted her about not selling the house so we could move back inside." And that had been what—two days ago?

"Then she goes on the list." His tone was brisk. "Did you get the laptop up?"

"Yeah," She tucked the phone into her shoulder and created the email, attached a decent picture of Janelle and sent it off. "It's on the way. Oh, here's another one. I'll send that too."

"Good. Now work on the list."

"Right." She pulled out a chair and sat down. "I can't just create this in a minute, you know?"

She added her Realtor to the list.

"That's fine. The email is here." His voice turned gentle.

"She's stunning."

Tears filled her eyes. "Yes, she is." She sniffled. "She's got her mother's dark Spanish good looks. There's no resemblance to me or her father—until you get to know her. She's her father in her stubborn personality."

"And the second picture?" His voice changed, cooled. "When was that one from?"

"That was this last weekend with Pete. They went fishing." She studied the picture on her laptop. "She was so excited about catching the fish. She threw up such a stink at going in the first place. Now look at her."

"And the man?"

She raised an eyebrow. "That's Pete."

Silence.

Damn, she was hearing that a lot lately. "I guess you never met him."

"Oh, I think maybe I did."

She sat back, only just now catching the weird tone in his voice. "Oh, at the second dump site of course. He was one of the guys with the chainsaws. Sorry, I'm just really distracted."

"Sure, I saw him there, but he was in full gear, and I never met him. He left before I arrived." He took a deep breath. "I believe, and I could be wrong because it's been so long ago, and he was in bad shape then, but, Jesus,… *no*, I have to be wrong."

"What are you talking about? Pete has lived with me for close to over ten years. Of course, it's possible for you to have met him before. I'm sorry I didn't introduce you."

"No. You don't understand. Hell, I don't either, but I swear he looks like Pero."

STEPHANIE STUMBLED THROUGH the weird door in her world. She knew she was dying. She wasn't happy about it but had gotten past the point of caring.

Except about Bruce—he would be her regret. She loved the big idiot and always had. And they'd been star-crossed lovers since Cia.

Damn that woman anyway. Her getting herself killed had messed up Stephanie's life. She should have been married to Bruce and have two perfect kids.

Now that wouldn't happen.

There was no one to save Stephanie. There never was.

A noise outside her mind caught her attention. With great difficulty, she rolled her head sideways, letting it hit the cement on the other side. She had to try. "Help," she said, but the words came out in a barest of croaks. She tried again. "Help …"

"Hello?" Then came sounds of running feet and a strangled yell, as someone dropped to her side.

"Stephanie, hang on," Bruce said. His face had never looked so good. She didn't know what he was doing here, especially in this ghetto of an alley.

"I was following you, hoping you wouldn't go to your dealer. Then I lost you." His gentle hand cupped her cheek. "Now I've found you again. Please, don't do this anymore."

Tears trickled from her burning eyes. "Bruce, I …"

"*Shush*, don't try to talk. I'm getting help." He was busy punching numbers on his cell phone.

She smiled. Look at that. This time, there *was* someone to help. "Bruce, I didn't do this."

"What?" he exclaimed. "Then who did?"

But the cloud of consciousness moved over her, and she passed out.

Chapter 21

MEG REARED BACK. "What?" she asked cautiously, studying the picture she sent him. "Pero, as in Anto's brother?"

He cleared his throat. "This is the only picture I have seen of Pete. Do you have some older ones?" Meg's gaze zeroed in on the wall, where she'd hung a picture of her and Pete from their first year together, from back in happier times. She kept it there more to remember Cia now than as a reminder of Pete. "I have lots, but I have to find them. Most are on the computer. Hold on."

"I didn't mean to shock you."

"Well, you did," she snapped. "And so what if he is? It's not as if I'd seen him for years, and I hadn't known him back then, as it were." But it *did* matter. She knew it did, and inside her heart raced. She so didn't need more shocks right now.

Her fingers were busy clicking through her laptop folders, selecting and attaching pictures to send. "I'm sending more pictures."

"And it might have something to do with Janelle's disappearance. You say it wasn't Pete's signature. Was it a man's handwriting?"

"How would I know?" she snapped, hating the suspicion. "I saw him yesterday. Remember? He was helping us clear away that downed tree, one of the guys with chain-saws."

"I remember. I also remember that we made it back in lots of time and so could he."

"But why? There's no logical explanation for why he'd have taken Janelle, particularly in secret. He doesn't even like her!" she finished, her voice rising to a shrill tone at the end.

"He doesn't?" There was a heavy pause, as Chad digested that news. "How could he not? She's just a child. And she's hurting."

"Yeah, well, he doesn't. Or maybe it's the whole situation he doesn't like. Years ago he wanted a family, but later admitted it was more to keep me at home. While my brother was alive, Pete and Janelle got along famously. They used to do movie-and-popcorn nights, and I swear they were more about popcorn fights than anything." Her voice thickened at the happy memories. "Then my brother died, and Janelle's stay became permanent, and everything changed."

"Sometimes, when a situation is forced on people, it takes time for them to adapt."

"Yeah, well, he didn't adapt well," she said shortly. "Maybe if we'd lasted, he might have, but I wasn't prepared to put Janelle through more trauma and abandonment."

She closed all the folders on her desktop. Her mind raced through the possibilities of where Janelle could be, as well as Pete and Janelle's turbulent relationship. Then she realized he wasn't speaking. "Chad?"

"I'm here."

He might be there, but his voice was aged, weary. As if he'd seen too much in life. "And?"

She stared at the series of pictures she'd sent him. They were memories of happier days. Sadness filled her. She scrubbed her eyes with her sleeve. She hated feeling out of control and so emotionally done. But, since her brother's death, life had been one roller coaster after another of pain. She needed life to come a halt. She needed things to work out for once. She needed Janelle home, safe and sound. "What are you thinking?" she asked Chad.

"I'm thinking that Pete is a dead ringer for or actually is Pero."

She shook her head. "No, he'd have told me."

"Why?"

"Because …" She didn't have an answer. They'd shared so little. If they'd known each other back then, wouldn't he have said something? Hell, she'd walked away from them all because she wanted nothing more to do with anyone from that time period. They all had in some ways. So maybe he had to. Maybe he hadn't recognized her?

Chad spoke again. "He was in that car accident. It damaged his shoulders. He used to stand so tall and straight. But then, after the accident, he lost his take on the world, as well as his happy attitude."

At a weak attempt to diffuse the tension, she joked, "At least he was the nicer brother."

"Yeah, he was decent."

"He is decent."

"His hair was jet-black back then."

She remembered that. "Why would it be black now but without that strong jet-black look?"

"Probably because of the accident. He was in the hospital for months." Chad added thoughtfully, "Was he heavily scarred?"

"No. He had some, probably more than a lot of people, but not all over." She tried to cast her mind back, but years of conversations were hard to remember. "I did ask him once about them, and he said something about being in an accident. But he never elaborated."

"Does Pete have any family?"

"His dad died in a car accident and he had an uncle who passed away a few years back. Pete inherited the cabin from him."

"Ah."

A wealth of subtle information filled his tone that she didn't like. "What does that have to do with anything?"

"The brothers were related to Bruce. Remember? They were all cousins. And we were at the lake because Bruce knew about the place, as he and his family owned several cabins there."

And now she *did* remember. Bile rose up the back of her throat. Blindly she walked to the sink, where she filled a glass with water. She took several sips, trying to ease back the nausea.

Either Pete or Pero—it didn't make a difference. And, if she kept telling herself that, she might believe it. Somehow if he were Pero, it was a betrayal. Yet she just didn't understand how.

"That would be pretty sad, considering I spent the last ten years trying to stay a long way away from anyone associated with that part of my life." She gave a half snort. "Not nice to think I'd hooked up with one of the main players and never knew it."

"And maybe he didn't either."

But Chad's tone of voice said he didn't believe it.

"That's quite possible. You changed the form of your name."

They both said together, "So did he …"

"Have you got the photo still up where Pete and Janelle are fishing?"

She clicked several times to bring up the picture in question. "Yeah. What about it?"

"The look in Pete's eyes …"

Her breath caught back a sob. "What are you talking about?" She bent to study the look in his eye and then relaxed. She'd seen that look often lately. It was directed at her—almost as if he hated her. "Yeah, he's not been real happy lately, especially with me."

More silence came.

"As I look at that picture, I realize just how unhappy he is." Meg rubbed her forehead, wondering what she was missing. "Look. I know I'm tired and not functioning on all brain cells at the moment, but you have to spell this out for me. What are you seeing that I'm not?"

"You are the one who took the picture, correct?"

"Yes," she snapped impatiently.

"So, … he's not looking at you."

Oh God.

CHAD KNEW THAT look in Pete's eyes. There was more than anger in that gaze. There was hate. Pete hated Meg's niece. The missing Janelle.

"Was anyone else around when you took that photo?" he asked casually, already knowing the answer but needing her to confirm it. He was already searching his database for Pero's details. What had Mack said about not getting a hold of him?

If they assumed Pero and Pete were the same man, did Mack know this? Or did he only know Pero, not that he was living with Meg as Pete? Could someone hide in plain sight for over a decade? Not that Pero was hiding—he had just avoided his family. It's not as if he was doing anything illegal. But, according to Meg, Pete came to the cabin a lot. According to Mack, he barely saw his nephew, yet both had cabins at the same lake.

And a lot of nastiness was going on at that lake.

"No." Meg was breathing heavy. She said suddenly, "I'll call you back."

Chad stared down at his dead phone and slowly laid it on his desk. Poor Meg, this was not an awareness everyone could handle. She was better prepared than most, but it was different when your family was in danger.

Family. He sat back and considered that. Family threaded through this whole mess. Was Pero the one who'd killed Cia? The Pero Chad had known years ago hadn't seemed like that type of guy. He'd been real popular with the girls, real popular with everyone, in fact. It was his brother who had been morose, broody even, and not as friendly or open.

That Anto had died so young had been so sad and such a waste.

After his accident Pero had been bitter and angry and seriously depressed. He'd resembled his brother a lot during his recovery. Then Chad had lost track of him.

Maybe that's why Meg had gravitated to him, even if she hadn't known. Not that they knew now. Honestly Pero's face had been shattered in the accident. He didn't look like he used to. The surgeons hadn't gone in and put his face back together. They'd left things to heal on their own, as was common in some cases. But nothing had healed like before.

He wasn't disfigured; he was just … different looking. And, in all fairness to Meg, he was just different enough to make Chad himself question if he really was Pero.

And just because he might have hooked up with Meg and had a cabin at the same lake where Cia had gone missing didn't make him guilty. Any more than Mack was guilty for having been at his cabin that weekend either.

And wanting it to be so didn't make it so.

He needed to connect with Bruce. Maybe he could identify Pero from this picture. They were cousins after all. But he knew Bruce had had little to do with his family now, especially Mack.

Chad walked over to his wall, where he had the case photos up and notes to look at the timeline. He'd only had a chance to put down yesterday that they'd found the other bodies. But, according to Meg, they would all have been deceased close to the same time as Cia—within a few years. And that *within a few years* was frustrating. Until they had identifications on these women, there was no way to narrow that down. This left both Anto and Pero/Pete as viable suspects.

So, in theory, Pero could have killed those women, and then been incapacitated, and that would have stopped the killing spree. He would have hooked up with Meg soon after his recovery and could have turned over a new leaf as Pete. A happy relationship might have been enough to keep him from returning to his murderous ways.

Maybe …

He ran a search on Pete and got the make and model of his truck, then sent out a regional BOLO alert. Better to be safe. … He added Janelle's picture and a basic description of both Pete and Janelle.

Next he ran a search for missing women in the age that Meg had stated, from two years before Cia's death to five years afterward. He ran it for the whole state. That would give him a place from which to start.

Within minutes he'd found thirteen hits. He bent to read the details.

MEG VERY CAREFULLY set her phone on the kitchen table. Then taking a deep, controlled breath, she screamed. And screamed, then screamed again, as fear and anger burned hot like a poker into her heart. The sound went on and on, and she couldn't stop it.

Shuddering in the aftermath, her mind still frozen and lost, her rage still bubbling, she finally calmed enough to catch her breath and to swallow the sobs, until they only rippled down her spine, instead of quaking through her.

She couldn't stand the thought of Pete hating Janelle with the level of viciousness that Meg had seen in his eyes in that photo.

What kind of man hated a child? With her arms wrapped around her belly, she rocked in place, trying to get through the horror to where she could deal with the reality on the other side. Janelle had been living with them for six months. Had Pete felt like that before then? Or was it recent?

She cast her mind back carefully, going from weekend to weekend, month to month, wondering and worrying if she'd left them alone. Was that why Janelle was so afraid of him? Did she know how Pete felt? She must have known subconsciously at least. Had he said anything to her? Threatened her? Hurt her?

Even if Pete had let his guard down in this photo, that didn't mean he'd kidnapped Janelle from school. But he was the one person who Janelle would have left with. She wouldn't know not to. She would have assumed that Pete and Meg were friendly, maybe even back together again. Who knew what story Pete might have told her.

He could have even said he was taking her to meet Meg.

And he might be innocent.

God, this was making her nuts.

There was one thing though. If he'd taken Janelle, and that was a big *if*, then Meg had one advantage. She knew Pete like no one else did. And that was always the key to hunting predators; getting inside their minds and thinking like them.

Where would he have gone?

To the cabin of course. She closed her eyes and realized how much of her life revolved around that damn lake. She reached for the phone.

"Chad. If Pete has taken Janelle, he'd take her to his cabin." She took a deep breath. "I'm driving up there to look."

"Whoa. You're not thinking straight. And you're not in any shape to drive. I have men still up there. I'll contact them and have them keep a look out for Pete and Janelle." He took a deep breath. "Give me a moment to get a hold of them, and I'll call you right back."

"Wait. I need to do something. How can I help?"

"By doing what you do best." He added, "I'm sending you some files."

And he hung up.

CHAD THOUGHT ABOUT calling Mack and realized Mack wouldn't likely take his call. With any luck, Daniel was still there. He was one of Mack's cronies but appeared to be a straight shooter.

"Chad, what's up? Are you still hanging around, or did you head back to town?"

"No, I drove back. Probably should've stayed, given this latest development."

"Oh, what's up?"

"A child is missing. The Amber Alert has gone out, but we have reason to believe she might be at the lake." Chad proceeded to bring him up to speed on what he knew. "Pete's cabin is on the same side as the crime scene but down farther. Mack should know which one, if he's still there."

"Yeah, he is." Daniel cleared his throat. "I'll see if I can track him down to help."

"Good. A door-to-door search is ideal. The girl is twelve years old and is only four foot six and maybe seventy pounds. Long black hair and very pretty, a china doll sort of look. I have pictures. I'm sending them to your email now."

"Good."

"There's also a picture of Pete. He's a long-time summer resident, and he was one of the men who helped out with cutting up that tree on-site."

"In that case, I can call the guy who hired him. If we can confirm he's been here all day. No way he ran all the way back to Seattle to snatch a little girl."

"Any confirmation either way would help out a lot."

"Right, I'm on it."

"There is one more issue." And he proceeded to explain the Pero/Pete mess and their connection to the case and … to Mack.

MEG WONDERED WHAT Chad was talking about, when an email came in with photos.

She read the short note. He'd found thirteen cases of missing women who fit the general profile of those missing in a ten-year period, with the day Cia had gone missing in the middle. She opened the first one, and her mind stalled.

She studied the photo, the shakes starting all over again.

This so couldn't be.

But, as she read the case number, she noted the name. Brenda Durnet.

She picked up her phone, then realized she needed to be at Chad's office for this. This would be a long night, and she didn't want to be alone, especially not now. She grabbed her purse and laptop, sent him a quick text, telling him to expect her, and ran out the door. The traffic had picked up unfortunately. It took her close to twenty minutes to cross town. She was more frustrated than anxious by the time she arrived. Her mind was locked on the one image she'd looked at. She should have taken the time to check out the others but had wanted to see Chad first. Maybe they could look at them together to both deal with the shocks she knew were coming.

Damn it. She really didn't want to be alone right now.

She walked into the station, phone out to call him, but he was waiting for her.

"Meg, are you okay?" he asked, his concern rolling over her in warm waves.

She shook her head. "No, I'm really not." She took a deep breath. "Anything on Janelle?"

"No, not yet. Come on back to my office," he said, wrapping an arm around her shoulders. "Do you want a hot drink? A coffee? A hot chocolate?"

"Maybe later," she murmured, hating her weakness. Now that she was here, that weakness just wanted to invade her body. She hated relying on anyone. For years she'd stood on her own two feet, and now she felt like she had none to stand on.

"Come. Sit down." He led her to the spare chair in his office; at least, she presumed that it was his space. He disappeared. "I'm just getting you a hot drink," he called back.

"Fine." She opened her laptop and turned it on. By the time he returned with two cups of steaming liquid, she had the laptop up and running. He placed a hot cup down beside her.

"So I spoke with Daniel, and they are doing a door-to-door search, looking for Janelle and Pete. He'll talk to Mack and show him Pete's picture. As his uncle, he should be able to identify him." He paused. "Let's find that much out for sure."

Meg just nodded. The theories had been coming in fast, but they were still just theories. They needed facts. And that was something she might have. "You sent me some photos."

"Is that why you came running down here? You could have stayed home. I'd have stopped off at the end of the shift and brought you up-to-date anyway."

"Yeah, well, I can't just stand around waiting for news, so I went to work." She turned the laptop around, the first picture loaded up for him to see. "Remember this photo?"

He pulled his chair around the corner of his desk beside her and sat down. He studied the picture and nodded. "Sure, it's one of the case files I pulled. Why? Do you recognize her?"

"Yes. And you should too."

His gaze flew up to lock on hers. "Why?" He studied the picture again. "And I don't."

"You went to school with her. So did I."

"No way."

He strode to his computer and tapped lightly on his keyboard. "I'm bringing up her file."

"Do that. Her name is Brenda Durnet. I was in her English class."

"How can you remember anyone from school?" He shook his head. "I certainly can't."

"Think nerd. Chess club, student leadership, et cetera. And the reason I remember her is my brother was sweet on her for a while."

Chad raised a brow. "And so someone else we know is missing. That's sad again."

"Yes, but it's also good. She's one of the girls we just found."

That relaxed gaze locked down and hardened instantly. "What?"

"See the teeth pattern?" Meg stared down at the smile and the very crooked teeth on the bottom jaw. "That is damn-near identical to the last skull we found."

Chad stared so hard at Meg that she could almost hear the spinning of his brain cells, as he processed the information and the implications.

"Do you have her dental records on file?" she asked.

He checked the file. "Yes. They were added in. And they are digital." He frowned. "We're lucky there. With lots of these old files, we'd be digging around in the storage units for something like that otherwise."

"Send the X-rays to Stacy and ask her to match it. She'll know which one."

With a nod, he tapped on the keys.

She waited, staring down at her old school friend. They

hadn't been close, but they'd been friendly. Brenda was the type to be friendly to everyone all the time. Well, someone hadn't been so friendly back to her.

"Done."

And her breath whooshed out, surprising her. She hadn't realized she'd been holding it in. "Good. That's one."

"You're that certain."

"Yes. The teeth caught my interest. I spent quite a bit of time studying that jaw bone."

"Okay, what about the others?"

"I honestly haven't looked. I came here instead."

"Good. Have a drink of that hot chocolate. It will make you feel better." He rolled his chair closer. "Now, let's go over these other photos together, and maybe we'll get lucky with another one."

Meg would have nodded, but she was busy sipping greedily away at her hot chocolate. It had been years since she'd had any. It wasn't great as far as hot chocolate went, but, for the shocks she'd been dealt lately, it was warm and soothing. When the cup was half empty, she replaced it on the desk and turned her attention to the photos.

She brought up the second one. Both studied the blonde, and Meg said, "I don't remember ever seeing her. And there's nothing distinctive about her that's catching my eye."

"Next."

They went through several more, when one photo jarred Meg out of her comfort zone—yet again.

She tapped the screen with a long nail. "I know her."

"You do?" Chad leaned closer to study the pretty young woman. She must have been in her early twenties. I've never seen her." He got up and went to his computer. "Her name is …"

"Cynthia. She was my old neighbor. Moved away, … oh, maybe nine, ten years ago."

"Was last seen leaving her condo just over ten years ago. She never showed up for work on Monday morning. No one knows her whereabouts from that Friday after work through the weekend." He studied Meg's face. "How do you know her?"

"She lived in the condo beside us. Well, I hadn't moved in yet, as I was still dating Pete, but I'd met her a couple times, coming and going. She seemed really nice. She moved out a couple months after I moved in."

When he didn't say anything, she looked up. At the look in his eyes, she was filled with dread. "What are you thinking?"

He pursed his lips. "I'm thinking it all comes back to the same person—you, and, therefore, maybe … Pete."

MACK SAW DANIEL before he saw him.

"There you are." Daniel called to Mack. "I've been looking all over for you. We've got a problem, and I need your help."

"What's up?" Mack might not be at his best—in fact, he was still pissed—but Daniel was good people, and, if he said there was a problem, then there was a problem.

"Missing child and the guy who might have taken her was helping us at the crime scene and has a cabin on the lake."

"Shit." Mack's stomach knotted. "Explain."

Daniel launched into the explanation he'd been given. "That's all Chad had. He's hoping we can go door-to-door and find either or both. Or at least confirm that Pete was here all day and couldn't have made it to Seattle and back again."

"Sounds as if Meg just had a tiff with him. It's probably nothing."

"Oh, I don't think so. According to Chad the two of them split this last weekend, and Meg and her niece moved out. You know how that goes. I say, we find this Pete and find out for sure." Daniel hesitated, and then launched into the rest of Chad's message. "Chad says there's some confusion about whether this Pete could be your nephew Pero."

Mack's face froze, and his gaze turned glacial.

Damn. Daniel tried to bring up Pete's picture. "It's not showing up very well." He held it out for Mack to see.

His gut twisted. Mack stared at the piss-poor image. "Who can say anything about *that* picture? It's so damn small. Besides, I haven't seen my nephew in years—a lot of years at that."

"Yeah, it's hard to see anything."

The expression on his old friend's face never changed. Daniel took a deep breath and forged on. "Chad also said you might know which cabin is his."

Daniel had turned to look at the cabins that Chad had mentioned.

Clearing his voice, Mack said, "Yeah, Pero's cabin is that old one over there."

"Good. Let's go. That little girl is quite a looker. Sure hate to see anything happen to her." He brought up the photo from his email. "Look at her."

Mack glanced down and was surprised to see a beautiful child staring out at him. "That's Meg's niece? Never would have thought it. No family resemblance there."

"No, apparently she takes after her mother, who died quite a few years back. Then her father was killed in a car accident, and she moved in with Meg and Pete."

"Maybe Pete just wanted to spend some time with her, explain that the relationship has changed and that they'd still be seeing each other." Daniel glanced at him, not commenting on the Pero/Pete issue thankfully.

"Maybe, but you and I both know a lot of other reasons for some guy to be picking up a beauty like this. And most of those beauties aren't quite so pretty by the time these assholes are done with them."

"Let's hope this is all a false alarm." But, inside his gut, Mack had a pretty good idea that things were not quite as innocent as he'd like them to be.

"I've already called a Jim Sutton." Daniel added, "He's the guy who hired Pete for the chainsaw work. Said Pete's well-known in the area for lending a hand. He hasn't seen him all day; thought he'd headed into town this morning."

Mack nodded, feeling a push of inevitability. Damn. Some things fate just insisted on controlling. "Let's go see if he's home."

Chapter 22

MEG WAS TIRED by the time they got through all the files that Chad had found. And underneath all the activity was an insidious fear, as she waited for news about Janelle.

Every time the phone rang, her heart jumped, and her stomach wanted to heave. She wanted to go to the cabin and find Pete. She'd texted him several times and had tried calling, but he never answered. She wanted to ask him herself.

To pass the time constructively, she had Brenda's file open in front of her. And Cynthia Wood's sat beside her. Both women had gone missing abruptly—just as if they dropped off the face of the earth. Neither had had a steady boyfriend; one friend thought Brenda had one, but, if she did, Brenda hadn't shared any details about him.

As for Pete's old neighbor, Cynthia, she'd dumped her boyfriend months before. The police had looked at him closely but ended up taking him off the suspect list.

Meg had little to go on with Cynthia's case. With Brenda, X-rays showed she had broken her left femur as a child and had two cracked ribs from a fall off a horse as a teenager. Those breaks would be fundamental to her identification, and all the information was immediately dispatched to Stacy, as she would find out if one of the skeletons had similar injuries. Meg hoped so.

Seven women were in the morgue, one most likely Cia, and Meg had thirteen missing persons case files, counting Cia. So many families would be watching and waiting by the phone, hoping for news of their loved ones. Six families would be disappointed, unless the police could find another dump site. But how many women would one man kill?

She flipped through the thirteen cases; the two women she had recognized were brunettes, like Cia and Meg herself. They were both young, like Cia, although Pete's neighbor was a couple years older. Of the other women, only four were similar. Two of the women she discarded from the group were overweight and didn't fit the pattern. One was quite a bit older, and another was into a lifestyle that was rough and also didn't fit the pattern. No, as she studied the women, she realized she'd picked out her particular six to match the bones in the morgue. And she could only hope that Cia matched the first set.

"We haven't discussed one other issue."

Meg checked the time on her cell phone for the zillionth time in the last hour. "And what's that?"

"The necklaces."

"They found four, yet six victims—not counting Cia and her necklace. Maybe we missed a couple, or they could still show up."

Chad added, "You're thinking that the killer had a half dozen or more made up and made his victims wear them?"

"Yeah, that's the most disgusting thing I could imagine, considering they have my name on them." Meg hated to think someone had so much anger toward her that these women had paid the price for it.

"It's unlikely that we'll track down whoever bought the

necklaces, but I'm hoping the person who did the inscriptions might still be around."

"Jorgensen's Jewelers." The name just blew out of her mouth. "That's where Josh bought mine."

"Excellent. Let's see if they are still around."

"They are." She smiled. "We walked in there a few years back. Pete bought me some earrings for my birthday."

Chad was already on the computer. "Found them." He picked up the phone. "I wonder if they still do inscriptions." He checked the time. "They closed down a few years ago. Damn."

"Doesn't that figure." She swallowed. "Your teammates haven't checked in yet."

Just then his phone rang. "Oh, good. It's Daniel."

"DANIEL, WHAT DID you find?" Chad asked.

"Nothing as yet. Mack can't tell from the picture if that's Pero—says he hasn't seen him in forever. But we went to Pete's cabin, which was empty, and Mack says it's Pero's cabin. He inherited it when his brother died. Mack searched inside, but no sign of Pete or the girl." He added, "A door-to-door search is underway, and we've got a couple people looking to track down Pete. Everyone we've spoken to says that he's been here all day."

"But you haven't been able to confirm it?"

"No. No one can say when they saw him or where. I'll give you a call in a bit."

"Thanks." Chad hung up and turned to face Meg. The crestfallen look on her face tugged at him, as he watched her clench her fists.

"They haven't found her, have they?"

He watched her lower lip tremble, then firm, as he answered, "No. Daniel has spoken to a couple people who believe they've seen Pete today at the lake but can't say when or where for sure." He took a deep breath. "Pete's cabin is the same cabin as Mack's brother left to his nephew, Pero."

She stood still, a frown wrinkling her forehead. "Really?" At his nod, she shrugged. "So maybe he is Pero."

And that was it. Chad stood. "It's a waiting game now. Yet we also need to keep up our strength. Do you want to go out and grab some food or shall I order pizza in?"

"Pizza," she said so quickly that he raised a brow.

"I don't want to leave," she said. "Just in case …"

He nodded. "I'll go put in an order. Back in a moment."

She nodded. "I want to see where these women were living at their last-known residences."

SHE WALKED OVER to the map of the state of Washington on the wall and found a map of Seattle nearby on the table. Grabbing a few pins, she posted the second map up on the wall beside the first. Then, using the files, she placed a blue pin where Brenda had lived, then a second one for where Cynthia had lived. Approximately thirty condos were at that address. That alone offered many potential suspects. Walking back to the files, Meg picked up her next four choices for the remains she'd found and took a different-colored pin and placed one at each last-known residence. She also took a red pin and placed it at Cia's address.

Then she stepped back. The cluster was close together—except for one. Cia's.

What did that mean?

Shaking her head, she retrieved the pages on the other

seven girls from the missing persons' case files Chad had found, and, choosing white pins for them, marked their residences as well.

She'd just finished, when Chad walked back in. From the look on his face, he didn't have any good news.

"No pizza?" she asked lightly. "It took you long enough."

He managed a smile. "Sorry, it will take twenty minutes."

"Ah." She placed the last pin and stepped back several feet to study the change.

"What have you found?" He stood beside her. "Is there a meaning to the colors?"

"White are those missing women I have no idea about." And, true enough, if there was a pattern to the white pins' locations, she couldn't see it. "The red pin is for Cia. Blue is for the two women I'm fairly sure of. The yellow pins are for the four women that I picked out from the files you gave me, as potential matches for the other four sets of remains."

She turned to glance at him, noting the surprise on his face. "What? You told me to do what I do best."

"And apparently you did." He pointed out the blue and yellow pins with one white pin. "These are very close together."

"Yes, but this map isn't the best. One of just this neighborhood would help us take a closer look." She motioned to the white pins that were sprawled across the city. "These can't be ruled out, but they aren't so likely."

"Interesting that you picked four yellows and three are in close proximity to the right area, and this one isn't. You're almost eerily accurate. How the hell do you do it?" Chad's phone rang. "Hi, Stacy. I thought you were long gone for the day."

"No, working late, it's almost the norm these days. Tell Meg that she is right about Brenda Durnet. That's a positive ID on our first one."

Chad turned to Meg. "Stacy says that's a yes on Brenda."

"Oh, Stacy is still working?" She held out her hand for Chad's phone. "Hey, Stacy, that's great. I have another one for you. Cynthia Wood." Meg looked at Chad. "We sent the information a while ago and …" She walked back over to the stack of four, removed the one located out of the hot spot, and read off the names of the other three missing women.

"Wow, that's fast," Stacy said. "Let's see what we have to make the ID with. We may need a family member's DNA."

"Hopefully it won't be necessary, if we can grab dental records."

"I'm on it," Chad said from behind her.

Meg turned and realized she'd walked to the end of the room to stand in front of the map again.

"Good," Stacy replied. "I think we might have dental records for one of these. I remember her case. Her parents come in regularly, bringing bits and pieces. We've called them once over a potential match, but it didn't turn out to be their daughter. I'll have to check." Stacy hung up without saying goodbye.

Meg laughed, as she handed the phone back to Chad. "She's as bad as I am."

"Yes, she is. And that's a good thing." He was busy clicking away on his keyboard.

Meg assumed he was helping Stacy on the case material.

"Interesting."

"What?"

"Just a second." He wrote something down on a scratch

pad, then clicked again, then wrote something else. She waited, staring at the pins. So many victims and these were just the brunettes. So sad.

"Okay. Here we go." He got up and walked around his desk, with a notepad in hand. "Here is everyone's home address from the camping trip." He stopped opened a drawer and pulled out black pins. "Let's add this to the grid and see what we have."

Chad put in his, then Josh's and Bruce's addresses. Meg grabbed two more and put them on Stephanie's address, then Cia's.

They all went to the same school, so it made sense that they would be living close together. On the map, the pins made a strong visual effect. Once Chad had finished with the last ones, he stepped back and handed her a pin. "Now put in your old home."

With an inner tension radiating through her, and yet another glance at the clock, hoping for some news on Janelle, she took a black pin, found her old family home, and pinned it.

Hers was right in the middle of the cluster. She stared at it, wondering what it meant.

Then he defined it. "It all centers on you."

MEG STARED BLINDLY out of the window. Chad's office overlooked the parking lot. Rain filled the sky, while tears filled her heart. *It all centers on you.*

These were hard words to hear and to bear. The necklaces had already said she was involved in a big way, but seeing it visually on the map …

She couldn't get the image of her home in the middle of

the dots. She spun around, and picked up another black pin and placed it at the second place she'd lived at, then placed a third at Pete's condo, where she'd been living over the last decade.

If anything, that put her even more in the center. She hadn't realized how close to home she'd stayed. As she looked at it, how close to Cia. She'd instinctively stayed close to the problem and, it seemed, may have subconsciously chosen a boyfriend from the same group. If Pete was Pero, that is.

Would Pete have remembered her? She hadn't changed much—at least she hadn't been through a severe car accident. But, as she hadn't known him back then, it followed that he hadn't known her either, surely …

So they were two strangers who had a past connection which neither had remembered.

That theory worked for her but maybe only because she wanted it to work.

The worry, the tension coiling tighter inside, left her wanting to pace the room—or to hit something. For the first time in years she felt the need to run, to run as hard and as fast as she could and to wear out this pulsing fear.

"Are you okay?"

She spun around to face him and opened her mouth to blast him, when a voice at the doorway said, "Chad, the pizza is here."

She closed her eyes and waited for the voice of reason to cool down her temper enough to speak calmly. Chad walked past her, and a strong warm hand landed on her shoulder for a gentle squeeze.

She focused on her deep breathing, trying to regain control. Then the aroma of pepperoni pizza filled the air, and tears filled her eyes. God, he'd remembered. She hated all pizza but one, ... pepperoni.

And just like that, memories once again flooded her psyche. Evenings spent sitting on his parents' deck, cuddling, while watching the rain, pizza and popcorn beside them. Early morning after a night of heavy lovemaking, swimming in the early dawn, their bodies still heated from their passion so recently spent.

God, *those* had been the days.

She wanted them back.

That sense of freedom, of knowing you owned the world and your life would go the way you had planned it. The rash arrogance of believing the world was theirs to do with as they wished.

How wrong could she have been? She bowed her head. She wanted to feel young again, to feel loved, and to feel vibrant and full of life again. She had to think about all the years with Pete. Why had he stayed with her? Sure, they'd been good together, comfortable together, like a well-worn pair of shoes. You hated to get rid of them because you knew how hard it was to break in a new pair, even though you knew the old pair were bad for you. In the same way, she had stayed with Pete—he just wasn't bad enough to get rid of ... yet.

And how sad was that?

Her relationship with Pete had slipped into the *old shoe* category, comfy but just not exciting. It had taken her brother's death to make the changes she'd been unwilling to make before.

She bowed her head. *Janelle*. Dear God, please let her be safe.

CHAD SET DOWN the hot pizza on an open spot on his desk. He went to say something lighthearted to help her get over this, when he saw her shoulders shake. Damn.

He walked up behind her, making sure she'd heard him, wrapped his arms around her shoulders, and tugged her backward against his chest to squeeze her gently. "Easy, sweetheart."

She caught back a sob, but her shoulders continued to shake.

"*Shush*. Easy." Chad turned her around gently and wrapped her into a gentle hug. She snuggled in closer and burrowed her face against his chest and bawled.

He held her close and waited out the storm, loving the feel of her in his arms again. Yet her inherent strength had taken on a new fragility that scared him. She'd had so many shocks. She had held it all together, almost in a cold way. Several of the guys had made comments about her demeanor. But Chad knew the real reason for the coolness. Control. Meg was all about control because so much of her life had gone out of control and had stayed that way.

He rubbed her back gently, easing the tension from her spine. But no one could keep this much emotion locked down for so long. This release was good for her and for him. He rested his head on her cheek and held her close. A part of him wanted this moment to never end, and another wanted it to stop immediately, so that she wouldn't be in pain anymore.

Finally her tears stopped flowing, and her sobs quieted to the occasional hiccough.

"Feeling better?"

She leaned back slightly and gave him a watery smile. "Yes, thank you. And I'm slightly embarrassed."

Reluctantly he let her step back. He brushed her hair off her face, then leaned in and kissed her on the forehead. "Don't be. You had to release this tension. You've been under horrible pressure for days."

"Make that weeks, months even." She stepped back, wiping her eyes gently. "Ever since my brother's death."

"And today has just finished it."

She sniffled, tears welling up again at the reminder. She took a big gasping breath and asked, "Any news?"

He shook his head. "Not yet. But we will find her."

To take her mind off her missing niece, he said, "Let's eat, while we have a moment. When the calls start coming in, it'll become bedlam."

Her eyes brightened at the thought of calls coming in with news. She walked over to the pizza box and opened it and smiled. "How could you remember?" She picked up the biggest slice and took a bite.

"How could I forget? Or forget that you always took the biggest piece?"

She laughed. "That's because I eat so little. It's slightly fairer this way."

"Yep, the same twisted logic as the old Megs."

That brought real humor and wonderful memories to her mind. "Oh, I do remember those many arguments."

"Good. I hope you remember the many great times of making up as well." He smiled, pouring as much heat into his gaze as he could. She *had* to remember. They'd been thunder and lightning together, different, unique, but perfect—a matched set. As they should always be.

She lifted her gaze and caught his. Her eyes widened, and she almost gasped. Pink flushed across her cheeks, and he'd never seen anything more charming or sexy. God, how he wanted her, yet this was so not the time or the place. Yet he wanted it to be. He wanted to tear off her clothes and take her on his desk, like he'd done once in his home so long ago.

He swallowed. Then he swallowed again. He clenched his fists.

She took a step closer, her pizza forgotten in her hand. She swayed toward him.

"Damn," he whispered hoarsely. "I really suck at timing."

Her lips tilted. "You never used to have a problem in that area before."

He closed his eyes, willing them to another world, where he could take her in his arms and remind her of what they'd had. What they could have again.

When he opened his eyes again, she stood before him, with a warm, loving smile on her lips. "As we can't feed one appetite, then I suggest we feed another one." With a smirk, she popped the pizza to his lips.

"Definitely not the same thing," he mumbled, his mouth full of hot deliciousness.

"Later," she said, with a sexy twinkle in her eyes. "Much later …"

And his heart swelled at her words. "Is that a promise?"

She laughed and shoved the pizza into his mouth. "We'll take it slowly and see."

"Not too slow," he mumbled around his mouthful, then swallowed. "You've got until the weekend."

Chapter 23

MEG GASPED IN shocked laughter. How typical of Chad. "I don't think so. That is so *not* going slow."

"Get used to it. I've given you fair warning." He eyed her pizza slice.

She leaned in to search his gaze but moved her pizza farther out of his reach. "You're not serious?"

He grinned, walked to the desk to snag a piece of pizza of his own. "I am so serious." He took a big bite. "We have a lot of time to make up for."

She gazed at him, her heart racing in shock and excitement. Chad had always been like this. Taking charge, been commanding, and then so very caring.

"That gives us this week to wrap up our history and get started on our future."

And then his phone rang.

She raced over, excitement and fear rippling through her. *Please let it be good news.*

Chad answered, his gaze zeroing in on Meg's face, all the fun dropping from his expression. "What? Really? Yes. Thank you. We'll be there in"—he checked his cell phone for the time—"twenty minutes." He disconnected but held up a hand to stop her.

"What? What is it?" Inside her stomach was jumping in panic. "Please."

"It's not Janelle."

Her stomach bottomed out like a cement pillar in the ocean. "Then what is it?"

"It's Stephanie. She's in Emergency."

"Oh God."

"They're working on her right now. They said we could see her in twenty minutes or so."

"Good. Let's eat first and then go."

THE HOSPITAL SCREAMED chaos as they entered. Meg stood at the front entranceway, hating having to even enter. Dozens of people had to be in there. Chad tugged her close, wrapping an arm around her shoulders. "There's been a major pileup on the highway." He motioned through the crowd. "Let's go this way."

She followed blindly, hating the smell of fear and sorrow, panic and pain. God, one never forgot it. Her brother's accident had paralyzed her, and, in a small way, she'd blamed the hospital. It had been so difficult to deal with the shock of his death, the harried nurses, the forms to fill out. Where was the person to hold her and to tell her it would be all okay?

Oh, wait, that had been her job for Janelle, who had been at school. Meg had tried to get her to the hospital in time for her to say goodbye to her father. They hadn't made it.

If only they'd been called just that little bit earlier, if only the traffic had been just a little bit lighter, … only God hadn't been so generous that night.

Chad reached a hand back and grabbed hers, tugging her up behind him. "She's up here." He led her to a long hallway that was almost graveyard quiet in comparison to the waiting room they'd just passed through.

Meg could walk beside him now.

"Has she woken up?" Meg asked.

"She hadn't when I called before leaving. She has been stabilized though."

"Good. I'd hate to see her finally succeed in killing herself, now that we're close to solving this hell."

He stopped at a large room with double doors. He peered into the window. "She's in here."

Meg looked in and saw rows of beds on either side of the room, green curtains partially concealing the occupants. Yeah, it was a typical hospital ward. He pushed open the door and walked to the right bed. Stephanie lay quiet, asleep. Her breathing was calm and stable. A man sat beside the bedside. A man she didn't recognize.

"She's so pale," Chad said.

Meg's attention was drawn to Stephanie. She walked closer.

"But she's alive," said the other man.

That voice. Meg lifted her head to study Stephanie's visitor. Then she recognized him. "Bruce?"

He stared at her blankly, and then a smile broke across his worried features. "Megan? Megs?"

She smiled. "It's Meg these days." She studied his features. He'd been such a fun-loving guy back then. He and Stephanie had had big plans. Then, they all had.

Chad smacked Bruce on the shoulder. "Everyone's been trying to reach you. Where the hell have you been?"

Bruce snorted. "Trying to save Stephanie."

Meg turned her attention back to her old friend, prone on the bed. In fact, she looked as white as the sheets around her. And her neck looked uncomfortably swollen. Tubes ran in and out of her arms, and that stillness to her had Meg wondering if she wasn't still standing with one foot in her grave.

"She won't wake up tonight," Bruce said.

"What happened?"

"God only knows. She was supposed to meet me for coffee, but she called it off. Said she was going to meet someone else. I was pissed. Then I got a text from her—all garbled and making no sense. Something about being scared." He sighed. "I'd followed her to see who she was meeting. Only she drove into a parking lot and sat there and waited for a long time, then took off. She drove downtown, parked, and started walking. I followed. Then she went really freaky and ran away."

"Jesus," Chad said. "Any idea who she'd planned to meet?"

Bruce shook his head. "After she ran away, I spent hours trying to find her. When I did, this is the shape she was in."

"She found her dealer then, I guess," Chad said, staring down at Stephanie.

"I don't know that she did. I asked her to stop doing this to herself, and she said she didn't do it." He frowned down at the silent woman. "Then she passed out. She hasn't been awake since."

"What?" Chad exclaimed. "She didn't do this to herself?"

Bruce stared at him. "No. She didn't."

"Then who the hell did?"

A SHORT WHILE later, back out in the parking lot, Chad wrapped an arm around Meg's shoulders, wanting to tuck her in his damn pocket and keep her safe, but that was so not possible.

"No news on Janelle?" Meg asked in a subdued tone.

He winced, pulled out his phone to check, even though he'd just checked a few moments ago. "No. Not yet."

The barest of shivers rippled down her back.

"Are you cold?" he asked.

"No. Scared. Bordering on panicked. I want her back, safe and sound."

"If Pete has taken her, do you think he'd hurt her?"

She lowered her head, her hair hiding her expression. Speaking slowly, thoughtfully, she said, "I wouldn't think so. But the Pete I know is not the killer we are hunting. If they are the same person, then obviously the answer is"—she took a deep breath—"yes."

On cue, Chad's phone rang.

Meg stiffened, she turned to face him, hope … and fear warring across her face.

MEG DIDN'T DARE breathe. Please. Please. *Please, let this be good news.*

Chad said, "Really? Where?"

He glanced at his watch. "We can be there in just under an hour and a half." His gaze locked on Meg's, a question in his eyes.

"Yes," she said. "Have they found Janelle?"

He shook his head. "Just Pete's truck. And it's been hidden away."

"Wait." Her heart plummeted. "What if he doesn't have her? We can't leave here and find out someone else has taken her."

Chad hung up. "Do you want to stay here then?"

"No!" She closed her eyes and took a deep breath. "I just wish it wasn't so far away."

"Everyone is out looking for her, but, if there is any chance that Pete has taken her, we need to find him. His truck was found in the bush, a few miles from the campsite."

She gasped; her skin flushed with an iciness she knew wouldn't leave, not until she had Janelle back in her arms.

"What?" He grabbed her shoulders. "Do you know of another place he'd have stashed her?"

"Not really," she whispered, her mind racing. "He hunts and has spoken of having blinds at various places." She shook her head. "But why would he be a few miles into the bush?" Shudders racked her body. "I can't stop thinking about the dump site."

"Think about this logically." He stared at the sky for a long moment and then glanced back at her. "Whoever took her was someone she knew well enough to leave with. That someone must have known where she was at the time, and, even more important, … that particular someone must have known they could sign her out of school and not raise any suspicions in doing so." His gaze, caring and somber, rested on her. "What does your gut say?"

At his words, her gut clenched so tightly, she was left gasping. "When you put it that way …" God, what a betrayal. Still, she had to get the word out. "*Pete.*"

"Exactly."

Chapter 24

THEY MADE IT faster than they had expected, with Chad stretching the speed limit to get there quickly. But, for Meg, sitting in the passenger seat, her knuckles gripped white, it wasn't fast enough.

According to Daniel, the vehicle had been parked, not run off the road. It didn't appear to be damaged in any way. Apparently the owner of the truck stop café knew of a couple of Pete's spots and had driven around to check. He'd been trying to prove that Pete hadn't done anything wrong.

The same owner had also said he'd never seen a kid in Pete's care.

Then Janelle hadn't been with Pete all that long, and, according to Meg, he'd never been alone with her. And he'd never taken her on a trip out of town. And, if he had her now, she could have been unconscious and hidden, where no one could have seen her.

Not that Chad would mention any of those suggestions.

Meg sat motionless beside him. Too quiet. He knew what thoughts were running through her head. He couldn't imagine the feelings, but he'd been with victims' families enough to know this would be one of the most horrible scenarios he could imagine.

He wanted to say something comforting but couldn't think of anything to say.

So he said nothing.

His phone rang again. He had it in his holder on the dash. He pushed the Talk button. "Hello."

"Chad, Daniel again." Daniel took a deep breath. "We're not sure from when, but there is a child's sweater in the back of the truck."

Meg gasped; she stared at Chad, her eyes huge.

"What color?" he asked.

"It's a deep purple, with a turquoise trim on the sleeves."

Meg nodded, her eyes closed. "That's Janelle's."

Chad hated this, but he needed to ask. "Meg, Janelle was at the cabin on the weekend. Did you drive up in Pete's truck?"

"Yes."

"Did Janelle have that sweater with her at that time?"

Her eyes widened in understanding. "Oh, I'm not sure."

"We need you to be sure." He cast another glance in her direction. "Think. She must have had some kind of warm clothing with her?"

"Sure. We all did. The mornings are brutal, and there is no central heat in his place. It's on his To Do list."

"And was that sweater one of those items she'd have taken?"

Meg sat back and took a deep breath. "Give me a moment. I'll go through it in my mind."

Chad said, "Daniel, I'll call you back."

"Good enough."

The silence was long and thick, as Chad waited for Meg to go through the events in her mind.

"I can't place it that weekend," she whispered. "I can't focus. I'm so scared."

"I know you are, honey. Stay focused. Did she have that

sweater on this morning?"

She turned to look at him. "I don't know. She was at the sleepover."

"Then call the mother and ask." He waited patiently, as Meg dialed her niece's friend's house and asked.

"Right. I know Linette loved the color of that sweater. Purple is always a hit, isn't it? Thanks, I'll pass this on to the police." She hung up the phone. "According to Deirdre, Janelle had the sweater in her backpack. She wasn't wearing it this morning, but it was in her bag, when she walked out the door." She leaned back and closed her eyes. "And therefore—"

"If it had been left in the truck from last weekend at the cabin, she couldn't have had it with her this morning." He added, his voice grim, "Now we have something concrete to go by. And Pete has just moved up the suspect list."

MEG NEVER SAID another word, as they raced toward Pete's truck. Her mind flit from shock to shock, and she couldn't bring the churning washing machine of emotions back under control. She could barely breathe. But passing out in Chad's truck was not an option.

She sensed his glances coming her way, and she knew he was worried. But, if Janelle were hurt—or worse, dead— nothing he could do about it, for her or for Janelle. And Meg was likely to get up and run—a long, long way away.

She didn't dare think about Janelle being hurt. She'd been picked up at 2:30 p.m. Pete had had her for over four hours.

Her mind refused to think about all the things a man could do to a child in that time period. Meg had to try and stay focused.

She had to be strong for Janelle's sake.

That little girl needed her. Now more than ever.

They turned one last corner, barely noticing the GPS on Chad's truck flashing the final destination. Dozens of vehicles had pulled up behind Pete's vehicle, and, sure enough, it was his truck. She would have recognized it anywhere.

"Will you be okay?" Chad asked, as he pulled up behind the cop car on the shoulder and turned off the engine.

"Find her. Kill him. Then I'll be okay," she snarled and bolted from the truck.

"Hey, wait up." With Chad racing behind, Meg dashed toward the truck and the group of men standing there.

Snagging her arm, Chad snapped, "Meg, easy."

She froze in place and realized she'd almost blundered ahead and compromised the scene. That scared her more than anything. She had to be smart. As smart as, even smarter than, Pete.

Chad gripped her shoulder, and whispered, "If you are not in control, you will have to leave. This isn't me saying this. It's the men here handling the case, who will order you to be taken back to the station."

She took a deep breath, froze all her emotions, like she'd learned to do a long time ago, and nodded. "Got it." She walked forward carefully, aware they'd attracted the group's attention. "And thanks."

She should have brought gloves. As if reading her mind, Chad handed her a pair from a box sitting on the ground. Blue gloves. She smiled at the color. She'd used similar ones on her last job. Just the reminder of her own professional history helped steady her. She could do this. *She could do this.* "Anything useful inside?" she asked casually.

The first man motioned to the sweater displayed on a rock. "That."

Chad spoke from behind her. "What do you have so far?"

"The suspect has been hunting in those woods for a lot of years. Apparently he has favorite spots. We're assuming he has the little girl with him. To that end, we have two dog teams coming in."

"Dogs are good," Chad said. "I presume his cabin has been thoroughly checked."

"Yes, it has."

That voice sounded familiar. She turned to face it. *Mack.* She nodded. "Good. And search parties?" She opened the truck door, stood up on the running board, and peered inside.

"We know what we're doing. Too bad you're forced back here. It's not exactly your favorite place."

She froze. Then, very slowly, she turned to look back at the man who'd terrified her so long ago. Her voice biting, she said, "No, it's not. But it is yours, I believe."

His face turned a ruddy red. A second man at his side tugged Mack out of the way.

"Easy tiger," murmured Chad, stationing himself beside her protectively.

The second man spoke up. "Hey, Chad."

"Daniel."

Meg assessed the man who'd called Chad on the phone about the sweater. She gave him a five-second assessment and realized he was a different type of fish than Mack.

His gaze was steady and clear, with intelligence gleaming through its depths.

"Is it hers?" he asked her.

Meg nodded. "Yes, it is."

"You didn't even examine it, so how could you know?" he asked gently.

"I sewed the turquoise trim on it," she said quietly, staring directly at Daniel. She needed someone besides Chad on her team. She had no idea how far Mack's influence had spread.

As proof went, it was hard to beat. Daniel studied her, his eyes narrowed, his gaze intent. Then he nodded, and Meg knew she'd passed some kind of test.

She turned back to peruse the inside of Pete's truck. It looked the same as last time, except for a take-out bag from the café. She handed them off to Chad. "Did anyone see Janelle in the truck when he bought this?"

"I'll ask." Chad took the bag from her. "The techs will be here in a few minutes."

She nodded. "I know, but we have no time to waste. I just can't see him forcing Janelle out in the woods here."

The men were silent, no one wanting to voice the other options. She sighed. "Most likely he has convinced her another cabin was through here, or either she was unconscious or ..." She set her lips together, refusing to say the last option.

"Do we know what's on the other side of these trees?" Chad asked.

"The lake, ... *duh*." It was Mack again.

As Meg was about to blister him, she caught sight of Chad's face. Right. Let him deal with the asshole. She turned and ignored the harsh words. Daniel's voice rose in the melee, but she was more concerned about the small notebook on the footwall of the passenger side.

Leaning forward, she plucked it up and pulled it open. It was Janelle's. She used it to keep track of her homework, a necessary step for the less-than-stellar student. She made it to the last page and read Janelle's note. *Leaving early. Yay! Pete is picking me up. Boo. We're meeting Meg. Yay! We're going to the cabin again. Boo! I get to miss school. Double yay!*

Silently she held out the book to Chad, so thankful she'd ended up coming. Janelle was here somewhere. "That answers that question."

He took it from her, read it, then read it aloud for the others to hear. "So we know he picked her up from school and brought her out here. From the sweater, we know she got into his truck. The question is, where has he taken her and why?"

"There are lots of places on the lake." This came from a man in the back. "Too many options."

Meg spoke to him. "Do you know other places on the lake where Pete might be hanging out? Maybe other cabins owned by relatives? Or friends?"

"Pete's a bit of a loner, but he often goes fishing with some of the locals. Their cabins aren't too far from here."

"Is there a path through here at all?" Chad asked. "Any reason for him to have parked here?"

"Pete likes to hunt wild mushrooms. He's got spots all over the place," said the same man at the back of the group.

Chad looked at Meg for confirmation.

She felt like an idiot, but she shook her head. She hadn't known. She also didn't think he'd ever eaten any he'd picked. "Does anyone know if it's mushroom season?" she asked. "And, if so, what kind of mushrooms?"

There was a scramble, as men pulled out phones and moved slightly away to hear.

Daniel walked closer. "We've already followed this direction to the lake, and we didn't see or hear anything."

Meg stared at the woods in front of her. "How far is it to the lake?"

"A few hundred yards, maybe a bit more."

She nodded. "How about a fishing dock?"

"One. It looks like there used to be a cabin a long time ago, with the dock still there, but it's rickety."

"Pete has a boat up at his cabin."

Daniel shook his head. "No boat when we were there." He turned and talked to someone beside him. "Bill is taking another run up to the cabin to double-check."

"Not alone," Chad said. "If Pete's gone there from here, he's looking for privacy. Doesn't want anyone to know that he's there or that he has a passenger." Chad studied the trees. "The truck is pulled far enough off the road for a purpose."

"And that's about the only reason to do it this way." Daniel studied the truck. "So no one would know."

Meg did another quick search inside the truck and came up empty. "I can't see anything else here."

"Good. The techs had just arrived. They'll do a once-over, then tow it back to town."

She nodded and jumped down. Walking around the front of the truck, she studied the trees and the ground, searching for the pathway. The dogs should have been out here already. Yet she knew that, if they didn't live in the vicinity, it could take precious time.

Time Janelle didn't have. Would Pete keep her at the cabin? No one knew about him. But he was always planning ahead, always thinking down the road. She couldn't help but think he'd have a secondary place to take Janelle.

Another cabin? He'd been ecstatic when he got this one.

He wasn't flush. He did well doing construction work, but it wasn't making him rich, and these cabins weren't cheap. So then what? He could build what he wanted. He had the know-how and the strength. However, he couldn't be obvious about it.

"Has he done any repairs on cabins around here? Is he known to help his neighbors out at all?" She turned to ask Daniel. "And, no, I don't know. The first time I was here with him at his cabin was this last weekend."

Daniel nodded. "He's been known to help others. Several neighbors have commented on that. He helped put a roof on one house and separated a basement into a suite. That type of thing."

"What about building a safe space in someone's cabin?" she asked calmly, thinking of all the empty summer homes. Who'd know?

"And how could he do that? The owners are obviously going to notice." Daniel snorted. "Not to mention having a girl screaming in their basement."

"Unless they don't live there," Chad said quietly. "And Pete might know some of the absentee owners. He might have done some work on their places."

"Pero did and more." Mack stepped forward, his ruddy face working furiously. "He's a caretaker for one of the Williamsons. Jackie Williamson is out of Germany. He owns the summer place at the far end. I'd heard a long time ago that Pero had been keeping an eye on it. The owner hasn't been here for years." He added, his eyebrows beetling together, "If not for decades."

Chad looked at him, wanting a definitive answer. "And would that be Pete or Pero?"

Mack's face chilled. "I guess we'll have to see, won't we?

I don't know Pete."

MEG WATCHED FROM inside Chad's truck. With Mack on board, the men scattered in organized chaos. The techs were here to deal with the truck, as she waited for Chad, who was lining up last-minute details. She wanted to be first on the scene at the Williamsons' cabin, but, at the same time, she was terrified of what she'd find.

Chad opened the truck door and hopped in. "Sorry for the delay. We have to do this right."

Meg was glad she wasn't in law enforcement. She'd bust down every door in her way, if it meant finding Janelle. And to hell with the law. "Are the other men going to continue to search here?"

"And at Pete's cabin. Don't worry. Daniel is coordinating all the efforts. He's good at it. If she's here, we'll find her."

Meg leaned back against the bench seat, hating the constant tension that lived under her skin. That sense of being coiled so tight that she'd break if she heard the wrong thing. Fear was under that tension and also a rage like she'd never felt before, that lifted the fear higher and higher to the surface. A rage that would demand answers, if someone had hurt Janelle.

She'd been angry before, but she'd never felt *this* emotion before.

That it sat just under her skin was scary because she knew the casing keeping it contained was fragile and so incapable of holding it back if it decided to blow.

And she didn't know what she'd do if it did. She knew now, after feeling that rage, that if she had to, she could kill.

That she was no better than any of the other animals Chad had spent his life trying to lock away.

The only difference between her and them was that thin protective shell.

And what would happen if she could no longer control it?

CHAD CAST A concerned look at Meg. She had a look on her face that he'd never seen before. Not on her face. But he understood it. He'd seen it before on parents who'd found out about atrocities committed on their children. Under the horror was a rage so horrific it had to be experienced to be understood. And it had always scared the parents. The emotions were so rare and so shocking when they flushed through the system that few people knew how to handle them. Hence, crimes of passion were committed.

And Meg looked to be dealing with her own right now.

"Are you okay?" he asked gently.

She shook her head. "Not really."

He sighed. He knew exactly what was going on. "You can't do it, you know?"

She made no attempt to misunderstand. "Yes, I can."

He stayed quiet for a long moment, wondering how to reach her and how to diffuse that rage.

"And what about Janelle? She's lost everyone already. Does she have to lose you too? Just so you get your revenge?"

"It's not about revenge."

Her voice, so cold and clipped, made him wince. "I've seen parents say the same thing over and over again. The problem is that killing Pete won't change anything he's done. It will only make you feel better—for that one moment in time—only for that. Then, there is the rest of your life."

"How could he?" she cried out, her voice breaking. She rounded on Chad. "She's so little. So fragile. How could anyone want to hurt her? She's done nothing to him."

"It's not about what she's done. It's about this person being ill."

"That's an excuse. We coddle these people and smack their hands, telling them they did a bad thing. These assholes say they are sorry, do a year or two in jail, and then get out on good behavior. Where is the justice in that?"

"For some it's not much, but it's the system we have. It's what we can do. And you know he won't get just a year or two. We'll build this case so he's not going anywhere for a long time."

She laughed.

A broken sound that shattered his heart. God, she'd been through so much already. And the night wasn't over yet.

"You don't know that. Look at how broken our justice system is. Killers walk all the time. Rapists rarely get caught, and so many others aren't even given a decent sentence."

"And many killers never see freedom again. Thousands of rapists are taken off the street every day, and so many more are paying the price for their actions." He reached over and grabbed her hand. "You have to believe in the good. In the right. You can't focus on all the wrong in the world. We've been hit with the shitty side of life, but it could have been so much worse. Cia paid the ultimate price from that trip so long ago, but we've been paying too, every single day, and it's tainted everything in our world. We have to let it go. We have to move on."

"Can you?" she whispered.

He pulled the truck over and parked it beside several

other trucks. "We're here." He squeezed her hand. "To answer your question, yes, I can. And so can you."

"No, Chad. I don't think I can." She looked him in the eye, her voice cool. "Not until I have Janelle back, safe and sound." She turned to scramble out of the truck. "Only then will I move forward and leave this all behind."

Chapter 25

MACK WAS SPEAKING with four other men when they arrived. Meg opened the truck door and hopped out. They'd parked at the neighbor's house and now stood at the edge of the Williamsons' property—just out of sight. She studied the location carefully. This lot was larger and more secluded than the ones they had passed on the way in. Large mature trees offered shade, and a huge cedar hedge ran down either side of the property. In other words, there was total privacy.

Then she turned to face the cabin. Maybe *summer palace* was a better description. It was huge. And anyone looking at it would assume it held expensive items worth stealing.

No sounds came from inside. No banging, talking, no music or sounds of activity. It looked empty. And she so hoped it wasn't.

If Janelle were in there, she'd be kicking up a ruckus—if she were able to.

Meg walked over to Chad, who was deep in conversation with the others. He reached out and pulled her closer, letting her into the discussion. "We're going to split up and go in from the two entrances. I want you to stay here."

She stiffened. "No—"

"Yes," he said firmly. "I want you to stay here to see if anyone flees from the house, while we go in." He shot her a warning look. "Do not go after him or her. Do you under-stand?"

Damn. Still, she nodded quickly. And he was right. If they all went inside, someone could flee the place, and they wouldn't know. He continued to search her face, as if remembering their earlier conversation.

Thankfully that rage had dissipated between then and now. As much as she wanted this asshole dead, she wanted Janelle home, safe and sound first. "I'm fine."

He gave one short nod, then went back to making plans. Within minutes, the group had broken up and headed toward the house.

After a strong hug and a gentle kiss to her forehead, Chad followed them.

Meg took a deep breath, whispered a silent prayer to the God she'd hoped was there but had lost faith in a long time ago, and slipped to the hedge, so she could do her part.

The five men scattered, trying to cover all the doors on the main floor in the house.

The cry came from the far side. "Police, open up."

One cop on this side tested the door. Finding it locked, he backed up, then rammed forward. The door popped open, and he fell inside.

An eerie silence surrounded the house. She could no longer see anyone. And that disturbed her more than anything else. It was as if she was alone in a bizarre science-fiction film—only the plot made it a horror movie instead. She bit her bottom lip, worrying and hoping she'd see them soon.

More shouts came from inside, but they sounded like the men speaking to each other.

Shit. Her nerves were knotting her inside. She rubbed

her sweaty palms on her jeans. Where was Janelle? She had to be here. Her heart raced, then slowed. She didn't know where else to look.

"Meg!"

She looked up. Chad was in an upstairs bedroom, his hands cupped around his mouth, getting ready to call her again.

She ran, "What?"

"You can come in. We're searching the house, but it appears empty."

Shit.

CHAD LOOKED OUT the window and watched as Meg raced forward, then went back to his room-by-room search. "Anything?" he called out to the team in general.

"No, except someone has been here recently. And food's in the fridge."

Interesting. The owners hadn't been here in years, so who was using it? Squatters? Or Pete? Chad finished checking out the closet and then ducked down to search under the bed. Nothing.

In the hallway, he heard Meg racing up the stairs. "Are you sure?" she called out.

"We're going room by room," said Chad. "This bedroom is empty."

Meg turned to the closet closest to her and opened it, full-on shelves but no Janelle. He watched Meg for a moment to confirm that she'd be okay. Not only was she okay but she pulled a small flashlight out of her pocket and searched the top of the closet for an opening. Disappointed, she faced him. "We'll have to find the attic too."

He nodded. "And we will." He walked into the next bedroom and repeated the process. By the time he'd completed a thorough search, he found Meg standing anxiously at the doorway.

"Next level," she said and bolted down the stairs. He raced after her. Downstairs, all the men were moving through the house in organized efficiency.

They only had the basement left.

Finally the team raced down the stairs. Meg could hardly breathe, and her side ached fiercely, but that was nothing to the massive disappointment that clutched at her heart and squeezed it when she realized the basement was just a big open room.

"Nothing," she whispered, tears gathering in the corner of her eyes, her heart breaking slowly, piece by piece. "Nothing's here."

"Hold on. Let's take a closer look." He walked to the wall closest to him and tapped. The others spread out and did the same, but all the walls appeared to be made of solid concrete. And that's what she had expected.

She walked behind the stairs and searched. Nothing was here. She wanted to crawl away and hide, be someplace alone, and let her tears pour out. Instead this horrible tension gripped her tight and made her want to scream.

The shakes started at her shoulders, and, by the time they'd hit her hips, she couldn't stop them. She stood in place and waited for the men to finish.

"Hey, over here."

Meg spun around. Two men, Daniel and someone she thought was called John, were at the far side, heads together.

Everyone ran toward them. Meg, walking very carefully, too scared to hope, and yet desperate for good news, was on their heels.

"A crack is in the wall here."

"It's wood. Painted with cement-like paint to blend in.'

"Looks like he painted the whole foundation here in the same paint."

"Let's get it open."

"Can't see a handle."

Meg closed her eyes, willing them to hurry. "Why not just bust the thing down?" she whispered, praying for patience.

"Because they don't want to hurt anyone inside," Chad murmured at her side. "They've got it now. Hold on."

She gasped for another breath and held it, as the door popped open, almost spilling the men inside. A shout went up.

"She's here."

And pandemonium ensued.

MEG GASPED IN joy. The relief was so great she could hardly draw another breath. Oh, *thank God.* She reached the open door and bolted through it. And came to a dead stop.

A single bed was in the corner of a long narrow room and a rough-plumbed bathroom at the other. The men crowded around the still form in the center of the bed. Meg walked closer, as if in running she'd lose control. She struggled to keep her composure. They'd found Janelle—but had they been in time?

Janelle lay fully dressed in her purple jeans and T-shirt, her runners still on. Meg choked back a gasp, her hand jumping up to cover her mouth—and the scream wanting to escape it.

Chad stepped toward Meg. "Easy. She's just unconscious."

"Just?" Meg took a long gasping breath, dropped her clenched hands, and slowly stepped up to the side of the bed. Daniel was checking Janelle's vitals. "That doesn't look like a normal unconsciousness."

"She's been drugged." Chad wrapped an arm around Meg's shoulders. "There are needle marks on her arms."

"Oh God." She covered her mouth with both hands and stared at him with wide eyes. "Poor Janelle."

"Yes … and lucky Janelle." He squeezed Meg's shoulders and tugged her in closer for a long moment. "We found her. And she's safe. She doesn't appear to have been physically hurt. We got to her in time." He let out a huge breath. "Take a deep breath. She's safe. We made it. And an ambulance is on the way."

"Thank God." She let out a shaky breath and nodded. "Right. Thank you."

"Don't thank me. It was a group effort."

Meg sat down on the edge of the bed, as the men made room for her. Gently she picked up Janelle's limp hand and held it tenderly in her own. Even in that position, she saw the round reddened mark on the inside of Janelle's elbow. Her eyes wandered to Janelle's pale face. Her normal porcelain skin looked waxy; her hair was tousled and knotted.

"The ambulance has been called." Daniel straightened up. "She doesn't have any other visible trauma, so I'm presuming at this point she's been drugged and is still under. If we're lucky, she'll stay that way until we get her to the hospital, where she can be more thoroughly checked over."

Meg closed her eyes at that. They were talking rape. The

doctors would need to be sure she hadn't been, and, if she had a rape kit, it would be done. God. That was hard enough to explain to a traumatized adult, but to a child? … Meg could only hope the drugs were ones that weren't going to hurt her, beyond keeping her subdued.

Impossible to think of Pete knowing about such things.

As if he'd read her mind, Chad asked, "Meg, does Pete have any experience with drugs? Would he know how to give them to someone?"

She hated to not know. She forced her mind to think back. "I can't imagine how." Then something twigged. "He's done some work on large animals and helped with horses. Maybe he would have had some experience through that."

"Who with?" Daniel had a notepad opened.

She shrugged. "I'm not sure of the names. He spent a spring helping someone around here do some work. About forty, fifty miles away maybe."

"Good enough, that can't be too hard to confirm." Daniel snapped shut his notebook and walked away.

"How are you holding up?" Chad asked.

"Fine." She gave him a watery smile. "More than fine." She lifted Janelle's hands. "We'll both be great. Now."

"We have to find Pete before he leaves the state," Chad said, his tone dark. "If he escapes this area, he could restart somewhere else."

"And who knows what else he's done here," she said, her gaze on Janelle. "But Cia could have been with Pete … or Anto. They were brothers. And both could have been involved."

"That's possible." Chad nodded. "Lots to sort out yet."

"But the biggest panic is over." Meg pressed Janelle's hand against her cheek, so grateful to know she was safe.

They had a long road ahead of them. And that was okay.

For the first time in hours, she knew they would have a road to travel.

CHAD WATCHED THE ambulance pull away, with Meg sitting at Janelle's side. He hated to be separated from them, but they had an all-out manhunt going on here.

And for all he knew, Pete could have gone back to Seattle by now.

And that had Chad calling for security for Janelle and Meg from the minute they arrived at the hospital.

"Are you ready, Chad?" Daniel called over to him. "We're splitting up the grid and calling in the local law. Roadblocks are up."

"Pete could be driving anything at this point or"—Chad turned to study the terrain around them—"he could have crossed over to Canada from here already."

"Yep, if he's smart, he's long gone, but, if he's still here, then we'll find him."

"I'm wondering if Janelle is safe in the ambulance," Chad said, staring down the empty road.

"At this point, I doubt he'd go after her again. More likely he's cut and run."

Chad agreed, but, if Pete was also their serial killer, he had a lot of history here, and he might not be so ready to let it go.

Daniel was speaking again. "We have a team coming to go over this room. Lock down the case tight, so this asshole can't wiggle loose."

"Right." Chad turned back to Daniel. "We can get prints from here and match them to Cia's case. We all voluntarily offered our prints way back when. His should be on file."

"Good. That would be one step crossed off."

"Let's get to it. It'll be a long night. Again."

MEG HAD TO sit opposite Janelle in the ambulance. She stared down at the little girl, alternating between wishing she'd wake up and wishing she'd sleep through the next couple hours. The red spot on her arm, where they'd assumed she'd been injected, looked angry. Her breathing was raspy, having gone from deep comatose to uneven and ragged.

The paramedic was keeping a close eye on Janelle and on the machines monitoring her vital signs. She was doing poorly, and Meg didn't need to be a medical professional to know that.

She sat back and closed her eyes, finding herself wishing she had religious beliefs to help her through this time. She'd only ever had herself. She'd been close to her brother Darren. He'd been a huge help to her years ago, knowing many of the people she'd gone camping with. He'd been a couple years older than her, close to Pero's age. In fact, he and Pero had been friends—until Pero's accident. Meg hadn't kept track; she just remembered the odd bits and pieces of conversation she'd heard.

And ... she sat back. Her brother had met Pete. He'd never mentioned anything about thinking Pete reminded him of anyone. And her brother definitely would have done so. Even Mack was Pero's family, and, although he was still waffling, considering where and how they'd found Janelle, he'd finally been forced to admit they might be one and the same man.

She noticed a road sign as they went by. They'd be at the hospital within minutes. She was surprised when, all of a sudden, the sirens went on and the vehicle sped through the lights ahead. She turned to look at Janelle, but the paramedic was leaning over her, right in front of Meg, blocking her view.

Shit. Was something wrong?

The ambulance peeled to a stop. The doors were flung open, and Janelle's stretcher was wheeled out, disappearing into the depths of the hospital. Meg got out slowly. They were at the same hospital as Stephanie. God, how many hours ago had that been? She glanced down at her cell phone to check the time. It was past midnight.

She stared up at the starry sky, with a full moon enhancing their brightness. Add the artificial lights from the hospital, and it was practically evening out here. She walked into the hospital, stopping for one last look out into the balmy night.

Easy for Pete to see in this light.

And easy too, for the cops to hunt their prey.

Chapter 26

MEG LOOKED UP from the chair she'd been sitting in for hours. *Chad.* With a gasp, she rushed over to him and threw herself into his open arms. "I wondered when you'd get here."

He swung her into a tight embrace. She snuggled deeper, laying her cheek against his heart. It felt so right to be here. His arms tightened, and then released her. Reluctantly she stepped back to look up into his tired face.

And knew he didn't have good news. "He's still out there, isn't he?"

"Yes, the search is ongoing. The roadblocks are up …" He shrugged. "We're doing what we can."

"He's smart. If he wants to leave the country, he will."

"Not likely at this point. We've alerted the airports and border patrol."

There wasn't any point in saying more. The hunt was on. If Pete had made it out, he had made it out. Little anyone could do that wasn't already being done.

"How is Janelle?" Chad asked.

"It was pretty dicey there for a while. She seems to have had a bad time with the drugs. The doctors say she's stable now, but she'll be out of it for a long time."

"Good. Then come home with me. We both need showers and some sleep. We'll come back after a rest and check up on her."

Meg stared at Janelle, undecided.

"You can't take care of her if you aren't in any reasonable shape."

That was hard to argue with. Finally she nodded. "A shower sounds good."

He wrapped an arm around her shoulders and tugged her toward the front doors of the hospital. "I've already set it up for the hospital to call us if there's any change in her condition. Or if there's news on the manhunt."

"Are the others still out there?"

Chad snorted. "We have teams all over the place."

They were in his truck and on the way home, when she realized he was taking her home to his place.

And that was just where she wanted to be.

He pulled the truck up into the driveway of a small bungalow of cedar and glass, and she loved it immediately. "This is beautiful," she said, a yawn catching her sideways.

"Thanks. Come on in. Let's get you cleaned up and settled for whatever is left of the night." He unlocked the front door and stepped in.

Meg trailed behind. She wanted nothing more than a quick shower and a bed.

He led her to a small bedroom, stopping at a closet, pulling out several towels. "Here's your room and towels and a washcloth. You have a bathroom in your room, so you should have all you need."

Except you, her mind screamed. And she'd have laughed out loud if she could have. Of all the nights she didn't have any energy for relationships, tonight was it. She smiled good night, walked inside, and closed the door. He never said a word, just headed on down to his own room presumably.

The hot water was breathtakingly soothing. If only she had some nightclothes to wear. She searched the room and found some T-shirts in the dresser. She pulled one on, letting it drop past her hips. As it was long enough to double as a sleep shirt, she crawled into bed. Turning out the lights, she then fell into a deep sleep.

CHAD SCRUBBED THE grime out of his hair. It looked like he'd been crawling through the brush and dirt for days, not hours. He'd been glad to make it back home. Swinging by the hospital had been instinctive. He knew Meg would still be there, watching over Janelle. He would be too in the same situation.

It was, in fact, what he was doing with Meg right now. Watching over her. He wished she was in his bed, but it was too early for that. Besides, he'd said he'd give her until the weekend. And he had meant it.

But it was damn hard.

He just wanted to hold her close. Could he? Would she be upset if she woke up to find him sleeping beside her?

Or was that pushing the line?

Deciding he'd better not push the issue, he went to his own bed and turned out the lights. But he wasn't able to sleep, as the unsolved issues on the case kept his mind churning through the information. All the possibilities … There were just too many of them. He lay here for a full hour, trying to go to sleep, then gave up. Just as he turned his light on and reached for a book to read, he heard it.

Meg. Crying.

Shit. Talk about something guaranteed to break his heart.

He got out of bed slowly, pulled on a pair of boxers, and walked to his door. Should he go to her? He didn't want to intrude if she needed privacy, but he hated to see anyone in pain—Meg, most of all. Calling himself all kinds of a fool, he walked over to Meg's door and knocked lightly. No response.

He stood undecided, then rapped again, a little harder.

The door opened under his hand. He peered around the corner. She lay still, her breathing broken by sobs. She was crying in her sleep.

His heart melted. She'd been through so much and had remained so strong for Janelle's sake. But who was being strong for her?

Knowing it was beyond him to walk away, he gave in. Walking over to the empty side of the bed, he crawled under the covers. Settling in, he tugged Meg into his arms. Instantly her sobs eased. She snuggled in deeper, took a long broken breath, and slept on.

Holding her close, he slipped off to sleep right afterward.

MEG WOKE UP, tangled in the covers and incredibly hot. She threw back the covers and lay half asleep, as her body cooled down. It was summer, but normally she didn't wake up this way. Then she heard it. Breathing. She twisted around to look and found Chad, asleep in her bed.

She glanced around the room, reorienting herself. Here she was in Chad's house, in his spare bedroom, and in his spare bed, her bed for the night.

And his too apparently. Yet it felt so right. As she lay here, she realized how well he'd aged. In the past, she used to watch him as he slept. She had always woken up before him.

It used to make him mad. She would just laugh. But here they were again, together, as if all those seventeen years hadn't happened.

This was where she belonged. Why had she ever left? When had the doubts become bigger than the knowing that they were right together?

Mack was likely to blame for that. Then again, he'd only shown up the cracks in the relationship; and she'd been the one to turn it into a rift. It was as if she'd been waiting all this time to come back home.

And he'd been here, arms open, welcoming her back. Luckily he wasn't married with a family of his own. None of her camping group had managed a *normal* life like that either.

They had all wanted it, but none had achieved it.

"What are you thinking?" he murmured beside her, his voice sleepy, sexy.

"That this feels like a homecoming." She twisted around again so she could look into his eyes. Eyes that were now open and so very welcoming.

He smiled a slow, slumber-filled smile that sent her pulse tattooing against her chest.

"That's because it is. It's taken you a long time to find your way back to me."

She stared at him, realizing it was time to shine a light on another long-held and discarded truth. She whispered, "You were supposed to come after me."

He leaned on his elbow to look at her in dismayed shock. "Shit." He dropped his forehead gently onto hers. "I didn't know. I thought you wanted to leave us all behind."

"I was confused. Scared. And I wanted you and needed you. But, at the same time, I couldn't stay here. So I left," she whispered, knowing it was the time to bare the truth. They'd already lost so much time. "I ran as far and as fast as I could. But I was hoping … that you'd come after me."

"And I would have—if I'd thought there was any chance that I was welcome." He closed his eyes. "When I think of all those lost years …" He hugged her close, rocking her gently, as a warm silence filled the room.

"Thank you," she whispered.

He lifted his head, his gaze narrowed thoughtfully as he looked at her. "For what?"

"For waiting for *me*." She pushed herself up onto her elbow, then leaned over and kissed him.

Meg couldn't believe how swiftly the years slipped away. It seemed so natural, so right, to be in bed with Chad. She deepened the kiss and sighed with pleasure, as his hands stroked up her arms, … gentle, accepting, loving.

She broke the kiss and dropped her forehead to rest against his.

"You're welcome," he whispered, the warmth of his breath floating soothingly against her cheek. "I'm just so glad it's finally our time." He reached up and captured her lips for a second loving kiss. She smiled against his lips. "You said you'd give me until the weekend."

He lowered his head and closed his eyes. "I did, didn't I? Foolish me."

"Of course I didn't say how long I'd give you," she whispered teasingly.

His eyes flew open. He stared at her hopefully. "No, you didn't. And I'm a fast learner. I don't need until the weekend to adjust."

"Are you sure?" She dropped gentle little kisses on his nose, his cheekbones, his chin. "I wouldn't want to rush you or to take advantage of the situation."

He swallowed hard. "You wouldn't? No, of course you wouldn't."

She smiled and dropped kisses down his neck to his broad shoulders. His fingers strolled her shoulders, always staying in contact, but compliant to her wishes.

"Not if you aren't ready to take this step," she murmured, stroking her tongue across his collarbone. "I'd hate to push you."

"It might be hard, but I think I'll be fine." He gasped as her tongue dipped into the hollow of his neck. "It will be a challenge, but I'm up for it."

She stilled, and then she smoothed her hand slowly down his chest to his belly, loving the way his muscles rippled under her touch. She curled her fingers gently into the thick V of hair that disappeared below the boxers. *Boxers.* They were new. Then so was her sleep shirt. She slid down the bed to allow herself more access, moving the blankets down, trailing her lips across his chest to his nipple. "Are you sure?"

Her finger danced along the edge of the boxers, then slipping under the soft material and feeling Chad's breath catch in his throat, he released it in a gust, as she removed her fingers.

"I'm sure," he gasped.

"*Hmm.* Maybe I should check it out further." She nipped at his nipple; his fingers clenched her arms. She did it again. Then again.

Shivers rippled down his skin. "Witch," he muttered thickly.

She chuckled. She rose up on one elbow, so she could

see his face. "I could stop." She toyed with the waistband on his boxers. Then she stroked down the surface of the material, loving the way it jumped under her fingers. "I'd hate for you to feel pressured."

"Oh, I'm feeling the pressure all right."

She wrapped her fingers around the long length of him and squeezed gently.

He groaned—a loud, guttural sound of relief and pain. "God, you're killing me."

She smiled lovingly. "So not. But I am having fun."

"Good. Then I want to play too."

She found herself suddenly flipped over on her back, Chad resting between her sprawled legs and holding himself just above her. He stared down at her, an odd look in his gaze.

She tilted her head slightly. "What?"

He smiled sheepishly. "Have you any idea how long I have waited for this?" The longing in his voice, his need, brought tears to her eyes.

"I'm so sorry."

He placed his fingers over her lips. "*Shush*. Don't be. I always knew you'd come back. I'm just so grateful that it has finally happened."

She sniffled, his words warming the lonely corners in her heart, making her aware of just how empty her life had been.

"Don't." He dropped gentle kisses on her cheeks, trailing down to her ears. Shivers slipped across her skin, which chilled, then heated, under his ministrations. "None of it matters. I loved you back then, and I've loved you every day since."

Now the tears ran in a gentle, slow stream. God, those

words, … the love in his voice … And she'd walked away from him and had suffered every day since. And here he was, forgiving her, wanting her, and—so, so precious—*loving her.*

After all she'd done.

"Stop. Please stop crying, Megs." And the use of his old nickname made her smile through the tears.

He lowered his head and took her lips in a deep, drugging kiss, full of memories and renewal. It was so familiar and yet so different that her senses swelled in response. She tugged him down, loving the weight of his body on hers, loving the emotional connection of his words, but needing as well the physical blending of their bodies.

His kiss deepened, as he slid his tongue inside her mouth to tango with her own. She wrapped her legs around his hips, hating the material still between them. Then felt his hand slide up between them, smoothing into her waist and up over her ribs. She shifted restlessly, waiting, wanting so much more.

But he didn't give it to her. His hand stayed just below, so teasingly close to her breast, yet out of touch. She smiled against his lips and dug her claws into his back.

He stiffened and cupped her breast. She moaned, arching at the exquisite feeling. It had been so long. His touch was so new and so needed.

"More?"

"So much more," she whispered. "I want it all."

He leaned back, a slightly worried look in his eyes.

"Stop trying to do the right thing," she whispered. "And love me."

That opened the firestorm, and, when he lowered his head this time, there was no hesitation. No doubt. He drove his tongue inside her mouth, as he plunged his hips deeper into the hollow between her legs.

She arched higher and rotated her hips slightly. He still had on his boxers, and those needed to go. She hooked her thumbs into the waistband and tugged them downward. He shifted to the side, reached down, and slipped them off. He kicked the tangled bedding to the floor.

When he turned back to her, she'd lifted the T-shirt over her head.

His eyes gleamed in the early morning light, as he stared down at her, lowering her to her back again. One hand cupped her breast, and he leaned over and suckled the nipple deep into his mouth. She cried out, cradling his head, as her body pulsed with heat. He shifted to the other breast, giving it more attention, loving the tip, and brushing the early morning growth of beard so gently across the pouting nub.

"Oh," she cried out again, the slight pain of his stubble instantly soothed by the moist heat of his mouth. She reached for him, wanting, needing to touch him.

"I don't think I can let you go this time," he murmured. "I've wanted you for so long."

Shifting slightly, he slipped his hand between their slick bodies and drove his fingers into her moist curls. She lifted her hips, then shuddered helplessly, as he found the pulsing nub.

"Please, let the first time be both of us together," she cried out, as need and heat twisted inside. She was already so close. "I don't want to fly solo—come with me."

He rose higher, hooked her leg up over his hip, and, with him sitting at her entrance, he leaned over and whispered, "Together."

And he drove home.

She cried out, as emotions and sensations surged through her. He withdrew slightly and then drove in again. She rose to meet every thrust, as she shifted, taking him yet deeper.

Tension twisted higher and higher.

She cried out, "Chad."

"I'm here. You're safe."

And her world exploded.

Dimly in the background, she heard him groan, as he followed her into oblivion, and collapsed softly beside her.

PETE STARED INTO the shadows of the bedroom, rage coiling *inside.*

She'd gone to him, to Chad. He'd seen her work with him at the site. Had noted that caring attitude that went far beyond their being professional colleagues. And had watched them from outside the house, when they'd found Janelle. The noise of their cheers was painful to his hopes and dreams. He'd stayed behind, until Chad had left, and had followed him back to town and straight to the hospital. Pete hadn't had time to decide his next actions, when the two had come out and had gotten into Chad's truck. He'd followed them.

To here. To this.

He couldn't believe it of Meg.

He didn't want to believe it of her.

Hadn't ten, almost eleven years with him pushed Chad into the category called history? To never be revisited? Apparently not.

Chad had coaxed her back into his bed—so easily—just like he had done when they were teens.

Pete had watched, hating that Meg had never looked at

him, had never even seen him. She'd been friendly, but then she was friendly to everyone. He was nothing special.

It had always been Chad.

When Pete had finally managed to woo her into his bed, and into his life, after years of trying, he'd done everything he could to make the relationship work. She hadn't recognized him, and that was good. He'd worked hard to keep it that way. He'd never complained about her trips away—and some of them had been for months on end. He'd never complained about her inability to commit to a more permanent relationship. He understood she was still affected by that camping trip. So he'd never brought it up. That he'd been the cause of it all had never bothered him. It had caused the rift between her and Chad, and that had been a wonderful side benefit.

Now, as if all those years with him hadn't mattered, she'd fallen right back into Chad's arms, as if she'd never left him.

Bitch.

Whore.

And yet still he loved her.

This was Janelle's fault. She'd driven a wedge between them. She'd turned Meg away from him. He'd been just about to take care of that little problem, when he realized he'd been found out. He wanted to blame Janelle but figured he could place the blame at Chad's feet for that. Losing Janelle would have sent Meg back into Pete's arms.

But instead Chad had saved Janelle, and Meg had fallen into his bed.

Or had it happened before?

When had she turned to Chad? She hadn't had time with that Janelle bitch living with them. Christ, that kid had taken all Meg's attention and all her love.

He hated that little slut-in-the-making.

He would have gotten his revenge on her too—if it hadn't

been for that bastard Chad.

Now look at the two of them. Cozy as anything.

Like hell. Rage—too long submerged—rose to the surface, clear, hot, and cutting.

He walked to the truck he'd used earlier for working the site. Chainsaws were still in the back of it.

And gas.

He opened the lid to the gas cans.

Chapter 27

M EG WOKE TO a sensation of rosy warmth, snuggled deep into Chad's arms. Janelle was safe. Meg was back with Chad, and it was even better than before—but then there was Pete. Yet, as Chad had said, "The police are on to him."

She smiled, loving the strong male scent.

Her nose wrinkled at something else.

Smoke?

Jesus. She bolted upright. "Fire!"

Flames were licking up the window side of the bedroom. That crackling sound of a good flame was just getting a stronghold on the wood. The air was filling with smoke.

"Chad, wake up." She gave him a hard shove, already reaching for her phone to call 9-1-1.

"What the fuck?" Chad bolted from bed and into his boxers and disappeared, making her realize she would be running out of the house nude in a moment. She threw the T-shirt back on and her jeans, grabbed her purse and her shoes, slipping them on as she ran. Thick smoke filled the room so badly that she could hardly see.

"Let's go." He was dressed, his truck keys in his hand. He grabbed her hand and raced to the front of the house.

Then she started to cough.

He shoved her to her knees. "Crawl to the garage. The

flames are all around us. Go, go, *go*."

Still coughing, her shirt pulled up over her mouth, she crawled on all fours behind him. By the time they had reached the garage, all she could hear was the roaring fire and the sounds of sirens—too far away to save them.

She hoped Chad had a plan.

The garage door was locked, but he managed to reach up and get it unlocked, and tugged it open. Through the gray smoke, she watched him motion her through the door, as a bit of fresh air came out from the garage. She coughed and gasped, struggling to make the short distance, but couldn't catch her breath. Then she didn't have to.

She was picked up and shoved in the front seat of the truck.

The whole garage was in flames around them.

He ran around to the other side, hopped in and fired up the truck. He didn't even wait to open the garage door, he put the truck in Reverse and blasted through it and out onto the street. Wood shattered, sending chunks onto the windshield. Her window automatically opened, and she gasped and coughed in fresh air.

Pulling the truck off to one side, he parked and turned off the engine. He coughed several times. "Are you okay?"

Tears ran from his reddened eyes, but the look of fury on his face had her answering quickly. "I'm fine, but smoke inhalation is not the best way to wake up."

He grinned, reached over, and kissed her hard. "Good. Let's go. I want the paramedics to check you out."

She went to speak and ended up coughing again. He exited the truck and came around to her side and opened the door. At last, she heard the sirens round the corner. An ambulance stopped in the middle of the road. Chad led her, still coughing, to the driver.

"Look after her." And he disappeared to speak with the firemen.

Meg let herself be led to the back, where she was given oxygen. After a bad coughing spell, she could finally breathe.

"Was anyone else in the house?" the paramedic asked.

"Just Chad and me." She closed her eyes and worked on breathing. Now that she was safe, the shakes were starting. She was pushed gently onto the bench inside the ambulance. A blanket was wrapped around her shoulders. She sank deeper into its folds, whispering, "Thank you."

"No problem. Stay here and rest."

Chad appeared in front of her. "Meg?"

She smiled at him. She lowered the oxygen mask. "I'm fine."

"It was arson."

"Yeah, I got that." In fact, she also thought she knew who it was who had done it. "Pete?"

Chad nodded. "He'd be my first choice. I gather he wasn't real happy about you breaking up with him."

"He would have been more upset if he had seen us in bed." She shrugged. "It was over a long time ago. Just waiting for the ink to dry, so to speak."

Chad glared at his house, well past saving now.

She followed her gaze, realizing belatedly what he'd lost personally. "I'm sorry."

He glanced down at her. "So am I, but this is not your fault."

That was debatable, but she didn't have the energy. "Is Janelle safe?"

He pulled out his phone. "I had security on her all night. As I haven't gotten a call, I'm presuming all is well, but I'll check."

She hadn't known. "Thank you."

He moved away slightly to talk. She stared at the mess around her. The fire trucks, the ambulance, the cops, the neighbors, everyone watching. She just wanted to hide away until all this was over.

Her gaze wandered, her mind lost on the chaos. She caught sight of something, her mind slow to compute just what, when Chad stepped in front of her.

"Janelle is fine," he said, with a big smile. "She's awake."

She blinked and got it, then said, "Don't look around. Pete is in the crowd, behind you to the left."

Chad froze. "Are you sure?" he asked hoarsely. He had his cell phone out. At her nod, he texted someone. "Men are moving into position." He looked up at her. "Get ready. All hell is going to break loose soon."

His cell phone beeped. "Is he still there?" he asked Meg.

She didn't want to look and alert Pete but knew it would be impossible not to. "He's on the move, going behind you now."

"Stay put."

And just then someone in the crowd screamed. Chad spun and ran, and it looked as if the crowd had scattered. Meg hunched lower, trying to sort through the chaos. Her gaze darted left, then right, frantically searching for Pete and Chad. There they were, in the distance. She watched Pete dart between several people, then dash behind a car, with Chad hot on his trail.

Several other cops converged on the same spot. Shouts rang out, and then the crowd dispersed. She watched the cops split and disappear and realized Pete must have slipped through. *Damn.* She needed him to answer for Janelle. She didn't know if he was also responsible for Cia and the other victims as well, but this had to stop.

The crowd grew in volume again and then receded. Her nerves were shot. She couldn't watch anymore. She shuffled backward to lean against the side of the ambulance bench and closed her eyes. Her eyes still burned, and the tearing had slowed down, but her throat swore it had been rubbed with sandpaper. Not to mention the smell. Smoke coated everything, and that nasty burning smell permeated the air around them.

She wanted all this to go away and everything to return to normal. She needed Pete caught and safely put away behind bars. God, how did he keep evading the cops?

"Meg."

And there he was, right in front of her, a baseball cap on his head, tugged low, hiding his features. He hopped inside the ambulance to sit beside her, slamming and locking the doors behind him.

She shifted, the movement, bringing on yet another coughing fit. He patted her on the back, even as she tried to evade his touch. His hand slipped up to her neck and squeezed gently. She turned on him. "Hello, Pete. Or should I say Pero?"

She tried to stay calm and interested, when all she wanted was to claw his eyes out. The men had to be not far away. Pete wasn't a damn ghost. Surely someone had seen him. Surely someone would come. She slipped her cell phone to one side, hitting the Redial button to call Chad. She coughed hard, not having to fake it, to cover her actions.

Surprise lit his features. "Figured that out, did you?"

"Somewhere around the time you kidnapped Janelle." The pain of that betrayal caused her to cry out, "Why did you hurt her?"

"That bitch. She's the reason our relationship was in trouble. After your brother died, it's like you became this milksop nanny. Anything Janelle wanted, Janelle got. We didn't have a relationship anymore. I tried to give you space, … anything to make it work." He shook his head. "Then you found that damn skull, and I knew it was the end."

"I'm sorry." She took a deep breath, surprised to realize that, after all this, she really was sorry. "At the time, I was hurting from losing my brother and knew Janelle was hurting too. It was natural to turn to her for comfort and to give comfort to her."

"*Right.*"

His tone was so derisive that she wondered how he'd kept his emotions in check all those months. Stalling for time, she asked him just that.

"Easy. I spent our entire relationship waiting for you to get off standby and into the game. But no matter how patient I was, how understanding, you never engaged in the relationship."

She gasped. "That's not fair." God, where was Chad?

"Yes. It is. I hated that you loved Chad all those years ago. When we got together, I figured it was finally *my* time. Instead all I got was the shell he left behind."

In spite of everything, she felt a pang for all his pain and some guilt for her actions. It was all such a waste. She'd been hurting everyone, when she had tried so hard to avoid doing just that. And also to avoid being hurt herself again. Pete didn't deserve her apology, not after all he'd done. But maybe an apology would help appease his anger. "I'm sorry." She whispered, "I never realized."

"No, of course you didn't. You weren't aware of anything. You stayed locked inside and never came out. A coward."

Stung, she fired back. "Is that why you killed Cia? Did she spurn you too?"

He laughed. "That bitch did the opposite. She was free for the taking. Anytime, anywhere."

"No, that's not true," Meg said. "Cia didn't want Anto. She hated him."

"Ha." But his tone of voice changed, got colder, nastier. "She did not hate him."

She stared at him. God, the look on his face. … She didn't recognize him. And his reaction was so … off. What was going on? She said slowly, "Cia loved Cia. Your brother terrified her. Hell, he terrified me."

And then Pete smiled; a creepy smile that seemed to start in his eyes and then to twist him into someone else. Shivers slipped down her spine, and instinctively she tried to shuffle farther away from him, but he had her pinned against the corner.

"And yet you've been sleeping with him for the last ten years."

She stared at him in horror. And then she got it. *Finally.*

Bile rose up the back of her throat, and she vomited over the edge of the stretcher in the ambulance.

And he laughed and laughed; a maniacal sound of sheer enjoyment that had her heaving a second time.

"You and your high-and-mighty attitude. Chad this and Chad that. Cia was the same, only it was Pero this and Pero that. Well, I knocked that out of the bitch fast, when she realized I was the one meeting her in the woods and not my brother."

"You killed her?" She gasped, hating the shocks that were continuously sending her off balance. She could hardly think. She desperately wanted Chad to come; surely he could hear the conversation.

He shrugged. "I was going to take what she'd been offering around so freely, but, when she saw me, she pulled the offer." He smiled coldly. "As if I was going to accept that. I just clamped my hands around her throat and squeezed. She died so easily. I didn't think it would be that simple." He smiled in reminiscence. "I raced to the cabin and stashed her in there, until the hoopla went away. I'd just got my license that summer and had wheels to borrow. Came up a few days later and buried her up top."

Meg, her stomach still heaving, shuddered. She had to keep him talking. Give Chad time. "And what about the others?"

"It's addictive, you know?" His tone was now conversational and thoughtful. "And did you notice they all looked like you?"

She hadn't thought they looked anything like her. "And the necklaces?"

"I wanted them to wear it. Cia had yours on. The bitch. But, after her, I was afraid it wouldn't be the same anymore. So I had them made to allow me to pretend, ... at least for a little while."

And her stomach heaved again. "Oh God. You kept them alive?"

"Not for very long. I hate tantrums and tears." He shrugged. "I kept them at the cabin. My uncle never knew. Neither did Uncle Mack. I did wonder though, so I laid enough doubt that it was probably his precious Bruce," he added thoughtfully. "Then the accident happened. Recovery was hard. There was the grief over my brother, whom I loved. Then I hooked up with you, and I realized that stage of my life was over. It had been all about you. You were my love, my reason. I didn't need those girls anymore. After all, my dream had come true," he mocked. "Until Janelle arrived …"

"How could you kill those women?" she whispered, feeling really odd, her thoughts foggy, distant. "Are there more?"

"No, but I'd planned for more. I went to a lot of trouble to build that room at the Williamsons' house. It was an easy solution for Janelle and any future others. Only, when I got her there, I realized I didn't want her. There was only one woman for me. You were mine for almost eleven years. I'm not willing to let you go. And if I can't have you …"

His voice changed. Softened. And that was just wrong. She tried to see into his eyes. Only she couldn't focus. "What have you done?"

And when? When he'd first arrived and squeezed her neck? Could he have done something to her then? So fast?

Her vision started to waver.

"Pressure syringes are the greatest invention and so easy to get a hold of," Pete said, tugging her into his arms. "I have you again. No one can take you away from me. Ever. It's a perfect ending."

Black spots appeared in her eyes. She heard shouts from the crowd outside the ambulance. "Why?"

He sighed happily content. "Because you are mine. *Forever.*"

No. It couldn't be.

"Meg. I love you. I always have." And Pete slumped over her, his weight pressing down heavily on her shoulders.

She tried to scream. Tried to call for help. But her voice

didn't work.

Her vision wavered—the world around her blurring.

Then she blacked out.

CHAD SAT AT Meg's bedside, her hand cradled in his. He'd damn-near been paralyzed by fear when he'd finally realized what he was hearing on his cell phone. He'd raced to the ambulance, unable to contact anyone else because he couldn't break the connection of Meg's call to him.

The panic run to the ambulance and the even faster race to the hospital had been heart-stopping.

The doctors had done everything they could, but Pete had injected himself with a massive dose, and he hadn't made it.

Good thing. Chad would have killed him if he hadn't.

And he didn't want to spend the next ten years behind bars, not when he could spend them with Meg instead.

Now if only she'd wake up. The doctors appeared confident that she would. They'd done everything possible and appeared satisfied with her condition.

Only there was so much they didn't know.

Then that went with this bizarre case too. So many strings to tie up. The paperwork involved would be days, weeks, in the making. Mack had been with him, as they tried to open the doors. The two had heard most of Pete's no make that Anto's confession on the cell phone. If, … when, … Meg woke up, she'd fill in the blanks hopefully.

The fingerprints from the truck had verified Anto's identity. He'd taken his brother's spot after the accident and had started a new life soon afterward with Meg. To the best of anyone's knowledge at this stage, he'd never killed again. But they had a lot more evidence to go through before anyone was comfortable making that statement with any certainty. The secret room was being printed now. Hopefully they'd get a better idea of who'd been forced in there—if, indeed, anyone.

Mack had been horrified. He'd stayed behind to clean up the mess of what was left of Chad's house. They would need to talk. Eventually.

Right now, Chad had no plans to leave Meg's side. Daniel had already come by and had dropped off Chad's laptop, which he'd forgotten in his truck overnight.

His case board, his years of notes, clippings, maps—everything else at home—gone. Maybe that was for the best at this point. They now knew who'd killed Cia and the other girls. Now Chad could move on.

Still, he'd loved his home. But not as much as he loved Meg.

And Meg loved Janelle. He'd taken a quick trip to see Janelle, who'd burst into tears at the news about her aunt. He'd been quick to reassure her that the doctors had said Meg would pull through, but Janelle had been desperate to see for herself. And, if Meg didn't surface soon, he might go get Janelle and bring her here. That little girl had been through enough, and, if seeing Meg would make her feel better, then he was all for it.

When he'd told her about Anto, Janelle had gone really quiet. Then she'd said, "Good. Maybe I can sleep at night again."

He'd wanted to ask more, but she'd rolled over and closed her eyes.

He'd taken a long look at the beautiful girl and had returned to Meg, his heart heavy, knowing what Anto had intended. Janelle must have known something was wrong, if she couldn't sleep at night. Thank God, Meg had gotten wise and had moved them out in time.

And he'd heard from Bruce. Stephanie had woken up. She was still groggy about the turn of events that had landed her on death's door, but she did confirm that she'd planned to meet Pete or Pero, as she knew him, for coffee. Then she had changed her mind and had run. Bruce was sticking pretty close to her side, especially now that he knew she'd most likely not been going back to her dealer.

Chad wished them well. Maybe, with Cia's case solved, they could all move on together.

Now, if only Meg would wake up.

Then a soft voice whispered, "Hey."

He glanced around. The room was empty. He looked at Meg, and she smiled at him, a frail small one but a smile nevertheless. His breath gusted free, and he gave her a brilliant smile in response. "Oh, Lord, is it good to hear your voice. You scared me."

"Scared myself," she murmured, her smile tremulous and hopeful. "Pete? God it's hard to say Anto."

"He didn't make it. He gave himself a large dose of whatever drug he was using."

Tears collected at the corners of her eyes. He didn't know if from relief or regret, but, knowing her compassionate heart, probably a bit of both.

"The doctors worked on you for a long time." He grinned sheepishly, lifting her hand to kiss her knuckles. "They said you'd pull through, but I wasn't so sure."

She squeezed his hand. "I'm here. Can't say I feel very good though."

"To be expected." He leaned over and kissed her cheek,

needing to be closer. If he had his way, he'd lie down beside her and tug her into his arms. Instead he said, "I don't think the doctors would recommend anyone racing out of a burning house, then being drugged to the point of death."

She smirked. "You forgot about being ravished first."

He chuckled, loving her bright spirit after all she'd been through. "There is that."

Her gaze widened, as something else hit her. "Janelle?"

Ah, he wondered when she'd remember. At least now he knew her brain was alert and firing properly. "Awake," he said quickly, "and wants to see you."

Meg smiled. "Good." Meg looked around the room, as if searching for her clothing to make a run for it. "When can we get out of here and go home?"

He patted her hand. "Not happening. You're not going anywhere until the doctors clear you. They went through a lot to keep you alive."

"Oh." Her head dropped back onto the pillow. "So not likely today?"

"I wouldn't think so." He leaned over and kissed her gently. "You need to recuperate from this week from hell."

"In bed preferably." She winked. "Join me?"

"Oh, gross!"

The words from the doorway had them both turning to see Janelle walking independently, but holding on to a nurse's arm.

"Janelle!" Meg struggled to sit up, only to collapse back, her arms wide open.

Janelle raced to the bed, where Chad scooped her up and laid her down beside Meg. The two females wrapped their arms around each other and burst into tears. Chad stepped back toward the doorway to give them some privacy and to keep watch. The nurse stepped out into the hallway.

Mack approached from the other direction. "How is Meg?"

"Alive," Chad said, his voice cool. "And she appears to be fine." Chad turned to nod at the two females cuddling on the bed.

"Good, good." Mack stared at the happy reunion. "It will be a long road ahead for the little one."

"And for Meg." Chad forced himself not to add, *No thanks to you.*

"For all of us, in a way," Mack mumbled under his breath. "What a shitty trip."

Chad heard and understood Mack was talking about the journey from Cia's death to now. "You going to be okay?"

Mack stared at him in surprise. Then gave a curt nod. "Yeah. With that asshole no longer able to play games with my head, I'll be fine." After another long moment of silence, he sighed heavily. "I'm sorry."

It was Chad's turn to stare at Mack in surprise. Then he nodded. "Apology accepted."

Mack turned and walked away, his shoulders bowed. Chad watched him. Mack would have to live with his actions over the past too. None were criminal, but they wouldn't make him shine either. Then that was his problem. Chad had enough of his own to deal with now.

He turned back to find both Meg and Janelle smiling at him. He snorted. "All right. What are you two up to? With those looks in your eyes, I'm sure it's trouble."

Meg laughed. "So not. Besides, we were just having some girl talk about you."

And damn if he didn't feel some heat climb his throat.

Janelle giggled a delightfully free sound that had Meg

tugging her back into a rocking hug. They looked so enchanting that Chad wished he could join them. He paused in thought, as he stared at the two females, who were now such a huge part of his life.

Then he figured he might as well start as he meant to go in life.

In two strides, he arrived at the side of the bed. Ignoring their laughing protests, he snagged them both into a big bear hug.

With Janelle's laughter ringing in his ears, and Meg's loving gaze locked on his, Chad knew he'd never been so lucky.

Life was good again. *Finally.*

This concludes Book 2 of By Death: *Haunted by Death.*
Read the first chapter of Chilled by Death: By Death,
Book 3

By Death: Chilled by Death (Book #3)

After losing two close friends three years ago in a snowboarding accident, Stacy Carter has become a loner and can't seem to make peace with this loss, not when Death intrudes upon her personal life again and takes two more people she loves. Meeting new people and trying to make a normal life for herself proves to be harder than anything else she's done. Meanwhile, in her career, being a forensic pathologist puts her in close contact with the dead. While fascinating and never dull, it isn't exactly a cozy conversation starter. When her brother tries to coax her out for a mountain vacation to help her heal, she has reservations, even as she tells herself rationally that she needs to face this. Reservations and rationale, however, were in short supply the last time she saw Royce O'Connell at that mountain …

Royce is floored when Stacy finally returns to the spot where she lost her two best friends, intending to deal with the depression that she's battled for some time. Royce and Stacy have been longtime friends, but Royce wants so much more between them. Yet he's well aware that he blew their last time together. Stacy makes it clear she's not looking for reconciliation. However, he can't help seeing her reappearance in their tight-knit group as a second chance, maybe his *only* chance.

Out in their winter wonderland, the vacation atmosphere shifts from merry to mayhem in a hurry, when they come across a dead man. Then, not long afterward, Stacy's brother goes missing. The nightmare is only just beginning, as the realization settles in that they can't trust anyone.

Maybe not even each other …

Find Book 3 here!
To find out more visit Dale Mayer's website.
http://geni.us/DMchilled

By Death: Chilled by Death
(Book #3)
Chapter 1

Three Years Ago

STACY CARTER SLID across the fresh white powder to come to a rest on the top of the small rise. She smiled up at the stunning blue sky and tall evergreen trees dusted in white.

It was a gorgeous day at Blackcomb Ski Resort in BC. A place she and her brother and their friends considered their home away from home. Their winter and summer play home was close enough to Seattle to make it an easy drive and far enough away to make it a change.

They were staying at her brother's friend's cabin, one they'd come to many times over the years. It was perfect. The day. The mountains. The situation.

Her best friends—they were like sisters really—Francine and Janice were up ahead. Or they should be. They'd been boarding.

However, Stacy hadn't been feeling well and had been in town all morning. Feeling better, she'd come out to meet them at the top of Gorman's Peak. It was a well-known run that could take one farther into the backcountry, and, yes, out-of-bounds if they wanted to—and her friends often wanted to. Stacy wasn't like that. She hated breaking the rules. But so many of the others loved to ski and to board the pure, untouched runs down the backside. They'd been doing it for years, and conforming to the new rules and regulations was difficult. And not appreciated in many cases. Areas that her friends had played in for years were carefully watched now.

Many of the tougher runs had been closed all week due to avalanche hazards. Although that disappointed several of her friends, Stacy didn't mind. She'd been skiing this resort since forever. There were lots of runs to keep her interest.

Then she was calmer, more relaxed, when compared to the other two women. They were the play-hard-and-love-harder variety.

Stacy was much gentler. More safety conscious and much more laid-back. She would have been happy to grab a coffee and to sit at the top of the run to just enjoy the moment. She worked hard at her job and preferred to relax when on vacation. Life was about balance.

Her two friends were both dashing raise-a-little-hell modern women. Stacy had never understood just what drew the three of them together, but something had, and it worked. They were opposites who complemented each other. They'd been friends for close to a decade. They'd changed over the years that they had known each other, with Stacy becoming more laid-back over time, whereas her friends had gotten wilder, becoming even more daredevilish.

The men loved it. Loved them.

Stacy had watched in bemusement, as Janice ate up a lifetime quota of men before she was twenty-nine. With her long black hair, a slightly olive tint to her skin, and massive brown eyes with long lashes and pouty lips, all on top of long and lean physical perfection, yeah, she could have any man anytime. And she did. Often. She also never let her heart get involved.

Francine was a slightly curvier and shorter version, but just as much of a go-getter. She'd been following in Janice's tracks since forever. Not quite as good as Janice in boarding, or with men, but Francine never seemed to care. She was content to take second place. However, she'd never slide to third. No, that was always Stacy's spot.

Not that Stacy cared. She'd always felt slightly out of sync with the other two, but they all loved each other.

It was all good.

Her phone beeped.

She pulled it from her pocket and smiled. *Janice.* She read the text, and her smile fell away.

Damn it. Janice wanted to end the day with a splash on the long back trail and cut to the cabin at the right time. Only that run was out-of-bounds. According to the text, the two would meet Stacy in a few moments.

She quickly texted a reply. **Back runs closed due to avalanche hazard.**

And waited.

She didn't have to wait long. The next text read **Phoo-ey.**

That was it. Stacy stared down at it, chewing on her bottom lip, and wondered. Out loud, she murmured, "Phooey what, Janice? As in phooey that's too bad, or phooey like that'll matter?"

Stacy shifted positions, so she could see her friends ride up the lifts. They'd be about ten minutes, if there wasn't much of a line at the bottom.

She sat back to relax.

Francine texted her next, asking where she was. She answered. Then deciding it was better to ask than worry, she texted Janice and asked, **Which run do you want to take down? The face looks great.**

She knew her attempt to convince Janice to go down the sheer drop in the front of the mountain wouldn't likely work if she was set on going down the back to the bowl, but the face would be perfect. Usually no one was there, leaving them lots of space to take jumps, to weave through the trees, or to just cut a narrow strip, racing to the bottom.

Her phone beeped again. *Janice.* **I want to take Gopher Run to the bowl.**

Damn it. **The bowl is closed too.** The bowl was an in-bounds area—as long as the weather cooperated. When it didn't, it was a closed area. Like everything connected to the resort and winter sports, safety was paramount. They had a great medical center here, and the search and rescue teams were second to none. Thankfully Stacy hadn't had any reason to use either.

She studied the chairs swinging in the gentle breeze, as the lifts toiled upward, carrying the many groups of happy winter enthusiasts.

"Stacy!"

Stacy turned in the direction of the yell, then smiled at Janice and Francine and waved.

Hearing her name again, she caught sight of her brother and two of his friends, who were also her coworkers, Mark and Stevie, several chairs below the women. "Hey," she yelled back.

Within five minutes, they all stood in a group at the top of the runs, just out of the way of the others getting off the lift.

"We're going for another run. See you in the cabin in an hour or so." With a big wave and lots of hoots and laughter, the three men jumped over the steepest part of the face.

Stacy grinned at their antics. They were all incredibly skilled and a joy to watch. "Awesome! We'll follow." With a big grin still on her face, Stacy turned her skis, planning to follow the guys off the top edge. "Come on, women. Let's go." She slid forward slightly, then twisted to make sure Janice and Francine were following.

They weren't.

Shit.

Awkwardly Stacy flipped her skis around, now facing the direction where the women stood, and Stacy struggled back the short distance to where she'd left them.

And reached only their trails, from where they'd plunged over the back of the mountain to the bowl. "Damn it, Janice. Why don't you ever listen?" she cried out to the vast white expanse in front of her. "That whole area is a bad deal right now."

Then Janice had always done as she pleased. Stacy wished she'd said more in her texts. Had she made it clear how dangerous the area was? It was closed. Avalanche warnings. Surely that spoke volumes about the snow conditions. She studied the pristine area in front of her, looking for their tracks. The women were already halfway down.

"Fine, then I'll catch you on the upside again." Although, as frustrated as she was right now, maybe she'd just head toward the cabin. She was in perfect alignment to cut across to a run that would take her back there.

She hated to see them do this. They were always taking unnecessary risks.

Like wild birds that had to be free to do their own thing.

Sure, Stacy had more understanding of the risks than most people, given her job. So many ended up on her table at the morgue because they made the wrong decision.

Given her experience with accidents and death, was it any wonder she worried about them?

Decision made.

She pushed off and glided along the ridge. She could see the women a long way down the slope. They should be turning right to head to the bowl and connect to several other runs lower down to bring them back around to the bottom of the chair lift they'd just gotten off of. Stacy debated waiting for the two to make their way back up again but decided she had already spent a lot of her time waiting for them.

She carried on for a few more feet, when she glanced down at the women, she saw them cut to the left.

Into the out-of-bounds area. And away from the chair that would bring them back up to where Stacy was. Would they turn left lower down and head toward the cabin? There was a run that cut off and would take them back home.

Her heart damn-near clogged up her throat, as she watched their devil-may-care attitude, while they raced across the mountain face and started the beautiful long zigzag pattern. "Damn it, Janice. Why do you always have to push it?"

She wanted to turn away and to ski her own path down to the cabin, but she couldn't tear her gaze away from the two women. They were incredible boarders, so graceful they looked like birds floating in the sky, crossing the mountain-scape below.

As Stacy watched, she thought she heard something. A

muted, deep booming sound. And a gentle rumble. She glanced around, but no one else was close by, and those farther away were busy laughing with their own friends. Several groups came off the lift and never stopped, skiing right on down again.

She glanced back at her girlfriends. Her gaze struggled to catch sight of them racing far below. They should be wrapping around the mountain to the left to catch the run toward the cabin. Only they were still going straight down the mountain.

And then Stacy saw the reason for the rumble.

One of the hard crusted overhangs of snow at the top of the peak had finally let go of its tenuous hold on the rock and had pounded onto the snow below. The impact started the massive sheet of snow to shift in a slow-motion slide that picked up speed the lower it went.

Within seconds, an avalanche raced downhill.

Down to her friends.

"Janice, move it!" Stacy screamed, her hands cupped around her mouth, but they couldn't hear her. Of course they couldn't. No way her voice could be heard over the noise of the destruction racing toward them.

Neither could she stop screaming at them to move faster.

The women needed to turn left. Now. And, once again, they had to take it to the limit and go down even farther. Finally they started the curve to the left, away from the cliff edge ahead of them.

"Jesus."

Stacy could only watch in terror as the two women suddenly noticed what was bearing down on them. Both women crouched down and raced as fast as they could out of the oncoming path of the avalanche.

"Faster," Stacy screamed. "Faster."

And faster it was.

The avalanche picked up speed …

And picked up the two women …

And tossed them into the white snowy melee.

As Stacy stood in horror and watched, the massive wall of snow and women slipped off the rock edge and out of her sight.

Forever.

Find Book 3 here!

To find out more visit Dale Mayer's website.

http://geni.us/DMchilled

Simon Says... HIDE: Kate Morgan (Book #1)

Welcome to a new thriller series from *USA Today* Best-Selling Author Dale Mayer. Set in Vancouver, BC, the team of Detective Kate Morgan and Simon St. Laurant, an unwilling psychic, marries all the elements of Dale's work that you've come to love, plus so much more.

Detective Kate Morgan, newly promoted to the Vancouver PD Homicide Department, stands for the victims in her world. She was once a victim herself, just as her mother had been a victim, and then her brother—an unsolved missing child's case—was yet another victim. She can't stand those who take advantage of others, and the worst ones are those who prey on the hopes of desperate people to line their own pockets.

So, when she finds a connection between a current case and more than a half-dozen cold cases, where a child's life hangs in the balance, Kate would make a deal with the devil himself to find the culprit and to save the child.

Simon St. Laurant's grandmother had the Sight and had

warned him that, once he used it, he could never walk away. Until now, her caution had made it easy to avoid that first step. But, when nightmares of his own past are triggered, Simon can't stand back and watch child after child be abused. Not without offering his help to those chasing the monsters.

Even if it means dealing with the cranky and critical Detective Kate Morgan …

Find Simon Says… Hide here!
To find out more visit Dale Mayer's website.
https://geni.us/DMSSHideUniversal

Simon Says... HIDE: Kate Morgan (Book #1)
Chapter 1

Vancouver, First Monday in June ...

NEWLY MINTED HOMICIDE detective Kate Morgan sat on one of the many benches positioned in this child-friendly park, watching the kids play on the swings in downtown Vancouver. She'd passed her first three months in her new position amid the craziness of too many murder cases to count. Vancouver, BC, was like any big city around the world and had its share of criminal activity. The city had its issues—just being on the coast and blending many different nationalities—yet somehow it all worked. Plus it was home for her. Always had been.

Because of those life-and-death issues, Vancouver had three homicide units, usually with six or seven detectives in each unit. She chuckled. At one time, the two other units called themselves Team Canuck or Team Flames, showing how hockey crazy Canada got. She didn't know what her unit used to call themselves, as she was the odd-one-out still. New enough to know her place and not so new to misunderstand the team needed time to meld.

Her ever-assessing gaze watched two men on a bench on the far side of the park. One got up, tossed a bright yellow ball at the other and then, with a raised hand, turned and walked away.

Her focus flitted to the storm approaching in the distance, assessed its threat, and dismissed it. Rain was part of the reality when living on the coast. The more pressing threats in her world were the two-legged predators. She'd known the dangers ever since her younger brother had disappeared, even now, twenty-five years later with still no trace of him. She kept a copy of his file on her desk, as a reminder of the work she'd dedicated herself to. Timmy was always close to her heart. She could only hope to get closure, as she worked to give closure to others.

Sudden movement on her left had her watching a lean man of average height, walking into the park and staring at the kids on the swing. Something about his gaze set her nerves on edge. He was slightly turned away from her, only letting her see his jeans and well-worn jacket with the upturned collar. He perched on a nearby bench seat, seemingly fascinated by the boys' antics.

The single male on the far side stood suddenly and strode her way, tossing the yellow ball and catching it smoothly with every step. He gazed at the street beside her, unconcerned for the kids or other adults. His focus was internal. From the power suit he wore, business deals most likely.

As she turned back to the other man, he'd disappeared. Her gaze zipped to the boys at the swings. They were still there. Relaxing slightly, she studied the park exits. Both men had left at the same time. From opposite sides of the park.

It shouldn't have meant anything.

But it felt like it did.

Her phone rang just then. Rodney, one of her team.

"We found another one. Prepare yourself. It's a little boy."

Tuesday

SIMON ST. LAURANT had had a bad week. He twisted in bed, kicking off the blanket. His body shimmered with sweat. He drifted in and out of sleep. He'd been up until two in the morning in one of his friendlier gambling games and had crashed soon afterward. Now it was five in the morning, and the last thing he wanted was to be awake. He rolled over, pulled the sheet over his sweating body, and closed his eyes.

As he tried to fall asleep again, he drifted down the same godforsaken dark street, just a halo of light coming from the streetlamps across on the other side. A small man, holding the hand of a very young boy at his side, walked quietly down the street. The little boy asked, "When will we be there?"

"We'll be there soon," the older man promised.

Something was just so damn wrong about that picture that Simon kept telling the little boy to run, wanting to reach out and drag him to safety. But, even as Simon reached out a hand, he saw that it wasn't real, that he wasn't there, that he couldn't grab that little boy and escape. As the older man walked under the streetlamp, Simon caught the hungry look on the man's face. A predator's look. Yet not clear enough to identify him.

Simon woke immediately, sat up, and groaned in frustration. "Why that same goddamn freaking nightmare?" he cried out, before flopping to his back yet again.

He was exhausted, his mind overwhelmed, as he drifted once again into the deepness of sleep. This time he landed in a small room, with lots of toys on the bed and on the floor.

A bed that broke his heart because it had a plastic sheet for the little kids who might wet themselves. A blanket was atop the bed but was otherwise empty. Simon's mind knew that a light was on the side of the room and that Simon would see the child soon, but he didn't want to go there. He kicked himself out of the dream, sitting up again, shuddering in the dark. "Damn it," he muttered, rubbing his eyes. "What fresh hell is this?"

Almost as if by asking that question, his body stiffened. He fell backward again, and this time he was in a different room, and the bed was bigger. It had little pink roses around the base and unicorns across the headboard. A little girl sobbed her eyes out, curled up into a tiny ball, hugging a teddy bear. The problem was that fancy little bed was completely out of place, surrounded by bare concrete walls and old cracked floors. The lack of carpet or any other niceties suggested this would not be a nice little home for her.

Instead Simon saw the bloodstains on the mattress around her, the pain and the terror in her heart, and the loneliness in her soul. He wanted to hold her and to tell her that it would be okay. But the same words rippled through his mind: *Hide. He's coming.*

Then everything went dark …

When he woke again, he lay in his bed, staring at the ceiling, dry-eyed, but felt as if he'd bawled his entire life away. Every part of his body hurt, especially his soul. He sat up, felt like he was thirty years older than his thirty-seven years on this planet. Thirty-seven years of pain and fighting to get the upper hand, trying to ensure that he wouldn't be a victim in this world again.

Years ago he'd sworn to be a victor instead. He played

the game, but he didn't let others play him. That wasn't part of his new reality. Not anymore—not for a long time. He looked down at his bed, the bottom sheet literally pulled off the mattress and twisted beneath him, while the top sheet was crumpled on the floor beside him.

"Looks like I had a party—and not the fun kind," he muttered, as he slowly straightened. He stretched, turned to get the kinks out of his neck and his back. A bad night had the effect of turning his spine into a pretzel that he could spend hours trying to untwist. He needed a hot shower to complete the job. Yet every time he went under the water, he kept seeing images of the boy that he'd seen in the first nightmare this morning.

It made no sense, when he'd seen many other children throughout his lifetime of nightmares, but, for some reason, he identified with that one. That night terror always upset him because he didn't know that child. It wasn't Simon as a child, and he didn't understand the dialogue, didn't remember it from his own life. What he did know was that these nightmares had to stop.

If he had a friend who was a doctor, he might have talked to him or her, but unfortunately he didn't even have that. In truth, speaking out loud of this weakness, … in the wrong hands, that knowledge could crush Simon. As he walked naked to the shower, he knew something had to change; he couldn't keep going on this way. The nightmares had restarted suddenly, for no current reason, and they were getting stronger, clearer, and more traumatic to view.

He should get away for a few days. Book a gambling cruise to take his mind off this mess. Maybe see Yale there. Simon's gaze caught sight of the yellow child's ball that Yale had tossed to Simon, the two men out of the blue both at the park yesterday.

Simon often walked that corridor and had come upon his old friend, looking sad and depressed. It had been nice to see Yale unexpectedly. Normally they'd be in on the same poker games or cruises, but he hadn't seen his old college friend in over six months.

Much happier after their visit, Yale had laughed, as he'd tossed him the ball, and said, "For old times' sake."

With a shrug, Simon stepped under the rain showerhead and let the hot water slosh over his head and down his back to the tiles below.

As soon as he was dry and dressed in lightweight pants with a linen shirt, perfect for summers in Vancouver, he picked up his blazer, flipped it over his shoulder, and headed out. He needed coffee in a big way, but he also had to escape the solitude of his own thoughts, preferably out in public, where he could disappear into the crowds. He walked off the elevator, crossed the lobby, and headed toward the front door, held open by the doorman.

Once outside, he stopped for a long moment, lifted his head, and sniffed the early morning Vancouver air. The nearby harbor, with that scent of salt, plus the noise and the bustle of city life, all of it melded together beautifully. With a smile he turned and headed toward his favorite coffee shop.

Find Simon Says... Hide here!

To find out more visit Dale Mayer's website.

https://geni.us/DMSSHideUniversal

Author's Note

Thank you for reading Haunted by Death! If you enjoyed my book, I'd appreciate it if you'd leave a review.

Dear reader,

I love to hear from readers, and you can contact me at my website: www.dalemayer.com or at my Facebook author page. To be informed of new releases and special offers, sign up for my newsletter or follow me on BookBub. And if you are interested in joining Dale Mayer's Reader Group, here is the Facebook sign up page.
http://geni.us/DaleMayerFBGroup

Cheers,
Dale Mayer

About the Author

Dale Mayer is a *USA Today* best-selling author, best known for her SEALs military romances, her Psychic Visions series, and her Lovely Lethal Garden cozy series. Her contemporary romances are raw and full of passion and emotion (Broken But … Mending, Hathaway House series). Her thrillers will keep you guessing (Kate Morgan, By Death series), and her romantic comedies will keep you giggling (*It's a Dog's Life*, a stand-alone novella; and the Broken Protocols series, starring Charming Marvin, the cat).

Dale honors the stories that come to her—and some of them are crazy, break all the rules and cross multiple genres!

To go with her fiction, she also writes nonfiction in many different fields, with books available on résumé writing, companion gardening, and the US mortgage system. All her books are available in print and ebook format.

Connect with Dale Mayer Online

Dale's Website – www.dalemayer.com
Twitter – @DaleMayer
Facebook Page – geni.us/DaleMayerFBFanPage
Facebook Group – geni.us/DaleMayerFBGroup
BookBub – geni.us/DaleMayerBookbub
Instagram – geni.us/DaleMayerInstagram
Goodreads – geni.us/DaleMayerGoodreads
Newsletter – geni.us/DaleNews

Also by Dale Mayer

Published Adult Books:

Shadow Recon

Magnus, Book 1

Bullard's Battle

Ryland's Reach, Book 1

Cain's Cross, Book 2

Eton's Escape, Book 3

Garret's Gambit, Book 4

Kano's Keep, Book 5

Fallon's Flaw, Book 6

Quinn's Quest, Book 7

Bullard's Beauty, Book 8

Bullard's Best, Book 9

Bullard's Battle, Books 1–2

Bullard's Battle, Books 3–4

Bullard's Battle, Books 5–6

Bullard's Battle, Books 7–8

Terkel's Team

Damon's Deal, Book 1

Wade's War, Book 2

Gage's Goal, Book 3

Calum's Contact, Book 4

Rick's Road, Book 5

Scott's Summit, Book 6

Brody's Beast, Book 7

Terkel's Twist, Book 8

Terkel's Triumph, Book 9

Terkel's Guardian

Radar, Book 1

Kate Morgan

Simon Says… Hide, Book 1

Simon Says… Jump, Book 2

Simon Says… Ride, Book 3

Simon Says… Scream, Book 4

Simon Says… Run, Book 5

Simon Says… Walk, Book 6

Hathaway House

Aaron, Book 1

Brock, Book 2

Cole, Book 3

Denton, Book 4

Elliot, Book 5

Finn, Book 6

Gregory, Book 7

Heath, Book 8

Iain, Book 9

Jaden, Book 10

The K9 Files

Jenner, Book 16

Rhys, Book 17

Landon, Book 18

Harper, Book 19

Kascius, Book 20

The K9 Files, Books 1–2

The K9 Files, Books 3–4

The K9 Files, Books 5–6

The K9 Files, Books 7–8

The K9 Files, Books 9–10

The K9 Files, Books 11–12

Lovely Lethal Gardens

Arsenic in the Azaleas, Book 1

Bones in the Begonias, Book 2

Corpse in the Carnations, Book 3

Daggers in the Dahlias, Book 4

Evidence in the Echinacea, Book 5

Footprints in the Ferns, Book 6

Gun in the Gardenias, Book 7

Handcuffs in the Heather, Book 8

Ice Pick in the Ivy, Book 9

Jewels in the Juniper, Book 10

Killer in the Kiwis, Book 11

Lifeless in the Lilies, Book 12

Murder in the Marigolds, Book 13

Nabbed in the Nasturtiums, Book 14

Offed in the Orchids, Book 15

Poison in the Pansies, Book 16

Quarry in the Quince, Book 17

Revenge in the Roses, Book 18

Silenced in the Sunflowers, Book 19

Toes in the Tulips, Book 20

Lovely Lethal Gardens, Books 1–2

Lovely Lethal Gardens, Books 3–4

Lovely Lethal Gardens, Books 5–6

Lovely Lethal Gardens, Books 7–8

Lovely Lethal Gardens, Books 9–10

Psychic Vision Series

Tuesday's Child

Hide 'n Go Seek

Maddy's Floor

Garden of Sorrow

Knock Knock…

Rare Find

Eyes to the Soul

Now You See Her

Shattered

Into the Abyss

Seeds of Malice

Eye of the Falcon

Itsy-Bitsy Spider

Unmasked

Deep Beneath

From the Ashes

Stroke of Death

Ice Maiden

Snap, Crackle…
What If…
Talking Bones
String of Tears
Inked Forever
Psychic Visions Books 1–3
Psychic Visions Books 4–6
Psychic Visions Books 7–9

By Death Series
Touched by Death
Haunted by Death
Chilled by Death
By Death Books 1–3

Broken Protocols – Romantic Comedy Series
Cat's Meow
Cat's Pajamas
Cat's Cradle
Cat's Claus
Broken Protocols 1-4

Broken and… Mending
Skin
Scars
Scales (of Justice)
Broken but… Mending 1-3

Glory
Genesis

Tori

Celeste

Glory Trilogy

Biker Blues

Morgan: Biker Blues, Volume 1

Cash: Biker Blues, Volume 2

SEALs of Honor

Mason: SEALs of Honor, Book 1

Hawk: SEALs of Honor, Book 2

Dane: SEALs of Honor, Book 3

Swede: SEALs of Honor, Book 4

Shadow: SEALs of Honor, Book 5

Cooper: SEALs of Honor, Book 6

Markus: SEALs of Honor, Book 7

Evan: SEALs of Honor, Book 8

Mason's Wish: SEALs of Honor, Book 9

Chase: SEALs of Honor, Book 10

Brett: SEALs of Honor, Book 11

Devlin: SEALs of Honor, Book 12

Easton: SEALs of Honor, Book 13

Ryder: SEALs of Honor, Book 14

Macklin: SEALs of Honor, Book 15

Corey: SEALs of Honor, Book 16

Warrick: SEALs of Honor, Book 17

Tanner: SEALs of Honor, Book 18

Jackson: SEALs of Honor, Book 19

Kanen: SEALs of Honor, Book 20

Nelson: SEALs of Honor, Book 21

Taylor: SEALs of Honor, Book 22

Colton: SEALs of Honor, Book 23

Troy: SEALs of Honor, Book 24

Axel: SEALs of Honor, Book 25

Baylor: SEALs of Honor, Book 26

Hudson: SEALs of Honor, Book 27

Lachlan: SEALs of Honor, Book 28

Paxton: SEALs of Honor, Book 29

Bronson: SEALs of Honor, Book 30

Hale: SEALs of Honor, Book 31

SEALs of Honor, Books 1–3

SEALs of Honor, Books 4–6

SEALs of Honor, Books 7–10

SEALs of Honor, Books 11–13

SEALs of Honor, Books 14–16

SEALs of Honor, Books 17–19

SEALs of Honor, Books 20–22

SEALs of Honor, Books 23–25

Heroes for Hire

Levi's Legend: Heroes for Hire, Book 1

Stone's Surrender: Heroes for Hire, Book 2

Merk's Mistake: Heroes for Hire, Book 3

Rhodes's Reward: Heroes for Hire, Book 4

Flynn's Firecracker: Heroes for Hire, Book 5

Logan's Light: Heroes for Hire, Book 6

Harrison's Heart: Heroes for Hire, Book 7

Saul's Sweetheart: Heroes for Hire, Book 8

SEALs of Steel

Badger: SEALs of Steel, Book 1
Erick: SEALs of Steel, Book 2
Cade: SEALs of Steel, Book 3
Talon: SEALs of Steel, Book 4
Laszlo: SEALs of Steel, Book 5
Geir: SEALs of Steel, Book 6
Jager: SEALs of Steel, Book 7
The Final Reveal: SEALs of Steel, Book 8
SEALs of Steel, Books 1–4
SEALs of Steel, Books 5–8
SEALs of Steel, Books 1–8

The Mavericks

Kerrick, Book 1
Griffin, Book 2
Jax, Book 3
Beau, Book 4
Asher, Book 5
Ryker, Book 6
Miles, Book 7
Nico, Book 8
Keane, Book 9
Lennox, Book 10
Gavin, Book 11
Shane, Book 12
Diesel, Book 13
Jerricho, Book 14
Killian, Book 15

Hatch, Book 16

Corbin, Book 17

Aiden, Book 18

The Mavericks, Books 1–2

The Mavericks, Books 3–4

The Mavericks, Books 5–6

The Mavericks, Books 7–8

The Mavericks, Books 9–10

The Mavericks, Books 11–12

Standalone Novellas

It's a Dog's Life

Riana's Revenge

Second Chances

Published Young Adult Books:

Family Blood Ties Series

Vampire in Denial

Vampire in Distress

Vampire in Design

Vampire in Deceit

Vampire in Defiance

Vampire in Conflict

Vampire in Chaos

Vampire in Crisis

Vampire in Control

Vampire in Charge

Family Blood Ties Set 1–3

Family Blood Ties Set 1–5

Family Blood Ties Set 4–6

Family Blood Ties Set 7–9

Sian's Solution, A Family Blood Ties Series Prequel
Novelette

Design series

Dangerous Designs

Deadly Designs

Darkest Designs

Design Series Trilogy

Standalone

In Cassie's Corner

Gem Stone (a Gemma Stone Mystery)

Time Thieves

Published Non-Fiction Books:

Career Essentials

Career Essentials: The Résumé

Career Essentials: The Cover Letter

Career Essentials: The Interview

Career Essentials: 3 in 1